The most dif_____at
first novel pub_____no
matter what wr_____e,
most publishers _____ant to take the risk of
putting out a novel by an "unknown."

Hence, *Ben Bova's Discoveries.* There's a wealth of talent in the science fiction field waiting for the chance to get their first novels to you, the reader. The *Discoveries* series will present novels by such writers: many of them experienced authors of short fiction or nonfiction, others brand-new writers who have never published anything before.

As editor of the *Discoveries* series, I promise you the same high standards I insisted on when I edited *Analog* and *Omni* magazines: science fiction that entertains you with bold new ideas and high-quality writing.

Hayford Peirce is known for his urbane, witty short stories. In *Napoleon Disentimed,* his first novel, he displays the dark humor and sophistication of a new Kurt Vonnegut. And the dazzling ability to traipse through alternate worlds and time zones, too!

—BEN BOVA

BEN BOVA'S DISCOVERIES

BECOMING ALIEN by Rebecca Ore
NAPOLEON DISENTIMED by Hayford Peirce

BEN BOVA'S
DISCOVERIES

NAPOLEON DISENTIMED

HAYFORD PEIRCE

A TOM DOHERTY ASSOCIATES BOOK

NAPOLEON DISENTIMED

Copyright © 1987 by Hayford Peirce Living Trust

First printing: November 1987

A TOR Book

Published by Tom Doherty Associates, Inc.
49 West 24 Street
New York, N.Y. 10010

ISBN: 0-812-54898-1
CAN. ED.: 0-812-54899-X

Printed in the United States of America

0 9 8 7 6 5 4 3 2 1

To
ROBERT A. HEINLEIN

CHAPTER
== 1 ==

Sɪʀ Kᴇᴠɪɴ Dᴇᴀɴᴇ ᴅᴇ Cᴏᴜʀᴛɴᴇʏ MᴀᴄNᴀɪʀ ᴏꜰ MᴀᴄNᴀɪʀ had been severely skimped by an unkind Nature in terms of mere physical size. Even the finest of handcrafted elevator shoes, those purveyed by Messrs. Rooney & Waggoner of Savile Row, Bespoke Bottiers to His Late Majesty Edward VII, were unable to totally conceal the galling fact that the MacNair of MacNair measured a trifle less than even the most average of his fellowmen.

In spite of this nettlesome affliction, he was the inevitable center of attraction of whatever gathering he chose to favor with his presence, for the MacNair radiated a dynamism and vitality as well as a superb urbanity totally disproportionate to his bantam-cock size. His suits were purchased exclusively from Monteleoni in Rome, his ties from Marsouin on the Rue de Rivoli, while his tiepin and personal jewelry were the province of Blumberg de Genève. He carried his spare frame with regal bearing and lofty self-confidence, and his nobly proportioned head drew looks of envy from other men and of frank admiration from their women.

Flashing brown eyes sparkled beneath an unlined forehead that was both broad and lofty and, together with a mobile, firmly chiseled mouth of surprisingly full and sensual lips, hinted at the powerful if mercurial intelligence that lay behind them. The MacNair's lustrous hair was thick and brown and combed straight back in a high

1

cresting wave that only served to emphasize the nobility of his brow. It was complemented by a glossy Vandyke beard of luxuriant thickness which he trimmed daily to rigorous precision on cheek and jaw with an old-fashioned cutthroat razor bequeathed to him by his paternal grandfather. Thrice a day the beard was vigorously brushed by heavy silver brushes until the MacNair was satisfied that it came to a rakish point keen enough to pierce an ineptly handled slice of bread.

The MacNair resolutely refused to let the twin handicaps of his modest size and of his birth in equally modest circumstances fetter his grandiose imagination or circumscribe the startling range of his activities. . . .

His dynamism he had inherited from his paternal grandfather, a well-known gentleman-about-town in Inverness and a familiar figure upon the numerous racecourses of Ireland and Scotland. After stoically enduring a particularly perverse run of bizarre finishes throughout the autumn of 1937, he had bid a definitive—though discreetly unspoken—farewell to his numerous racetrack creditors by surreptitiously gathering up his family one stormy evening and taking them across the ocean to settle in the cool dark forests of central Maine. Here the transplanted Scotsman contentedly passed the rest of his days as the proprietor of a harness-racing track in the mosquito-filled New England summers and of a moderately honest nonstop poker game in the top of his barn throughout the long icy winters.

The MacNair's motivation had come from his father, a shy, innocent scholar who to the family's astonishment had inexplicably enrolled in the Bangor Theological Seminary and become a man of the cloth. Kevin's memories of his kindly, soft-spoken parent were those of a slight, pale man of delicate health with a constant cough who suffered incessantly through the harsh northern winters. . . .

In the particularly glacial winter of 1957, when Kevin was nine years old, his father had triumphantly invested most of his own personal assets along with whatever he could raise from the members of his congregation in the purchase of a twenty-acre plot of orange groves in sunny, eternally warm central Florida. The real estate promoter who sold the land was kind enough to recommend a contractor to put up the first of several buildings planned to house the elderly retired parishioners who would come to Florida to spend their final years far from the icy northern gales. The lawyer in the small town of Frostproof who represented Kevin's father in the transaction arranged for the necessary additional financing through a local bank of which he himself was serendipitously a director.

It was only when the half-completed building collapsed into a sinkhole that the finances of Kevin's father and his unlucky parishioners began to collapse as well. From the rubble of the half-million-dollar building the contractor received the court-afforded protection of bankruptcy. Upon presentation of the claim for damages to the insurance company, it was discovered that title to the land was derisory, while the title-insurance company involved had failed to purchase the policy which would have saved their investment. Soon the bank stepped in to seize the property for failure to meet the schedule of payments upon the ruined building, and on the perjured testimony of the land promoter Kevin's father was indicted by a grand jury in Jacksonville for criminal conspiracy.

The family home and remaining assets were sold to pay for legal costs and to partially reimburse those of the congregation who found themselves in even more desperate straits than their pastor. The three-year struggle of his bewildered father to defend his faultless intentions was burned inalterably into the mind and soul of the sensitive youth, and when his father collapsed and died one winter's day in the midst of his ordeal, the thirteen-year-old swore bitterly that one day he would have vengeance on all of those who had struck his father down and condemned his beloved mother to grinding poverty.

Long ago the MacNair had extracted a measured revenge upon those he deemed responsible for the death of his father and the disruption of his life, and then without further reflection had turned his attention to others of their ilk. As the years passed, the MacNair had finally lost track of the countless identities he had fleetingly assumed in the course of predatory forays from one unexploited and still unwary continent to the next. Now in the prime of life of his middle forties, the early years of bitterness were largely forgotten and he occasionally looked back with nostalgic fondness upon some of the more picaresque exploits of an ebullient youth.

As Sir Kevin Bleake he had purveyed tolerably authentic Gauguins of the Breton period to a number of Florida lawyers; as Saraf Mozaffar od-Din, an Iranian refugee from the Ayatollah Khomeini, he had bilked a Beverly Hills real estate agency from what they anxiously awaited as the $700,000 down payment in cash on a $7-million mansion on Mulholland Drive; as Aristide Beaumont de la Bonninière he had solicited several hundred million yen from Japanese insurance executives to open a replica on the Ginza in Tokyo of his celebrated three-star gastronomic shrine in Cancon, the sublime Relais des Quatres Petites Brebis.

Now the MacNair hummed softly to himself behind the wheel of his rented Cadillac as he pulled away from the Shelburne Museum on the banks of Lake Champlain, a few miles south of Burlington, Vermont. It was a torrid summer day in late July with a high blue sky and a brilliant midafternoon sun which poured dazzling light upon the fields and meadows, the small dark clumps of forest and the gently rolling hills. Even the MacNair, who was far from sharing the sentiment of that Poet who *loved not Man the less, but Nature more,* felt a mild sense of contentment and well-being as the pastoral New England landscape flowed smoothly past his windows.

He wiggled himself into a more comfortable position on the firm cushion he was obliged to use when driving and let his thoughts wander to that retired title-insurance broker on Sunapee Lake in southwestern New Hampshire who would be his host for the indeterminate future. Sheldon MacMurray was a pink-skinned, shiny-scalped old buffer who had amassed a sizable fortune in Miami Beach by virtue of unlimited rapacity and preternatural shrewdness. In retirement to the cool dark forests of New England he had retained his keen native wit until the fateful day he had come to learn of his distant descent from the House of Hanover and King George III of England.

The obsession rapidly grew that in some manner yet to be determined he was closely, albeit clandestinely, related to

Queen Elizabeth and the present-day Royal Family. To the despair of his friends and relatives he mobilized a considerable portion of his fortune to establish proof of this elusive relationship, and eventually left for London to pursue his hobbyhorse.

In London Sheldon MacMurray had been coldly rebuffed in his initial faltering attempts to put flesh to his fantasy, but as he sat despondently one evening in the cocktail lounge of Simpson's-in-the-Strand, he made the acquaintance of a small but superlatively well-turned-out gentleman who, after a quick, barely noticeable glance around the room, introduced himself as Sir Kevin Deane de Courtney MacNair of MacNair, Knight Escutcheon of the Order of the Primrose and Senior Equerry to the Queen herself.

Over smoked Scottish salmon followed by roast beef and the traditional accompaniments of boiled brussels sprouts and Yorkshire pudding, Sir Kevin effortlessly drew out the broker's confidence, then confided with some diffidence that a certain part of his largely hereditary duties at the Palace consisted precisely of genealogical research. He was, unfortunately, off to France the following dawn for an extended mission of some delicacy for the Royal Family, but if chance should ever bring him to the colonies he would take the keenest pleasure in aiding MacMurray in what appeared to be his quite reasonable quest.

So now, eight months later in the summer of 1991, the MacNair was at the wheel of the most imposing automobile he had been able to rent, driving pensively through central Vermont. Three months devoted to enticing a shopping-mall contractor in Cleveland, Ohio, to part with a modest portion of his assets had ultimately yielded little more than pocket money, and among his prospects for the future only this addled insurance broker seemed at all promising.

The MacNair was still far from certain what his actual method of operation would be, but a week's intensive study of the science of genealogy in general and of the British Royal Family in particular had prepared him for a number of eventualities. A small smile played across what the MacNair considered his sharply honed features, although others, he was always baffled to learn, particularly women, occasionally professed to find in them a certain cherubic roundness, and he tugged contentedly at the tip of his stylish beard. If he couldn't inveigle a crooked insurance salesman named Sheldon MacMurray into ruining himself with unseemly haste, he was unfit to sport the glorious name of MacNair!

His smile faltered for only an instant as there came to mind the unbidden outcome of a number of his more ill-considered ventures. But the MacNair had been an inveterate optimist since birth. In retrospect he could dismiss those occasional unsolicited spells of enforced retirement from the hustle-bustle of the workaday world as little more than unusually fruitful opportunities to expand his mind by long hours of profound study in prison libraries around the world. . . .

He had elected to drive slowly south to Green Mountain National Forest, then wind his way leisurely through the back roads of Vermont in order to arrive precisely on time for cocktails. He had just passed Brandon Gap and was now moving east through the National Forest. The narrow road was climbing steadily, with trees lining both sides of the twisting route, and it was only through occasional clearings that he could make out the peaks of Bread Loaf Mountain to the north and Bloodroot to the south. There was little traffic to keep him alert, and the car had become uncomfortably warm. He yawned broadly and turned up the air conditioner.

Two hours until the sun was over the yardarm: nearly time for the first bracing glass of schnapps of the day. What did a senior equerry to the Queen drink? he mused, raising a hand to suppress another yawn. A pink gin? So excruciatingly British, so unmistakably upper-class, so veddy, veddy naval. Could he once have been a messmate of the Duke of Edinburgh in the Royal Navy? Possibly, possibly. . . .

Fully absorbed by these vagrant thoughts, he failed to notice the small grey sedan that had come up behind him and was now attempting to pass on his left. A horn suddenly blared in his ear and he awoke with a violent start. The heavy Cadillac veered toward the center of the road and with a terrifying clang bounced against the smaller Toyota. Heart pounding, the MacNair fought to bring the careening monster under control. A hundred yards farther and he at last brought it to a jerky halt on the narrow shoulder.

What on earth was *that?* he asked himself wildly as he looked back along the road. There was nothing to be seen but the empty road stretching through the forest. A moment later a red pickup truck rounded a distant bend, drew quickly closer, and rushed past in a gust of wind. The MacNair shook his head. Surely he couldn't have imagined that horrible noise? Could a deer have run into the car? No. Of course not. That had definitely been an automobile horn that so desperately surprised him.

Lips pursed, he slid out from behind the wheel and examined the scratches and dents on the side of his once immaculate Cadillac. Uttering an elaborate curse, he reluctantly began the slow trek back along the deserted highway, his slight bearded figure clad in a grey herringbone suit disconcertingly out of place on the shoulder of this lonely country road.

A dense forest of pine and fir grew on either side of the road and the warm summer air was redolent of the dried needles that lay like a thick brown carpet between their trunks. His glossy black shoes from the lasts of Rooney & Waggoner raised soft clouds of dust as he trudged along, and under the prickly heat of the summer sun he tugged irritably at the constraints of his exquisitely tailored grey weskit and sober red and blue tie.

In spite of the thick cover of forest it was evident that here the road had been cut into the side of a hill, for on the north side of the highway the slope fell away so sharply that in places the MacNair found himself looking directly into the upper branches of the trees. His misgivings grew.

Fifty yards farther on, as he shook his head in perplexity, he suddenly came upon what appeared to be a number of damaged trees and a small gap in the otherwise virgin forest. The MacNair squatted and peered down into the gloom. There, forty feet below at the bottom of a moderately steep slope, almost entirely hidden by the forest, lay a small grey sedan upside down on its crumpled roof. A human arm protruded pathetically from an open window.

His first impulse was to turn and run. No one had seen the accident. More important—no one had seen *him*. The whole unfortunate incident, after all, was clearly the other's fault, as he had tried to pass on what was virtually a blind corner. Well, *almost* a blind corner. He glanced back at his glossy black Cadillac, gleaming in an errant shaft of sunlight that angled through the forest. In thirty seconds he could be away, and no one the wiser. . . .

There was a long agonized moan from below, and with a profound sigh the MacNair began to make his way carefully down the slope. A senior equerry to the Queen could never shirk his duty. . . .

CHAPTER
=== 2 ===

As THE MACNAIR APPROACHED the upside-down car along the path it had cleaved through the broken trees and underbrush, he saw to his enormous relief that no shattered limbs or severed heads lay piecemeal on the soft forest floor, for in spite of a number of disagreeable incidents that had befallen him around the world, he had never grown fond of the sight of blood.

Brushing away a thick pine branch, he knelt and saw that two men were still inside the battered vehicle, hanging awkwardly from their safety harnesses. To his relief they were groaning intermittently and stirring feebly. The MacNair drew a deep breath and began gingerly to extricate their unconscious forms. When he had them stretched out on the ground some distance from the car, he paused to reflect dispassionately upon the situation.

The late afternoon sun pierced the dark forest with narrow golden rays, dappling the faces of the two supine figures. The driver, the MacNair judged, was tall and youthful, his passenger squat and middle-aged. Both seemed fit and hard and were dressed with rather surprising elegance for this rustic corner of New England in dark grey suits and narrow black ties. In spite of their occasional groans neither seemed critically injured in any readily apparent fashion. But even in repose the cast of their faces was unmistakably and disquietingly grim.

The MacNair tugged pensively at his beard. Somewhere a bird trilled sharply, followed by an answering call from the other side of the small clearing where he stood motionlessly in the shadows of a large fir. The MacNair started nervously, feeling distinctly ill at ease in this unremittingly sylvan atmosphere. Were there still bears, he wondered, in the Vermont woods? And were they lashed into a killing frenzy by the smell of blood? He looked uneasily over his shoulder into the sinister darkness of the forest around him. Or was that sharks?

He shivered, and directed an impatient glance down at the cause of his discomfort. For their own welfare, he told himself, it would be far better to leave them here and go report the accident to the state police by phone rather than try to carry them up to his car. An ambulance would be here in a trice and then the MacNair could be on his way.

The MacNair ran his fingers through his beard. In fact—now that he paused to seriously consider the matter—it might actually be wiser to phone in the accident under a *nom de guerre* and *then* be on his way. After all, even for senior equerries there were clearly drawn limits to just how far duty had to extend. . . .

He was about to turn up the slope when a sharp metallic noise startled him. He jumped involuntarily, then saw that the battered rear trunk of the overturned car had chosen this moment to come unsprung. As the MacNair watched, it slowly stretched open toward the ground. A cardboard carton tumbled out and turned twice to stop nearly at his feet. With a muttered imprecation at his jumpiness he instinctively reached down and raised the package to his chest. Above the soft whispering of the wind in the trees he could hear the blood pounding in his ears.

Stop being so *jumpy,* he commanded himself. Nothing—

"Hey, whataya doing?" The sudden cry whirled him about, the carton cradled in his arms, his heart throbbing violently. The heavyset passenger had rolled over onto his stomach and half lifted himself up. He seemed to be fumbling at the inside of his jacket.

"Nothing at all," replied the MacNair with instinctive hauteur, indignantly drawing himself up at the other's peremptory tone.

"What's that you got in your arms?"

The MacNair glanced down at it in surprise. "Merely a carton that fell from your trunk. Where would you like me to place it?"

"Over here, next to me. Yeah, that's it. Right there." He raised himself painfully to a sitting position and ran his hands over the carton. "Yeah, it seems to be okay," he breathed softly.

"You have no idea how you set my mind at rest," replied the MacNair icily. "Now that all is well I shall just be stepping along. An ambulance will arrive shortly to tend to your needs." He inclined his head curtly. "Gentlemen: good day."

"Hold it a second," growled the other, unmollified by the MacNair's unfailing courtesy and oblivious of the dangerous glint in his flashing brown eyes. "Aren't you the something-or-other who tried to kill us?"

"Kill you? Whatever do you mean?"

"Who drove us off the road—that's what I mean!"

The MacNair's eyebrows shot up. *"I?* Certainly not, my good man. I merely happened to chance along and—"

"What kinda car ya driving?"

"Car? Why a Cad—a Khaddafi Special, of course, why do you ask?"

"A Cadillac!" His already grim features grew grimmer yet. "You *were* trying to hijack us!"

"Hijack you? Nonsense!"

"For the . . . that carton there."

The MacNair's eyes turned to the ordinary-looking brown carton. It was heavily taped and about two feet around. Nothing could have been more banal in appearance. How tiresome this fellow was! Already he appeared to have forgotten that it was the MacNair who had undoubtedly saved his wretched life by pulling him from the shattered wreckage! Here was true ingratitude!

"Kill you for *this?*" said the MacNair with all the considerable disdain at his command, reaching down to lift the carton and juggle it scornfully in his hands.

"Yeah, this," growled the other, reaching inside his coat and bringing out a small automatic pistol which he fired at the MacNair from point-blank range.

But the MacNair had already cast himself in one direction and the carton in another. The bullet penetrated the box with a tortured whine as of crystal shattering. An instant later the carton caught the gunman full in the face. As he fell sideways with a muffled cry, the gun sailed from his hand to land in the depths of a bush.

With a sharp cry of triumph a jubilant MacNair leapt to his feet and vented a portion of his rage and terror by earnestly kicking his assailant three times in the head. Breathing heavily, he drew back his foot yet again. . . .

Enough! The man was clearly unconscious. The MacNair retrieved the automatic from the middle of the bushes, activated its safety, and stuffed it into the top of his trousers. Then he stared grimly down at the two sprawled figures. By rights, he supposed, he ought to shoot them out of hand. If not in the head, at the very least in the kneecap. Wasn't that almost *de rigueur* among gangsters and terrorists these days?

He snorted derisivily at his fantasy. Was he Sir Kevin Deane de Courtney MacNair of MacNair, Knight Escutcheon of the Order of the Primrose, Senior Equerry to the Queen, or was he a third-rate Al Capone? The matter needed no further reflection.

He reached down and for the third time lifted the carton in his arms. It would be chastisement enough to transport this contentious carton to some distant remove where these churlish oafs would be at some pains to recover it.

Imagine: trying to shoot the MacNair of MacNair, the original Good Samaritan!

After a brief stop in the tiny hamlet of Stockbridge to phone the state police, the MacNair turned his Cadillac south to skirt the eastern edge of the Forest, all the while looking for an unobtrusive spot in which to examine the package that had so nearly gotten him killed. At last he spied an inconspicuous dirt road half overgrown with brush disappearing into the forest and with some trepidation bounced the Cadillac slowly along its ruts until he was well out of sight of the highway. He continued another hundred yards until he found a widening where he was able to maneuver the car around to face the way he had come, then with a sigh switched off the motor. Already he was regretting his tiresomely quixotic gesture of petty revenge. Far simpler to have shot the rascals out of hand!

He reached into the back seat to gather up the carton. He had nearly been murdered because of it. Would it contain the Pentagon's secret plans for its latest communications satellite, with which Russian spies had been fleeing to Canada? Or would it turn out to be a package of dirty laundry possessing enormous sentimental value for its befuddled owner?

The MacNair pulled a Swiss Army knife from his pocket and carefully cut the tape away. The flaps opened to reveal nothing but white Styrofoam packing bits. He grimaced and plunged his hands into them. Immediately he felt a single large object. Heedless of the plastic bits cascading over the seat and floor, he pulled it out impatiently. All this trouble over—a Tiffany lamp?

But this was no lamp that he held in his hands, at least from what he could see of it through the semitransparent layers of bubble-wrapping that swathed it tightly. Once again he used his blade to cut away the wrapping. As it came away, his eyes widened, and when at last he saw clearly what he had so casually sauntered away with from the wrecked Toyota, he knew that his mouth must be hanging open.

His eyes flickered wildly around the forest that hid the car and the MacNair from prying eyes—or so he devoutly hoped. For what he held in his hands was worth more than any man's life. Or those of any *dozen* men.

Glinting and sparkling with a million coruscating flames from its more than 30,000 diamonds was the Gathering, Organizing, and Dispersing Holistically Extratemporal Autonomous Device of the Tirthankara Mardumjar, better known to the world as the GODHEAD.

CHAPTER
= 3 =

THE TIRTHANKARA MARDUMJAR WAS a man of striking, if eclectic, appearance. Golden locks of a precise and regular curl fell well past his shoulders, and his pale blue eyes were those of a Viking raider. But in spite of the magnificent Nordic head his muscular surfer's body was a gleaming mahogany brown which seemed to glow as if animated by its own inner power source. A large red ruby sat in the middle of his broad forehead, while the eight incisors in the Tirthankara's mouth had been replaced by eight glittering sapphires which were only a shade darker than his intolerably penetrating eyes.

His customary apparel was an all-enveloping cloak of rich crimson velour festooned with black and white symbols celebrating the intrinsicality of the yin and yang. It was fastened at the neck with an ornate silver clasp just above the great expanse of his smooth bare chest. For even in the most inclement weather all other clothing was disdained save for a pair of skintight black leotards with a yellow sash at the waist and fourteen small golden bells which dangled at each ankle.

The Tirthankara's feet were equally bare, for footwear he proclaimed an extravagant and overly ostentatious superfluity for one whose humble origins in the lowliest villages of the East must never be long forgotten. In any case, his feet were now virtually useless appendages, for his habitual means of locomotion from even one side of a room to the other was a cream and gold Louis XIII sedan chair lovingly shouldered by four devout neophytes.

The Tirthankara Mardumjar was the first and most notable of the scientific swamis to appear at the end of the 1980s. His proclaimed goal was to synthesize the technological disciplines of the materialistic West with the spiritual realities of the mystic East, and from them derive a single new Greater Truth. From his temple in Stimson Beach, a small seaside community just north of San Francisco, the message he preached to his disciples was simple enough to be understood by anyone in Marin County with a BMW and a taste for Brie and Pinot Chardonnay.

Salvation was to be found through the intermediary of the sleek and graceful form of the smiling bottlenose dolphin, life's highest form on earth. There were but two steps on the road to paradise for a disciple, or Dumjar, of the Tirthankara Mardumjar. The first was to ensure the transmigration of the Dumjar's persona to the physical body of a dolphin. The second step would follow automatically, for upon the eventual demise of his aquatic body the Dumjar's persona would then be translated to the indescribable joys of eternal bliss.

What puzzled nonbelievers was how the Tirthankara Mardumjar could function as an interface between humans and dolphins, and it was here that the Master's creative genius had flowered to its fullest degree in its sublime marriage of mysticism to microchip. The miracle was wrought by means of an elaborate electronic crown commonly called the GODHEAD.

In a temple sanctum which owed more to IBM and Mission Control Center than the incense and prayer wheels of the East, the Tirthankara donned the Gathering, Organizing, and Dispersing Holistically Extratemporal Autonomous Device for three full hours a day on behalf of the salvation of his disciples' souls. A switch was flipped on the unit's self-contained power supply and the GODHEAD was activated.

Even nonbelievers avowed that the ensuing effect was spectacular, for the bulky headset was adorned with microchips and circuitry of surpassing complexity, and now it began to glitter brilliantly with flashing lights of intense reds, blues, yellows, and oranges.

What distinguished the GODHEAD from more prosaic electronic effects was the fact that its sparkling colors flashed and glittered in the midst of 30,000-odd identically cut one-carat diamonds. For each disciple there was a single stone, emblematic of his commitment to the Tirthankara and the quest for eternal life.

Every working day additional diamonds were added to the platinum crown as hopeful new Dumjars purchased them at cost from the sect's single authorized dealer—the Tirthankara's holy brother-in-law, the Rajasthani Sahibdin, more prosaically known to his old friends in Bronxville, New York, as Louis Zweig.

Once set in the Tirthankara's crown, each diamond became a storage device into which the Dumjar's persona was focused by the Master's ineffable spiritual powers, then inalterably recorded there for the ages. Augmented a millionfold by the complex electronic circuitry of the GODHEAD, the recorded persona was later ceremoniously beamed to its joyous recipient, a bottlenose dolphin somewhere in the grey Pacific, who thereby became the standby repository for the Dumjar's soul until such time as he cast off his human body.

Such were the beguiling tenets of Dumjarism.

The MacNair had encountered this marvelous scam for the first time in the pages of the *Los Angeles Times* in late September of 1989. Almost without conscious thought he had reached for his pocket computer and calculated that the weight of the 23,874 one-carat diamonds mentioned in the article was 10.526 pounds. . . .

At an ultraconservative $3,000 per carat, the GODHEAD was worth a minimum of $71,622,000.

The MacNair could only shake his head in mingled fury and envy. It was particularly irksome that it had taken an ex–theology student from North Crossett, Arkansas, named Orville Tavery to conceive and implement this splendid gaff. The MacNair twitched with vexation. How could a hayseed from the depths of the Ozarks have given birth to a concept of such stark beauty?

He tossed the newspaper away with a scowl. Perhaps it wouldn't hurt to make a few discreet inquiries about how one had one's skin toned a rich, glowing brown. . . .

In January of 1991 the Tirthankara Mardumjar decided that his operation had now outgrown the confines of the West Coast. He traveled east, where he began preparations for a temple near Midland Beach on Staten Island, just across the Verrazano Narrows Bridge from Brooklyn. Soon he began to appear widely on local television, his head nearly obscured by the size and brilliance of the diamond-studded crown.

Guglielmo Aldobrandini was a second-generation New Yorker in his late sixties who was proud of his membership in the Italo-American Anti-Defamation League. Officially he owned nothing more than a used-car lot on Roosevelt Avenue, but in fact he also directed a wide variety of other activities in New York and parts of the neighboring six states. In the paneled den of his four-story house in central Queens he took note of the Tirthankara's appearance late one evening on a celebrity talk show. It was the first that Aldobrandini had heard of the scientific swami, and he was duly impressed.

The following day he summoned his *consigliori* and three *caporegimes* and began to issue instructions. What foresight he had shown, Aldobrandini told himself smugly, in arranging years ago for a brilliant but hungry young lawyer to take the bar exams for the near-cretinous brother-in-law of his wife's second cousin. Now that very brother-in-law was contentedly serving out his third term as state senator in upstate Albany. . . .

* * *

Three weeks later the Tirthankara Mardumjar was subpoenaed to appear before a Senate committee in Albany which had been recently convened to investigate quackery in New York State. Included in the subpoena was the requirement to produce upon demand that diamond-studded crown which was the purported instrumentality of the Tirthankara's so-called magical powers.

The Tirthankara Mardumjar and a modest retinue of armed disciples accordingly made their reluctant way to Albany by sedan chair, armored limousine, and chartered jet. At Albany County Airport they were unexpectedly joined by a large escort of state troopers and motorcycle outriders, all of whom were heavily armed. Surrounded by their escort, the Tirthankara's entourage left the airport by an inconspicuous side exit and turned toward the capital.

Almost immediately they were obliged to detour because of an overturned oil tanker on the main road. Shepherding them along at high speed, the police escort led the procession through a series of baffling maneuvers which came to a sudden stop when the cavalcade swung around the side of a deserted factory and straight into the darkened interior of an enormous warehouse. A moment later the doors closed ominously behind the Tirthankara Mardumjar and his astonished bodyguard of California yuppies. . . .

Now Sir Kevin Deane de Courtney MacNair of MacNair sat pensively against the base of a very large maple, the pistol gripped tightly in his hand. The carton containing the Tirthankara's GODHEAD was concealed in a bush somewhere behind him, while the Cadillac was out of sight a hundred yards to his right. The MacNair rubbed his back against the rough bark of the maple. Or was it a pine? Odd that a native son of the Pine Tree State should be unable to recognize one. But what he *did* recognize was that the gloomy depths of a lonely forest composed of any kind of tree at all was absolutely the safest place in the world for him to be at the present time. What matter that he started at the rustling of every leaf and the sudden call of every bird? His pounding heart might deny it, but here at least he was *safe*.

Or so he tried to convince himself.

The question was: for how long?

After gaping in stupefaction at the dazzling glitter of the Tirthankara's crown the MacNair's first gesture had been to turn on the Cadillac's radio. Only seven minutes had been needed to find a radio account of the daring theft of the Master's priceless crown earlier in the day a hundred miles to the west. In spite of himself, the MacNair had been obscurely pleased to learn that the Tirthankara himself had emerged intact from his ordeal. A man of such genius should be treasured as a national asset!

The MacNair twirled the gun nervously in his hands, wondering uneasily at what time it would start getting dark. Would nighttime be an advantage? He shivered in spite of the late afternoon heat. The thought of sitting here alone in the northern woods while darkness fell and unseen animals scurried about and wolves began to howl was far from comforting.

But what else could he do until he had come to some firm decision one way or the other? Whoever was responsible for the Tirthankara's hijacking, the CIA or the Mafia or even the Committee of Rational Skeptics, was bound to be upset by the MacNair's wholly impromptu intervention. More than upset: furious. It would be useless to point out their own folly in confiding the GODHEAD to such feckless bumblers as those the MacNair had so inadvertently stumbled upon. No, far better to avoid any attempts to reason with them!

What then was the alternative?

The MacNair tugged fretfully at the end of his beard, twisting its point between his thumb and forefinger. A speedy departure for Europe perhaps? England, Germany, France, Italy? All were countries whose customs he knew, whose languages he could speak. But how? He could be readily traced through the use of his credit cards. His liquid funds were nearly at an end. What irony that the possessor of limitless wealth should be unable to put it to practical use!

The MacNair considered the gun in his hand with distaste, then began to tap it rhythmically against his thigh. He looked up aimlessly through the tops of the trees. Were the few patches of clear blue sky that were visible through the dense foliage beginning to darken in sinister fashion? He pulled impatiently on the knuckles of his fingers, snapping them noisily. What other possibilities suggested themselves?

Surely such an object as the GODHEAD must be insured. There would be an enormous reward for its return, one substantial enough for even a MacNair to retire upon. But would even the MacNair of MacNair be adroit enough to negotiate its return without in some way coming to the attention of the Tirthankara Mardumjar and his army of yuppie fanatics, the FBI and the police, and whoever had stolen it in the first place? Did he *really* want the Mafia after him for the rest of his life? The MacNair shuddered.

But on the *other* hand, by the holy memory of his saintly father, there was no chance in a trillion that he—the MacNair of MacNair!—was going to walk away from this preposterously valuable artifact without in some material way benefiting from it! He straightened up against the tree, his slight frame rigid with determination.

He was far from greedy, the MacNair told himself dispassionately. He disdained as illusory the notion that he might ever realize the GODHEAD's actual value of more than $100 million.

No. A modest $50 million would be more than adequate to meet his immediate personal needs and to serve as recompense for the aggravation he had so recently suffered.

But how to realize even *this* diminished sum?

But wait! The diamonds. Perhaps he could prize off a dozen or so this very moment and quickly unload them on the addled Sheldon MacMurray as having been the favorite stones of Queen Victoria or something of the like. . . . With whatever he might raise from MacMurray he could then afford to reconsider the whole matter somewhat more leisurely from the vantage point of Europe or even Australia.

The MacNair leapt to his feet. Yes, why not? He would remove a few diamonds, carefully secure the GODHEAD against future need by burying it here in the Vermont woods, then continue on his way. And perhaps by tomorrow a better plan would have presented itself.

The gun still in his hand, he burrowed through the undergrowth to retrieve the carton from its hiding place in the bushes. Returning to the tiny clearing, he carefully unpacked its contents. Once again he found himself half stunned by the glittering brilliance of the crown's thousands of precious stones. Turning it over in his hands, he scrutinized it closely.

Was that tangle of broken electronic circuitry the spot where the gangster's bullet had penetrated the carton's soft packaging instead of his own equally soft and yielding body? He shuddered convulsively at the vivid image of a bullet ripping through yielding red flesh and felt the sudden prickle of sweat beading his forehead as the harsh evidence of the damaged GODHEAD brought home the closeness of his escape. Had this ridiculous artifact actually saved his life? If so, then surely it was his good-luck talisman!

The MacNair poked at the jagged bullet hole with the tip of his finger. The bullet had certainly made a mess of some of the circuitry but seemed to have left undamaged all of his precious diamonds. With a soft chuckle the MacNair impulsively raised the preposterous device to his head. What would it be like to talk to the Lords of the Earth, the bottlenose dolphins?

He laughed aloud at the whimsical notion and settled the crown about his head. What a genius was Orville Tavery, aka the Tirthankara Mardumjar! It was almost a shame that title to his extraordinary Gathering, Organizing, and Dispersing Holistically Extratemporal Autonomous Device had now passed irrevocably to another, far more deserving owner.

"Harken unto me, O Dolphins!" he cried sardonically, heedless of whoever else might be in the woods.

But the dolphins remained obstinately silent.

After a while the MacNair removed the crown and was about to begin the serious business of removing a dozen or so diamonds when his eye was caught by a small on-off switch discreetly hidden by a tangle of microcircuitry. Could this be the toggle that made the GODHEAD light up like a berserk Disneyland fireworks display? Tentatively the MacNair fingered the switch.

And the lights came on!

He nearly dropped the GODHEAD, so startling was the sudden display of laserlike intensities. His eyes widened as he held it in his hands. Never had he beheld anything so beautiful!

Slowly, almost reverently, he raised the pulsing, glowing crown and brought it down upon his head. "There," he murmured, strangely elated. "Perhaps now I can talk to the dol—"

CHAPTER
= 4 =

AT THE FATEFUL INSTANT of the MacNair's lowering of the flashing GODHEAD upon his brow a strangely disparate group of men in three widely scattered European cities were setting into motion a chain of events which would have the most momentous consequences not only for the MacNair but for all those other billions with whom he shared the planet.

These three cities were London, Düsseldorf, and Paris. . . .

The great sprawl of London lies some 3,400 miles to the east of central Vermont. The local time was close to midnight and the pale half-moon was barely visible in the gritty mist of fog and coal dust that blanketed the few remaining lights of the British capital. Not far from the Edgeware Road on the northeast corner of Hyde Park, in a tall narrow building of eighteenth-century construction but undistinguished design, Alfred St. John Wester, 7th Earl of Kensington, grudgingly poured the last of the port into the crystal glass tendered by Sir Norvil Dennett, the Master of Garnaway.

"A noble year," allowed Wester, lifting the empty bottle of Compton's Imperial Ruby to study its label by the soft yellow glow of the old-fashioned gas brackets on the paneled walls of the upstairs smoking room. Two hundred cases of the great wine, a 1905, had been laid down in the deep cellars of Les Amis des Grands Vins de Bordeaux nearly half a century before the birth of the present Earl. Now he patted his ample paunch with smug pleasure, a stout but muscular gentleman of early middle age whose shiny bald head was partially compensated for by a thick growth of muttonchop whiskers on the ruddy cheeks of his rotund face. "I believe there's still a case or two of it left."

"I should fervently hope so," said Sir Norvil, who was tall and thin to the point of gauntness, with a high shiny dome of a forehead and a great puff of salt-and-pepper whiskers. As the Earl had foreseen, Dennett had arrived at the club for dinner in his usual disreputable yellow tweed motoring suit and scruffy brown boots. *Scientists!* muttered the Earl crossly, himself turned out as befit a gentleman in close-fitting dark evening attire of a boiled white shirt, floppy black tie, and discreet red epaulettes with short golden tassels. You'd think that just *once* Dennett might have the courtesy to—

"You know what *I* shall do when we have our own little time machine?" confided Sir Norvil with drunken owlishness. He stirred in the depths of his dark red leather armchair just enough to tap Wester on his plump knee. "*I* shall use the jolly old thing to transport myself back to the year 1905, where I shall purchase a case, no, a *hundred* cases of—"

"For heaven's sake!" muttered the Earl furiously between his teeth, directing a ferocious glance at the intolerable Dennett. "Keep your voice *down!*"

Sir Norvil's pale grey eyes blinked behind their glittering

half-moon spectacles. "You think someone might overhear us?"

"No more than half of London, I daresay."

"But here at the club, Les Amis . . ."

"You *know* that most of them are totally unaware of what we're doing!" The Earl glanced uneasily around the empty smoking room. "For them, the club is exactly what it purports to be, an association devoted to the great wines of Bordeaux. I *beg* you to remember that!"

"Of course, my dear fellow, of course."

But would he? wondered the Earl of Kensington uneasily. *Could* he? It was all very well telling themselves that Dennett was one of the half-dozen men in the world purporting to understand Einstein's Special Theory of General Equivalency in its totality, but aside from that the man had no more common sense than a chicken. "Spies," hissed the Earl. "Any one of the club servants could be a *spy.*"

Sir Norvil fell back in his chair as if astounded by the novelty of the proposition. "Spies! From Napoleon?"

The Earl of Kensington snorted derisively. "Our own implacable goal is the destruction of Napoleon, is it not? But surely our keen appreciation of human nature tells us that Napoleon will doggedly resist being destroyed, if only from spite or general perversity. And just as we wish to preempt the creation of the French Empire, so the French will wish to preempt the construction of our time machine."

"I never thought of it in quite that light," conceded the Master of Garnaway pensively.

"I beg you to do so in the future, and to suit your behavior accordingly."

"You . . . you surely don't think that I . . . that *we* may be in actual physical *danger?*"

Wester glanced furtively over his shoulder. An ancient servant was discreetly emptying the great brass ashtrays arrayed about the room for the convenience of the club's members. He waited until the servant had tottered out the door, then lowered his voice. "You recall what happened last week to Sir Francis Gifford and Harold Detterling? As well as to their entire families—both wives and all seven children?"

Sir Norvil Dennett frowned. "Of course, a shocking tragedy, shocking! Drowned, all of them. In a boating accident."

"On an absolutely still day on the Thames near Guildford? On a Sunday afternoon with a thousand people on the water beside them? With no trace of water in their lungs?"

"But—"

The Earl of Kensington leaned close. "I have received confidential information from the assistant coroner who performed the postmortems. They were not drowned: they were *murdered!* The knowledge has been adjudged too dangerous to be revealed to the public. Another act of cowardly infamy by those who rule us in the name of England."

"But—"

"But consider this carefully, my dear Dennett. Two Members of Parliament, both of them Yeoman Sons of Essex, brazenly murdered in the heart of England by French agents! If even *they* are not safe from the ferocity of Napoleon and his hangman the Marquis of Vézelay, then what of ourselves?"

Sir Norvil Dennett hastily gulped the remainder of his port while Wester watched sardonically. Just how, the Earl wondered, did Dennett think the Napoleonic tyranny had maintained itself for nearly two centuries now, dominating all of Europe west of the Ottoman Empire? By sweetness and reason? By appeal to the good nature of its subject races? The man was an idiot!

Wester ran his fingers through his luxurious growth of side-whiskers, his lips pursed. And yet clearly the man was also a patriot. Why else would he have joined the Yeoman Sons of Essex long before the movement had obtained its first seats in Parliament? No, Dennett was far from being one of those Johnny-come-latelies who had recently jumped onto their bandwagon by the thousands and sent two dozen members of the Sons of Essex to Parliament in the last election. Obviously, like Wester himself, he yearned for that untrammeled freedom which had been the birthright of

every Englishman for those centuries before the catastrophic battle of the Cotswold Encirclement had led to the abject
surrender to Bonaparte by mad King George and the traitor
Fox.

The Earl of Kensington shook his head in despair mingled with puzzlement. Ever since the loss of the American
colonies two centuries before, followed hard by the crush-
ing defeat inflicted by Bonaparte, the once mighty British
Empire had been little more than a memory. *And yet no one
seemed to care!*

Had Englishmen lost that steely resolve that had once
defeated the Armada and sent their sons and daughters to
bring the benefits of British rule to the farthest corners of
the globe? Was there no one but himself—and the Yeoman
Sons of Essex—who recognized the monstrousness of having had the bastard House of Bonaparte-Hanover on the
throne in Buckingham Palace for 105 years now? How
could the vast majority of the millions of true-born Englishmen stomach the insult of paying homage to a so-called
British sovereign named—His Royal Majesty King
Auguste-François!

Wester's lips tightened. Soon, he vowed, how very soon,
the French would pay at last for the indignities and miseries
they had inflicted on his beloved England!

How they would pay!

Three hundred and thirty miles to the east of London in a
quiet park on the outskirts of Düsseldorf, Herr Doctor
Professor and Director Sigismund Hubmaier tossed sleep-
lessly in his elaborately carved mahogany bed on the third
floor of the pale granite building that housed Die Freunde
der Goethe Vereinigung—the Friends of Goethe Society.
An owl hooted softly from one of the great elms that shaded
the spacious grounds of the Society, and the warm evening
breeze brought the unmistakable smell of impending rain
through the open windows of his bedroom. From far away
came the mournful call of barges moving up and down the
Rhine.

For most of the day the Herr Doctor Professor had been
absorbed in the study of a hand-delivered missive from his

colleague Sir Norvil Dennett in England detailing the theoretical flaws in the Goethe Society's approach to the goal that beckoned them both—the construction of a time machine. Sir Dennett's arguments were, Hubmaier had to concede, both logical and closely reasoned, but he was, nonetheless, still convinced that they were somehow subtly wrong. Or, if not actually wrong, then at least totally irrelevant. For surely the immortal Einstein's noble theory of equivalency was broad enough to permit of *two* possible paths to the same goal!

And Sir Dennett's objections, Hubmaier reassured himself, were purely theoretical in nature. Did he, Sir Dennett, have an actual apparatus constructed, in actual operation, as was the machine in the subbasement of the Society's headquarters?

No! A thousand times no!

The Herr Doctor Professor turned restlessly in his bed. And yet—if his own theories were correct—why wasn't the machine *working?* This was the question that had tormented him for three days and nights now, ever since his team of scientists had made their last adjustments to the machine whose very existence was unknown to their English colleagues, and with apparent success sent a 67-kilogram package of recording devices into what they had calculated would be the early seventh century B.C. The sturdy package had suddenly vanished—that was indisputable! Let Sir Dennett explain *that* away!

But why then—oh, why—after three full days with the machine in continuous operation, hadn't the instrumentation returned?

Could Sir Dennett's niggardly objections somehow be right?

Hubmaier replumped the wrinkled pillow behind his head. Tomorrow they would have to dismantle the machine and see if they could find some mechanical fault. In the meantime, a junior member of the team named Müller had been assigned the dreary night watch in the increasingly dim hope that the machine might unexpectedly deliver—something.

Outside his window the owl hooted derisively.

* * *

The fabled City of Light, the greatest metropolis in the world as well as the capital of Le Grand Empire des Etats-Unis de l'Europe, lay glowing 290 miles to the south-west of Düsseldorf, its brightly lighted boulevards and cafés still thronged with festive merrymakers from the entire empire. In a quiet, treelined street a few hundred yards from the Seine and the Place de la Concorde, Gérard Philippe Edouard de Bounias, 6th Marquis of Vézelay, sat in his high-ceilinged office of gilt and silk-paneled walls on the Avenue de Marigny in the 8th Arrondissement.

The formal gardens of the Elysée Palace lay directly across the street from his third-story window, so that by turning his head he could look down upon the rows of trees and ornamental bushes softly illuminated at night by cunningly hidden red, blue, and orange spotlights. In the grandiose marble building at the end of the park, the Marquis knew, the old man who was Napoleon V, Emperor of All the French and of the Great Empire of the United States of Europe, lay deep in untroubled sleep.

The Marquis yawned, and reached for the half-empty glass of red wine which with a platter of two dozen different cheeses had constituted his evening meal, taken, as so many of them were these days, at his desk while he worked steadily through the great mountain of paperwork he found awaiting him every morning.

In order that our beloved Emperor might rest untroubled, he muttered sardonically.

Now he scanned the report from a newly recruited agent in Düsseldorf, a native German who had—by his own assertion—penetrated some obscure cultural association called Die Freunde der Goethe Vereinigung in the guise of a second footman. The Marquis snorted. Penetrated indeed! The man *was* a second footman! What self-important airs these fools could give themselves!

He lay the report aside with a snort, paused for a moment, then reached for it anew. How curious the glorious French tongue could be when written by a German!

At last the secrets of the apparatus contrived in the caverns of the building have I disemboweled! Not an engine for the propagation of the tonalations of the 200-piece symphonic orchestrations as is fervently hoped to be supposed, but an instrumentality of temporal remission it is! For revelationcy of such astoundingness, the remittance in urgency of 2,000 francs will—

An instrumentality of temporal remission, repeated the Marquis of Vézelay to himself. What on earth could the fool imagine that he was reporting?

With a final sigh he pushed the remaining papers to one side and rose wearily to his feet, a slight man in late middle age with thinning brown hair and a long narrow face whose aristocratic mien and pointed brown beard imparted an air of Satanic sardonicism. He brushed a few obstinate crumbs from the exquisitely tailored pin-striped grey suit with extra-wide lapels and two rows of silver buttons for which he traveled yearly to Savile Row in London to be fitted by Perkins & Sons, bespoke tailors to four generations of the Royal Family, and picked up his straw boater and silver-tipped walking stick. The Empire would surely stand another day while the director of His Imperial Majesty's Special Directorate snatched a few hours' sleep. But as he rang for his chauffeur, the nagging thought recurred to him: What *was* an instrumentality of temporal remission?

The question was far too intriguing for the hyperactive sense of curiosity which had tormented him all his life. Tomorrow he would have to find out. . . .

CHAPTER
=== 5 ===

."—PHINS."

The MacNair half choked on the last syllable.

No longer was he standing in the cool shade of a New England forest, hoisting the Tirthankara Mardumjar's diamond-studded crown to his head. Now, to his utter stupefaction, he found himself entangled in the midst of a complicated piece of machinery in the glare of what appeared to be a fully equipped electrical research laboratory. His ears were assaulted by the sharp whine of a million demented bees apparently buzzing about his head, while a sharp piece of metal jabbed painfully into his side. His hands, he saw, still reached up to grip the pulsating GODHEAD on the top of his head, but that was his sole article of clothing. Aside from the bejeweled crown, he was now suddenly and utterly naked.

Somewhere in the distance an unseen alarm began to howl.

Sir Kevin Deane de Courtney MacNair of MacNair squeezed his eyes shut until sparkling stars began to move across the blackness. What kind of a nightmare could he be having? Warily he reopened his eyes. He was still naked. He was still in a laboratory. He still felt the GODHEAD's heavy weight upon his head.

It was awkward trying to turn his head while burdened with the unwieldy crown as well as being constrained by this strange grid of chromium tubing all around him. But by shuffling his feet in tiny back-and-forth movements he eventually managed to turn his entire body about in a complete circle, satisfying himself that at least for the moment the spacious, brightly lighted laboratory was completely deserted. A glass-paneled door at the far side of the room seemed to reveal a dim corridor from which the appalling noise of the alarm was emanating.

His heart thumped loudly. Was that *movement* beyond the door, a white face peering in? Impossible to tell with the glare of the GODHEAD's lights flashing only inches away. With trembling hands he reached up and removed the crown. A moment later he had found the switch that cut off its remarkable light show. With a sigh of relief he sagged back against the metal restraints of his cage, then almost instantly bounced forward again.

He had to get *out* of here!

Both hands were needed to extricate his naked form from the bowels of the peculiar machinery which enclosed him, so he was first obliged to set the crown on the tiny wrought-iron platform beneath his feet. Horribly aware of his ridiculous and undignified exhibition of naked flesh, the MacNair crawled awkwardly through the chromium tubing, then turned to retrieve the swami's diamond-studded crown. A moment later he stood hugging the GODHEAD tightly against his bare belly. In spite of the wail of the alarm, he could still hear behind him the high-pitched hum of the bizarre machinery which had held him prisoner. He grit his teeth and took an indecisive step forward.

That ghastly buzzer! It was still ringing, seemingly louder than ever! How long before someone arrived to see what the commotion was? Someone, perhaps, with a gun. . . .

A gun! He stared aghast at the crown in his hands. However he had come to find himself in this madman's nightmare, it was absolutely imperative that he not be found standing stark naked holding a stolen crown worth $100 million!

Desperately he looked about the laboratory. Were those shouts he suddenly heard? *There!* In the far corner . . . dull white wooden cupboards and storage shelves that spilled over with a jumble of mechanical parts and tools. He leapt across the room, then frantically yanked open one cupboard after another until he found a half-empty wooden box just large enough to hold the GODHEAD. Dumping out its contents, he jammed the crown inside, then hastily covered it with what appeared to be solenoids, coils of insulated wiring, and a rusty panel of switches. A moment later the crate was shoved to the back of the cupboard, concealed by two more boxes and a tattered smock.

As the MacNair dashed madly to the other side of the laboratory where he had spotted three gleaming white smocks hanging from the wall, he asked himself wildly why all the boxes he had come across should have had their labels in—German!

A wooden desk covered with pages of scribbled mathematical calculations caught his eye as he reached for a smock. Stunned, he stared down at the clutter of papers, unable to move. Everything he saw was in German! Hardly daring to breathe, the alarm's clangor harsh in his ears, he pulled open one desk drawer after another. Letterheads, forms, invoices, everything without exception was in German. If his faltering wits could be trusted, he was in the laboratory of something calling itself Die Freunde der Goethe Vereinigung!

Now he *did* hear the sound of excited voices, and he leapt away from the desk. When the door from the corridor burst open and three men in pajamas and dressing gowns crowded through, they stopped short in astonishment at the sight of a small naked man in early middle age desperately trying to pull one of their large starched laboratory smocks around his pale white shoulders.

"Please don't be afraid," murmured the Herr Doctor Professor and Director Sigismund Hubmaier in soothing Germanic tones. "We are your *friends.*"

All very likely, admitted the MacNair to himself. At least this short, stout, red-faced German *looked* enough like a jolly, beardless Kriss Kringle to inspire trust and friendship in almost anyone but a professional skeptic like himself. But at the moment he was not about to trust *anyone.* Until he knew what was going on around him, he was revealing nothing—not even his knowledge of reasonably adequate German acquired some years before during an enforced sabbatical of nine and a half months in a federal retirement center just outside Baden-Baden.

He turned his eyes away from the eager face of Director Hubmaier and back to the mug of hot oxtail soup which had been tentatively handed to him along with a heavy silver spoon. Buried in the folds of his ridiculous smock, the MacNair sat on a hard wooden chair beside the director's desk, stirring the steaming soup and pretending to ignore the babble of voices around him.

As he sipped cautiously at the hot broth, he counted eleven men in various kinds of nightclothes clustered around the desk. One of them, he gathered by listening to a long litany of loud recrimination, was supposed to have been on watch in the laboratory at the time he had suddenly materialized. But the straw-headed youth named Müller, to the MacNair's everlasting thanks, had chosen that moment to visit the kitchen on the floor above to prepare himself an evening snack of leftover sauerbraten and the very soup the MacNair was now savoring. His head still whirling with the terrifying implications of his situation, the MacNair used the silver spoon to pick out a large piece of tender marrow. He swallowed it hungrily, reflecting dourly that in addition to whatever else might be happening to him his stomach was anxiously telling him that it was dinnertime.

Ah, these blessed Germans! Oxtail soup was all very well, but couldn't they have handed him a triple shot of Scotch instead?

The conversation around him was growing increasingly loud and acrimonious. "He is obviously a man from the past!" cried a white-haired gentleman wearing a red flannel nightgown and a floppy grey nightcap that dangled from his head. "From so far in the past that German is not yet even spoken!"

"*Quatsch!* Just look at him! His haircut, his body, his demeanor. See how he uses a spoon as if it were second nature! He's obviously a man of our own era."

"Spoons were in common use in seventh-century Greece —are you forgetting the era to which we sent the machine?"

"But not to Greece! It was to stay here in Germany! Look at him, his manicured fingernails and toenails, that carefully barbered beard! Does that look like the handiwork of our revered Germanic ancestors in the seventh-century-B.C. Black Forest?"

"You are making ridiculous objections! You were always against the project! Avow it: Time travel is a reality!"

"So you say! But why, in that case, do we find before us seventy kilograms of living human male instead of sixty-seven kilograms of inert instrumentation?"

"What will you wager that he weighs exactly sixty-seven kilograms?"

"Ha!" cried Herr Doctor Professor and Director Hubmaier. "At last a grain of sense in all this nonsense! Quickly, to the scales, before he drinks any more soup!"

While his protective smock was apologetically removed and he was being carefully weighed, the MacNair turned matters over in his mind and came to a number of tentative conclusions.

First: By some miracle undoubtedly associated with the apparatus in which he had initially found himself, he was definitely in Germany. It was far too difficult to deny the obvious: the evidence of the papers on the desk, the language of the men around him, all the hidden boxes he had seen in the cupboards. And the large clock on the wall: it now read 1:34. Assuming that was 1:34 *A.M.*, a logical assumption in view of the nightclothes of all these excitable Germans, that would jibe with the time difference between western Europe and the eastern United States.

Second: Whatever the hopes of these earnest Teutonic savants, their time machine was clearly no time machine at all, at least as it concerned the MacNair. For there on the very desk at which he had been sitting was a thick calendar of the sort from which you ripped away a single page per day to reveal the following day's date. Even in Gothic script it was easy enough to read the date: July 22, 1991.

Third: He was almost certainly not an amnesiac, or the victim of some inconceivably elaborate hoax, or a madman confined in an asylum with a clutch of fellow lunatics, for the simple reason that no time at all had elapsed in which he could have lost either his memory or his reason. If the desk calendar had read July 22, 1992, that would be a different matter. But as it was—

But his thoughts were interrupted as he was reclothed

and led back to his chair by a solicitous Director Hubmaier.

"Excellent thinking, my dear Gregor," burbled the Herr Doctor Professor. "He does indeed weigh precisely sixty-seven kilograms—plus, of course, the forty grams or so of soup he has just ingested. Obviously, for reasons which we do not yet understand, the machinery mistook this unfortunate gentleman for our package of instrumentation and deposited him here in the middle of our laboratory."

"Sir Dennett must be informed at once."

"No, no, not Dennett—Kensington," said Hubmaier firmly. "He, after all, is their leader, and protocol dictates that—"

"But Kensington is in Scotland on a fortnight's shoot with the King! It would be far too dangerous to send a message to him while—"

"Auguste-François?" snorted Hubmaier, his three chins quivering violently and his nostrils flaring. *"That* miserable excuse for a king? I ask myself how a true patriot such as Kensington can bring himself to toady to such a creature, even in a noble cause! How *can* the British put up with the House of Bonaparte-Hanover? How truly *spineless* they are!"

"But how else could Napoleon trust the English to—"

"How can we *Germans* put up with the Bonapartes?"

"Why doesn't Kensington simply grab Auguste-François by the neck and choke him to death?" yelled another gleefully.

"Or push him into Loch Ness and let the monster get him?" wondered a third.

"Enough of this childishness!" shouted Hubmaier, smiling in spite of himself at the boisterousness which animated his colleagues. "We are all participants in one of the world-historical moments and must conduct ourselves accordingly. And we must carefully consider our next step. Whatever we feel about the so-called English Royal Family, and of Kensington's relationship with it, he is, after all, the leader of our project, even more so than Prince Konrad, and it goes without saying that he should be immediately notified. He is *not* with His so-called Royal Majesty in Scotland, for the shooting trip has been postponed. We must—"

The MacNair's head whirled with excitement. Auguste-François King of *England?* How very extraordinary! The House of Bonaparte-Hanover? Real, live Bonapartes? Could it possibly be true? If so, how absolutely thought-provoking for a man of ready wit and steely resolve! Quickly he reviewed the situation in his mind, the circumstances of his arrival, the physical evidence of the laboratory, the implications of the scraps of conversation he had so cunningly contrived to overhear. Unless he actually *was* somehow trapped in a freakish dream, there seemed but one conceivable explanation for all of this, extraordinary as it might be. In which case, did even *he* dare to . . . ?

Sir Kevin Deane de Courtney MacNair of MacNair set down his empty mug, inhaled deeply, and offered up a silent prayer to whatever gods might choose to receive it. *Sir Kevin Deane de Courtney MacNair of MacNair,* he murmured to himself, I will miss you. . . .

"I say," he interrupted in the clipped, precise tones of Eton and Oxford, "do any of you chaps speak English?"

A sudden hush fell. The Herr Doctor Professor and Director Hubmaier's twinkling blue eyes widened. "But . . . but of course."

"Indeed. You might have done so before, you know. Saved me considerable worry."

The crowd around the MacNair pressed closer, their faces reflecting astonishment and curiosity mingled with disappointment and bafflement. *"Mein Herr* is *English?"* exclaimed the director with only the hint of an accent, his cherubic round face quivering with a wealth of conflicting emotions. "A tourist, perhaps?"

"A tourist?" cried the MacNair indignantly. "Of course I'm not a tourist! I'm—" He broke off suddenly and stared about him with growing suspicion. "Is that *Russian* you're speaking?"

"Russian?" The Herr Doctor Professor turned to exchange looks of bafflement with his pajamaed colleagues. "Who can speak Russian? No one in Europe has spoken Russian for three hundred years! We were speaking German."

The MacNair's eyes widened. "German? Why the bloody

hell are you speaking *German?"*

"But what else would we speak in Düsseldorf?" asked Hubmaier apologetically.

"Düsseldorf? You're simply not making sense, man! What the devil am I doing in Düsseldorf?"

"Precisely that is what we too would like to know, *mein Herr.* If I may ask: Where were you before you were . . . transported here?" There was a sudden hush as the group of Germans huddled around the MacNair awaited his momentous answer. The MacNair drew a deep breath. . . .

In the dimly lit corridor outside the laboratory Siegfried Kleinmutter, second footman to the Friends of Goethe Society, peered cautiously around the edge of the partially opened door, ears straining to catch every word. How absolutely infuriating! Just as the man from the past began to speak, they had changed languages! How maddening! Was that possibly English? Kleinmutter clenched his fists in anger. Whatever it was, he could no longer understand a word! And where, the second footman suddenly asked himself belatedly, was the wondrous sparkling crown of such breathtaking beauty he had momentarily glimpsed?

Slowly the MacNair exhaled the air from his lungs. "Where was I?" he repeated. "Why, in my bath, of course, at the Palace. Why else do you suppose I'm absolutely starkers?"

"The Palace?" murmured Hubmaier. "Which palace is that, *mein Herr?"*

"Bloody flaming hell!" roared the MacNair, angrily slapping his empty mug onto the top of the desk. *"Buckingham* Palace, of course! Where else would you expect to find me?" He glared at each astonished German in turn. "I should have thought that even in *Düsseldorf* there might be someone who could recognize Prince William Ernest Augustus, Duke of York, third in succession to the throne of Great Britain and Ireland!"

CHAPTER
=== 6 ===

A MAN FROM the *past?* muttered the Marquis of Vézelay incredulously. As naked as a worm and wearing a great golden crown with a million jewels and ten thousand flashing lights? At least this man Kleinmutter showed no lack of imagination!

Irritably he rang the buzzer on his desk to summon his aide. "Put me through to Berlin," he said to Colonel Etournaud when he had marched stiffly into the room.

"By telephone, sir?" The colonel's eyebrows shot up.

"Yes, by telephone!" The Marquis sighed. Why was the Emperor so convinced that the telephone was only a fad of the Americans, unfit for the dignified business of Empire? Didn't he know that an empire extending from Lapland in the north to Gibraltar and Sicily in the south and as far east as Vienna could make practical use of the accursed instrument? Hadn't it been in operation for over a hundred years now? Why, even the *Turks* used it throughout their own vast empire!

But no. The telephone hadn't been invented by a Frenchman, so long ago Alexine I had hindered its installation in France, even during the dark days of the Great War of 1910 when its use against the Ottomans might have been decisive. The Marquis of Vézelay toyed pensively with the tip of his beard while he waited for Etournaud to return. Thank God that *that* particular pigheaded Bonaparte had been assassinated by a crazed anarchist seven long months after

37

the initiation of hostilities. If her son Napoleon IV hadn't acceded to the throne, the war might *still* be dragging on.

In spite of the shafts of bright sunlight that angled through the tall narrow windows of his office, the Marquis of Vézelay shuddered. The Great War had come to its stalemated, inconclusive end long before his birth, but in his youth he had spoken with veterans who had survived its carnage. This single monstrous exception to the two centuries of European peace which had been the legacy of the magnificent Bonaparte had left dead a full quarter of a million soldiers!

To the Marquis the figure was something beyond the grasp of the human mind. Never again could the horrors of war be allowed to ravage Europe! To that end, he had pledged his life, his fortune, his sacred honor to the service of His Imperial Majesty. God and the Marquis of Vézelay willing, it *would* not happen again!

"Berlin?" he shouted at last into the ornate gilt and bronze telephone which his aide brought to his desk on a silver tray. "Is this Marcus? I can hardly hear you." The Marquis blew sharply into the instrument, then tapped it on his desk. "Listen, *mon cher* Marcus, you are undoubtedly working too hard in Berlin. I want you to take a little vacation. Yes, yes, a vacation! To Düssel— Damn!" The Marquis of Vézelay grimaced at Colonel Etournaud. "Cut off! *Mince alors!* Try to get through again. *Mince!* Imagine: Even the *English* use the telephone!"

"Third in line to the throne of England!" The Earl of Kensington goggled at the thick sheets of creamy paper as if they had suddenly turned to wriggling snakes in his hands. "Can Hubmaier have lost his *mind?*"

"For heaven's sake, man, don't stop now," snapped Sir Norvil Dennett. "What else does he say?"

"Yes, yes," agreed Lord Avery of Eventon, "do go on."

"It's simply preposterous," snorted the Earl, turning away to the broad French windows that opened from the morning room onto the south terrace. Behind his stocky figure could be glimpsed a long row of graceful marble nymphs running along the terrace as far as the broad steps that led down to the vast park with its cold grey lake. Even on a bright summer's morning the dark green forest of Scotch pine that flanked the lake looked gloomy and uninviting, and the graceful white swans that floated on the still surface of the chilly waters, Kensington knew from sad experience, were as surly as the dour Scotsmen who tended the grounds of Dennett's enormous domain. Grimacing, the Earl of Kensington returned his attention to the two men who stood watching him impatiently. Here at Garnaway Castle, the 16,000-acre estate in Morayshire in northern Scotland where Dennett carried out his research, Wester found the scientist's manner far more imperious and even more trying than in London.

"Listen to this," said Kensington with sardonic skepticism. *"We know, of course, that part two of Einstein's Special Theory of General Equivalency theoretically allows for movement in either direction across Time as well as across Space. It now appears as if Space, in this sense, must be construed to encompass what we may term Parallel Worlds, or Alternate Universes. What, for example, might our own present world be like if Suleiman the Savage had* not *defeated the Russians in the Battle of Krasnodar in 1697, and in consequence the Ottoman Empire had* not *expanded into Siberia and Central Europe? What—"*

"Please," protested Sir Norvil, "does he take us for ninnies? Get to the *meat* of it!"

"But that was really most interesting," protested Lord Eventon. "I've never—"

"I will give you a kindergarten course about parallel worlds at some future date," snapped the Master of Garnaway, his eyes flashing behind his half-moon spectacles. "Kensington: continue."

"Very well," muttered Wester, rapidly scanning the tight Germanic penmanship. "Here: *If not a time traveler, our unexpected guest can only be a visitor somehow brought to our world from some neighboring or parallel universe. This, in fact, is confirmed by him. He is, he states, and I have no reason to gainsay him, Prince William Ernest Augustus Henley, Duke of York, third in succession to the English throne. In* his *world his father King Frederick IV occupies the throne, for not only did the first Bonaparte* not *invade England, but the tyrant's direct family line soon died out.*

Princess Yvonne, the youngest daughter of Napoleon III, never married the Prince of Wales in 1886, for the good and sufficient reason that she never existed. The original House of Hanover, therefore, occupies the British throne to this day."

There was a gasp from Lord Eventon. "No Bonaparte? But this is incredible! The coincidence is simply too—"

"No, no," corrected Kensington irritably, "that is *not* what he says. Listen: *In Prince William's world, as in ours, Napoleon Bonaparte attempted to conquer Europe. But in this other world he was forced to fight a number of wars against a succession of coalitions which included a great Russian power. He never seriously attempted to invade England, and in 1815 he was decisively defeated at an obscure locale in Belgium called Waterloo, then sent into lifelong exile. England subsequently went on to become the world's mightiest empire, while our own many Germanic states and principalities were eventually united in the middle of the nineteenth century into a single powerful nation. To our horror and dismay, Prince William informs us that early this century a militant Germany, led by tyrants fully worthy of assuming the foul mantle of the evil Bonaparte himself, waged two terrible wars of aggression against England, France, Russia, and the United States. In both cases Germany was ultimately defeated but the destructiveness of these wars eventually weakened all of Europe to the point where the world's two great Powers are now Russia and the United States of America."*

"Germany?" snorted Sir Norvil Dennett. "Two hundred princelings in search of a king simultaneously fighting England, France, and the United States? Ridiculous!"

"What utter nonsense!" spluttered Lord Eventon. "Didn't Hubmaier speak of Russia? Why, that's like saying . . . like saying that the kingdom of the *Visigoths* is the world's greatest power! There *is* no Russia!"

The Earl of Kensington sighed wearily as he tapped the rolled-up letter against the knuckles of his meaty left hand. "In *our* world Russia no longer exists," he enunciated carefully, "but in *his* world there *is* still a Russia. That is why they are called alternate universes."

"Ah. Ah, I begin to see." Lord Avery of Eventon looked

thoughtfully out at the dark forest that ringed the bright green meadowland of the park before imperceptibly merging with the far-off hills. "I say, Kensington . . . Does this mean you actually might *believe* . . . this . . . ?"

Alfred St. John Wester tugged fretfully at his ample red jowls. "I must say, now that I have read the entire letter, there *is* a certain coherence to—"

"It *sounds* preposterous," said Sir Norvil Dennett slowly, "but after all, isn't all of this our very goal: a world without Napoleon? A world in which the British Empire has regained its rightful place?" He came to a sudden decision. "I say, Kensington, I must see this so-called prince for myself!"

Siegfried Kleinmutter, second footman to Die Freunde der Goethe Vereinigung and part-time French agent, crept nervously along the darkened corridors and down the rear staircases of the five-story building that housed the Society and its Fellows. Berlin, he knew, had been skeptical about what he had so ardently reported. "What kind of schnapps have you been drinking, Kleinmutter?" his contact here in Düsseldorf had asked him rudely. "You think I dare pass on a story like this to Berlin and Paris? They'll take us for madmen—or worse! Have you ever heard what the French do to *agents provocateurs?*"

Kleinmutter shuddered in the darkness as he halted momentarily on the third-floor landing with the French library to his left and the English library to his right. He *didn't* know what the French did to *agents provocateurs* but he had heard fearsome tales of the devilish Marquis of Vézelay and had no trouble at all believing anything sufficiently horrible about the great tyranny to the west that kept his own native Germany divided into a host of impotent petty kingdoms. He could feel his heart thudding rapidly in his chest and with a soft sigh leaned back against the stairway wall to wait for his nerves to steady. If only he didn't need the francs that only the French could provide . . .

But he would show them! he swore with sudden resolution. He would *prove* that he hadn't been imagining things, that he actually *had* seen the man from the past with his great golden crown, its thousands of dazzling lights, its millions of diamonds. He would show them so that even *Paris* would hear of Siegfried Kleinmutter!

The second footman, still in his green and gold livery, stopped outside the darkened laboratory, where he listened for a long moment, then cautiously stepped inside. Ha! It was as he had foreseen, entirely deserted! But then who would be here at three in the morning? He flipped on the tiny battery-powered flashlight he had purchased that afternoon, then slowly and methodically, though the blood was pounding in his ears, began to search the laboratory for that wondrous crown he had glimpsed for a few unforgettable seconds when the man from the past had suddenly materialized.

From what he had seen from the corridor while the herr doctor professors talked to the man from the past and then subsequently led him off to bed in the red room, he knew that the strange creature hadn't left the laboratory with the crown. And since none of the learned Fellows seemed even remotely aware of its existence, it followed that for reasons of his own the man from the past must have hidden it just before the others had burst into the laboratory.

And where else could he have hidden it except in this very laboratory? The second footman grinned triumphantly in the darkness. What a coup it would be when he held it in his very hands!

CHAPTER
=== 7 ===

"THE DIAMONDS, THE diamonds," chortled the MacNair to himself as he crept cautiously down the stairs, "whatever shall I do with the diamonds?" It was all very well being third in line to the throne of Ireland and Great Britain, but as a hedge against the uncertainties of inflation and old age there was nothing to equal the possession of 30,000 flawless diamonds!

For, he reflected as he peeked around the edge of the doorway into the darkened laboratory, it was still to be seen just how far he could travel with this newfound persona of bonny Prince William, the jolly old Duke of York. He grinned wolfishly. Up to this point it had hardly been a fair contest to pit the MacNair against these poor addled Teutons. It would be far different when the major-leaguers —the real English nobility—began to pour in to examine him. A MacNair would never panic in the face of adversity, of course, but it never hurt to have some sort of contingency plan either. And a quick examination of the Encyclopaedia Britannica in the English library on the third floor had told him that diamonds were just as much a girl's best friend in this particular universe as in his own. Thank goodness that *some* things hadn't changed!

Boldly he turned on the laboratory lights. Who would dare question a British prince of the realm about his activities at even three in the morning? Certainly no one had bothered him the previous afternoon as he had snooped around the spacious elm-shaded grounds of the Society. . . .

As the MacNair strolled slowly through the immaculately manicured park, his head bent as if in melancholy meditation, he could hear the faint sounds of trolley cars clanking by on the road in front of the Society's imposing granite headquarters and the occasional horn of this world's boxy black automobiles that looked like refugees from 1930 movies. Threatening black thunderheads were piling up in the sky just to the north of Düsseldorf, but here the hot July sun still shone brilliantly. The MacNair paused to remove the round blue bowler which the Herr Doctor Professor had pressed upon him and wiped the sweat from his lofty brow. He flicked a drop of perspiration from the tip of his carefully trimmed Vandyke, then let his fastidious eye move once again from the dark blue bowler in his hand to the excruciatingly garish orange of the hairy tweed suit which had been proudly offered him yesterday morning. "So very English, is it not?" had exclaimed Herr Scientist Rausenberger as he and the establishment's butler held it up for the MacNair's astonished inspection. "His Regal Highness will feel deliciously at home in it!"

With a heartfelt sigh the MacNair replaced the grotesque bowler and moved deeper into the park. In a secluded corner of the garden, hidden in the deep dark shade of an enormous horse chestnut tree, he found to his delight an old and curiously neglected gazebo of superb gingerbread design. The MacNair stepped cautiously into its refreshing coolness and sank slowly into a dusty wicker chair. Thoughtfully he considered the summerhouse's worn coconut matting, the warped and partially broken floorboards. A quick glance showed that no one else was about in the park. He knelt on the wooden floor and carefully lifted a corner of the coconut matting. . . .

Now the MacNair paused for a moment beside the desk at which he had announced to the astonished cream of Teutonic science that he was in actuality Prince William Ernest Augustus, late of Buckingham Palace, and grinned even more wolfishly than before. For now he had a hidey-hole beneath a loosely fitting floorboard which would do very nicely indeed for the temporary concealment of a modestly sized object worth some hundreds of millions of dollars. Let even the editors of Debrett's *Peerage* themselves come to question his royal pedigree—the MacNair would still have his diamonds!

He cast an appraising glance around the brightly lighted laboratory, then stepped jauntily past the curious machine which had so brusquely removed him from his own familiar world and knelt before the cupboard where his natural resourcefulness had led him to hide the GODHEAD three nights before. Yes, here were the two wooden boxes (curious that cardboard cartons seemed almost unknown in this world; it definitely lagged behind his own in a number of unexpected ways), here was the wadded-up old rag of a smock, here was his own beautiful crate. . . .

With loving hands he removed the panel of switches, the coils of wire, the half-dozen rusty solenoids and found . . . the bottom of the crate! The MacNair's eyes bulged and his heart lurched. The GODHEAD was gone!

Siegfried Kleinmutter had grown increasingly nervous as well as hungry as he sat in the bare anteroom, a small wooden box on his knees, contemptuously eyed by an enormous blond Gascon in a tight-fitting blue suit who sat behind an equally bare desk smoking one foul French cigarette after another. Kleinmutter's stomach protested noisily. It had been barely dawn when he hastily downed a meager breakfast of cheese and pickles, and for hours now he had been tormented by the pungent smells of braised sauerkraut and roasting pork rising from the kitchen below. . . .

For to Kleinmutter's surprise and dismay, it was not the grandiose French Mission that he had found after a morning spent on the new electrified train to Berlin, but a modest French bistro serving Alsatian cuisine. Could Knickmeyer have treacherously given him a spurious address made up at random? He had known that he was taking a desperate risk in bullying his cutout in Düsseldorf into disclosing the address of their superior in Berlin and clearly recognized that he was making a mortal enemy of Knickmeyer. But all that had been easy enough to dismiss as he contemplated the rewards that would be his alone when first Berlin, and then Paris, beheld the wonders of the crown. . . .

Once again he had examined the apparently ordinary restaurant, its lacy curtains in the windows, its elaborate French menu posted on each side of the door. With a baffled shrug Kleinmutter had stepped into the restaurant. It was just before lunchtime and waiters scurried about repolishing already gleaming glasses and arranging silverware and small vases of flowers. The maître d'hôtel, still in his shirt sleeves, had stepped forward, eyebrows raised. They had risen even higher when Kleinmutter inquired hesitantly for a certain Monsieur Sitjar. A moment later he had been almost surreptitiously rushed up a staircase and into this depressing room with its brute of a guard. A long afternoon had been spent waiting with neither food nor drink while he listened avidly to the sounds of revelry that rang out throughout the interminable lunch hour. Now it was nearly dinnertime and—

A door behind the watchdog at the desk suddenly opened. "Idiot!" cried an angry voice in French. "Yes, you! Come in here at once!" Siegfried Kleinmutter's heart leapt in panic. With dragging footsteps he let himself be shoved by the enormous French guard into a small, starkly furnished office glowing with the last orange rays of the setting sun. A red-faced Frenchman with a bristling ginger mustache glared at him from behind a drab metal desk. "Idiot!" repeated Marcus Sitjar furiously. "It's *you* I've been chasing around for all over Düsseldorf!"

Kleinmutter recoiled in horror as the awesome Frenchman rose to his feet and shook a clenched fist under his nose. "Your coming here is a breach of every *conceivable* rule! Your cutout Knickmeyer is already on his way to France, where I trust that twenty years of harvesting sugar beets will teach him the nature of discretion." As Kleinmutter paled, the terrifying Frenchman leaned forward and smiled with genuine pleasure. "I have been in touch directly with Monsieur le Marquis de Vézelay, Herr Kleinmutter, so I can assure you with great pleasure that if whatever you are carrying under your arm does *not* measure up to your world-shaking claims for it, I have express permission to send you off on your *own* little trip. *Not* back to Düsseldorf, my dear Kleinmutter, but to a sunny southern island: *Devil's* Island!"

Siegfried Kleinmutter fainted.

"You say you've sent him off to Devil's Island?" muttered Captain LeFleur without looking up from his examination of the extraordinary object which his longtime acquaintance Marcus Sitjar had brought earlier this evening just as he was preparing for bed. Now, with growing astonishment, he leaned over a table in the cramped laboratory of the Grunewald Barracks just outside the heart of Berlin where the Imperial French Army maintained a symbolic presence of a single ceremonial regiment.

"A small joke," murmured Sitjar, nearly awed into silence by the sight of the coruscating fires of the thousands of diamonds as they flashed and glittered under the high-intensity beams directed downward by Captain LeFleur, "at least for the moment. Right now he's in a holding cell here in the barracks until I decide what to do with him."

"If he really brought you *this*," murmured Captain Le-Fleur softly, "then I suggest you make him president of the Senate."

"It *is* a beauty, isn't it?"

"It's extraordinary!" grunted Captain LeFleur as he turned the crown over and over in his long pale hands. "Not only are these genuine diamonds, my dear Sitjar, but look at these incredible—well, I don't know what to call them—*devices*, all about it." He pointed at an array of tiny multicolored microchips. "I've never seen anything quite like them. They are obviously man-made, clearly purposeful rather than decorative in character, and quite probably electrical in nature. But they are of a size that at least for the moment would rule out any function I can imagine."

"Could they account for the brilliant flashing lights that Kleinmutter spoke of?"

LeFleur shrugged and placed the tip of a finger on a minuscule red bulb. "Frankly, I don't understand how a thousand bulbs as tiny as these could produce any light at all. And where would the power come from?"

"But it's *not* a joke of some sort, a hoax?" asked Sitjar anxiously, tugging at the end of his ginger mustache. "It's not just a contrivance that—"

"Good heavens! On such a scale? It would be like building a full-scale copy of St. Peter's Basilica out of papier-mâché in the middle of your backyard. It might be done, I suppose, but why would anyone bother?"

"Hmmm. So you think that all of these . . . devices on it are there for some *purpose."* Marcus Sitjar bent closer. "For instance, this little switch here. *That* seems straightforward enough." He tugged again at the tip of his mustache. "What do you suppose would happen if we just . . . flipped it over?" His finger darted out.

"Stop!" cried Captain LeFleur, far too late.

Several years earlier in the wet and gloomy spring of 1987, Sir Walter Courtney, the immediate predecessor to the MacNair of MacNair, had purchased a bankrupt and deserted distillery in the bleak hills of central Scotland and spent two expensive months suitably adorning it for subsequent resale to an Oklahoma real estate developer as the celebrated Chivas Regal Distillery. The shock to the Mac-Nair's central nervous system when the cretinous Tulsan handed him the shiny badge of the Edinburgh bunco squad instead of a cashier's check in the amount of three million pounds sterling had been no greater than the one that had just rocked him in the basement. . . .

Even now, an hour later, he still lay rigidly on his bed on the fourth floor of the Friends of Goethe Society in a state of near catatonia. The lights were off in his room, and even in the predawn darkness he felt half stifled by the warm damp summer air that lay heavily over the sleeping city. He wiped away a sheen of perspiration. Why couldn't this wretched world that lagged so far behind his own in technological development have devoted its precious resources to inventing air-conditioning instead of parallel-world machines? he wondered glumly before his thoughts drifted off to even bleaker questions.

Where, he wanted to scream aloud, *is my crown?*

How could he fend off these terrible Englishmen who were on their way to examine him, *real* members of the British nobility?

The MacNair clenched his fists until his fingernails dug painfully into the palms of his hands. What had *possessed* him to pose as English royalty in a world where England was little more than a vassal state? Could it be that in his forty-fourth year he was at last beginning to lose his once-steely grip? He sighed explosively and kicked the tangled bedclothes irritably to the floor.

And what was to be done with Hubmaier, a positive pest with his physical examinations and probing questions about the exact circumstances in which His Royal Highness had found himself transported from universe to universe? Once again this evening's dinner with all the scientists of the Society had consisted of yet another minute examination of the differences between their two worlds. "Who reigns in Paris?" asked the Herr Doctor Professor and Director eagerly after an elaborate discussion of the fate of what had once been Russia before its disappearance into the maw of the Ottoman and Polish Empires. "If not Napoleon, then who *is* Emperor?"

The MacNair had hesitated for only the barest instant. Who *did* reign in Paris? he asked himself desperately. Wasn't Monsieur le Président de la République some wretched worm of a vegetarian? "Philippe VII," he said easily. "A dear friend of mine, and the son of Charles XI, who was commonly called Le Nez, The Nose. The monarchy was restored after the Second World War, you know, and the House of De Gaulle has reigned ever since."

And let them try to prove otherwise! the MacNair told himself with a faint smirk as his naturally ebullient spirits began to reassert themselves. He sat up in bed and began to rearrange the pillows behind him. But all joking aside, what *was* he going to do to recover his precious GODHEAD?

Surely it couldn't be Herr Hubmaier who had sequestered it—that tubby, red-faced cherub was far too transparent to have lent himself to such an unscrupulous breach of trust. Nor, he decided, could it be any of the other scientists of the Society, if only because by now they would all be

openly exclaiming about its marvels. No, it was almost
certainly one of the servants. Perhaps that rather sinister-
looking butler who had chosen that ghastly orange suit for
him. . . . Or even more probably that oafish young footman
named Kleinmutter whose beady eyes never seemed to
leave the MacNair—the one who had actually spilled the
tureen of applesauce on him at dinner two evenings before!

The MacNair suddenly sat up straight in bed, his fists
clenched in rage. If only the yielding flesh of Kleinmutter's
throat were in his hands! How he would teach the beastly
Teuton to profane the MacNair's crown with his unclean
touch! The glowing image of his GODHEAD was sharp and
brilliant in the MacNair's mind. If only he had his crown
and its dia—

Even as the words flashed across his mind the room came
suddenly alive with the dazzling brilliance of the GOD-
HEAD's thousands of glittering lights.

As if in a dream the MacNair slowly lifted his hands.

His crown was sitting securely on his head.

CHAPTER
== 8 ==

FOR THE THIRD TIME in four days the Marquis of Vézelay was
on the telephone to Berlin, an absolute record. "You say it
vanished?"

"Utterly and completely," replied Marcus Sitjar nervously from his office above Le Petit Coin d'Alsace.

"Impossible!"

"Precisely our own reaction. That is why I have called *you*, Monsieur le Marquis."

"So very kind of you." The director of the Special Directorate drummed his fingers rapidly on his desk. "Captain LeFleur will of course corroborate this preposterous story?"

"Of course. And we also have several photographs of the crown."

"Before it vanished."

"Before it vanished."

"I see," said the Marquis of Vézelay thoughtfully. "Very well. Prepare a room. I shall be there for dinner."

Prince William Ernest Augustus acknowledged the greetings of the Earl of Kensington with aloof dignity, then indicated by a curt nod that he might be seated. Herr Hubmaier rushed forward with a sturdy chair of pale blue plush and the Earl subsided heavily into it.

Rocking back and forth on his heels before the broad windows of the sunny downstairs drawing room, the MacNair clasped his hands behind his back and pursed his lips as he silently considered the Earl. He saw a large stout man of early middle age with quick, darting eyes, a shiny bald skull, and thick muttonchop whiskers that framed a broad, florid face. He was dressed in the heavy tweeds and baggy trousers that the MacNair associated with old pictures of the Duke of Windsor in the 1920s or '30s. Altogether, a formidable-looking character, the MacNair decided. He sniffed loudly and turned his attention to the fingernails of his left hand.

The Englishman waited patiently until the butler had swung shut the two broad doors of the drawing room, then leaned forward to whisper eagerly, "Is it true, Your Highness, that Bonaparte never invaded England in your world, that there's no Napoleon in Paris, that the House of Hanover still reigns?"

"Our father Frederick IV is King of England," stated the MacNair austerely. "We are still in direct descent from George I and the House of Hanover, although we fear that it was adjudged expedient during the first war with the

Germans to Anglicize the name to Henley."*

Alfred St. John Wester sat back and tugged thoughtfully at his curly brown side-whiskers. Was it just conceivable that this pretentious popinjay really *was* a prince of the realm? His manner, his bearing, his accent, his arrogance, none of these seemed totally spurious. He was short and wiry, with none of the fleshy corpulence the Earl associated with paintings of those distant Germans who had ruled England at the end of the eighteenth century with such disastrous consequences. Still, it was hardly fair to judge a man outfitted as he was in one of those strange three-piece suits of hairy orange plaids which his poor German associates of the Goethe Society seemed to consider so quintessentially English. And there *was* something disturbingly familiar about the rather plump face, the dark flashing eyes—something which unmistakably suggested the Royal Family. . . . "You have some notion of the state of affairs in our own poor world?" asked the Earl.

"Up to a point," replied the MacNair cautiously, essentially indifferent as to whether or not all of Europe writhed, as Hubmaier had so colorfully expressed it, under the jackboot of the tyrant Bonaparte. "Herr Hubmaier informs us that circumstances in England are not precisely as we might expect them to be."

The Earl sighed deeply. "What is there to say other than that the sixth Napoleon is now upon the throne in Paris and the entire world must suffer the whims of the French tyranny."†

"And England herself is ruled by Bonapartes?"

"They call themselves Bonaparte-Hanover, but it comes to quite the same thing: the darkest tyranny prevails."

"Hard to fully comprehend," muttered the MacNair. "What a remarkable man the first Napoleon must have been. Wicked, to be sure, but still: to have conquered all of Europe—remarkable!"

"Perhaps. To me the fact of his wickedness far exceeds his remarkableness." The Earl of Kensington scowled. "But

*For a fuller explanation of the royal lineage of Prince William Ernest Augustus, Duke of York, see Appendix I.

†See Appendix II for the genealogy of the Imperial House of Bonaparte.

then again, what should one expect from a man whose sole contribution to Western civilization is the invention of the flush toilet?"

"And who is that?" asked the MacNair, bewildered by the strange turn this conversation had suddenly taken.

"Why, Napoleon Bonaparte, of course. You mean you don't go to the bonny in your own world?"

"If ever you should decide to retire from the unthankful task of ensuring our beloved emperor's security, my dear Sitjar," said the Marquis of Vézelay as he allowed himself to be poured another glass of Piersporter, "you have a brilliant future as a restaurateur. But in the meantime we have this matter of the disappearing crown to consider. You say it was simply sitting there on the bench when it suddenly vanished?"

Marcus Sitjar looked up from his plate of venison fillets in red-currant sauce. His usually florid face was only a touch redder than usual. "Precisely. We were exceedingly careful not to disturb it in any way." No need, he thought, to go into the actual tedious details. And if LeFleur doesn't back me up, it's a six-year stint for him studying penguins in the Antarctic. . . .

The Marquis of Vézelay ran his fingers along his gaunt cheeks and bearded chin. "So it's possible that these beastly Germans have actually invented a time machine?"

"Kleinmutter certainly *believes* that they have. And this vanishing crown would seem to—"

"—offer a certain corroboration." The Marquis leaned forward. "You realize, of course, that this would be the most terrible weapon ever invented."

"In the wrong hands it could be . . . mischievous, yes."

"I think then we shall have to nip this little Goethe Society neatly in the bud." The Marquis's face hardened. "Or we may find ourselves with no tomorrows at all."

"You believe he is real, then?" asked Hubmaier as he and the Earl of Kensington strolled slowly through the gardens in the cool of the early evening.

"At least it's *possible,*" allowed the Earl. "His genealogy is coherent enough, and fully detailed. The history of his world is grossly improbable—can you *imagine* this fellow Hitler trying to rid the world of Jews, or Staleen, or this notion called Darxism—it's all so improbable that even a Shakespeare couldn't invent it. It must be real!"

"And His Highness along with it?" said the German slowly. "I can't imagine that anyone would dare—"

"Exactly!" cried the Earl. "You've put your finger on it precisely. Who would *dare* pretend to royalty if he weren't?" He stopped, and tapped Hubmaier solemnly on his shoulder. "We must take every step to protect our royal friend—and your machine in the basement. As I keep trying to tell Dennett—Napoleon's spies are everywhere!"

"Indeed they are. But at least not here in the Society. But have no fear—I have already secured a hundred kilograms of blasting caps to the apparatus in the basement. No agent of Napoleon will ever seize it as his own."

How thoroughly Teutonic, thought the Earl of Kensington glumly. I only hope he's seen to it that we don't somehow blow *ourselves* to smithereens. . . .

The MacNair sighed faintly as he shut volume 14 of the Encyclopaedia Britannica. In this world the preposterous appeared to be commonplace: Napoleon Bonaparte, l'Empéreur de Tous les Français et du Grand Empire des Etats-Unis de l'Europe, had indeed snatched a moment from his monumental labors to invent the modern indoor flush toilet. Or so the Britannica article on plumbing solemnly assured him.

He pushed the heavy volume back onto the library shelves and dropped listlessly into a brown leather chair. For once in his life the MacNair felt curiously indecisive— adrift and at the mercy of elements far beyond his control.

The miracle of the GODHEAD's sudden materialization upon his head two nights before had left him baffled and frightened, bereft of rational explanation. Could the electronic crown—obviously damaged in unknown ways by the passage of the gangster's bullet—have developed some strange affinity for his own unique electrical pattern during their simultaneous transit from one universe to another? The MacNair supposed it was possible, but even this was an explanation which raised as many new questions as it answered. Questions which would interest Herr Hubmaier, no doubt, but which the MacNair intended him never to have the opportunity to raise.

For by now the GODHEAD was at last safely tucked away in the dark recesses beneath the gazebo; it had been the MacNair's original plan to begin his first discreet inquiries among the city's jewelers the following day. For America, it seemed, still maintained a lofty independence from the affairs of old Europe. And after his first two hours spent face-to-face with the Earl of Kensington fending off one question after another, his once-playful notion of incorporating himself into the House of Hanover had seemed more and more absurd. As soon as he could sell enough diamonds for first-class passage to America . . .

But just as they had settled down for the previous evening's dinner, Kensington had suddenly turned the MacNair's world upside down once again. "Then His Highness will do whatever is in his power to aid us in our quest to remove the French yoke of tyranny?"

"Up to a point, of course," replied the MacNair cautiously, far from anxious to do battle with an entire armed continent. He raised a finger. "As long as it is in a manner consonant with the dignity of our position."

"That is something less than boundless enthusiasm."

"You must pardon us," said the MacNair coldly, "but we are still not yet entirely cognizant of the affairs of your world."

"No matter," said the Earl. "Once Your Highness has assumed the throne, you will have more than ample time to digest all the history you wish."

CHAPTER
=== 9 ===

"THE THRONE?" THE MacNair repeated numbly. "You wish us to assume the throne?"

"You know our aim: to eliminate the pestilent Bonapartes and restore freedom and human dignity. An inevitable consequence of our triumph will be the removal of the French usurpers from Buckingham Palace."

"By the use of this so-called time machine of yours?"

The Earl of Kensington nodded. "Your Highness will appreciate the infinite possibilities that a time machine will allow us."

"And you want *us* on the throne?"

"But surely you *belong* there, do you not?" asked the Earl, frowning at the MacNair's muted enthusiasm. "Surely you find the notion of a House of Bonaparte-Hanover as repugnant as I, or any other true Englishman? Who else in all the world can trace his descent directly from the House of Hanover before it became so vilely corrupted."

"Of course, of course," muttered the MacNair uneasily, his thoughts racing. Could this entire conversation be some infinitely subtle trap being laid for him by this cunning fat man? "This puts a somewhat different light upon the matter," he temporized. "We shall have to consider your proposal with the most careful scrutiny. It is not a decision to be taken lightly."

The Earl of Kensington nodded grudging approval.

"And while we are of course greatly in your debt for the hospitality you have shown us to this point," the MacNair continued, buttering a slice of pumpernickel bread and neatly arranging a morsel of smoked eel on it, "it would be a wanton disregard of reality to totally ignore the fact that it was through your own manipulations of the space-time fabric that our person has been untimely ripped from our own beloved world, family, and friends, quite probably never to return." The MacNair allowed a soft sigh to shake his bosom. "We know you share our sentiments in this matter and that your natural impulse is to make what restitution you can."

Alfred St. John Wester frowned in perplexity. "I should have thought that the throne of England—"

"Of course, of course," said the MacNair, holding up a hand. "Your generosity does you credit. But as we understand the situation, there may well be objections to your proposal by the present incumbent of the throne, to say nothing of your tyrants in Paris."

"You are forgetting our time machine."

The MacNair raised an eyebrow. "Are we? But it doesn't *work,* you know. *We* are the proof of that."

"*This* one doesn't work," pointed out the Earl of Kensington irritably. "In England we are proceeding along somewhat different lines. We have the highest hopes for our own machine."

"Then your two societies, the Friends of Goethe and the Friends of Bordeaux Wine, intend to use this machine to wage a revolution all over Europe?"

The Earl of Kensington laid a finger alongside his ample nose. "Revolution is perhaps too forceful a word. Perhaps I have subtly misled you by the vehemence of my feelings on the subject. I must avow that the French do not actually impose their rule on England and Germany by armed soldiers in the streets. Their domination is far more subtle, and far more difficult to combat than if that were the case. They must be fought by equally subtle means."

The MacNair drummed his fingers impatiently on the edge of his gold-rimmed plate upon which a footman in green and gold livery had just served a generous portion of wild boar in plum sauce. "Such as going back in your time machine and assassinating old Boney's mother, that sort of thing, eh?"

"I should hope that we would *never* contemplate anything so crude," protested Herr Hubmaier, while the Earl of Kensington stared impassively at the golden glow of the setting sun on the massive green foliage of the elms in the park outside the dining room windows, "but in general, yes, that would be the thrust of it."

"But none of this activity is actually scheduled to transpire within the next twenty-four hours or so?"

The Earl frowned. "More likely it will be months, or even years. For to be perfectly frank, Your Highness's presence, while of course extraordinarily welcome, is nevertheless the proof of a grave setback to our project."

"Not at all!" cried Herr Hubmaier indignantly. "It—"

But the Earl of Kensington waved him imperiously to silence, then fixed a beady stare on the man who styled himself Prince William Ernest Augustus. "In England Dennett and his team have been occupying themselves—or twiddling their thumbs, you might say—with so-called purely theoretical research. It now appears that the estimable Hubmaier's own efforts, carried out in the greatest secrecy, have led him off in a rather different and, to my mind, entirely futile direction. It may be that all of his efforts here in Germany have been absolutely for nothing. I feel very strongly therefore that the pace of our own work in Scotland must be stepped up vigorously. This is why I left Dennett and the others to apply themselves to what they know best rather than bringing them along to greet Your Highness, which was, of course, their dearest wish."

"We are touched, of course, but—"

"You are much too quick to cast aside the fruits of our research," protested Hubmaier, his three chins quivering indignantly. "Even a parallel-worlds machine can be an engine of enormous power if properly focused!"

"Indeed?" countered the Earl skeptically. "How then would you focus it, and to what end?"

"There's the rub," sighed the Herr Doctor Professor with disarming honesty. "Like the force of a mighty ocean pounding against the coastline, the parallel-worlds machine is an instrument of enormous power, this I know! The sole problem consists in *harnessing* that power."

"No matter," said the MacNair firmly, cutting short their tedious debate. "What it all means is that we shall not be assuming our rightful duties on the throne of England in the immediate future. But in the meantime, we remind you, a man must live." He tapped his pursed lips pensively. "We suppose that a modest *Schloss* of ten bedrooms or so in the Bavarian Alps, with perhaps a dozen staff, would be tolerable enough until you can arrange for something more befitting our position."

The Earl of Kensington's eyes narrowed.

"Or, of course," added the MacNair judiciously, "in England we have always enjoyed Sussex. A few thousand acres, a small trout stream, a manor suitable for occasional receptions, a modest stipend to meet those minor financial obliga—"

"Of course, Your Highness," interrupted the Earl firmly. "These are matters which obviously must be seen to. I feel certain, for instance, that our estate in Scotland will more than meet your most exquisitely demanding requirements."

"Scotland?" The MacNair scowled at unhappy memories of that bleak land. "Cold and dreary. Quite out of the question."

The Earl of Kensington bit his lip to still an angry retort. There was no longer any question about it at all: this ludicrous popinjay was incontestably as stupid and arrogant as any of his distant Hanoverian ancestors! Still, he reminded himself with a certain smug satisfaction at his own cleverness as he raised a glass of Armagnac to his lips, a liberated England would certainly need a king, and there was much to be argued in favor of a monarch of sharply limited capacities. Especially if there was such a man as Alfred St. John Wester, 7th Earl of Kensington, close at hand to guide him in his duties. . . .

Now the MacNair stood brooding by the third-story window of the English library, watching the sparse traffic of boxy black cars slowly passing on the treelined street at the front of the building. As he pondered why this world under the stewardship of the imperial Bonapartes had not progressed as quickly in matters of technology as his own, he idly watched the Herr Doctor Professor and the Earl of Kensington descend from a high black taxi and stroll up the walkway to the Society. What utter loonies they were! One intended to build a time machine, while the other placed his faith in a parallel-worlds machine! Did Herr Hubmaier hope to bring additional troops for his lunatic cause one by one from parallel worlds? If so, this seemed a singularly ineffectual means of overturning a mighty empire which had enforced its Pax Gallica over much of the world for nearly two centuries!

The minutes slowly passed as the MacNair stood motionlessly by the window contemplating the uncertainties of the future. A car drew up at the sidewalk, and then another. A third came to a halt, and a fourth. Soon there were a dozen or more parked under the trees. Was this the Friends of Goethe Society's weekly meeting? he wondered. If so, why don't they leave their cars?

A peculiar bunch of people, he muttered, coming at last to an irrevocable decision. Delightful as it might be to accede to the throne of Ireland and Great Britain, mature judgment clearly dictated that he leave these lunatic Englishmen and Germans to their own devices, even if—

But now a number of hard-faced men wearing light tan overcoats in spite of the sultry July heat had gotten out of the cars and were spreading out in purposeful fashion around the Goethe Society. Six of them marched up the entranceway, and with a sudden catch in his throat the MacNair saw that they were drawing automatic pistols as they advanced.

He heard himself gulp noisily. Were these the dreaded French secret police whose grim exploits held an entire continent in thrall?

Unable to tear himself away from the window, the MacNair stared in horrid fascination as they approached the columned portico that sheltered the formal entrance to the Society. What madness had possessed him to place the accursed GODHEAD of the Tirthankara Mardumjar on his head in the depths of the Vermont woods?

Dimly he heard a soft buzzer ringing somewhere deep in

the building and then the muffled pounding of fists. A moment later the echoes of three separate shots came to him, followed by a veritable fusillade. His paralysis left him instantly and he ran briskly across the room to a small built-in cupboard beneath the long shelves which housed the collected works of Dickens. Here he pulled open the doors and frantically pushed aside a number of enormous old leather-bound folios until he could wriggle himself into the space within. Hastily pulling the heavy volumes back into the cupboard, he began arranging them to hide him from anything but the most determined search.

He was in the act of reaching out to pull the cupboard doors shut when his entire body shook to a tremendous explosion. The floor beneath his darkened hideout trembled violently and he was slammed mercilessly against something hard and unyielding. The sound of an even greater explosion enveloped him, and then with a dazzling burst of light in his eyes he was battered into unconsciousness.

CHAPTER
= 10 =

"AWAKE AT LAST," OBSERVED the Marquis of Vézelay.

"Am I?" murmured the MacNair groggily as his blurry eyes moved slowly around a plain white chamber whose single article of furniture appeared to be the hard narrow bed in which he was lying. A powerful odor of disinfectant filled the room. His head throbbed, and he blinked painfully at the beams of sunlight which flooded around the tattered shade drawn before the lone window. Outlined against the light was the silhouette of a small dapper figure in a dark grey double-breasted suit which glittered with an improbable number of large silver buttons. A bright red rose was set jauntily in his lapel, and he twirled a broad-brimmed grey hat impatiently in his left hand.

"Do you speak French?" asked the Marquis, stepping forward to peer down at the MacNair. Except for his pointed brown beard, his pale white skin was closely shaven, and the sharp tangs of talcum and eau de cologne assailed the MacNair's fastidious nostrils. The cast of his gaunt features and his cold grey eyes brought to mind all the policemen the MacNair had ever encountered in the course of a hectic life.

"No," said the MacNair, vaguely recalling some nebulous occasion where it had once somehow proved beneficial to conceal his knowledge of German. "Not a word. You must be confusing me with somebody else."

"Tiens!" The Frenchman's eyebrows lifted in mock astonishment. "In what language, then, do you imagine we are now conversing?"

"Oh," said the MacNair feebly, his heart suddenly pounding wildly in his chest. The French! Somehow he had fallen into the hands of the French! Without actually apprehending the exact reason, he knew that somehow this was a catastrophe of the first order. "What I meant," he continued in English, "was that I don't speak it very well."

"Nevertheless—let us continue in French. You have a charming accent of—Toulouse perhaps? If there is something you don't understand, you have only to say so." The Marquis stepped to the door and rattled its handle. He grimaced, then rapped it sharply with his walking stick. The MacNair watched it swing open. A stiff figure in a dark blue uniform of military cut stepped into the room and saluted smartly. "You may bring in a chair now," said the Marquis. "If our friend here uses it to assault me, you may be certain that I shall scream loudly."

"Oui, monsieur," said the soldier without the flicker of a smile.

"Now, then," said the Marquis of Vézelay after the door had been secured and he had seated himself in a straight-backed wooden chair just by the MacNair's right elbow. "You're the man from the past, are you?" He leaned closer and scrutinized the MacNair minutely. His eyebrows knit and his long pale fingers tugged pensively at his bearded chin. "You seem strangely familiar to me somehow. Are you someone famous, I wonder, a personage I ought to know?" He shook his head quizzically and his thin lips twisted into a faint smile. "How curious if you should turn out to be some celebrated character such as Jamieson Floyd that I've read about in history books all my life! Now, then, my dear fellow, just what year would 'the past' actually be?"

"Say that again, more slowly please," temporized the MacNair in dogged English while a million disjointed thoughts ran raggedly through his mind as the events of the last few minutes suddenly returned to him. He had been pulling himself into a cupboard when—

The GODHEAD!

What had become of his crown?

Sweat suddenly beaded his forehead. Above all he must keep this diabolical Frenchman from finding out about his crown!

"I don't know what you mean by 'year' or 'man from the past,'" attacked the MacNair desperately, wriggling himself into an upright position against his pillows, "nor do I know who *you* are, nor where I am, nor how I came to be here. It would appear to be a hospital room. Are you, then, my doctor? If so, I think I should inform you that your bedside manner leaves much to be desired."

"So you don't recall how you came to be here," marveled the Marquis in soft French. "Then you don't recall a certain building in Düsseldorf?"

"Düsseldorf?" The MacNair frowned. He shook his head uncertainly, then lifted his hand to delicately explore a large tender bump on the left side of his forehead. "I seem to have hit my head somewhere. Perhaps my memory—"

"—is playing you tricks," concluded the Marquis with a sardonic smile. "Then let me set your mind to rest about certain matters. You *are* in a hospital: the Military Hospital of St. Jerome and the Fallen Comrades in the city of Metz. Metz, you may or may not recall with your impaired memory, is in the country of France in the department of

Moselle, not too many miles south of Düsseldorf and the Rhine. For your own personal safety, we concluded it was best to bring you here."

"For my own safety?"

"Wouldn't any place be safer than Germany?" asked the Marquis of Vézelay reasonably. "Here at least, I think I can assure you, no one will be blowing up buildings around you."

"Someone blew up a building?"

"To smithereens," said the Marquis with grim relish, unwittingly echoing the dire premonition of the Earl of Kensington. "So far as we know, *you* were the sole survivor, though at this time we are still picking through the rubble." His aristocratic features suddenly lost any trace of amiability. "Aside from an indeterminate number of dead Germans, I also lost a number of friends and associates. And of the machine that brought you here there is not the barest trace. I would be very pleased indeed to place my hands on the perpetrators of this irresponsible carnage."

"You're *not* a doctor," muttered the MacNair uneasily.

The Marquis pursed his lips. "Hmmm. In truth I am Gérard Philippe Edouard de Bounias, 6th Marquis of Vézelay. Am I a doctor, you ask? Perhaps, perhaps, in the sense of one who watches over the health of the body politic. Sometimes in the course of my duties I must uncover, examine, and even occasionally extirpate potentially harmful bacteria."

He smiled engagingly as he scratched idly at his beard. "Take yourself, for instance. We know that you stepped forth, naked as a worm, from a so-called instrumentality of temporal remission. We know further that you subsequently spent several days in earnest conversation with the learned Fellows of the Society, these conversations unfortunately being conducted exclusively in English, a language which our informant is quite unable to understand. And we know finally that none of these Fellows are in a position to aid us in our investigations, no matter how earnestly we solicit them, being, as I mentioned to you, now reduced to a number of small, disjointed segments. From all of this we are inexorably led to conclude that you yourself are almost certainly the single most important human being alive."

The MacNair groaned weakly and raised his hand feebly to his sweaty forehead. "Hrmph," he muttered crossly while his thoughts raced. What was it he had once read in a book of wartime memoirs uncountable eons ago? That the best time to escape from the enemy was as soon as possible after your capture?

"What we *don't* know," continued the Marquis, "is whether in this particular case you yourself are a harmful bacterium to be ruthlessly segregated and if necessary destroyed, or merely some benign intruder of no particular consequence, to be studied and then left alone. This, you may take it, is my task to determine."

The MacNair let his bruised and aching body slip down from his pillows deep into the bed. Never had he encountered anyone who so exuded such cold-blooded menace! "All very well," he protested, "but *I* had absolutely nothing to do with this . . . building that exploded, you say? Which building was that?"

The Marquis leaned forward until his nose almost touched that of the MacNair. "Why, the building in which you yourself were found, my dear fellow, dressed in a fine suit of orange plaid such as would be worn by *un grand sporting milord,* concealed in the rubble in a particularly stout cupboard, surrounded by enormous nineteenth-century folios which almost certainly absorbed enough of the blasts to save your life."

The MacNair gulped. "In a cupboard, you say?"

"I do indeed. What all of us from the Emperor on down are now asking ourselves is this: Just what were you, the honored guest of the Friends of Goethe, actually *doing* in that cupboard? Surely you weren't searching *there* for your crown?" A wintry smile tugged at the Marquis's lips. "Unless, of course, the explosion somehow hurled it out of the cupboard to where it landed under the floorboards of that delightful summerhouse?"

A second, far more genuine, moan of anguish escaped the lips of the dismayed MacNair. "The crown? You've found the *crown?*"

"Ha!" The Marquis of Vézelay grinned satanically. "I *thought* that might elicit some reaction! Yes, it's already in

Paris, my dear fellow. How it made its way from Berlin to Düsseldorf I must confess is a total mystery. But one thing is certain: It will not be vanishing from the vaults of the Curie Institute!"

"You say it vanished from *Berlin?*" The MacNair shook his head in bewilderment.

"So it seems. Unfortunately, both witnesses to its sudden disappearance perished in the same explosion which landed *you* in our hospital, so the exact circumstances are somewhat hazy. But I feel confident that eventually you yourself will be happy to shed additional light on this puzzling episode."

The MacNair's eyes drooped shut and his breathing thickened as despair gripped him. The crown was in Paris. He himself was in some sort of military hospital, about to be put to the question by some titled Torquemada of the French secret police. Could any circumstances be more disheartening?

All of this seemed to leave but a single desperate expedient. He sighed heavily and ran his fingers through his disheveled Vandyke beard. How fortunate that he and this wretched Marquis were much of a size. . . .

"You want to know about the crown?" the MacNair whispered raggedly.

"Among other things."

"In . . . in a moment. . . . First . . . is there a . . . you know. . . . The shock has been too much. . . ."

"Is there a—ah, of course." The Marquis stooped to reach under the bed. "I perfectly understand. Here, my dear fellow."

"Thank you," murmured the MacNair weakly, taking the heavy enamel bedpan from the Frenchman's fingers and using both hands to smash it down with a terrible ringing clang upon the top of his head.

The Marquis's broad-brimmed hat pulled low on his forehead, the MacNair rapped smartly on the locked door with the silver ferrule of his benefactor's walking stick. He wriggled his toes uncomfortably in the loose-fitting black shoes so unlike his own superb creations from Rooney & Waggoner and reflected for an instant on the word *flatfoot*

—what an enormous foot this rather moderately sized secret-police man seemed to have!

As he listened to the guard fumbling with the lock, he pulled nervously at his pearl-grey cravat and turned to cast a final glance upon the slight form huddled beneath the coarse grey sheets. From the doorway only a tangle of light brown hair on the back of a head was clearly visible. With any luck at all it would be several hours before anyone looked in to find the Marquis of Vézelay trussed and gagged like a holiday turkey.

How vexed he will be! the MacNair reflected uneasily, now plucking at one of the silver buttons that festooned the herringbone suit which sat a trifle loosely upon his frame. He heard the door opening at his back. . . .

"Until tomorrow, then, my dear fellow," he chirped with as much of a Parisian accent as he could muster, his body turned sideways to the open doorway. He sketched a half salute which only served to further conceal his face from the impassive guard, then spun around with a soft grunt and walked rapidly down the dark wooden flooring of the long gloomy corridor that lay before him, the walking stick of the Marquis of Vézelay tap-tapping loudly in the melancholy silence of the hospital.

CHAPTER
⹀ 11 ⹀

AS THE MACNAIR hobbled unchallenged from the Hôpital Militaire de St.-Jérôme et les Camarades Tombés with as much panache as his assorted aches and bruises allowed, his head seethed with possible courses of action. But ultimately none of them seemed any more feasible than the first, and simplest, to have presented itself—which was to fly for the sanctuary of England with all possible speed.

He stepped past a uniformed guard at an imposing wrought-iron gate which swung between two granite posts topped by white marble angels and out into the city of Metz. He found himself on a shady treelined boulevard of elegant nineteenth-century three-story residences with intricate metal balconies and ornate stone carvings.

The noontime sun pierced the canopy of trees overhead with bright shafts of light, and a poignant odor of slowly simmering onions and garlic came to his nostrils. Electrified trolleys and streetcars clanked by noisily amidst a light scattering of the standard black automobiles which he had come to expect in this world. As he stood indecisively for a moment on the sidewalk, conscious of the painful throbbing of his head and of a growing void in his stomach, he was jostled by impatient Frenchmen in dark suits and a variety of peculiar hats hurrying home for lunch with crusty loaves of long golden bread tucked beneath their arms. His mouth suddenly watering, the MacNair turned without further hesitation against the flow of the crowd and hobbled off in what he hoped would be the direction of downtown Metz.

Twenty minutes of wandering the crowded streets while he devoured an enormous sandwich of smoked pork purchased in a busy *charcuterie* took him past an immense Gothic cathedral, a curving river with meticulously laid-out gardens along either side, and then unexpectedly to his goal: the grimy marble splendor of the city's railway terminal.

Half an hour later he was watching the drab brown and grey houses of the outskirts of Metz move past his window from the comfort of a first-class compartment. How thoughtful it had been of the Marquis of Vézelay to garnish his hand-tooled wallet with a fine selection of variously denominated bank notes of different sizes and colors, each one adorned with the stern classical features of one imperial Bonaparte or another!

For tyranny or not, the MacNair had discovered that the formalities of travel, at least here in the very heart of the French Empire, appeared to be as casual as those he recalled of his far-off youth. He had seen only two sleepy-looking *agents de police* in wrinkled blue uniforms wandering lackadaisically through the station, and a few minutes' observation quickly revealed that railroad tickets were procured by the simple presentation of a sufficient number of francs. Without further hesitation he had joined a group of people knotted around the window marked Paris. By judicious use of his elbows and the Marquis's invaluable walking stick he had fought his way to the *guichet* and purchased a thirteen-franc round-trip ticket. Unlike the whimsically named democratic republics of his own officious world, in this particular tyranny no proof of identity was required, nor official permission to travel, and he had boarded the long dark green carriage of Compagnie Internationale des Wagons Lits a few minutes later by merely surrendering his ticket to the clearly uninterested conductor.

Alone in his first-class compartment, he pulled down the lace curtain to screen himself from view of the corridor and let his aching body sink deep into the soft comfort of his seat. Carefully he examined the contents of the Marquis of

Vézelay's pigskin wallet. Aside from an imposing thickness of bank notes, there were none of the credit cards and assorted pieces of identification which made his own world's wallets so uncomfortably bulky. But what little he found was of compelling interest to a man of the MacNair's eclectic tastes.

What a trusting world this appeared to be! The driver's license issued twenty-two years before in the name of Gérard Philippe Edouard de Bounias, Marquis of Vézelay, was unmarred by either thumbprint or photograph. And the engraved card which austerely identified him as Director of His Imperial Majesty's Special Directorate did nothing more than that; no mention of height, age, or physical characteristics sullied its pristine beauty. The MacNair tapped his walking stick thoughtfully against the floor. Certainly he had ample food for thought. . . .

As the train pulled into Paris two hours later he stared anxiously along the platform for anything that might resemble a reception committee such as might be organized by an infuriated head of the French secret police. But nothing more than a single uniformed policeman at the end of the platform was apparent and the MacNair stepped awkwardly down from his compartment, adjusted the broad-brimmed hat of the Marquis of Vézelay to a jaunty angle, and with the help of his walking stick stepped as briskly as he could into the crowd of fellow passengers making their way into the cavernous station.

The station, he found, was the Gare des Allemagnes somewhere in the east of Paris. Apparently even the mighty Bonaparte himself had been unable to bring a measure of rationality to the French railway system by decreeing the construction of a single central station. The MacNair shrugged with Gallic resignation. *Plus les mondes changent,* he murmured, *plus ils sont les mêmes choses!* and let himself be swallowed up by the noisy mob of Parisians battling each other for the services of a long line of patiently waiting taxis.

Eventually he engaged a taxi of particularly antiquarian aspect and let it convey him to the Gare des Cotswolds on the northwest side of the capital. An airplane, of course, assuming that they even existed in this baffling world, would certainly be quicker, but upon careful consideration he had concluded that he would be far more conspicuous in some tiny 1920s-style airport in the middle of a suburban cow pasture than in the crowded anonymity of the gigantic metropolitan railway stations with which he was now fully at his ease. So onward to the Cotswold Station!

Nothing in this universe had changed the nature of the Parisian taxi driver, he thought desperately as the ancient vehicle careened madly in and out of heavy traffic at impossible speeds. As he bumped and slid from side to side in its dark interior, it was hard to see much of the Paris he had visited frequently over the years, but the Opéra was still there, as was the cathedral of Notre-Dame in all its splendor in the middle of the Seine. But as he peered out toward the hills of Montmartre he was astonished to find that the alabaster domes of Sacré Coeur had been replaced by nothing less than a replica of the glorious Arc de Triomphe which in his own world had been the culmination of the Champs-Elysées.

"The arch there on the hill," he asked in his most apologetic and rustic French, "what is it?"

The driver glanced contemptuously in his mirror at the hayseed behind him. "The Arc de Triomphe, uncle. What else would it be?"

"But what triumph was that?"

"Flûte! Doesn't anyone outside of Paris go to school? The Battle of the Cotswolds, uncle!"

"The Cotswolds?"

But the driver had thrown up both hands in despair to let the taxi sail untended beneath the nose of the largest truck the MacNair had ever seen. When at last he dared to open his eyes, it was to find with agonized relief that the taxi had slowed to swing into the courtyard of an even more imposing marble-faced edifice than the Station of the Germanies.

"Cotswold Station, *grandpère,"* muttered the taxi driver as he reluctantly made change and carefully deducted his tip. "Why don't you ask the ticket taker for your next history lesson?"

Ah! thought the MacNair with a bittersweet smile as he stepped down to the curb. How invigorating to be in Paris again! How little it had changed from his own world!

Correction! he told himself hastily as his eyes swept the familiar skyline of the City of Light. At least one more astonishing difference was now apparent: here no Eiffel Tower soared majestically over the self-proclaimed center of the civilized world!

Paris without an Eiffel Tower? Shaking his head in wonder, the MacNair limped slowly into the Cotswold Station.

He had long been a believer in the virtues of the simple as opposed to the overly elaborate. How, he had asked himself even as he hobbled through the echoing corridors of the Hospital of St. Jerome and the Fallen Comrades, would a typical Parisian, a true *boulevardier*, travel from Metz to the barbarity of the British Isles? The answer was simple: He would take the train to his own glorious city, the central hub of everything that was French, and then another to the English Channel, where in turn a ferry would ultimately transport him to England.

Then so would the MacNair.

Inside the Cotswold Station he purchased a first-class ticket for Calais, then a number of evening papers to beguile the two-hour journey. It was nearly dark before he stepped down into the cool salty air of the Channel port, and he wandered indecisively through the station while pondering the next and potentially most perilous step of his excursion since bidding farewell to the Marquis of Vézelay in his hospital room in Metz.

He watched a number of English tourists purchasing tickets for the last train of the evening for London while he tried to decide whether he could take the risk of joining them. At last he fortified himself with a glass of strong red wine at the buffet and came to a decision. It was true that he had no passport, but surely the papers of the Marquis of Vézelay would be enough to get him through any French formalities. And none of the Englishmen or Frenchmen who thronged the station seemed to have a passport or anything resembling one. Hadn't he once read that even in his own troubled world passports in Europe had been largely unknown before the outbreak of the First World

War? Here in a world which had known two hundred years of peace why should not the same circumstances obtain?

The MacNair hitched up the Marquis of Vézelay's somewhat loosely fitting pants and with an accelerated beating of his heart stepped forward to the bright red railway carriage that awaited him.

Three hours later he was in London, the entire trip having been agreeably spent in the dining car over a leisurely supper of Belon oysters and grilled Dover sole accompanied by an iced bottle of Graves and followed by several small glasses of aromatic *fine*. The transition into the Channel tunnel and then to England had gone completely unnoticed by the MacNair, and by the time he stepped down wearily from the train in the great echoing terminal at Elephant-and-Castle, the only official he had encountered since leaving Calais was a polite French conductor who had clipped his ticket.

He spotted a long orderly queue of Englishmen patiently lined up for the arrival of taxis and knew at once that he had left the Continent. Some things in England never changed—even, it appeared, under the austere rule of the Hanover-Bonapartes.

CHAPTER
= 12 =

"YOU SAY THE rascal got *away?*" muttered the Emperor of All the French and the United States of Europe, His Imperial Majesty Napoleon V, as he savored a mouthful of Hudson River caviar.

"A veritable desperado," explained the Marquis of Vézelay with simple dignity. "My men and I were absolutely no match for him. He hurled us about as if we were so many bowling pins!"

"A man from the *past?*" repeated the Archduchess Mireille of Luxembourg wonderingly. Her cornflower-blue eyes widened and the tip of her moist pink tongue peeked deliciously between her bright red lips. "You mean he's a *Neanderthal,*" she said huskily, her eyes glowing and her superb bosom rising and falling beneath her fluffy white blouse, "like those great hairy men from the caves?"

"Not entirely, Your Highness," murmured the Marquis indulgently, trying to suppress a strangled cough. Although still in the full flower of her youth, the exuberant Archduchess was already widely celebrated among *le tout Paris* for her taste for the exotic and *outré.* "Immensely powerful, of course, but aside from that, as far as I could tell, he was quite like you and me." He reached across the gleaming Louis XVI table for another wafer-thin slice of English fruitcake from Fortnum and Scott's.

"Harumph!" snorted His Imperial Majesty, clearly as disappointed as his niece, though for rather different rea-

74

sons. He set down the delicate gold-filigreed Limoges tea-cup from which he had been sipping his late afternoon tea in the baroque splendor of the small music room of the Elysée Palace and ran his fingers through his fluffy white mustache. "If he's not a caveman, then just what year *is* he from?"

The Marquis of Vézelay stroked his sleek brown beard while his eyes turned up to the glorious blue and gold frescoes that decorated the vaulted ceiling. "Clearly some time within the past few centuries," he said at last. "His French was thoroughly modern, and according to our informant he appeared absolutely at ease in his daily intercourse with the Fellows of the Society."

"These beastly Germans!" exclaimed the Archduchess peevishly. "You say they *destroyed* their machine! Why on earth would they have done *that?*"

The Marquis shifted uneasily in his chair under the sharp scrutiny of the Emperor. The whole episode was far from redounding to his credit. There was, in fact, much that he would prefer to keep strictly to himself. Already the two orderlies who had discovered him bound hand and foot by a torn-up nightgown had been persuaded to pursue their careers in the Republic of Equatorial Africa. But not everyone was so amenable to reason, and he knew that the balance of his career hung by a rapidly fraying thread. Thank goodness that this amiable if rather thick-witted Emperor *was* his second cousin and could most likely be counted on to stand by a kinsman. Up to a certain point. Beyond that . . . The Marquis of Vézelay's fingernails dug deep into his palms. If ever he laid hands on the person who had made such a fool of him . . .

"Apparently to keep anyone else, such as ourselves, from discovering what they were up to," he replied smoothly. "But in doing so, they inadvertently managed to destroy not only the machine but also themselves and all of their papers concerning it."

"How horrid they are!" The Archduchess wriggled angrily in her chair. "How *selfish!*"

"Then we have no possible means of reproducing their device?" asked the Emperor thoughtfully. "I must confess I find extremely distasteful the notion of a machine that would allow someone to go back forty years or more and spy upon some of my own more youthful escapades. . . ."

"Oh, Uncle!" The Archduchess smiled, tapping him playfully on the knee. "I think it's just *terrible* we don't have this machine. How beastly Germans are! Why don't you simply take a thousand of them—scientists, you know—and shoot them as an example? Then you could *command* all their other scientists to build us another machine. I'm sure they would listen." She sat back with a satisfied nod and quietly sipped her tea.

Napoleon V exchanged a baffled glance with the Marquis of Vézelay. How on earth had this appalling savage ever come to crop up among the rest of his placid nephews and nieces? What a throwback she was to his equally appalling grandmother, the tyrant Alexine who had so tirelessly prosecuted the Great War! "I fear that it might prove impractical to shoot that many Germans, my dear. The Senate would never allow that great an expenditure for bullets."

The Archduchess sighed scornfully. "Well, at least you know enough to keep them all apart in their own little states. Can you imagine how overbearing Germans would be if they all got together in a single country?"

"Impossible," declared the Emperor as he marveled anew at his beautiful but addled niece's wilder flights of fancy. "Germans are essentially poets, visionaries, and dreamers—they have absolutely no sense of the practical. Just look at how they invented this fantastic machine—only to destroy it, and themselves, out of sheer peevishness." The dark flashing eyes that had marked six generations of Bonapartes turned to the Marquis of Vézelay. "Then there is no hope at all of duplicating this so-called time machine?"

"None for the moment, I fear. It was utterly vaporized, first by the explosives which had been placed around it, and then by some further inner explosion of its own. We have but two possible paths to pursue. The so-called man from the past—"

"Who has disappeared," said the Emperor curtly, rising to his feet to indicate that the tête-à-tête was nearly over.

"—who has disappeared," ruefully admitted the Marquis

of Vézelay as he climbed wearily to his own feet and looked up to meet the skeptical eye of the towering, rawboned Emperor, who even in his dark blue afternoon lounge suit still looked as if he had just come in from milking the cows in the barn. "And, of course, there is the crown."

"The crown?"

"The crown?" exclaimed the Archduchess Mireille, jumping up and leaning forward eagerly so that her warm breath wafted delicately against the Marquis's cheek. "What crown is that?"

The Curie Institute for Research in the Physical Sciences was located in a block of sagging sixteenth-century houses just off the Place de la Bastille in the workingmen's quarter of Popincourt. Six days and nights of frenzied construction in the deepest basement of the seven adjoining buildings which made up the institute had resulted in a small but complete laboratory surrounded on all six sides by a multitude of precautions.

Six inches of total vacuum were sandwiched between a solid foot of lead shielding and three inches of armor plating such as that employed on the battleship *Duc d'Orléans*. Inside this initial barrier were four inches of compressed argon, two inches of high-carbon steel, and a final six inches of additional lead. Further consideration of the theoretical nature of possible telepathic signaling had resulted in a last-minute addition of a Faraway cage around the entire vault. This was a double thickness of copper mesh screening designed to shield the volume within from any conceivable type of electromagnetic waves, including the recently discovered so-called radio waves. This in turn had led to the introduction within the central vault itself of six radio noise generators, the theory being that the creation of such random static might block any telepathic signals which had somehow penetrated the outer defenses.

"And *that*," said the director of the Institute Giorgio Campinotti with some satisfaction as he surveyed his handiwork, "should take care of the problem of the so-called vanishing crown." He flashed his gleaming teeth at his handpicked team of scientists from all the distant corners of the Empire. "Now, then, *mesdames et messieurs*—to work. First: measurements, photographs, and meticulous reproductions. Then . . . well, let me see. . . . There would appear to be a small toggle switch just *here.* . . ."

"What a peculiar room this is!" exclaimed the Archduchess Mireille of Luxembourg to Dr. Campinotti after she and the Emperor Napoleon had been carefully ushered through a series of hermetically sealed air locks in order to reach the final fastness of the lead-lined laboratory far below the streets of Paris. "Are you *sure* you couldn't have just brought this crown to the Palace? Uncle is far too old to be gadding about like this."

The Emperor of All the French ran his hamlike hand through his great thatch of straw-colored hair and scowled angrily. How, he was asking himself for the hundredth time, had he conceived the incredible notion of bringing this nitwitted niece of his into the Palace to act as imperial hostess after the death of his beloved Empress Charlotte? How easy it was to see why this imbecile Archduchess had remained unmarried so long in spite of her blond good looks, royal breeding, and astonishing wealth!

"Quite impossible, Your Highness," interjected the Marquis of Vézelay smoothly. "Once you have seen the crown for yourself you will instantly appreciate the precautions that the good Dr. Campinotti has felt obliged to take to ensure its protection."

"Oh, very well. Where *is* this marvelous crown?" She turned her head impatiently from side to side to scrutinize the garishly lighted vault in which they found themselves hemmed in on all sides by a welter of mysterious machines and instruments.

"*Here,* Your Highness," smiled Dr. Campinotti, dramatically whisking away a blue silk foulard from an object on a small piecrust table of polished mahogany that was distinctly out of place in the harshly utilitarian laboratory.

At the sight of the GODHEAD's thousands of brilliantly glittering gems the Emperor's eyes widened and the Archduchess gasped sharply. "But . . . it's *beautiful!*" she whispered at last, awed nearly to silence.

The director of the Curie Institute beamed happily. "But

this is nothing," he said, holding up a palm. "Wait until Your Majesties see what happens *now!*" He bent forward and his hand made a subtle movement at the side of the crown. Instantly the laboratory was filled with the flashing beams of a thousand multicolored lights. Even the Archduchess Mireille was unable to utter as the four of them stared in wonder.

"All these lights are perfectly harmless?" ventured the Marquis of Vézelay at last.

"So far as we know. We have tried turning the lights on and off for several days now and our instruments have found absolutely no deleterious effects." He pursed his lips ruefully. "In fact, we are utterly unable to determine any purpose to them at all."

"Indeed, indeed," marveled the Emperor, his eyes glowing with entrancement. "It's stunning, absolutely stunning. I fully understand your precautions." He tore his eyes away from the brilliance of the crown to study the furnishings of the laboratory with a deeper appreciation. "It would be nothing short of criminal folly to permit—"

"Kindly let me have it at once," interrupted the Archduchess imperiously. She turned her gleaming cornflower-blue eyes upon the director of the Curie Institute. "I shall just try it on for the barest moment. I have always been told that diamonds become me particularly well."

The Emperor sighed inaudibly and nodded almost imperceptibly at Dr. Campinotti, who in turn managed a gallant smile. "I don't see why not," said the director of the Curie Institute as he carefully raised the glowing GOD-HEAD to the Archduchess's blond curls. "One beautiful object surely deserves another."

CHAPTER
= 13 =

THE ORIGINAL GARNAWAY Castle had been built as a rude
fortress in the late ninth century. Successive generations of
Farquhars, Stuarts, and McDougals had added an eclectic
assortment of towers, armories, banqueting halls, ball-
rooms, chapels, flying buttresses, porticos, terraces, formal
gardens, marble statues, and picturesque follies until the
shaggy clansman who had laid the first rough stone would
never have recognized it.

By 1805, the year of England's defeat at the Cotswold
Encirclement, its present tenant, the 4th Marquess of
Morayshire, derived the major part of his enormous fortune from shipping and mercantile interests in the West
Indies. As the British Empire dwindled and declined in the
decades following the establishment of French hegemony
over all of western Europe, so did the fortunes of the clan
McDougal. Finally, in 1891, five years after the accession to
the British throne of the Bonaparte-Hanovers, the eldest
son was obliged to settle his debts by selling the vast estate
to a French railroad magnate, the Duke of Eygalières. What
was left of the dispirited clan emigrated to Canada.

Two generations passed. The grandfather of Sir Norvil
Dennett made a fortune in timber in the western province
of Georgiana. An uncle quadrupled it by creating a chain of
newspapers and then returned in bitter triumph to the
Scotland he had never seen and purchased the McDougals'
ancestral home from the dissipated heirs of the Duke of

Eygalières. Four years later he and his immediate family perished in a train disaster in northern Italy and Mr. Norvil Dennett, an impoverished professor of physics at a redbrick university in Birmingham, came into the inheritance.

Wealthy now beyond calculation, his gaunt figure wandered the ancient stone passageways for nine brooding months, his thoughts turning always to the ninety years of shame in which the McDougals had been forced into cruel exile. Soon he joined the local branch of the fledgling political party the Yeoman Sons of Essex, whose proclaimed goal was the eradication of all French influence from English life. By the end of the year he had made the acquaintance of its secret founder, Alfred St. John Wester, Earl of Kensington. Two months later Sir Norvil began to study the possibility of constructing the world's first time machine.

This evening the bright red flag that flew over the highest tower of Garnaway Castle was at half-mast, as it had been ever since His Royal Highness Prince William Ernest Augustus had brought confirmation of the devastating death of the Earl of Kensington to the innumerable residents of the vast estate.

At the moment the person known as Prince William Ernest Augustus was gazing meditatively from his window high in Garnaway Castle at the dark green forest of Scotch pine which stretched out under a cold drizzling sky to the distant grey waters of the Firth of Moray. Even in his fine new suit of heavy grey Harris tweed he shivered slightly. For in spite of the splendid name he so proudly bore, ever since the ghastly fiasco of the Chivas Regal Distillery, Scotland was far from being the MacNair's favorite place. Even now in early August when the pale summer light of northern Morayshire lingered almost till midnight, this was a country of bleak and depressing mien.

And yet, he asked himself plaintively, what other choice had he? It was impossible to remain in France or Germany or any other place on the Continent where the power of the Bonapartes held sway. America, of course, was the ultimate goal. But two things precluded his instant flight to the New World.

First, his funds were limited to the francs which the

Marquis of Vézelay had so kindly contributed to the Mac-
Nair's retirement plan, and until he knew more about the
particularities of this strange world it would be best to keep
them in reserve. How many would be needed for travel to
America was still something to be determined.

And second, of course, was the GODHEAD.

Impossible to leave Europe without his beloved crown,
his security for all the years ahead!

Yes, the GODHEAD, murmured the MacNair to himself
as he paced the vast cold bedchamber he had been assigned
by the Master of Garnaway, its harsh stone walls only
partially covered by great faded tapestries that hung from
the dark molding far above. His distant royal forebear
George II had once spent the night in this very bed, Dennett
had informed him proudly. The MacNair snorted in disdain. Had anyone troubled to change the deplorable mattress in the two centuries since that notable event? would be
his question to Dennett on the morrow. He snapped his
fingers in irritation. But that was surely the most minor of
his problems! What was imperative now was the retrieval of
his GODHEAD.

But how?

What was it that awful Marquis had said: that now it was
secure in the vaults of the Curie Institute?

He flung himself impatiently into a chair beside the
fireplace in which a frugal fire of coke and peat gave off an
imperceptible heat and pressed his hands tightly to his
temples. It had been while concentrating upon the image of
the crown—like *this*—that it had suddenly materialized
upon his head that night in Germany. . . .

Twenty minutes later the MacNair gave it up. His forehead was beaded with sweat and his hands were trembling.
Perhaps that devilish Frenchman had been right—perhaps
it *was* forever beyond the reach of its rightful owner!

The MacNair resumed his pacing. How many miles was
Düsseldorf from Berlin? Perhaps the GODHEAD's magical
powers only operated within a certain radius. . . . Perhaps
he should have stayed in Paris after all. . . .

Perhaps, perhaps. . . .

He sighed and padded off to the bonny down the corridor
to brush his teeth for the night. On the whole he had

probably been right to seek out the London quarters of Les Amis des Grands Vins de Bordeaux and inveigle one of its members into placing a call to that Sir Norvil Dennett in Scotland whom Kensington had mentioned several times. At least now his most elementary needs had been met. He was apparently safe from the demon French, his food and drink were being seen to, and he had a roof over his head.

Tomorrow he would have to have a serious discussion with this chap Dennett about the proposal that the late Earl of Kensington had so graciously made just before his untimely demise, poor chap. For now that he was actually *in* Great Britain he was certain he could feel flowing within him some of the deep-seated patriotism which had so impelled that worthy man. . . .

How long, he addressed the bearded image in the mirror, could his native country writhe under the jackboot of the conqueror?

He gestured angrily with his toothbrush.

Yes, how long could the sole legitimate representative of the House of Hanover be denied his rightful place upon the throne of Ireland and Great Britain?

Even now, after numerous introductions and several meals shared with them in various of the castle's five dining rooms and banqueting halls, many of Garnaway's inhabitants were still only vaguely recognizable to the MacNair.

There were, he had been told by the Master of Garnaway, no fewer than eleven scientists collaborating with him in his research on the time machine, a shifting population of twice that number of Yeoman Sons of Essex who came and went on mysterious errands, and uncounted scores of servants ranging from a butler and bottle washers to tweenies and third underfootmen. Of this number, Sir Norvil informed him, no more than a bare half dozen of the inner circle were aware of Prince William's august identity.

"The full details of your illustrious identity were sent to us by Kensington only the day before his grievous death. Since then, I fear, we have all been too immersed in the aftermath to devote adequate time to yourself, my dear Prince William."

"Hmmm." The MacNair let his fingers run down the

keyboard of the eighteenth-century harpsichord with a soft tinkle. The somber grey light of midmorning cast deep shadows throughout the ladies' retiring room in which they now stood. "Did Kensington indicate to you what his ultimate plans were in regard to us and your time machine?"

The Master of Garnaway cleared his throat uneasily. "Only in the most circumspect of terms, Your Highness. I have touched upon it in brief discussions with the other members of our little group, but we have as yet come to no firm conclusions on the matter. Obviously, this is something we must go into very thoroughly with you in the days to come. In the meantime, would Your Highness like to continue on your tour of my modest premises? I can promise you a really splendid view from the Black Tower."

"Do carry on, my dear chap," replied the MacNair with lofty condescension. "We are finding your little place delightfully cozy."

"These were Kensington's private apartments when he chose to visit," said Sir Norvil sadly as he and the MacNair climbed the winding stone staircase that led to the top of the ancient Black Tower. He stopped on a narrow landing and indicated a thick oaken door. "This is his study—all his private papers are there—and up here on the very top is his bedroom."

He led the way to the uppermost landing and politely stepped aside to let the MacNair precede him through the stone archway. A moment later he had thrown open a small window in the narrow embrasure of the two-foot-thick walls of the tower and turned a melancholy eye upon the great green forest that stretched off to the sea. "How dearly poor Kensington loved to stand here and drink in the beauty of his beloved Scotland!"

The MacNair, too, was drinking in the beauty—but of the Earl of Kensington's superbly appointed living quarters. Here was warm radiant heating; here was a canopied bed with a mattress that seemed not to have been stuffed with straw from the stables of Bonny Prince Charlie; here were comfortable easy chairs; here was a dressing room filled with an array of apparel for every conceivable occasion;

here was a warm, brightly lighted bathroom with an enormous enameled tub carefully set into a wainscoting of brilliantly burnished dark oak.

The MacNair frowned, for the thought had leapt unbidden to mind: *This* was an apartment fit for a king!

"I say, Dennett, there is something we really must discuss."

The Master of Garnaway turned away from the narrow embrasure and ran his hand through his fluffy grey sidewhiskers. "Yes, Your Highness?"

"Yes. We feel quite sure that the Earl of—"

But the MacNair was interrupted by the sound of steps echoing on the stone staircase, and a moment later a grave footman in black and green livery stepped into the room. "Excuse me, your lordships. It's Lord Avery, Sir Norvil, with . . . with a person of *most* disreputable appearance. Benson has shown them into the blue drawing room. Lord Avery states that your presence is most urgently required."

"Bother," said Sir Norvil, "whatever can he want?" His shaggy eyebrows climbed like caterpillars up the shiny dome of his forehead. "After you, Your Highness. I am sure that this will take but a moment. Ah, but I was forgetting: you had something you wished to discuss. Shall we resume our conversation in—shall we say—the conservatory in an hour's time?"

"Oh, very well," conceded the MacNair testily as he marched down the narrow staircase, more eager than ever to move into these splendid quarters. "In the conservatory, then."

How vexing it was to be almost a king and yet be confined to this wretched cold bedroom, thought the MacNair angrily as he waited for Dennett to return from whatever foolish errand had called him away. If he were to *be* king, then he must learn to *act* like a king. What would a *real* king do in his position?

The answer was plain.

The MacNair strode from his bedroom and stalked regally down the long passageways of the castle until he came to the massive nail-studded door that opened onto the tower staircase. A *real* king would take immediate possession of the apartment and the devil take the hindmost!

As he bounced contentedly up and down on the side of the firmly sprung mattress of the canopied bed, it occurred to him that it was while lying in a similar bed in Düsseldorf that the Tirthankara's electronic GODHEAD had suddenly materialized upon his head. Even now the image of that incredible moment was indelibly engraved in his—

Once again he felt the weight of the miraculous crown as the entire room began to glow from its coruscating colors. His heart leaped up in exultation. "Ha!" he cried, and jumped to his feet in triumph.

He had removed the GODHEAD and just switched it off when his heart leaped again—but this time with paralyzing shock.

For surely those were footsteps he heard marching purposefully up the tower's single staircase. . . .

Unable to move, unable to shake off the utter blankness that suddenly gripped his mind, he stared numbly down at the jeweled crown he clutched against his breast.

The soft murmur of voices came to him from below, and now he could feel his knees beginning to tremble.

The steps grew nearer.

Wildly the MacNair cast his eye about the apartment. There was no way out of this terrible trap save a single tiny window hundreds of feet above the hard Scottish turf. . . .

"I tell you, the man's nothing but a spy!" came a sudden angry bellow from the staircase. "This so-called king is nothing but a spy for Napoleon!"

The MacNair's senses reeled and he clutched desperately at the back of a chair to keep from falling.

That voice! Surely . . . surely it could only belong to *the dead Earl of Kensington!*

CHAPTER
= 14 =

"A SPY? IT CAN'T be *possible!*" protested Dennett, coming to a sudden halt on the staircase just in front of the door to the Earl of Kensington's study.

Wester gripped his arm painfully. "Look! The door to my study is open! I wager this so-called Henley has been—"

"Do put your mind at rest, my dear fellow. The chambermaids have been cleaning all day. They must have inadvertently left the door ajar." He smiled wanly at the Earl of Kensington. Wester's prominent muttonchop whiskers had vanished and his upper lip now sported a straggly toothbrush mustache in the horrid fashion made popular in Germany in the 1940s by the pioneer transatlantic aviator Prince Siegfried von und zu Bodenheim. The swollen flesh around both eyes was a livid yellow and purple, and he walked with a perceptible limp. He wore a workman's tattered coverall of faded blue twill and heavy brown boots. The Master of Garnaway wrinkled his nose discreetly. This Earl of Kensington who was so shockingly different from the fastidiously turned-out gentleman who had embarked for Germany ten days before also badly needed a bath. . . .

"You must make allowances for the effects of the explosion on your central nervous sys—" began Dennett.

But the Earl had suddenly dashed into his study. He reappeared a minute later, his face flushed an angry red. "My papers have been disturbed: that spy has been among them!"

Sir Norvil Dennett could only shake his head as he watched his old companion stump furiously up the stairs to the open door of his apartment. A few days in bed would do the poor fellow a world of good. . . . He sighed, then followed him up the staircase.

Inside Kensington's chambers he found the Earl stalking intensely from one side of the room to the other. "He's been here, I tell you, I can *smell* him!" One by one Wester yanked open the doors to his cupboards and closets and studied their contents suspiciously. Growling softly, he moved into his dressing room to angrily push his clothes to and fro on their racks. Dennett followed him into the large empty bathroom, where the frustrated Earl stood glowering menacingly. "Perhaps a nice cup of bouillon," urged the Master of Garnaway soothingly.

The Earl of Kensington's eyes and fists squeezed tight in speechless fury—just as the MacNair clambered in from his terrifying perch on the crumbling stone sill 170 feet above the ground.

A quick glance at the bathroom to confirm that the two ghastly Englishmen were still distracted and in an instant the MacNair had bounded lightly across the thick red Persian carpets and down into the blessed sanctuary of the staircase.

"What's *that?*" cried Kensington, pushing Dennett aside to dash back into the bedroom. He looked wildly about the empty chamber. "Didn't you *hear* it?" he cried in anguish. "I tell you: I heard the sound of footsteps!"

Sir Norvil Dennett turned away sadly. Poor dear Kensington! The terrible explosion that had destroyed the Goethe Society had caught the Earl just as he was climbing unnoticed through a window in the pantry in the rear of the building. It had deposited him fifteen yards away in the depths of a commodious bush, where he had remained undetected until he could stagger away late that evening. It had been a miraculous escape, but obviously the lingering effects of the awful blast and of his desperate week in disguise while he sought to escape Germany had temporarily unhinged him. How fortunate that Lord Avery had come to spend the weekend! As head of the Royal Institute of Physicians he hadn't, of course, actually practiced in years,

ut certainly it shouldn't be beyond his modest capabilities
o administer a soothing injection of morphine. . . .

Back in the refuge of his own bedroom, the MacNair
ollapsed onto his sagging bed in total emotional exhaus-
ion, his arms and legs still trembling uncontrollably. In
pite of the castle's chill his body was damp with sweat, and
he pounding of the blood in his ears was like kettledrums.
Vith an incalculable effort of will he pushed away all
hought of the horrible moments he had just spent clinging
o the smooth stone walls of Garnaway Castle like some
normous tropical lizard. He who so detested heights! But
o let his mind linger on his sudden terrible venture into
ock-scaling would be to risk dropping dead of sheer
right. . . .

No, best to turn his thoughts to how he would reclaim his
eautiful GODHEAD, which had once again been so mer-
ilessly snatched from his grasp. At the moment, clearly,
nd for as long as that devil Kensington remained in
esidence, it was definitely out of reach. But if it were out of
each to *him*, he reasoned, then surely it was also safe from
asual discovery by anybody else. The thick layer of undis-
urbed dust that blanketed the surprisingly large space
eyond the small, barely perceptible hatchway in the oaken
vainscoting that gave access to the massive brass plumbing
eneath the Earl's enormous bathtub was surely proof of
hat.

But now the question became: Just *how* was he to get into
he bathroom past the manic vigilance of the pathological
Censington, that demented Kensington who had now de-
ided that *he*—the MacNair!—was a Napoleonic spy!

Could any circumstances be more grotesquely infuriat-
ng?

The MacNair gritted his teeth in rage.

What else did perverse Fate hold in store for him in this
naddening universe?

"You have no *idea* how beastly my uncle can be,"
omplained the Archduchess Mireille of Luxembourg to
er lady's maid that evening as she sat before her gilded
ressing table while her wavy shoulder-length hair received

its regular one hundred leisurely brush strokes.

"He was overly stern in his admonishments, Your Highness?" asked Mathilde sympathetically.

"He actually *shouted* at me! Can you imagine? As if were one of his armies or something. And all I did was te the Countess Simone about that magic crown from the pas and how it vanished from my very head!"

Mathilde's eyes widened perceptibly but the regula rhythm of her strokes never faltered. "It's all supposed to b some sort of secret, then?"

"That's what *he* says! He and that awful Marquis o Vézelay. They actually made me *promise* not to tell anyon about what we'd seen! Well, I haven't! I just barely *men tioned* it to the Countess Simone. She's my first cousin, isn' she? *That* isn't the same as telling some awful Turk, is it Mathilde?"

"Of *course* it isn't, Your Highness! I *do* think your uncle has reprimanded you *most* unfairly!" She reached for the silver jar of skin conditioner. "You say this crown actually vanished from your very head?"

The ensuing week was trying in the extreme for Prince William Ernest Augustus as he loftily tried to ignore the Earl of Kensington's incessant, and far from discreet efforts to convince his colleagues in the castle that the roya personage who so condescendingly suffered their mos lavish hospitality was actually nothing more than a particu larly daring *agent provocateur* slyly introduced into thei midst by the fiendishly cunning director of Napoleon' secret police, the Marquis of Vézelay.

The absurdity of the claim was so obvious that it wa curiously difficult to refute. Appeals to logic, commor sense, and Kensington's own previous conviction of the Prince's authenticity were of no avail. Even the exhaustive set of medical examinations which Lord Avery of Eventor had carried out upon the royal person made no impac upon Wester's rigidly held conviction.

"But his body contains trace elements which are com pletely unknown to this world!" protested Lord Avery plaintively at the breakfast table in the morning room "Already he has revolutionized all we know of chemistry

And his dentistry! Ah, his dentistry! Have you looked inside his mouth? It's—"

"Of course I haven't looked inside his mouth!" bellowed Kensington passionately, nearly beside himself at his inability to make these infernal chuckleheads see the obvious. "Do you take me for a bloody horse doctor?"

It was only after receiving an intricately coded message concealed in the middle of a two-pound block of truffled *foie gras* from Fauchon's in Paris that the truculent Earl was at last prevailed upon to moderate his views. For it was the Earl of Kensington himself who had painstakingly put together the cunning network of agents who reported back even the most recondite activities in what he scathingly referred to as the City of Darkness. And now their prime agent within the Elysée Palace itself had sent this stunning piece of information. . . .

"A crown," the Earl of Kensington muttered softly, running his hand back and forth over his gleaming scalp. "A diamond-covered crown that vanishes into thin air. . . ."

"Preposterous," said Sir Norvil Dennett flatly.

"Preposterous?" echoed the Earl angrily. "This, from one who has been championing the proposition of a man *appearing* out of thin air?" He turned to Lord Avery of Eventon. "I ask you, Eventon: Which of the two notions is the more absurd?"

Eventon pulled pensively at his nose and stared up at the Canaletto above the fireplace depicting a sunny morning on the Grand Canal. He walked to the far side of the afternoon sitting room and helped himself to a glass of pale estate-bottled whiskey. "It would appear to me that if *one* apparently preposterous notion is found acceptable it would be the utmost folly to dogmatically deny the possibility of the other without actually investigating it at first hand."

"Oh, very well," muttered Dennett testily. "I suppose that in *his* universe vanishing crowns are no more startling than buttered scones in ours."

"Buttered scones?" murmured the MacNair cheerfully, turning into the gloomy passageway that led from the west hall to the afternoon sitting room. "Did I hear someone mention buttered—"

"Then where *is* this blasted crown?" exclaimed the Earl of Kensington in exasperated tones that echoed along the castle's thick stone walls. The MacNair came to a sudden startled halt with one foot in the air and slunk unseen back into the shadowy passageway. "According to our informant, the French have actually held it in their very hands *twice* now. Each time it has suddenly vanished. And it seems that they invariably refer to it as *the crown of the man from the past.*" His sharp brown eyes moved meaningfully from Dennett to Eventon. "There is only *one* so-called man from the past. So where, then, is the crown? And what is its relationship to . . . *him?*"

"Yes," muttered Dennett, his eyes glittering behind his half-moon spectacles. "Yes, indeed. Do you realize that if this crown can actually be . . . *teleported* . . . it may well be of greater importance than the time machine itself?"

"Impossible!" cried the Earl of Kensington.

Sir Norvil raised a didactic finger. "I must remind you, my dear Kensington, of the following indisputable facts: One, that the time machine in Germany proved *not* to be a time machine at all. Two, that in any case that particular machine is now nothing more than a residue of vaporized atoms. Three, that our own machine is still in the planning stage. And four, that there is no guarantee that even *our* machine will work when actually built. For all these reasons, therefore, I suggest that while carrying on with our present project, we *also* devote some very concentrated consideration as to how we might possess ourselves of this astonishing crown."

"Hear, hear!" endorsed Eventon.

"But the one thing which we *do* possess," said the Earl of Kensington slowly, "and which the French do *not,* is—"

"—the actual person of His Royal Highness," completed Sir Norvil thoughtfully. "But I fear that this tale of the crown would seem to call into question his complete frankness and openness with us."

"Yes," said Eventon, "it *is* rather a bad show if all this time he has had some miraculous crown he's been concealing from us."

"He won't conceal it much longer," said the Earl in a grim voice which sent a cold tremor up the MacNair's spine. "There are any number of subbasements in this very building carefully designed by Dennett's ancestors for the express purpose of eliciting information from recalcitrant subjects. I suggest that if, by dinnertime, our royal jacka-napes has not answered all of our questions to our entire satis—"

But the MacNair heard no more, for he was already halfway up the staircase which led to the whispering gallery on his way to the winding staircase which climbed the Earl of Kensington's tower. If only he could get to the space beneath the bathtub for even a moment! A quick flip of his finger to switch on the crown for later retrieval and then—

But when he reached the nail-studded door that was the entrance to the Black Tower, he found the situation un-changed since Kensington's infernal return from the dead: an enormous liveried footman stood guard before the securely locked door. With a distant but gracious nod the MacNair continued sedately down the passageway. Before him, he knew, lay a staircase that would take him down through the kitchens into the basement garage, where a shiny fleet of powerful Delton automobiles awaited his pleasure.

Already he was wondering if he would be able to break his trail in Inverness by sinking the Delton he was about to borrow into the cold grey waters of the Firth of Moray before catching the first train out in any direction at all. . . .

CHAPTER
$=15=$

THE LATE AFTERNOON sun slanted into the Marquis of Vézelay's office from just above the long flat roofline of the Elysée Palace. From where he stood by the window he could look over the row of tall dark cypress that ran along this side of the formal gardens and see beyond it the tiny figure of the Archduchess Mireille running gaily back and forth along the croquet grounds with a dozen of her indolent friends.

Could the crown's disappearance somehow have been connected with that feather-brained woman putting it on her head? the Marquis asked himself peevishly. But if so, then how did that in turn relate to its disappearance from Berlin when it had been in the custody of Sitjar and LeFleur? And where was it now? Back in the hands of that outrageous man from the past? How he must be laughing at them!

The Marquis of Vézelay slammed his palm angrily against the desk. What a terrible shambles this entire *histoire* was! If word ever got out about it to the committees of dour senators who actually ran this enormous empire from their marble rooms in the grandiose Senate on the other side of the Seine, it would certainly mean the end of his career. The probing questions of the Emperor he could deflect; the baffled twitterings of the imbecile Archduchess he could ignore. But the senators who controlled the purse strings—*they* were all-powerful and totally unforgiving.

94

No, they must never, *never* learn of this!

Nor would they! Once again he banged his palm against the desk, but this time in triumph. For by now his agents in England had unexpectedly located his quarry!

But even in the midst of his triumph the Marquis suddenly felt his cheeks burning red with humiliation. For it was with *his* stolen documents and francs that this impudent scoundrel had purchased a ticket on yesterday's flight to America on the Royal Mail Line! Could anything be more gratuitously insulting?

But in doing so the fool had finally overreached himself.

For when he arrived in America handpicked agents, grim, tenacious, and resolute, would be waiting for him. Very soon now he would learn what it meant to wantonly smash the heads of totally inoffensive people with deadly enamel bedpans!

When the MacNair disembarked from the 600-foot dirigible *Marlborough* of the Royal Mail Line at Hamilton Fish Airship Station in North Queens three days later the credentials of the Marquis of Vézelay carried him past the mild scrutiny of the United States Border Control Agency without comment. A few minutes later he stood outside the small brick terminal in the warm August sunlight with his seventy fellow passengers awaiting transport into the city.

What, he wondered, would he find in this country he had once known so well? Already, he knew, it would be different. For as the great airship *Marlborough* had ponderously maneuvered above the Long Island coast, an anxiously straining MacNair was unable to spot any of the instantly recognizable features of the New York skyline: the World Trade Towers, the Statue of Liberty, the Empire State Building, the needlelike spire of the Chrysler Building. Even the glassy slab of the United Nations was gone. Other towering buildings had taken their place but on the whole the skyline seemed clearly less spectacular than what he remembered it as being.

The passengers with whom he had shared the fifty-three-hour trip from Runnymede Terminal were now supervising the loading of their steamer trunks into huge orange limousines. The MacNair was burdened only by the clothes on his back, the Marquis of Vézelay's wallet, and the trifling amount of dollars he had purchased from the dirigible's purser with his dwindling supply of francs. The MacNair stepped briskly through the crowd, and a few moments later his own cab—Mr. Timothy X. Flannery at the wheel —was moving slowly along the crowded four-lane road that led to Manhattan.

The MacNair slumped back with a sudden attack of acute depression. Was *this* the America he had known? Look at this very cab, with its two feet of legroom beyond the tips of his outstretched legs. A man of middle height such as himself could almost stand upright within its interior! When was the last decade in *his* America that anyone had concerned themselves with the comfort of paying passengers?

He sighed, and turned his gaze to the streets of central Queens through which they were now crawling from traffic light to traffic light. Here were no broad freeways or toll roads. Here were the same drab tenements and middle-class houses he had known in his own world, somehow transported in time back to the 1920s or '30s, where street peddlers still hawked their wares from pushcarts, where the sidewalks were crowded with women in long calico dresses, where the men still wore tightly buttoned dark suits and their heads were universally covered by a startling variety of homburgs, caps, fedoras, berets, and other designs which the MacNair was unable to identify.

Here were electric trolley cars running down the middle of the avenue, and over there in the next block the elaborate structure of an elevated railroad. For a few strange moments the MacNair wondered if by boarding the dirigible *Marlborough* after his precipitous flight from Scotland he hadn't somehow stepped into a *real* time machine, one which had set him down two days later in a long-vanished past. . . .

But no. He glanced down at the crumpled *Telegraph-Advocate* on the seat beside him: August 14, 1991, was the date. A grainy photograph on page 3 showed President Joseph P. Kennedy, Jr. receiving a barrel-shaped man in an elaborate flowing robe. He was further adorned with a tasseled fez, enormous dangling epaulettes, a curved scimitar, and slippers with six-inch pointed toes. This, read the caption, was His Serenity Mustafa Vefik Effendi, the new ambassador to the United States from the Ottoman Empire.

The MacNair tugged at his beard in astonishment. Joseph P. Kennedy? The father of JFK? Wouldn't he have to be at least a hundred years old? He looked again at the white-haired gentleman with the unmistakable Kennedy traits. Sixty-five or seventy, yes. A hundred, no! The terrifyingly frail-looking three-engined propeller planes that he had briefly glimpsed on the outskirts of London and which apparently managed to fly the Atlantic in competition with the stately dirigibles of the Royal Mail Line came suddenly to mind. Could a world which lagged so far behind his own in aeronautical technique be so advanced in medical science that a centenarian could still be Presi—

His speculations were interrupted by a sudden curse from Mr. Flannery. The MacNair looked up to see a small black coupé cruising beside the cab while two uniformed policemen peered intently in his direction. The MacNair's heart leapt up. Twenty minutes in America, and already the Gestapo was after him! It was not to be borne!

"Okay, Mac, pull it over," bellowed Angus McCarthy as he leaned into the wind that whistled between the squad car and the speeding taxi. He wondered if his partner at the wheel Fred Cooney was as uneasy about this business as he now was. It had *sounded* easy enough when the Frenchman with the thick wad of bank notes had proposed it to them the day before. All they had to do, he said, was get dressed up like cops, go out to Ham Fish, and pick up some pint-sized foreigner with a beard who would be getting off the *Marlborough*.

The money had seemed good, too, half now and half on delivery of the foreigner to a warehouse by the East River docks. Renting the uniforms and stealing an unattended Manhattan squad car hadn't been hard either. It was only after they'd crossed the Burr Bridge into Queens that they discovered that neither of them knew the way to the dirigible station. By the time they'd finally arrived the passengers had already disembarked and their taxis were beginning to pull away. The passengers in at least three of the cabs were clearly men with beards while the few remaining on the sidewalk were all starkly clean-shaven.

McCarthy and Cooney looked at each other in sudden despair. What were they to do *now?*

"Look," said McCarthy suddenly. "That little guy in that cab there. He might be the one."

"Maybe," grunted Cooney dubiously, but then shrugged unhappily. "What have we got to lose?"

They had followed the cab until it was out of the business section of Queens and was rolling smoothly along Alton Boulevard between an endless string of eight-story brick apartment buildings set in a drab parkland. The sidewalks on either side of the boulevard were deserted. The taxi slowed at McCarthy's command and with a sigh of relief he watched it pull over to the curb. A snatch in broad daylight on the main road into the city was not how he'd envisioned the afternoon's work. And the main problem still remained —they *still* didn't know if this was the guy they were supposed to snatch. . . .

The two hired agents, grim, tenacious, and resolute, climbed out of their small black squad car and strutted forward with studied arrogance to the orange cab, McCarthy to the passenger's side, Cooney to the driver's.

"License and hack papers," growled Cooney.

A broad red face as thoroughly Irish as Cooney's own and twice as truculent protruded through the window. "Indeed, now? In case you're lost, my fine boyo, Manhattan is *there,* while *here* where your oversized rump is impeding the flow of traffic happens to be the fine borough of Queens. So what, pray tell, is a Manhattan cop car doing hassling the good citizens of Queens?"

Cooney blinked beneath his stiff visor and glanced at McCarthy. "Hot pursuit," said McCarthy as he leaned over the hood and tried to make out the features of the passenger in the dark interior. But a tabloid newspaper shielded his face. . . .

"Hot pursuit," repeated Cooney. "We're in hot—"

"From the *dirigible* terminal? In hot pursuit. of *what,* Napoleon?"

Cooney gulped. How could this taxi driver know about

the Frenchman? "Whattaya mean, Napoleon?"

"I mean this ain't the flaming French Empire, your royal lordship. Here we got a set of rules. And the rules say you can't bust me in Queens. So why don't you guys just peddle your little wagon away?"

Desperately Cooney tried to compose his features. "Look. Just lemme see who your passenger is and—"

"Are you guys for *real?"* muttered Mr. Flannery, reaching for his dashboard radio. "Wait'll the dispatch—"

"Okay, out!" shouted Cooney, gripped by sudden panic. He thrust the barrel of his large blue revolver almost into the mouth of the startled hackie. "Back to the squad car with you!"

"Are you boyos ever gonna find yourselves in trouble," breathed Mr. Flannery wonderingly as he heaved himself out onto the pavement. He threw his shoulders back and Cooney's eyes widened. Mr. Flannery towered a good five inches over the top of his policeman's cap, and his shoulders and chest were broad in proportion. The French agent exchanged an uneasy glance with McCarthy, who after a moment's hesitation drew his own gun and came around the cab to join his partner.

"Back to the squad car with you," muttered Cooney, telling himself that maybe they could handcuff this monster to the wheel, then come back and drive off with his own cab, taking his passenger with them. "And don't even *move,* you!" he shouted at the dimly seen figure in the rear seat of the cab. "Okay, *march!"*

Mr. Flannery allowed himself to be marched back to the small black coupé. Just as they reached it and Cooney was asking himself what they were *really* going to do with this gorilla, the three of them looked up at the sound of a nearby engine roaring into life.

A sharp screech, the smell of burning rubber, and the gigantic orange cab roared backward directly at them. Before they could move, its heavy steel bumper had smashed deep into the middle of the coupé's tall narrow radiator. Water and steam instantly began to spurt. The grim, tenacious, and resolute French agents stared helplessly as the cab moved forward, darted suddenly into the flow of traffic, and was lost to sight.

"Well, now," murmured Timothy X. Flannery into the aching silence as he deftly plucked the two pistols from their unresisting hands. "Ain't that something?" The bananalike fingers of his great hands clamped around their necks and slowly began to tighten. . . .

CHAPTER
= 16 =

As THE MACNAIR wrested his borrowed behemoth through the clogged streets of downtown Manhattan vainly seeking a Central Park that no longer existed, his mind was working rapidly. If those were genuine policemen he had just escaped from, even now all of New York would be on the lookout for Mr. Flannery's stolen taxi.

And if they *weren't*—then who were they?

Agents of some sort, English, German, French? Suddenly he recalled the photo in the paper of President Kennedy receiving the Turkish ambassador. Or even thugs in the hire of the Ottoman Empire! Why not? Everyone else in this absurd universe seemed to be after the MacNair and his crown!

The MacNair came to a sudden decision: New York was no haven at all. He would have to put additional space between himself and his myriad enemies just across the Atlantic. There was no time to be lost; his funds were nearly depleted; what had served in one world should serve equally well here. It was near San Francisco that the Tirthankara Mardumjar had made his fortune with the

GODHEAD—California, here I come!

He left the taxi in the shadows of the elevated tracks that ran down Yorktown Avenue, strolled two blocks through a neighborhood that seemed to be predominantly Swedish, and hailed a cruising cab. "The station—the one with the trains for the West Coast."

"Hudson River Station, it is," muttered the cabbie, flipping the meter.

But as the MacNair walked uncertainly through the vast nineteenth-century structure overlooking the New Jersey Palisades, he was preoccupied by a second, far more astonishing idea that had suddenly come to him. Why had the great theoreticians and scientists Hubmaier and Dennett never mentioned the possibility? Because it *wasn't* possible? Or simply because it hadn't occurred to them? But what could be more logical?

The MacNair bounced nervously up and down on his heels in an agony of indecision. At last he made up his mind by counting the remaining dollars in his wallet. He had barely enough for a first-class compartment to San Francisco. Could the GODHEAD scam be counted on to begin producing revenues as soon as he stepped down from the train? In a world with which he was still barely acquainted? A risk, a terrible risk! Better at least to *try* this alternative which had such amazing possibilities. . . .

The MacNair replaced his pigskin wallet and set off decisively toward the ticket windows. In any case—which of his enemies would ever think of looking for him *there?*

He was obliged to taxi back to North Station on the Harlem River to catch the New York, Mystic & Plymouth north to Boston. Shortly after crossing the Bronx the train emerged into a bright Connecticut countryside curiously free of the endless suburbs of his own world, and the MacNair slouched back comfortably in his seat while his carriage rocked comfortingly across southern New England.

After arriving in Boston in the early evening he strolled for several restful hours through a city that seemed unchanged from the occasional visits of his youth. The bright green Common, the twisting lanes so ill adapted for modern traffic, the ancient buildings and graveyards, the innumerable historic churches, all of these were as he had known them. . . .

The night passed without incident at the Stevers House on Milk Street, and after a satisfying breakfast of codfish cakes and blueberry muffins in its paneled dining room he walked briskly through the financial district until he found Adams Station. The ticket seller looked at him curiously when he demanded a ticket for Bangor, Maine.

"Bangor, *where?*"

"Maine."

"Got a Bangor, Franklin, on the line, but no Maine. Take it or leave it."

The MacNair pursed his lips. "About two hundred miles north of here?"

"Yep."

"I'll take it," he said finally.

"$12.84. Say, you a foreigner of some kind?"

"A foreigner?" The MacNair looked slowly around the echoing station and its crowds of expensively dressed businessmen mingling with workingmen in tight brown suits and close-fitting caps. "Yes, I guess I am."

Fittingly enough as the steam locomotive of the Boston, Portland & Aroostook Line rolled sedately through the dark forests of central Franklin with its twelve passenger cars behind, the MacNair found himself absorbed by a thick book he had purchased at Adams Station, *Poor Richard's Almanac, 1991.* Yes, here was the State of Franklin, admitted to the Union in 1834 as part of President Clay's California Compromise which emancipated the slaves. Capital: Portland. Population: 735,498.

President Clay? The MacNair flipped through the pages of the *Almanac.* Hah, a list of Presidents! Washington, Adams, Jefferson, all the Founding Fathers were there. The middle of the nineteenth century: Jackson, Clay, Polk, Blaine, Adlai E. Stevenson. *Stevenson* but not Lincoln? Ah, no more slavery, no Civil War, no Abraham Lincoln. On to the twentieth century: William Jennings Bryan, followed by Charles W. Fairbanks, Philander C. Knox, Charles J. Bonaparte, Henry Cabot Lodge, Henry L. Stimson, Hamilton Fish, Joseph P. Kennedy, Hamilton Fish again. . . .

The MacNair frowned. Joseph P. Kennedy? Elected 1940, reelected 1944. But . . . ? His eye skimmed down the list. . . . Samuel J. Wilson, Joseph P. Kennedy, Jr., elected 1984, reelected 1988. . . . Joseph P. *Junior?* Could that be old Joe's *son?* The MacNair pursed his lips. The older brother of JFK, the one who was lost in the war? How much he had forgotten that once he had known. . . .

A sudden sharp image came to mind of a small thirteen-year-old boy huddled in front of his family's black and white television set in a tiny apartment on Hammond Street watching the inauguration in Washington of the vigorous young president with his great shock of hair. A spectacle he would never forget. The following morning his father had collapsed and died. . . .

The book fell unheeded to the seat beside him as he let himself be swept away by the flood of forgotten memories that these cool dark woods were so powerfully evoking. . . .

At last the train emerged from the endless pine forests to run beside a scattering of small farms and meadows. It slowed perceptibly and began a long gentle turn that brought it to the banks of the broad Penobscot River. The MacNair felt a strange constriction in his chest as they followed the river north to Bangor. What would he find at his destination?

A few minutes later they were creeping through the outskirts of southern Bangor. The MacNair pressed his nose eagerly to the window. Everything was as he remembered it: a small neat city of rivers and hills, weathered old buildings, enormous shade trees, and innumerable church spires cleaving through the lush green canopy. On the other side of the Penobscot from Bangor he could see the gigantic mountains of pulpwood that rose in front of the same great paper mills he had known as a child.

The MacNair's heart was pounding with excitement as the train jerked to a halt and he leapt down to the platform. Clouds of hissing steam billowed around the station and the air was filled with the familiar smells of the railroad yards of his youth. But as he stood mustering his disjointed thoughts, he slowly became aware that the railway station itself was subtly different. Yes, it seemed smaller, *much* smaller. And now he could see that it was clearly on the wrong side of the Kenduskeag Stream that flowed through the center of town to intersect the Penobscot in the heart of the commercial district. Fading gold letters on a long panel above the old brick waiting room told him that the long gaunt structure of wrought iron and grimy glass was no longer Union Station but now the Waldo Memorial Depot.

Tingling with a curious anticipation, the MacNair left the dark green coaches and the rumbling, smoking locomotive behind him and stepped out into the station's cobblestoned courtyard. His gaze moved slowly along the sagging old buildings of faded brick across from the station, past them to the rooftops of downtown Bangor gradually climbing the hills beyond, then finally came to rest on the dark green horizon of ancient trees silhouetted against the cloudy grey sky. A sudden gust of warm air blew against his cheek, bringing with it the heady aromas of steam and freshly baked bread. The MacNair took a deep breath of the rich redolent air and blinked away a light mist that had inexplicably blurred his eyes.

After twenty-five years he was home.

CHAPTER
= 17 =

MOTELS HAD NOT yet made their appearance in the Bangor, Franklin, of 1991. A discreet sign in the window of the old four-story Kenduskeag House on Exchange Street informed him that every room had a telephone and radio. The MacNair engaged a modest room with private bath, then eagerly picked up the thin grey telephone book that served Bangor and the neighboring counties. At last he threw it down on top of the scarred wooden radio console and roundly cursed his foolishness.

Why hadn't he remembered in New York that Americans moved constantly, that no one in the world was less attached to his place of birth? Look at himself, for instance: Was there anyplace less likely in the world to find the supremely cosmopolitan MacNair of MacNair than this small backwoods town of his birth? Why hadn't he thought of all this in New York before squandering two days of his precious capital on this obvious fool's errand?

But still—as long as he was here he might as well try all possible avenues. . . . With a quick glance in the mirror over the battered old dresser he straightened his dark blue tie and gave a cursory brushing to his already debonair beard. For even in the grotesquely misnamed state of Franklin appearances must be kept up!

The desk clerk directed him to the offices of the city's evening paper, the *Commercial,* and from there he strolled thoughtfully down Washington Street until he came to the old wooden building that housed the *Daily Guardian*. After he had transacted his business he continued his aimless rambling around the downtown streets.

How strange it was to be in a city he had once known so intimately and now to find everything about it nearly unrecognizable! The department stores, the sporting goods shop, the fish market, everything had changed, their sites, their names, the color of their paint. Even the beloved movie theaters of his youth, the Opera House, the Bijou, the Rat Hole, all had vanished. Only the hills, the streets, and the beautiful old trees were the same. He sighed deeply. Only now did he fully realize what it meant to be condemned to spend the rest of his life in a world which wasn't his. . . .

He stopped in front of the Penobscot Grill and studied the menu in the window. Baked stuffed lobster—$2.95. If nothing else, the prices in this world ought to be cause enough for cheer! His spirits already rising, he tugged twice at the end of his beard and stepped jauntily through the swinging doors.

Four days later the MacNair had given up all remaining hope and had informed the desk that he would be leaving in the morning. That evening he had an early meal of steamer clams and a boiled lobster accompanied by three frosty glasses of chilled ale. Undoing the buttons of his overly snug weskit, he stepped out of the Brass Rail and into the soft sultry air of the bright summer evening.

Slowly he walked through the small downtown business area that hugged the Kenduskeag Stream. The granite library and the post office had been interchanged and the Universalist Church on the hill across from the Taratine Club had become a two-story business college. A few steps farther and in his own world Bangor High had been just *here,* that same Bangor High where he himself had been the star shortstop and twice president of the Drama Club. Where he and little Ellen Mae Bickford had— The MacNair shook his head in wistful memory. Instead of an imposing brick school, he found a large wooden warehouse and a shabby tin building that housed a trucking concern. With a sigh he turned onto Colby Avenue and slowly climbed its steep hill for the final time.

He stopped across the street in the cool shade of a century-old oak and let his gaze linger once again on the even older three-story brick house with its wide wooden porch in front. The porch was a sparkling white while the brickwork had been painted a soft grey and the wooden shutters were a harmonious dark brown. How odd to think of someone like himself—a true citizen of the world, a veritable voyager across universes!—as having actually been born *there*, in that very house! How very improbable it now seemed. . . .

He wondered for a poignant moment who lived in this beautifully maintained old home he had known and loved as a child, the same home which in his own lost world his father had been obliged to sell in Kevin's eleventh year. He clucked his tongue against the roof of his mouth and with heavy footsteps moved slowly off. Years ago he repurchased his father's home with a portion of the funds which a Florida circuit-court judge had been kind enough to entrust to him, and had established an old people's retirement home for the members of his father's congregation. The stately red brick building wasn't as warm in the icy winters as their haven in Frostproof, Florida, might have been, but it would have to do, the MacNair told himself, it would have to do. . . .

Which reminded him: There was still time for one last glance at his father's old stone church under the elm trees on State Street. . . .

The jangling of the telephone roused the MacNair from a troubled sleep in the early hours of the morning. "Um?" he muttered groggily.

"This the fellow who placed that ad?" asked a soft Down East voice.

"Ad? Um, oh, the ad. Yes. Yes, I did." Suddenly the MacNair's heart began to pound with excitement.

"The one that says a certain Kevin Frost would learn something to his advantage?"

"Yes, that's what it says." The MacNair gripped the telephone tightly. "Are *you* Kevin Frost?"

"It may be that I could reach him. What exactly is the

something to his advantage?"

"What conceivable interest is that to anyone who isn't Kevin Frost? You've awakened me from a sound sleep. If that's all you have to—"

"Wait." There was a long pause while the MacNair listened to the humming of the wires. "This has nothing to do with . . . that affair in Portland?"

"Portland? I know nothing about Portland. This matter has nothing at all to do with Portland."

"Hmmm. Perhaps in that case I could prevail upon Kevin Frost to join us. But Kevin Frost is a man who cherishes his privacy. He would have to be certain that his liberty would not be impinged upon. Absolute discretion is his watchword!"

"Is it, now?" murmured the MacNair, his pulse racing. "I can appreciate *that* for I, too, am a man who treasures discretion and privacy. What, then, do you suggest?"

Even at three in the morning with only the meager yellow light of the occasional street lamp to mark his way, the streets were like old friends to the MacNair as he walked rapidly back and forth through the downtown business area. Carefully following instructions, he constantly doubled back on his trail, three times crossing the Kenduskeag Stream before at last turning up into the hills on the south side of the river with their century-old homes. As he moved from one street to the next, he saw that only their names had changed. Here was Ohio Street, where he had once fallen off his bicycle. Here was Union Street, where he used to catch the bus after playing baseball. Why were they now so improbably called French Street and Hillcrest Way? He shook his head and continued on to the next pool of light.

"Hsst!"

He jumped sharply at the sudden sound from the impenetrable mass of shadows to his left. "You MacNair?" came a soft whisper.

"I'm the MacNair."

"Quick, through here." A hand reached out of a clump of shrubbery and fixed itself around his wrist. He let himself be pulled through the bush itself, then along a darkened driveway and into the front seat of a small boxy sedan. It was impossible to make out his companion's features as he hunched over the steering wheel, his hands working feverishly beneath the dashboard. The MacNair raised his eyebrows but maintained a tactful silence.

The motor caught, throbbed softly, and the car moved off without headlights. A block later the driver switched them on and they began to move at high speed through the sleeping city, doubling back again and again on their tracks. The darkened streets were totally deserted and it was obvious that no one was following them. At least it was obvious to the MacNair, who sighed plaintively. How tiresome it was to be in the company of the incurably paranoid!

A few minutes later they sped out of town on the road south to Hampden and Belfast but before they reached the Hampden junction the driver slowed abruptly, switched off the lights, and in the sudden total darkness wrenched the car off the highway and onto what must have been the crudest sort of farm track.

As they bounced and tumbled for the next ten minutes in utter darkness, the MacNair felt that his insides were being shaken out. Where were they going? And how could the driver possibly see what he was doing? Just as he was about to demand an explanation, the car lurched a final time and came to an abrupt halt. "We're here."

"Yes," said the MacNair, "so I would hope."

He climbed down from the car and stood turning his head from side to side. The stars were bright in the clear moonless sky and his eyes had adjusted enough to distinguish fields to his right and the dark mass of a clump of woods to his left. He saw his companion move off to merge with an even darker mass that loomed up just in front of the car. A moment later the MacNair heard the creak of rusty hinges. A match suddenly flared, and then a flickering orange light began to glow in the interior of what was revealed to be a small tar-paper shack.

The MacNair walked through the door, barely able to keep his excitement from bubbling to the surface. "Your _pied-à-terre?_" he asked with genial interest.

"Only when I need absolute discretion." The driver set the kerosene lamp down on a wobbly table and swung around to face the MacNair. His smooth round face glowed orange like a Halloween pumpkin in the eerie light. His eye sockets were deep black holes and the MacNair saw with a sudden shock that a strange black line seemed to run up each cheek just to either side of his nose. The MacNair gulped softly. This *couldn't* be! *This* grotesque creature? Something was terribly wrong! His heart pounding fiercely, he reluctantly forced himself to step closer.

"Stop!"

The MacNair rocked to a halt, one foot in the air, and found himself looking into the end of a small black revolver which had miraculously materialized in the other's hand.

"I warn you, I am armed! Move no further! Now, then!" The fantastic shadows flickered across his Halloween-pumpkin face as his head bobbed up and down and his voice was suddenly shrill. "Now, then! You have something to offer to my advantage?"

"You yourself are Kevin Frost?"

"For the purposes of this discussion I acknowledge it."

"Born in Bangor on October 2nd, 1947?"

The other sighed plaintively. "I wonder what marvels would accrue to my advantage if such were the case?" He shook his head in sad resignation. "Ah, well, Kevin Frost is above all things devoted to the tenets of absolute truth. I was born in Orono on September 29th, 1947."

"Orono," murmured the MacNair. "I'd forgotten about Orono—yes, a few miles up the river. Your parents, then: Charles Kevin Frost and Françoise Thibodaux?"

The other's gun wavered. "Charles Frost and *Hélène* Thibodaux."

"Close enough." In spite of the unwavering revolver that was pointed at his midriff the MacNair stepped forward until he could feel the feeble heat of the glowing lamp on the table just before him. "Imagine me, if you will, without this beard, without my hair combed straight back, without—"

"My God," murmured Kevin Frost, his eyes widening, *"you're me!"*

CHAPTER
= 18 =

A FEW MONTHS short of his forty-fourth birthday Kevin Frost was small and wiry with a mobile face which reflected the mercurial nature of his character. He had flashing brown eyes with long soulful eyelashes, an unlined countenance, and thick brown hair clipped short in the Prussian fashion. A delicately formed handlebar mustache adorned his upper lip, culminating in two long waxed points that turned up like stilettos on either side of his nose and came nearly to his eyes. His laugh was merry and unforced, his wits nimble, his urbanity—despite his modest origins—a byword to those who knew him.

He was the only child of a shoe salesman in Beaver's Department Store in Bangor and of his young French-Canadian bride. His mother had died in giving him birth and his stricken father had turned to alcohol. Thereafter Kevin had been raised mostly by a succession of his mother's relatives. He passed his teenage years in Dover-Foxcroft Reform School and from there had gone on to five long years as a pharmacist's mate policing the banana republics of Central America on the coal-burning vessels of the Caribbean Fleet.

Upon returning to his native Franklin he had ventured into a wide field of activities: he had peddled patent medicines among the Indian reservations and the northern logging camps; he had distributed illicit pills from the back of an Augusta pharmacy; he had sold a nonexistent lake to a

111

syndicate of Philadelphia businessmen; he had set himself up as an investment counselor; he had obtained a number of ornately engraved diplomas and hung out a sign proclaiming himself a chartered public accountant. As such he had labored diligently on behalf of his clients with all the ingenuity he could bring to bear, his eyes gleaming with pleasure as he conceived a host of subtle fiscal ploys. Some of those stratagems relating to the depreciation of wasting assets, in this case Holstein cows, eventually had generated enough admiring attention to earn both him and his employee an unpaid leave of absence of seventeen months in a federal establishment in central Kansas. Undaunted by the experience, he had returned to Franklin with his head full of ambitious projects for the future. For none of his previous occupations, he felt, diverse as they had been, had done full justice to the lofty aspirations which surged within him.

Among his ambitions was the acquisition of a helpmeet and companion of the gentler sex capable of measuring up to his exigent standards. But here Kevin Frost set forth with a certain trepidation, for he had not entirely succeeded in completely obliterating the distasteful memories of his single previous venture into the uncertain shoals of love.

Franklin, in fact, was a state in which an alert caution in matters of the heart was generally advisable, for even now in 1991 it remained one of the nine states in which incurable insanity was the only grounds for divorce and one of the thirty-seven in which adultery remained a felony. Since simple fornication was a mere misdemeanor punishable by no more than six months' incarceration at the State Work Farm, Kevin Frost had never seriously contemplated the rigors of marriage until his thirty-fifth year.

Finally the prospect of another icy Franklin winter was more than he could face: he found himself, somewhat to his surprise, at the altar with a rather plain but astonishingly supple woman of his own age whose parents owned 3,000 acres of prime sugarcane in the French colony of Martinique in the sunny Caribbean.

This was a remarkable coincidence, in that *his* parents, so he told his prospective bride, owned a 16,000-acre plantation in Cuba. Due to political strife on that unhappy island, however, they were unable to attend their son's wedding. For similar reasons, it eventually transpired, neither were the parents of his inamorata, Mademoiselle Jacqueline Groussolles, able to take part in their joyous festivities. After a brief honeymoon in St. Augustine, Florida, the lovers returned to the farm outside Gardiner, Franklin, where Kevin Frost was engaged at the time in raising 70,000 white turkeys.

He was certain that it was only a matter of time before he was asked to take over the direction of his elderly in-laws' sugarcane plantation, but to his perplexed dismay his bride abruptly vanished from his life one rainy day in December with nothing more than a curt note in French pinned to the wooden door of the icebox.

Enough of your frauds and fantasies, it read, *I have returned to Martinique. For the sake of your earthly tegument do not follow me: you would be dealt with severely by my brothers. For the sake of your immortal soul renounce your ways of duplicity and restrict your activities to the honest cultivation of your white turkeys for which you are so well suited. . . .*

Now, eight years later, even as he listened to the Mac-Nair's weird tale, it was impossible for Kevin Frost to entirely suppress occasional stray thoughts of that lithe Martiniquaise. For astonishing as he found this incredible confrontation with an identical self from another world, events of a far more compelling immediacy were even now reaching a grim climax 120 miles to the south in the state capital of Portland. Events which had inexorably been set in motion nearly a decade before by the faithless Jacqueline Groussolles. . . .

"You will appreciate the need for the strictest confidentiality in regard to what I have just disclosed," concluded the MacNair. He added with a quizzical lift to his eyebrows: "Just as, I imagine, you may feel the need for discretion about your own 'affair in Portland.' "

Kevin Frost started abruptly at this apparent telepathic intrusion into his own thoughts, but recovered to make a small gesture of dismissal. "A tedious matter of no great consequence."

"I am happy to hear that. You live in Portland, then, or here in—wherever we are?" The MacNair denoted the shack's squalid interior with a wave of the hand.

"I am highly mobile. You are fortunate to have caught me. I had chanced to be in Bangor for a few hours on matters of pressing business before departing for a lengthy stay abroad when your notice caught my eye. But enough of my own insignificant affairs," said Kevin Frost, leaning forward with a sardonic smile, the wirelike points of his bizarre mustache and the shadows they cast wobbling eerily against his orange face. "Tell me this: Why, if we were born of the same parents in practically the same city in parallel worlds, do you call yourself by this preposterous name, the MacNair of MacNair? In *my* world, my father Charles Frost was far from being a Scottish nobleman. He was, in fact, an alcoholic barman on Exchange Street."

The MacNair scowled peevishly. "If you like, it is something in the nature of an honorific."

"An honorific," muttered Kevin Frost with heavy irony. "Well, well, I suppose anything's possible. But mine is a harsh world, full of unscrupulous characters, in which a misguided trust is invariably betrayed. I see it constantly in my profession."

"Which is? Gentleman farmer here in Bangor?"

Kevin Frost scowled in turn. "Stockbroker," he replied shortly. "You'd be amazed at how many people want something for nothing."

"I'm afraid the situation is much the same in my own world."

"Where your own profession is—"

"University president," said the MacNair with austere dignity. "Now, then," he continued briskly, "the situation is as I have explained. Through circumstances beyond my control I have been brought unexpectedly to this, your own world. A series of rather trivial misunderstandings has placed me in a somewhat equivocal position with regard to certain individuals in Europe. This world of yours is similar to, but in many important ways different from, my own. Until I have gained a fuller understanding of its workings it seemed best to seek the guidance and shelter of a person in whom I might place my entire confidence. Logic dictated that *you* might exist." His own winning smile easily matched Kevin Frost's for frankness and openness. "And as you see, I was lucky enough to find you. So now, dear brother, I humbly entrust my fate to your hands."

"I am of course deeply touched by your trust," murmured Kevin Frost as his thoughts whirled at a furious rate, "but I suppose that your financial position is—"

"Somewhat constrained," admitted the MacNair.

"A great pity." Kevin Frost rose from one of the two wooden chairs which with the table and a sagging cot were the shack's sole furnishings and paced slowly to the door and back. "I fear that at the moment I find myself unable to aid you in any material way. My house in Portland is rented, my funds have been transferred abroad, and, as I have already mentioned, I am about to depart on a lengthy trip of indeterminate duration."

"But surely," said the MacNair, "you can see the incalculable advantages of associating yourself with one from a more technically advanced world! Between us we can make a fortune, a *hundred* fortunes! This world of yours lacks any number of items which are commonplace in mine: television, jet propulsion, space travel, atomic energy, computers—"

"What is a computer?"

"A thinking machine. Photocopiers, transistors, auto—"

"And you yourself can actually design these marvels and implement their construction?" Kevin Frost pulled uncertainly at the tip of his Dali-like mustachios. "I suppose that as a university president that would be conceivable."

"Up to a point, perhaps," replied the MacNair cautiously. "That is to say, I will unstintingly supply the absolutely essential item, the requisite ideas. You, as a broker, should then have no trouble finding financial backers and capable technicians."

Kevin Frost glanced uneasily at the pale dawn that was now beginning to lighten the shack's single window. "An interesting proposal, but I fear that the press of affairs calls me away. I am, in fact, booked on this evening's airship for England and it will certainly be some little time before I return. Perhaps if you were to accompany me, together in Europe we could—"

"Out of the question! A number of regrettable misunder-standings quite preclude that possibility." The MacNair abruptly halted to marshal his thoughts. It was obvious that the Kevin Frost of this world—his own flesh and blood!—was far from being the exemplar of open-handed and unstinting generosity that he himself was. No doubt it could all be explained by the sad nature of his childhood. But be that as it may, he was obviously about to coldly abandon the MacNair to his fate.

He pursed his lips. But now his circumstances had actually *worsened* since his impulsive decision five days before to make for Maine rather than California. For not only was he still on the run, but now his wallet was almost totally depleted, and the crucial fact of his existence had been imparted to this rather loathsome Frost creature. What only hours before had been the merest theoretical speculation had now become dire necessity: somehow he must turn Kevin Frost into his firm ally.

The MacNair sighed. "Let us carefully reconsider the situation, for the news that you are going to England clearly changes the perspective. I see that I shall have to fill you in a little more clearly on the nature of certain of the events which have led me here."

CHAPTER
== 19 ==

"SO YOU'RE PRETENDING to be the heir to the British throne!" marveled Kevin Frost, his eyes wide with admiration. "Is this Frenchman, the Marquis of Vézelay, aware of this?"

"Not so far as I know."

"Hmmm. But he will be, you know. He's not just a mere secret-police man but the director himself. They say his agents are everywhere, even here in America."

The MacNair let out a little sigh as he thought again of the narrowness of his escape from the so-called policemen in New York City. "All the more reason to act quickly," he said urgently. "The sooner you get to Scotland, the sooner we'll be able to recover the crown."

"And split the proceeds equally, I believe you said?" pressed Kevin Frost.

The MacNair stared at him with wide guileless eyes. "But of course! You *are* myself, aren't you? How could it possibly be otherwise?"

Kevin Frost ran his fingers through the short stiff hair on the top of his scalp as he wondered how much faith he could put in this patently untrustworthy rascal who talked so glibly of other universes and unlimited riches. He glanced down surreptitiously at his watch. If he were to get to Boston to make the airship, he would have to be leaving soon. He grimaced as once again his thoughts strayed to Jacqueline Groussolles and from her moved on to southern Franklin, where the events of the past few days had clearly served to demonstrate the nature of his blunder in so carelessly turning his attentions to the city of Portland in his quest for a lady to share the joys and sorrows of his existence.

For it was there in the very shadows of the State House that he had made the acquaintance of a certain Mary Louise Babcock, the grieving widow of the late lieutenant governor of the state of Franklin. Her lamented husband, Lynwood W. Babcock, Kevin Frost soon learned, had come to a macabre end upon the antlers of a stuffed moose head which had fallen from its perch above the main fireplace of his hunting lodge on Third Roach Pond in central Franklin and neatly impaled him.

His widow had inherited the seventeen-room lodge in which he had met his bizarre fate as well as a wide circle of devout cronies, an enormous house in Portland, and a large portfolio of conservative securities administered in trust by the Fiduciary Bank of Salem, Massachusetts. Fifteen years her senior, Kevin Frost had fallen in love with her the glorious moment he chanced across the court records detailing the extent of the probated estate.

That the widow Babcock was tall and slim, with sparkling green eyes and glinting auburn hair that fell to her shoulders, was a welcome bonus. And even in the shapeless black clothes dictated by her year of mourning it was impossible to entirely conceal her youthful beauty and natural exuberance. Even the tiresome circle of cigar-smoking politicians and hearty woodsmen and fishermen who surrounded the lovely young widow were welcome to Kevin Frost, for he quickly realized they only served as a counterpoint to let his own raffish urbanity glitter the more brightly as he ardently pressed his suit.

Now he sighed as he contemplated the whirlwind courtship he had brought to so triumphant an end, and its unexpectedly poignant sequel. He glanced again at his wristwatch. Any moment now he would have to come to a decision of one sort or another. "Tell me more about this crown," he said hurriedly. "The whole situation is far from clear. Where actually is it hidden? If you can materialize it out of thin air, why don't you simply do so? It would save me the tedium and attendant dangers of going to Scotland to retrieve it."

"Its operation is occasionally somewhat haphazard by nature," temporized the MacNair, unwilling to tell this grotesquely disreputable version of himself any more of his priceless secrets. "I believe it has something to do with the proliferation of sunspots." If only he could somehow induce Kevin Frost to switch on the crown without being aware of what he was doing!

The MacNair drew a hand across his face. And if only he himself weren't so tired! For he had suddenly realized that he was no longer capable of sustaining coherent thought. Assuming that he could place his hands on it in the first place, what was to keep Kevin Frost from walking off with the GODHEAD and dismantling it diamond by diamond, never troubling to turn it on. . . . He shook his head in exasperation at his foolishness in disclosing as much as he already had. "I've been up all night," he muttered wearily, looking out the window at the pale light of early morning. "I'm hungry and thirsty. Haven't you—"

"An excellent idea!" exclaimed Kevin Frost with sudden enthusiasm, for he had just now come to a momentous decision. "There may be a few cans of beans. Let me see what I can find. In the meantime"—he drew a silver flask from his pale linen jacket—"perhaps a small nip of Dr. Frost's All-Purpose Restorative and Elixir Supreme to celebrate the occasion. Dear, dear, let me see if I can't find a clean glass for His Royal Excellency Prince William Ernest Augustus." As he bustled around in a dark corner of the shack, the MacNair felt his eyes closing for a few brief moments. . . .

He was shaken awake by Kevin Frost's hand on his shoulder. "A toast," cried Kevin Frost gaily, handing the MacNair a large smudged tumbler of gleaming amber liquid and simultaneously raising his own. "A toast to our meeting! And to our future!"

"A toast," muttered the MacNair, sipping cautiously at his drink. It was nothing as good as what he had recently grown accustomed to at Garnaway Castle in Morayshire but at least it was recognizably Scotch. He watched Kevin Frost down his own in a single long swallow, then with a stifled yawn threw back his head and let the fiery liquid course down his throat. . . .

A terrible pounding in his head and the sensation of being mercilessly shaken in a revolving cement mixer slowly brought the MacNair awake. He moaned and opened his eyes. The harsh light of day assaulted him. With a groan he threw his arm across his face and tried to nestle his head deeper into the hard pillow. What a peculiar dream! Inexplicably he seemed to be back in the seat of Kevin Frost's car, jouncing and bouncing across—

He opened his eyes again and rolled them blurrily from left to right. He *was* in a car. And he *was* being bounced around like a roulette ball in a casino's wheel. But *why* was he in a car? And why was he sitting between these two beefy men in dark green uniforms and hats like forest rangers?

He turned his head cautiously from side to side. Through the windows he could see that the car was bumping with agonizing jolts along a primitive track in the depths of a forest of tall dark pine. From the occasional rays of bright sunlight that slanted down through the trees the sun must now be high in the sky. But that was impossible! Only a bare moment ago the pale white dawn had been brightening the interior of Kevin Frost's miserable shack as the MacNair lifted a glass of whiskey in the company of his twin. . . .

The MacNair moaned and focused his eyes with difficulty on the orange and blue patch on the shoulder to his right: *Franklin State Police,* it read. The memory of the policemen in New York City suddenly returned and a terrible constriction gripped his chest. Could the Marquis of Vézelay have somehow traced him here to Maine? But if so, then where was his doppelgänger Kevin Frost? What could have happened to his other self? And—of far more consequence to the MacNair—what were they planning to do with *him?*

Desperately he ran his hand through his beard—and stopped short. The throbbing inside his head was ferocious —but enough to be indicative of a mind that had suddenly slipped its moorings? Bewildered, he scratched again at his bare, stubbly chin.

What had happened to his beard? And how had his magnificent head of hair suddenly become so short and scratchy?

"He's awake, is he?" For the first time the MacNair became fully aware of the two uniformed troopers in the front seat of the lurching vehicle. One of them had turned around and was eyeing him curiously. "That must be some party you give, mister. We had to carry you out like a sack of cement."

The MacNair shook his throbbing head feebly. "Where . . . where am I?" he heard himself muttering idiotically.

The trooper on his left guffawed appreciatively. "Where does it look like you are?"

"Yes, yes," said the MacNair testily, "I see quite plainly that I'm in your absurd police car. What I should have said is *why,* and where are we going?"

"You sure you couldn't guess, now?" wheedled the trooper in the front seat.

"I hate guessing games."

"Well, now, someone down to Portland sure must hate bigamists the same way you hate guessing games. The state's attorney himself was on the phone to the colonel out at the barracks in Newport to make certain we picked you up all safe and sound." He smiled smugly. "And I guess we did, all right, except maybe for a little bit of a hangover."

But the MacNair was struggling to make sense of these bewildering words. "What have bigamists got to do with *me?"* he asked at last.

The trooper shook his head admiringly. "What a rakehell you are!—for a runty little fellow, of course. Three weeks married to that beautiful widow Babcock down to Portland, with that other wife of yours sitting home somewhere maybe peeling potatoes and hoping you'll be home for your evening meal, and all the time here you are up to Bangor drinking and carousing all night long and maybe even angling to marry wife number three."

The MacNair felt as if his head had suddenly been inflated to the size of the dirigible *Marlborough* while simultaneously a steel band was being tightened around its enormous bloated girth just above his ears. Blood pounded loudly in his ears as he struggled to digest the absurd words.

He tried to protest. "But—"

"But we just can't let you do it," said the trooper sternly. "Even two wives at a time is one too many for the state's attorney and the People of the State of Franklin to swallow. Brokenhearted, she is, that poor little Babcock woman, and all because of a brute like you." He shook his finger admonishingly. "I tell you, Kevin Frost, your marrying days are over for the next five to ten years."

CHAPTER
= 20 =

"THERE'S A MAN who *wants* to see me?" repeated the Marquis of Vézelay. "How very extraordinary. I should have said offhand that of the 287 million citizens of the Empire approximately 286,999,000 most heartily *don't* want to see me. Obviously he's a madman. Tell him to go through channels like everyone else."

"I've already told him, sir," replied Colonel Etournaud, "but he is really most insistent. A foreigner of some sort—he speaks a most bizarre French. He seems to be saying something about a bedpan, but of course *that* can't be the case."

"Of course not," muttered the director of the Special Directorate, rapidly spinning his chair around to conceal from his aide the furious blush that had suddenly inflamed his cheeks. "Well, well," he said with forced joviality, "I suppose we bureaucrats must always be vigilant about becoming overly hidebound, slaves, as it were, to a pettifogging routine. We are, after all, here to serve the public."

"We are?" echoed Colonel Etournaud, unable to conceal his astonishment.

"In a manner of speaking, of course," said the Marquis of Vézelay crossly. "I should have thought the point was clear: Our duty to protect the Emperor and the Empire transcends any petty routine that we may have allowed ourselves to slip into." He spun around in his chair and made a broad movement with his open palm. "If only as a symbolic gesture against the dangers of bureaucratic rigor mortis, let us see this mysterious madman who comes to discuss bedpans with the director of His Imperial Majesty's secret police."

"You say you're Prince William Ernest Augustus, heir to the British throne?" repeated the Marquis of Vézelay incredulously. He leaned across his desk to study the madman who sat across from him so insouciantly twirling the ends of his preposterous mustache. His eyes were clear and untroubled, his mouth somehow subtly mocking. He wore a deftly tailored summer suit of pale cream linen, a silk foulard of a deep rich burgundy, and glossy brown shoes with cunningly devised elevator heels. The hair was definitely shorter, and the neat little beard had been replaced by these absurd mustachios, but otherwise he bore a striking resemblance to that so-called man from the past whom the Marquis of Vézelay so fervently wished to interview.

"But what are you doing *here?*" marveled the head of the French Empire's dreaded secret police.

Kevin Frost raised his eyebrows quizzically. "Surely you *are* the gentleman to whom I granted an audience some time ago in—could it have been Metz? I distinctly recall that rather ratty beard."

The Marquis of Vézelay inexplicably found himself uttering gobbling noises.

"I'm sorry, sir," said Kevin Frost calmly, "I am quite unable to follow your French. You'll simply have to enunciate more clearly."

With a terrible effort the Marquis of Vézelay brought himself back under control. "So you recall an . . . audience in Metz?" he murmured softly in tones of infinite menace, his eyes flashing.

"Only in the vaguest of terms," said Kevin Frost with a dismissive wave of his right hand. "I fear I was still suffering from the aftereffects of shock. I recall you broaching the subject of my crown, but after that—nothing!"

"Nothing?" shouted the Marquis de Vézelay, hardly able to believe the effrontery of this insolent jackanapes. "What do you mean, *nothing?*"

"Nothing," repeated Kevin Frost firmly. "It was only when I suddenly found myself standing on a street corner in downtown New York City with my head half-shaven and my beard missing that I realized that a number of days were missing from my life."

"You mean—you've lost your *memory?*" The Marquis of Vézelay stared with unconcealed loathing at the man who had pronounced himself to be Prince William Ernest Augustus.

"You find that peculiar? Put yourself in *my* place, if you will. Here I am quietly sitting in my bath at the Palace—"

"Buckingham, I presume?" muttered the Marquis between his teeth.

"Where else? I am sitting inoffensively in my bath, I say, when suddenly I am somehow dragooned from my own particular world through a myriad of universes and unceremoniously deposited totally naked in the basement of a building in Düsseldorf, Germany. The so-called scientists who have kidnaped me then inform me that it is frankly beyond their power to ever restore me to my universe, country, family, and friends. Imagine, sir, my shock and dismay! A few days later, as I meditate peacefully in the library, attempting to come to terms with this terrible catastrophe, the very building in which I am sitting is blown up around me!" Kevin Frost fixed the Marquis of Vézelay with a particularly cold gaze. "Is it any wonder, then, that I might later experience a few trifling lapses of memory?"

"I see," said the Marquis of Vézelay somewhat less menacingly. "You are saying, then, that you are not, as I had been led to believe, from the past, but from—"

"An alternate universe, or parallel world, where today's date is exactly the same as yours, that is to say, the 27th of August 1991."

The Marquis of Vézelay rose slowly to his feet and

padded softly across his office to the deep window embrasure where he stared down pensively into the imperial gardens across the Avenue de Marigny. "You speak remarkably fluent French," he said at last.

"Thank you. You may, incidentally, address me as Your Highness, or merely Sir," said Kevin Frost graciously.

The Marquis of Vézelay swung around with a dark scowl on his face. "If Your Highness will permit the observation, I distinctly recall commenting upon your charming accent of Toulouse during our previous conversation. Now, however, I would venture to say, without wishing to give offense in any way, that the accent has become rather more—"

"French Canadian?" The man who called himself Prince William Ernest Augustus sighed profoundly. "My dear old nanny, God bless her soul, was of French-Canadian background. The French I learned from her in the nursery has remained with me to this day."

"How peculiar that the entire British Isles were unequal to the task of procuring a genuine English nanny for the heir to the British throne."

"Isn't it, though?" agreed Kevin Frost blandly.

"And you say that you were sitting naked in your bath at the moment Your Highness was transported here to this world? How, then, did the crown—"

"Accompany me?" Kevin Frost shrugged massively. "I have not the faintest idea."

"And in your own world, does it also possess seemingly magical powers?"

"Magical powers? Whatever do you mean? By British standards it is a quite ordinary crown with some 36,000 inlaid diamonds and some rather banal communications equipment."

"The electrical connections on the crown are an aid to communications?"

"Certainly. How else could I communicate with my brother Prince George at our base on Mars, for instance?"

The Marquis of Vézelay's eyes widened. "You can talk to *Mars* with it? It's a sort of super radio?"

"If you wish," said Kevin Frost tolerantly, "but one doesn't of course *talk* into it, one *thinks* into—"

"Telepathy?" whispered the Marquis of Vézelay. "You

mean it's a . . . a telepathic augmentator?"

"Possibly, possibly," admitted Prince William without any great interest. "I am not, myself, technically inclined."

The Marquis of Vézelay could only marvel silently as he considered the impact of such a machine upon the Empire —or in the hands of its enemies. At last he raised his eyes to the remarkable specimen who sat so imperturbably across from him. "And might I ask just where this fabulous crown is at this very moment?"

Kevin Frost leaned forward in his chair. "But that, my dear sir, is precisely why I have come to see *you!* I have come, in fact, to recover my rightful property. You will recall, I trust, our previous conversation. If memory serves me well, you mentioned something to the effect of it being in safe hands in the vaults at the Curie Institute." He rose abruptly to his feet. "Perhaps it is wise to leave it there for temporary safekeeping, but I do think that I should stop by to make certain that—"

"Then you don't know that it has—vanished?"

"Vanished? How could it vanish?"

"That is what I intended to ask *you.*"

"How extraordinary!" Kevin Frost sank slowly back into his chair. "How on earth could I tell you how it vanished?" He pulled thoughtfully at the tip of his mustache. "What precisely were the circumstances under which it vanished?"

The Marquis of Vézelay looked up briefly at the elaborately gilded ceiling moldings, then down at his carefully manicured nails. *This* was supposed to be the most closely guarded of state secrets. But given the extraordinary circumstances . . . "We were showing it to the Emperor himself, deep in the vaults of the institute, when it suddenly disappeared in an instant."

Kevin Frost's eyes widened. "From the very hands of the Emperor?"

"Actually from the head of Her Exalted Highness the Archduchess Mireille of Luxembourg," the Marquis of Vézelay amended. "The lights had been turned on and she had just placed it on her head when—"

"Stop!" cried Prince William. His eyes flashed and his hands clutched the arms of his chair. "Did . . . did you say the . . . the Archduchess Mireille of *Luxembourg?*"

The Marquis of Vézelay frowned in bewilderment. "I did."

"But . . . but . . ." Prince William's eyes grew round. "She is about . . . so tall, with curly blond hair, blue eyes, a frolicsome though occasionally imperious manner?"

"Yes, I suppose one might say that. But why—"

"Why?" Prince William Ernest Augustus leapt once again to his feet, his chest rising and falling rapidly. "Why, you ask? Because in *my* world, don't you see, the Archduchess Mireille is my beloved wife!"

CHAPTER
= 21 =

"ISN'T IT THRILLING, Mathilde?" trilled the Archduchess Mireille of Luxembourg as she stepped daintily into the sudsy waters of her steaming bath. "The man from the past isn't from the past at all—he's from another universe!"

"Another universe, Your Highness?" murmured the raven-haired lady's maid, stepping back from the marble tub with the Archduchess's dressing gown. "I don't understand."

"Neither do I, entirely, but I haven't told you the best. This man—it seems he's *really* Prince William Ernest Augustus, the heir to the British throne, in the world in which he comes from—claims that he is actually married to—*me!*"

"I can't believe it! Do you think that it's true?"

The Archduchess Mireille began to soap herself languidly. "All I know is what that awful Marquis of Vézelay tells

Uncle. He didn't want Uncle to tell me, but once I saw he was trying to keep something from me it wasn't hard to worm it out of him."

"How thrilling! Have you seen him? Is he handsome? Is he tall and—"

The Archduchess laughed gaily. "Actually he's quite short, no taller than I am, but he's *quite* distinguished and he has such a . . . a royal air about him."

Mathilde clapped her hands in excitement. "Then you *have* seen him!" Her voice dropped to a whisper. "Did you—"

"Mathilde!" exclaimed the Archduchess, playfully tossing a handful of suds at the lady's maid. "I haven't even met him yet! Uncle showed me pictures of him taken when he was presented to him in private. He says that perhaps sometime next week, after Vézelay has investigated him more thoroughly, then I can—"

"Oh, Your Highness! Just imagine: your own little husband! What *fun* you can have. And no one will be able to say anything about it, since he—"

"—*is* my husband." The Archduchess Mireille cocked her fine blond head thoughtfully. "Or at least as long as I choose to let him play at it. Isn't that a delightful thought! What a pity we can't do that with *every* man. . . ."

Ah, this was how life was *intended* to be lived! reflected Kevin Frost as he watched the elderly sommelier refill his glass from one of the three remaining bottles in the world of the majestic 1929 Romanée-Conti. Across the table from him the Emperor of All the French, Napoleon V, looked up from his roast duckling Montmorency and smiled amiably beneath his fluffy white mustache before once again returning his attention to his plate to stab at a glazed cherry. What a joy to be here in the Elysée Palace as the privileged guest of the most powerful man in the world instead of in the cold backward hinterlands of Franklin!

As he swirled the noble Burgundy slowly around his crystal glass to release its magnificent aroma, he ran his eye admiringly around the indescribable profusion of priceless works of art and furniture in even this small private dining room where the two of them sat alone at a rosewood table inlaid with gleaming black pearl, attended only by the maître d'hôtel, the sommelier, and two footmen in dark blue livery. He was savoring the ripe fullness of the noble wine by gently swirling it about his mouth when he was suddenly startled from his reverie by a question from the elderly Emperor Charles-Pierre.

"The brontosaurus," he asked without preamble, "what precisely is the status of the brontosaurus in your world?"

"The bronto—"

"Surely the noblest of all beasts," continued the Emperor, oblivious of Kevin Frost's abject confusion. "I ask because it appears that travel is far more convenient than it is here, what with your rockets and jets. A trip across the Atlantic is nothing at all, a matter of hours! I imagine, then, that you have frequently visited the digs near Cross, Wyoming?"

"Not . . . er, recently," temporized Kevin Frost desperately, wondering what on earth the Emperor of All the French could be talking about.

"No?" The Emperor's thick white eyebrows rose in astonishment. "Why, even *I* have visited the sites twice now in spite of the grumbling it occasions from my security people." His craggy face cleared. "But of course, my dear fellow, I fear that every paleontologist has his own little hobbyhorse. My own, I fear, happens to be the brontosaurus. Your own sphere of interest, perhaps, is that of the diplodocus or even the allosaurus."

"That is to say—"

"Chacun à son goût," chuckled the Emperor, "even when it comes to dinosaurs! But what a boon for the paleontologist a time machine would be, and what a pity that what we apparently took to be a time machine turned out in actuality to be something entirely different!" He speared the last of his *pommes dauphines* and chewed it with gusto. "Imagine my disappointment when I learned that—" He halted in apparent confusion. "But, my dear fellow, I am sounding as if I am not grateful for the machine which has brought *you* to our world. Quite the contrary, quite the contrary!" He let the sommelier pour him another glass of

wine. "How different must be the study of the Jurassic and Triassic in your world, so much more advanced than ours. I have always felt, for instance, that regarding the brontosaurus much of what we have learned from the fossils in Wyoming is . . ."

As the Emperor of All the French continued his cheerful monologue, Kevin Frost allowed his mind to drift off in idle speculation of what might have become of the man from another universe who had first given him the inspiration for this audacious venture which had inexorably led to where he now sat in intimate *tête-à-tête* with the Emperor of France and the uncle of the divine Mireille.

Would the MacNair be meeting Mary Louise face-to-face? And if so, what on earth would they have to say to one another? Kevin Frost chuckled softly to himself. How useful were some of the tricks he had picked up along the way as a pharmacist's mate in the navy! Two of his special green tablets in a glass of whiskey and his bearded alter ego had been asleep almost before he could finish his drink.

A pity about having to leave Mary Louise so abruptly, of course, a charming woman in many ways. But certainly not worth going to jail for! And to even consider her in the same light as the incomparable Archduchess Mireille—ludicrous! For ever since the first photographs of the delectable blond teenager had begun to appear in the blurry rotogravures of the Sunday papers Kevin Frost's heart had been lost to the unattainable goddess. For years he avidly followed the course of her glamorous life from afar, consumed by the bitter knowledge that someday she would eventually commit herself in marriage to some unspeakably undeserving male other than himself.

What an unexpected godsend had been the so-called MacNair of MacNair with his preposterous tale of Prince William of England and his magical crown! Preposterous, but perhaps truly inspired by the gods! For as Kevin Frost had suddenly realized, why should he comb the lochs and forests of Scotland for problematical riches when everything he had ever desired could now be his for the simple asking? If only he dared . . .

Kevin Frost sipped the sixty-year-old wine and his heart

began to beat faster at the thought of his forthcoming encounter with the most irresistible beauty on earth, the only woman he had ever *truly* loved. Could the whispered rumors he had heard about her scandalous private behavior possibly be true? Would she—

"Do tell me more about the British base on Mars," invited the Emperor politely, interrupting Kevin Frost's increasingly gallant thoughts. "The concept of space travel is absolutely fascinating! Your fleet of rocketships, for instance, just how are they propelled?"

"Propelled?" Kevin Frost frowned in sudden anxious thought. "Ah, by great propellers, of course. Once they have been shot into space, that is to say. There is, as you know, no air between the planets for the rockets to push against, so propellers are necessary."

"I see," said Napoleon V with a slight frown. "Fascinating! Do go on!"

Sir Norvil Dennett was about to begin a series of tests on a massed array of glowing vacuum tubes on the workbench before him when the Earl of Kensington burst into the laboratory. A flimsy page of notepaper was clutched in his hand. "Look at this!" he cried, pushing the paper under Sir Norvil's nose.

"Your French is better than mine," said Dennett. "Why don't you just translate it for me?"

But the Earl of Kensington could only splutter. "That . . . that *traitor* . . . that . . . madman . . . that . . ."

With an irritated sigh the scientist pulled the paper from Kensington's grasp and perched himself on a high stool to slowly decipher its message. At last he looked up at the still seething Earl with bewilderment in his eyes. "If I understand this correctly, it says that Prince William has suddenly turned up at Napoleon's court. And that he is asking the Emperor to recognize the validity of his marriage in his original universe to the Archduchess Mireille!" He shook his head in puzzled dismay. "Can this be *possible?*"

"Is it possible that he's a madman? This is the proof! Is it possible that he's actually married to that nitwitted Archduchess? It's inconceivable!"

"But what can his *motives* be?" demanded the Master of Garnaway. "Could he actually be a French spy, just as you—"

"For pity's sake, Dennett!" snapped Kensington. "If he was a French spy, he wouldn't be trying to convince Napoleon that he was really a British prince, would he?"

"This whole thing is far beyond me," admitted Sir Norvil.

"It's not beyond *me!* First of all, it's clear proof that he really *is* who he says: Prince William Ernest Augustus!"

"But . . ." Sir Norvil Dennett frankly goggled. "But it was *you,* Kensington, who insisted that he was *not!*"

Alfred St. John Wester brushed aside the objection airily. "But nothing! There is no one in any *conceivable* world who would dare put himself at the mercy of Napoleon and his torturers with such a story unless it was actually true."

"But why—"

"—would he go to Napoleon in the first place? That's my second point. You physical scientists never try to understand the *psychology,* only the technique! What does this royal jackanapes with whom we were intimately closeted for several weeks actually *want* from life? Position, my dear Dennett, power, wealth, the throne of England!" He paused meaningfully. "Obviously he has now decided that he is more likely to attain all those things from the French than from us."

"But our machine—"

"—is so far nothing more than a collection of vacuum tubes and a lot of fine theory! Can you *blame* him for deciding to cast his lot with Napoleon?"

"But he knows all about our plans. He—"

"And that's my *third* point," growled Kensington, slamming his palm against the workbench. "A man like that will betray us in an instant. In fact he may have already. And the knowledge which he brings from his own universe is far too valuable to be shared with anyone but ourselves. So whether he has already betrayed us or not is in any case beside the point. The man must be silenced!"

"Silenced? In Paris? In the Elysée Palace? Surely—"

"—that would be difficult. *Too* difficult, unfortunately.

There is, however, another way of effectively silencing him."

"Which is?"

"By totally discrediting him."

Kevin Frost hummed happily to himself as he dabbed eau de cologne beneath his ears and stroked the tips of his magnificent stilettolike mustachios with the heavy silver brushes embossed with an ornate N that came with his regal apartment here in the Emperor's palace. Tonight, at long last, after nearly three weeks of intolerable waiting while he played cat and mouse with the Marquis of Vézelay, he was about to be presented to the sublime object of his most ardent fantasies, the ravishing Archduchess Mireille! Though it was only for dinner, and in the company of the Emperor himself, it was nevertheless a beginning. . . .

He gulped with sudden nervousness and peered anxiously into the dressing room mirror for any possible imperfection in his sleek black evening suit. Behind his dapper image the mirror revealed a corner of the broad canopied bed in the room beyond. At its sight a sudden prickle of sweat beaded his lofty brow as fanciful images of the Archduchess and himself engaged in amorous dalliance left him weak and quivering. The niece of the Emperor was reputedly totally without inhibitions. Could he hope that—

A quiet tapping came from the far side of the apartment. Reluctantly breaking off his reveries, Kevin Frost crossed the bedroom into the reception salon and from there into the small foyer with its Fragonard on the wall by the broad double doors. He pulled one open and his lips tightened as the Marquis of Vézelay stepped lightly past him.

"I fear you catch me on my way to dinner," said Kevin Frost with cool reserve. "If you have a matter to discuss, perhaps—"

The Marquis of Vézelay permitted himself a thin smile. "I in turn fear that your dinner engagement has been canceled."

"Canceled? But—"

"The Emperor was extremely upset."

"Upset? By what?"

"By the message which my agents intercepted from the Earl of Kensington in Scotland to one of his own agents here in the Palace."

"But how should that possibly concern *me?* What did the message say?"

"Beyond the fact that you are the crassest sort of impostor? Very little."

CHAPTER
= 22 =

IDLY THE MACNAIR watched the steel-plated door at the distant end of the corridor swing open. Two uniformed jailers stepped through, followed by the cadaverous figure of the state's attorney, two obvious lawyers with briefcases, and, somewhat more hesitantly, the tall slim figure of a beautiful auburn-haired woman in a white blouse and pale blue skirt. With mounting curiosity he watched them approach the model cell (1922 vintage) in which he had now been incarcerated for twenty-three days. Suddenly he sat up with a start as he realized who this unexpected vision of loveliness must be.

The mixed group stopped in front of the bars of his stark enclosure and Mary Louise Babcock peered timidly between them. Her sparkling green eyes ran over the MacNair and a small gasp escaped her lips. "But that's not my husband!" she cried.

"Ha!" cried the MacNair triumphantly, jumping to his feet and rapidly crossing the short distance to the bars. "Precisely what I have been patiently explaining to these lackwits all along!" He cocked his head with frank admiration as he looked up to meet the eyes of the troubled young beauty. He breathed deeply, wistfully, for her fresh summery smell instantly dispelled all the dismal institutional odors that surrounded him.

Her eyes probed deep into his own, and he saw her underlip quivering slightly. "Mrs. Babcock, I presume?" With his customary gallantry the MacNair reached between the bars to take her long slim hands in his but was instantly thwarted by the two jailers. "I beg you to accept my deepest condolences for the shameful deceit that has been played upon you. I assure you, however, that—"

"How strange," faltered Mary Louise, falling back a step. "He has exactly the same voice. And the same eyes. But—"

The state's attorney drew himself up in his dark three-piece suit with its tiny gold emblem of the State of Franklin on the lapel. "Yes, at some point he evidently thought to disguise himself by shaving off his mustache and hacking at his hair with some dull instrument or other. How different he looks without those enormous curly mustachios of which he used to be so proud!"

"Not so!" cried the MacNair indignantly. "Believe me, dear lady, this is all the most terrible misunderstand—"

"And of course he's started growing a beard," said the state's attorney with gloomy relish, the wattles of his stringy red neck quivering. "For a fact, he no longer looks like the debonair man-about-town we all used to know—or the shameless villain who wronged you so terribly."

"False! Palpably false! I—"

The state's attorney shook his head dolefully. "But I do wonder if the stress of being arrested might not have deranged him in some way."

"What do you mean?" quavered the betrayed wife of Kevin Frost, unable to tear her eyes away from the man in the cell.

"I mean that any *normal* person would at least admit who he was, once he'd been positively identified by his fingerprints!"

"You mean you've fingerprinted him, just as if he were some common criminal?"

The older of the two lawyers sighed. "But, my dear Mary

Louise, you must recognize the plain truth, painful as it is: This man has never been your lawful husband. He *is*, in fact, a common criminal."

A large tear welled up in her bright green eyes and slowly trickled down her cheek. "I suppose you're right," she murmured softly. "But I did love him—I *know* I did! Oh, why did all you spiteful people have to dig at him, and dig at him until you found out that . . . found out that he had . . . That was all so *long* ago! I *know* he didn't mean to hurt me!"

In spite of the delicacy of his own equivocal position the MacNair felt his heart reach out at the sight of her terrible distress. He found himself taking a step forward, while Mary Louise Babcock grasped two of the bars between her hands to pull her face between them. "Oh, Kevin," she whispered hoarsely, "why did you think you had to *marry* me? How happy we could have been without worrying about that worthless piece of paper. We could have . . . could have . . ."

She broke off, her small high breasts heaving fitfully beneath the ruffles of her snowy white blouse as she began to sob. One of the lawyers stepped forward and with his arm around her shoulders solicitously turned her away from the cell and down along the corridor. Unable to speak, the MacNair watched her stumble out, his mind a welter of conflicting emotions. Never had he encountered a more stunning creature! What a fool this Kevin Frost had been to have deserted a woman of such grace and loveliness! And yet—how could he be faulted for risking his liberty by marrying this superb beauty in the first place? What would it be like to be loved by such a—

The MacNair sighed plaintively as he was abruptly brought back to harsh reality by the state's attorney, who was considering him with open disdain. "Men like you, Frost, are worse than any murderers to my way of thinking. At least a murderer's victim only suffers for a moment." He pinched his thin lips together. "I've never really understood why the maximum penalty for bigamy is only thirteen years, but at least I can assure you that the full thirteen is what you'll be getting from Judge O'Ryan. Maximum Mike has already promised me that."

With a soft groan the MacNair sank back on his cot, the thick stubble of his renascent beard clutched between his hands, bitterly cursing the moment he had ever chosen to seek out that unspeakable caricature of himself who was this world's Kevin Frost.

Some thousands of miles to the east the thoughts of that unspeakable caricature were strikingly similar to those of the MacNair of MacNair. But while the model cell in Portland, Franklin, was dry and airy, temperature-controlled and aggressively hygienic, Kevin Frost's was buried deep in the damp subbasement of a crumbling edifice in the clutter of ancient buildings that surrounded the great central meat market of Paris and might easily have been left over from the days of Charlemagne so stark were its amenities.

Or so Kevin Frost told himself as he inventively reviled the habits and proclivities of that obvious madman from another world who was so directly responsible for his present ghastly predicament. For who could have imagined that in a space of a few short heartbeats he could have been cast down from the unimaginable luxury and glorious prospects of the Emperor's palace to a grim future in this damp, malodorous, ill-lighted, rat-ridden medieval dungeon?

The Marquis of Vézelay, however, had not appeared unduly surprised by the dramatic change of circumstance. "You must be mad, you know, to think you could have gotten away with it," he had observed almost sympathetically as he took a seat on a three-legged stool in the dark corridor outside the heavy iron bars. "A notorious confidence man from Glasgow who surreptitiously introduces himself into the basement of the Goethe Society in the hopes of extorting a few easy schillings from a group of gullible German scientists is one thing; the same affront played out for the Emperor of France is quite another."

"I can only repeat," said Kevin Frost with enormous dignity, "that I am who I represent myself to be. Why a person of your supposed intelligence and experience should choose to credit this so-called message from an obvious *agent provocateur* such as the Earl of Kensington is far beyond my understanding."

The Marquis of Vézelay smiled grimly. "As is your understanding of the dynamics of space travel, to cite but a single example. Propellers on rocketships, indeed! Don't you see, my dear fellow, that even without this perfectly genuine message from Kensington to one of his spies in the Palace, telling him to take no further notice of your antics, we would have shortly unmasked you by the accumulated evidence of your gross absurdities?"

"But what about my crown?" countered Kevin Frost with growing desperation. *"That* is not a gross absurdity! You yourself have seen it!" He lowered his voice to a confidential whisper. "Release me at once from these deplorable surroundings and I shall instantly retrieve it—*for the two of us."*

"Would you, now?" mused the Marquis of Vézelay thoughtfully. "I admit that this is a problem which remains unresolved. But I feel sure that eventually some simple explanation will turn up that does not involve parallel worlds and magical powers."

Kevin Frost shook the bars in exasperation. "But I tell you—"

Ignoring his expostulations, the head of the secret police reached into an inner pocket of his bright red jacket and brought forth a folded newspaper clipping. He passed it through the bars to Kevin Frost, who glanced at it curiously, then felt his heart lurch against his rib cage. "Trial of Bangor Bigamist Begins Next Week," read the caption at the top of the article from the *Portland Press Journal.* Below was an unflattering photograph of a disreputable-looking man of obvious criminal proclivities. In spite of the shadowy beginnings of a straggly beard the face in the picture was only too obviously his own.

"Why do you show me this?" asked Kevin Frost with casual disinterest as he handed back the clipping.

"Why? Do you never look in the mirror, man? Surely this archfiend bears a striking resemblance to his supposed highness, Prince William Ernest Augustus."

"I totally fail to see it."

The Marquis of Vézelay chuckled tolerantly. "It is, of course, well known that identical twins also possess identical fingerprints. Our colleagues in Portland, Franklin, have been kind enough to forward us the prints of this hardened and desperate criminal whom they are so wisely holding. Would it surprise you to learn that his fingerprints match your own exactly?"

"Oh, very well," said Kevin Frost with a heavy sigh, secure in the knowledge that the MacNair could never be brought to testify against him, incarcerated as he was in a Portland jail, totally beyond the reach of even the Emperor of France. "I avow that I felt a twinge of pity for the poor wretch and chose not to let any of my own possible notoriety rub off onto him. But I see now that I should have confided in you before: that poor devil in the paper is Kevin Frost, the man who in this strange world was born in the place of myself, Prince William of England."

The Marquis of Vézelay arched his eyebrows. "Indeed, indeed? Our scientists at the Curie Institute have formulated the possibility of just such a person existing. But what they did *not* consider, Your Royal Highness, was the possibility of the doppelgänger of British royalty being, in this world, a common Yankee criminal."

Kevin Frost cleared his throat hastily, aware too late of the terrible implications of his ill-conceived confession. "That is to say—"

"Nor are they able to explain just how it is that Prince William Ernest Augustus should come to make the acquaintance of this depraved criminal a mere three weeks after his arrival in this world!"

A leaden weight in his stomach, Kevin Frost watched the Marquis of Vézelay bounce lightly to his feet. His mind raced furiously. Surely there was a reasonable explanation for this slight discrepancy in logic. There *had* to be!

The Marquis of Vézelay smiled amiably from the darkened corridor. "Until this trifling matter of Kevin Frost is clearly elucidated, I am sure you will be happy to hold yourself at our disposition." His smile suddenly vanished. "And you should count yourself fortunate for the delay. The insolence of your imposture and the enormity of your demands are without precedent in modern history. Dining with the Emperor! Demanding the hand of the Archduchess Mireille! If it weren't for the chance discovery of this Kevin

Frost in Franklin, I assure you that you would have met a very bleak fate as an English spy some time ago."

With a brief nod he moved off into the darkness, leaving a limp and trembling Kevin Frost grasping the bars to keep from sagging to the damp stone floor.

CHAPTER
= 23 =

THREE DAYS BEFORE his scheduled trial in the courtroom of Maximum Mike O'Ryan the MacNair sat gloomily in his cell, preoccupied by what had now become an obsession: trying *not* to think of his diamond-encrusted, multimillion-dollar crown lying hidden in the dusty recesses beneath the plumbing of the Earl of Kensington's bathtub. For the notion had suddenly come to him with stunning clarity that aside from thirteen years of unmerited imprisonment the next greatest calamity that could befall him would be for the GODHEAD to be discovered and switched on. For then it would take but a single errant thought to ensure its instant materialization upon his head.

Here in the confines of the Portland Municipal Jail.

It was not a revelation that added to his peace of mind. How do you keep yourself from thinking of that which is of paramount importance? This was the question he was asking himself for the thousandth time when he was interrupted in his reveries by the appearance of two of the city jailers. To his surprised dismay he was shackled between them and escorted down the corridor to a small room furnished only with a scarred table and six metal chairs.

Three large men dressed in spite of the summer heat in cheap brown suits, woolen vests, and broad fedoras stood watching his entrance impassively.

One of them removed a cigar from his mouth and looked down at a paper in his hand. "This is the man Kevin Frost?"

"This is the man Kevin Frost. Sign here. And here. And here. And here." The city jailer squinted carefully at his sets of papers. "All right, he's yours. But only until five o'clock. It says so right here."

"We'll remember," said the other dryly. The MacNair's shackles were removed, but before he could begin to rub his wrists he was deftly handcuffed between the two large men who up till now had remained motionless.

"What's all this about?" the MacNair demanded of his municipal jailers, who at least had the virtue of familiarity. "Who are these men? Why am I being handcuffed?"

"Looks like you're off to the Federal Building," shrugged one of the jailers, "in the company of these here federal marshals. Seems like there's a federal grand jury looking into a drug-smuggling ring."

"What? Am I to go before the grand jury in these striped convict clothes? They'll convict me on sight!"

"Well, if you don't like the clothes, you shouldn't ought to have done it."

The MacNair was led away protesting loudly. For how many more heinous crimes of the nefarious Kevin Frost would he now be held to account?

Outside, he stood blinking in the bright sunlight before being shepherded into the rear seat of a large black automobile, where he sat uncomfortably handcuffed to the marshals on either side. The third marshal climbed behind the wheel and for five minutes drove carefully through the crowded streets of downtown Portland. The MacNair wriggled his wrists experimentally but it was evident that for the moment any attempt at escape would be fruitless. With a sigh he sat back and tried to compose his whirling thoughts.

The car slowed and turned into the sudden gloom of an underground basement. The garage door swung shut behind them, cutting off the busy sounds of the city, and the car came to a halt. Neither of the men beside him moved.

The MacNair watched with mounting tension as the driver slid out from behind the wheel to open the rear door. He climbed into the compartment, his hands busy with what appeared to be a small bottle and a large yellow sponge. Suddenly the sharp smell of ether filled the tight confines of the car.

The MacNair lashed out instantly with his feet in a futile attempt to disable the man before him but his arms were seized and in spite of his struggles the icy chill of the ether-soaked sponge was pressed firmly against his face. He gasped and choked, then tried to hold his breath, but as the seconds ticked away and a terrible pressure built up in his chest, he felt himself suddenly gasping, his head whirling, his body floating into the air and then . . .

The car bearing the MacNair of MacNair turned into the Avenue de Marigny and along the high stone wall that separated the gardens of the Elysée Palace from the gaily dressed Parisians and tourists who crowded the sidewalks this bright September morning. As it slowed to turn into the courtyard of the three-story building that housed the offices of the Marquis of Vézelay, it came to a sudden halt. An enormous red moving van had jammed itself immovably into the narrow archway that ran through the sixteenth-century building into the inner courtyard. With a muttered imprecation the driver pulled up on the sidewalk beside the noisy group of workmen and policemen who were ineffectually trying to extricate the tightly wedged truck.

At least, the MacNair thought as he was guided across the sidewalk by a brawny secret-police man on either side of him, he was no longer clad in that ghastly uniform of black and white stripes. His present costume of overly large blue serge pants and a rough cotton shirt was not precisely what he himself would have chosen, but now if the opportunity should ever present itself to make a dash for freedom, at least he would no longer be as conspicuous as a zebra in a herd of cows.

He was escorted through a side entrance and up a narrow rear staircase. Eventually a broad marble hallway filled with gilded mirrors and fragile Louis XVI chairs led to an ornate door set in a deep embrasure. A tall bald man of early middle age stood before it wearing a dark blue suit and a striped maroon tie. "This is the man?" asked Colonel Etournaud. "Excellent. Step right in." He threw the door open and allowed the MacNair to step past.

"You!" cried the MacNair, spying the Marquis of Vézelay seated behind his large gleaming desk on the far side of the room. "We should have known! For three days, sir, we have been held incommunicado, for three days we have—"

The Marquis of Vézelay grimaced and rose to his feet, a loud sigh escaping his lips. He stalked angrily across the carpet to confront the MacNair, who was still tightly hemmed in by his escort and Colonel Etournaud. For a long moment he studied him closely. *"You* at least seem to have the same beard—or at least you will have when it's fully grown out."

"Of course we have a beard," said the MacNair, running his hand through the thick brown tuft that now adorned his lower jaw. "Why shouldn't we? So did *you* the last time we met. And so you do now. What is remarkable about a beard?"

The Marquis of Vézelay blinked. "Nothing at all, except when it happens to become a mustache. Particularly a mustache with fantastic curly tips that could almost poke your eye out."

The MacNair felt his heart suddenly sink. This hateful policeman could only be referring to the egregious Kevin Frost! But how in the world could Kevin Frost be connected to the spymaster general of Napoleon's empire? Unless, of course . . .

His dismay increased as the Marquis of Vézelay glanced at his watch and turned impatiently to his aide. "And where's the other one? He was supposed to be here by now."

"Oui, mon directeur," muttered Colonel Etournaud, snapping to attention before rapidly leaving the room.

"It's just as I thought," mused the Marquis of Vézelay as he continued to study the outwardly unperturbable MacNair from every angle. "You *do* have an accent of Toulouse. That *other* one speaks French like a lumberjack from—"

He was interrupted by the reappearance of Colonel Etournaud. "He's here, sir, it's just that they've been delayed by that confounded furniture van that's gotten itself stuck in the courtyard."

"Stuck in the courtyard? Is *that* what all of that commotion is about?" The Marquis of Vézelay crossed to the center window and flung it open to peer out at the broad roof of the still immobile truck stuck in the building's entranceway two stories below. While he scowled at it peevishly with his back to the room the MacNair tried frantically to marshal his thoughts.

He had been kidnaped and drugged by agents of Napoleon: so much was clear. Smuggled clandestinely to France on a noisy, bumpy transport plane which apparently belonged to the French army, he was now in all likelihood about to be confronted by his insufferable alter ego, the ineffable Kevin Frost. Who, the moment he opened his mouth, could reveal once and for all that he, the glorious Sir Kevin Deane de Courtney MacNair of MacNair, occasionally harmlessly known as Prince William Ernest Augustus, third in line to the throne of Ireland and Great Britain, was actually nothing more than humble Kevin Frost of Bangor, Maine, whatever the world of his birth.

How, he wondered desperately, *could he silence Kevin Frost?*

"Ah, here he comes now," murmured Colonel Etournaud.

A uniformed guard to either side, his hands and ankles manacled by heavy shackles, Kevin Frost nevertheless marched into the room with regal dignity. His hair was long and matted, the tips of his once unrivaled mustachios limp and bedraggled, and he still wore the glossy black evening clothes in which he had once been about to attain his most cherished dreams. His eyes widened for a moment as they came to rest on the MacNair, then swept on across the rest of the room.

"Have them get that wretched truck out of there *at once,*" ordered the Marquis of Vézelay testily, turning away from the window to lean against his desk while his eyes moved rapidly from the MacNair to Kevin Frost and back again. "Ha!" he exclaimed happily. "As alike as two peas in a pod! Except for that grotesque mustache, of course."

Kevin Frost's hand unconsciously rose to stroke the

superb facial adornment in question but was brought to a halt by the heavy shackles which bound him to his guards. He glanced down at his fetters with astonished disdain, then cocked his head at the Marquis of Vézelay with a majestic sardonicism.

"Oh, very well," snorted Vézelay, "remove those confounded things."

"Is that wise, sir?" asked Colonel Etournaud.

Without troubling to reply, the Marquis seated himself behind his desk and turned his attention to the MacNair. "And I suppose that *you* would like to sit down as well," he muttered ungraciously, waving his hand. "Oh, very well, go ahead. Until I know which of you smashed me with a . . . well, smashed me, I suppose we might as well be civilized about it all."

"So kind of you, my dear chap," murmured Kevin Frost as he stepped gingerly out of his heavy black ankle rings and let his guardians remove those which enclosed his wrists. "I shall always think well of you." And with those words he bounded lightly across the room to vault unhesitatingly through the open window onto the top of the furniture van below.

By the time the stunned Colonel Etournaud had dashed to the window the small lithe figure of Kevin Frost had already merged with the noontime crowds and was lost to sight.

CHAPTER
$=24=$

"—AND $E=mc^2$," CONCLUDED the MacNair, "the theoretical basis for the construction of the atomic bomb."

"And it was *Einstein* who conceived all this?" marveled Giorgio Campinotti, director of the Curie Institute for Research in the Physical Sciences. "What a remarkable man he was, no matter which world he was in!"

"Surely nothing as remarkable as the Emperor Napoleon and his invention of the indoor flush toilet," muttered the MacNair sardonically, for he had grown increasingly weary of these tedious and interminable sessions with the leading scholastic lights of the French Empire.

In the course of a lifetime's wandering the MacNair's grasshopper mind had accumulated a startling number of haphazard facts and random misconceptions without any attempt at all to order them into a systematic classification. Now, ever since the news of his presence in Paris had begun to leak out, a thousand scientists, scholars, historians, and theoreticians of a hundred different disciplines vied for the chance to sweep the merest crumb from his disorganized intellectual table.

Today, the 16th of October 1991, here in the director's study on the topmost floor of the Curie Institute, the MacNair had come to conduct a seminar in theoretical nuclear physics as the consequence of a bargain struck only the evening before with the Marquis of Vézelay.

"If only you knew how well off you are without atomic

146

bombs," the MacNair had protested vehemently in the drawing room of his apartment on the second floor of the granite building at 14, Avenue de Marigny which housed the secret police of the French Empire. He pointedly refilled his glass from the dusty bottle of Grands Echézeaux '59 without heeding the Marquis's mutely imploring eye. "What on earth do you want them for? The Empire is the most powerful force on earth, there hasn't been a war in two hundred years—"

"You forget the Turks. We fought a terrible war with—"

The MacNair snorted irritably. "Eighty years ago! A war that lasted six months with a total of a quarter million dead on all sides! Tragic, to be sure. But in *our* world there were *fifty* million dead in the two wars with Germany, and the rulers of China and Russia have almost certainly murdered an equivalent number of their own countrymen! *That's* the kind of world you want here?"

"You willfully misrepresent the case," sighed the Marquis of Vézelay patiently. "That's the kind of world we want you to help us *prevent* from happening here."

"By helping you cook up your own atomic weapons? Six generations of Bonapartes seem to have done a perfectly adequate job of preserving the peace without any assistance from us. Why can't we be left alone to—"

"—join your friend Kevin Frost in England?" murmured the secret-police man coldly as he climbed to his feet and, ignoring the MacNair's scowl, poured himself the last of the ruby-hued Burgundy. "We caught sight of him for a moment last week in London, you know, but now he has utterly vanished from sight again." His lips tightened. "The two of you seem able to wander in and out of Europe as if it were your own private preserve!"

"A certain native resourcefulness, perhaps," murmured the MacNair, turning his back to conceal his elation at the news that his alter ego had somehow succeeded in putting at least the breadth of the English Channel between himself and the Grand Inquisitor of the French Empire. It was proving difficult enough to maintain his role of Prince William Ernest Augustus in the face of Vézelay's open skepticism without having to parry any further revelations which the unspeakably gauche Kevin Frost might witlessly disclose in the heat of purposeful interrogation. If only his worthless doppelgänger could be induced to put an even greater distance between himself and the agents of this rancorous Marquis, whose overly indulgent sense of amour propre still smarted from the contemptuous ease with which the mustachioed madman had chosen to take leave from his third-story office. Vézelay, the MacNair knew, would never rest quiet until he had his hands again on Kevin Frost.

"A native resourcefulness developed in your *other* universe, no doubt?" muttered the Marquis acidly. "While stalking the savage grizzly in the State of Franklin, perhaps?"

The MacNair sighed plaintively. "Surely this is an issue which can no longer be in doubt? We have been informed that the Emperor himself fully accepts the conclusions of the report from the Curie Insti—"

"Yes, yes, yes," interrupted the Marquis of Vézelay, "all of *them* are only too eager to accept your preposterous story in all its sublime glory. And all because of the fillings in your teeth!"

"That, too," said the MacNair with a tolerant smile. "But once we were interviewed by *qualified* persons, don't you know, it was inevitable that—"

"Do spare me the gloating," snapped the Marquis of Vézelay. "Without that wretched Kevin Frost I can't even prove that you're not the King of England!"

"Prince, my dear fellow, merely a prince."

"And you still maintain that this crown of yours is a communications—"

The MacNair uttered a short grunt of irritation. "Why do you persist in attempting to catch us out in your childish traps? *We* have never said anything of the sort. A dozen times we have told you that upon the ascension of our father Frederick to the throne in 1983 this ceremonial crown was financed by public subscription throughout the Empire and crafted for the occasion by Messrs. Rolls & Royce, the celebrated jewelers of Bond Street. So far as I know, the crown was never meant to be anything other than a ceremonial token of esteem to be displayed only upon occasions of state."

"On which occasions the lights are turned on and it glows merrily for the edification of the Great British Public?"

"How well you express it," said the MacNair dryly.

The Marquis of Vézelay fixed the empty bottle of wine with a reproachful eye. "And you yourself have never had occasion to put it on, nor are you able to account for its singular presence upon your head at the moment you materialized into our particular universe?"

The MacNair rolled his eyes and let out a long, low sigh of ironic relief. "How pleased we are that at long last you appear to have grasped these simple, fundamental truths."

The Marquis of Vézelay let pass the heavy-handed sarcasm. "But once it *was* in this world, you nevertheless were able upon occasion to teleport it to yourself. The evidence for this is clear: there can be no other explanation."

"Possibly, possibly," conceded the MacNair, rising to his feet to signify the conclusion of their *tête-à-tête*. "It is a matter of no great concern."

But the Marquis of Vézelay obstinately refused to budge from the depths of his yellow easy chair. "No great concern!" he cried. "It is easily the single most important concern in the world today!"

"Come, come, your exaggeration is touching, but outlandish."

"I tell you, the future security of the Empire itself may depend upon this crown!"

"Nonsense!" trumpeted the MacNair, hard put to contain his glee at the direction in which he had so deftly steered the conversation. "It is essentially a trinket. An elaborate trinket, to be sure, but nevertheless a trinket, and only a trinket."

"This is outrageous!" spluttered the Marquis of Vézelay. "Are you saying that you refuse to help in the search for—"

"Refuse?" The MacNair's eyes grew round with hurt bewilderment. "Why should we refuse to help recover what is, essentially, our own property?"

"Surely it belongs to the people of Great Britain?"

"As the sole legal representative in this particular world of *our* British Empire we are, of course, charged with holding it in trust."

"I see. Then you *do* know where it is! You teleported it

out of the Curie Institute and then you—"

"—hid it in great secrecy?" The MacNair stroked his full, luxuriant beard while his eyebrows rose quizzically. "So well, in fact, that we are now unable to retrieve it? Ridiculous! What a droll notion! As we have said, we consider it nothing more than a somewhat ostentatious geegaw, of no particular aesthetic or sentimental value."

"Interesting that you make no mention of its *material* value!"

The MacNair shrugged as if he had nothing further to say upon the subject.

"But you *would* assist in retrieving it—assuming of course that such was within Your Highness's power?" persisted the Marquis of Vézelay.

"Possibly, possibly. As you know, our time these days is thoroughly occupied by these most interesting sessions with your learned savants as we teach them the principles of everything from floppy disks to bowling balls. At first we were chary of it, we frankly admit it. But now that we have actually seen the stirring spectacle of an underdeveloped continental nation beginning at last to pull itself up from—"

"Oh, very well," conceded the Marquis of Vézelay with ill grace as he slumped deeper into his seat. "You know yourself protected by the Emperor and every worthless pen-pusher in the entire Empire—I have been explicitly told that it is infeasible to extract the truth from you by more robust methods. So then—how much do you want?"

"—in time, of course, duty will compel us to return to our native England, where we shall—"

"I said, *how much?*" cried the Frenchman, his eyes flashing.

"Oh, dear. Were you speaking to us? We fear we were already thinking about the Fellows of the Royal Society and how they—"

The Marquis of Vézelay spoke between clenched teeth. "How . . . much . . . do . . . you . . . want?"

"Want?" The MacNair waved his hand in a vague gesture. "What do we *want?* What an interesting question. . . ." He skillfully broached a second bottle of Grands Echézeaux and held it up suspiciously to the light to study its deep ruby glint. At last he uttered a soft grunt of satisfaction, then turned slowly with the bottle in his hand to face the Marquis of Vézelay. "Tell us this, my dear fellow: Just what do you have to offer?"

CHAPTER
= 25 =

"The Archduchess Mireille!" announced a rosy-cheeked herald in a powdered wig and glittering gold costume. Her blond hair drawn up into an elaborate tower crowned by a ruby-studded tiara, the first lady of France stepped regally into the grand ballroom of the Elysée Palace. She bestowed an impersonal smile upon the two hundred guests gathered together in small groups across the gilded ballroom, then glided through them in her stiff hoop skirt to the other side of the room where Napoleon V stood with a small group of intimates on a slightly raised dais beneath an elaborate pavilion of flags, bunting, and banners surmounted by a giant imperial gold eagle.

Creamy white breasts seemed ready to burst at any instant from the décolletage of a pale pink gown so tightly cinched about her tiny waist that the MacNair marveled that she was able to breathe. He tugged uneasily at the bright crimson sash that encircled his own midsection and threw back his shoulders. Was that the insidious beginning of a small but discernible potbelly he was developing since taking up residence here in the Palace? He must keep a sharper eye on his appetite in this world of resolutely *ancienne cuisine*.

A sixty-piece orchestra in gaudy red and blue military uniform at the far end of the ballroom struck up a lilting tune and the tall, rawboned figure of the Emperor stepped down gravely from the dais to lead his graceful niece awkwardly through the stylized patterns of the first dance of the evening. After an initial respectful pause another twenty couples joined them on the gleaming marble floor in what appeared to be a stately pavane. The MacNair stood pensively in a corner until the tune came to a sudden end with a brief flourish of horns, then took a glass of white wine in a tall crystal flute from the tray of a passing footman and let his eye wander over the guests, who mingled like brightly colored, loudly chattering tropical birds beneath the thousands of glittering lights in the great crystal chandeliers far overhead. The soft strains of an air with something of the suggestion of a waltz to it were barely discernible as the footmen circulated with silver trays and conversation grew increasingly noisy and uninhibited. With the men in their powdered perukes and the women in their enormous tulip-shaped hoop skirts it could easily have been a scene from the court of Louis XIV. The MacNair smiled appreciatively, his entire being suffused with a radiant sense of well-being. How wise had been his decision to join forces with the Emperor of All the French rather than cast his lot with those madmen in their drafty castle in Scotland!

He raised the glass to his lips and drank deeply.

"Ouf!" His tongue recoiled and he fought to keep from choking as the insipid yet cloying sweetness of the syrupy white wine caught him totally unawares. "What *is* it?" he demanded of a passing attendant.

"Château Bergeron '83, monsieur. Would monsieur care for another glass?"

"What a fanciful notion!" The MacNair set the half-empty flute on the footman's tray. "A glass of champagne to remove this execrable taste, at once! Very dry, very cold."

The footman looked at him oddly. "Monsieur desires a glass of *fine champagne*, very dry, very cold?"

"Not *fine champagne*, that's cognac! I said a glass of *champagne!*"

The footman blinked uneasily. "If monsieur will permit, I will fetch the maître d'hôtel immediately. I am certain he will be able to fulfill monsieur's wishes." He inclined his head and disappeared hastily into the crowd. The MacNair pursed his lips and tugged at the end of his beard. Was it possible that in this peculiar world—

"Champagne?" said a gay, lilting voice behind him. "*Do* tell me about champagne! Is it something which you drink in your *own* world?"

The MacNair turned to find himself looking down into the startling cleavage of two perfectly formed breasts in the décolletage of the Archduchess Mireille of Luxembourg. They thrust out straight before her and could easily have supported the small tray of caviar hors d'oeuvres which a passing footman held before him. The MacNair hastily raised his gaze from the smooth creamy flesh to meet cool blue eyes and slightly mocking lips. Bowing low, he brought the long slim fingers of her white-gloved hand nearly to his lips. He could feel his heart suddenly beating a little faster. So Vézelay had *not* been dissimulating: the notorious niece of the almighty Emperor *was* interested in him!

"Champagne is a dry, sparkling wine of indescribable verve and effervescence, Your Highness, to be drunk only upon very special occasions. Upon making the acquaintance, for instance, of a very special person such as—you!" He gently squeezed her fingers, then reluctantly released her hand.

Her laugh was loud and uninhibited, a deep contralto with a sharp trill that hovered on the unpleasant edge of shrillness. The long black eyelashes she had donned for the evening batted at him roguishly. "I'm so *happy* that you're a king and not a troglodyte."

The MacNair blinked in bewilderment. "A troglodyte?"

"Yes. Those great hairy men who used to live in caves, such as those down in Les Eyzies-de-Tayac. So strong, so hairy." A tiny tremor ran through her body and the MacNair stared in fascination as the bare tops of her incomparable breasts quivered delicately. How did they keep from popping out of the marvel of structural engineering that propped them up? he wondered. "Do you have cavemen in your world, too?" she continued eagerly.

"Only their skeletons, we fear."

"What a pity! When first they told me you were a

caveman I was *so* excited."

The MacNair quailed inwardly. Could the Archduchess really be as idiotic as she sounded, or was she playing some deep game, subtly mocking him, perhaps, for inscrutable motives of her own? He smiled at her blandly. Now that he had the opportunity to appraise her, it was evident that her fine blue eyes *were* set a tad too close together, that her small soft Cupid's mouth *was* perhaps a shade on the pouty side of unrestrained self-indulgence. . . .

But no matter, he rebuked himself hastily. Let us look on the other side of the coin. Without question she is young and nubile, tall and blond, and the mistress of one of the great fortunes of Europe—all pleasing characteristics which make it easy to overlook any trifling imperfections of the flesh. And to judge from the creamy perfection of her proudly displayed breasts and the graceful proportions of her bare shoulders and upper arms, who was to say that the rest of her body would not be equally flawless?

"But now?" he murmured. "When you find that we are *not* a great hairy caveman, but merely a banal old—"

"King of England?" The Archduchess Mireille stepped closer, so that the MacNair's trouser leg half vanished into the leading edge of her gown. "That's even *more* exciting. Do tell me about your crown! It was absolutely the most beautiful thing I have ever seen."

"The crown?" The MacNair glanced quickly over her bare shoulders as his eyes automatically swept the ballroom. Could anyone be listening to them? He lowered his voice. "The crown is supposed to be—"

"A secret? But how can it be a secret from me if I've already had it on my head?"

"You have?" The MacNair blinked in astonishment.

"Of course. Just before it vanished. We had gone to see it at the Curie Institute and once we saw how lovely it was Uncle promised me that I could have it. So then when I tried it on—"

"He promised you *our* crown?" spluttered the MacNair indignantly, his eyes widening in shock.

The Archduchess Mireille fluttered her eyelashes appealingly. "But that was before we knew it belonged to *you*, of course. That changes *everything!*"

"Ah," replied the MacNair dubiously, "of course."

"Of course it does. Even though it's vanished. For now we know that it belongs to a king, a king who can do anything, can't you?"

"Up to a point, perhaps," began the MacNair cautiously.

"So why don't you make it come back at once," she whispered breathlessly, "and I'll let *you* put it on my head!" She clapped her hands gaily.

"That, of course, would be our dearest wish," said the MacNair with austere reserve, "but we fear that for the present time the crown has been displaced into some unknown limbo, unattainable by any of us in spite of our most devout efforts."

The Archduchess's fine brown eyebrows twitched in vexation. "Oh, dear, I *did* love that crown. Well . . . perhaps someday. . . ." Her vivacious features instantly brightened. "What importance is a silly old crown; after all, it's the king that counts!" She leaned forward and fixed the MacNair with an unwavering blue eye. "I just *love* kings! Especially if they're *real* kings!"

The MacNair's lips tightened in sudden dismay. Was *this* why she was mocking him? Had the Marquis of Vézelay already poisoned the mind of this lovely but obviously featherbrained young person against him? Was this how the treacherous secret-police man lived up to his part in a bargain? "*Real* kings?" he temporized.

"Kings who *rule*," she whispered passionately. "Kings who are *kings*, not like poor old Uncle."

"Ah," sighed the MacNair with heartfelt relief. "But surely your uncle is the greatest emperor in the entire world?"

Her lips twisted into a sulky moue. "Oh, pooh! *That's* the Sultan of the Ottoman Empire. But how could any *civilized* woman be interested in a man who already has four wives and a thousand concubines? But Uncle isn't at all like the Sultan—he doesn't rule, he just does what all those awful deputies and senators tell him to do."

She squeezed his upper arm with her gloved fingers and inclined her head just enough for her pale blue eyes to become level with his. Her soft sweet breath fluttered against his face, and his nostrils were filled by the rich aromas of subtle powders and perfumes. In spite of himself he felt a sudden warmth pervade his body. He watched her bright pink tongue run around her lips. How, he wondered breathlessly, does one apply lipstick in the patriotic colors of the Tricolor—blue, white, and red—in such a regular pattern on such obviously passionate lips and have it remain unblemished? Her fingers tightened on his arm and his suddenly hypersensitive ears could hear her light breathing above the myriad sounds of the ballroom. *"Why,"* she demanded in a hoarse whisper, her eyes widening hypnotically as they stared unblinkingly into his own, *"why doesn't he just take them all out and shoot them?* That's what a *king* would do!"

The MacNair leaned closer over the tremendous obstacle of her hoop skirt so that his lips nearly touched hers. "And what would a mere prince do?" he whispered softly, his pulse racing at her nearness.

For a moment, still in the thrall of some compelling inner vision, she looked at him uncomprehendingly, then with a quick shake of her head visibly brought herself back to the ballroom. "A prince?" She tapped the back of his wrist with a playful finger and let her eyelashes flutter. "That all depends on the prince, wouldn't you say?"

"Indeed I would," declared the MacNair stoutly, drawing himself up to his full height. He lowered his voice to a confidential whisper and glanced carefully over both his shoulders before speaking. "As you may be aware, the world from which we come is deemed in many domains to be somewhat more advanced than your own." His gleaming brown eyes flashed and once again he took her hand. "Let us assure you that not all of these domains are necessarily in the rather tedious fields of technology. A considerable portion of our expertise may be said to fall among the, shall we say, *softer* sciences?"

"My, you *are* forward, aren't you?" The Archduchess Mireille frowned deliciously but left her hand where it was. "Are *all* the men in your world as saucy as you?"

"Only the troglodytes."

Her fingers tightened around his. "Actually, I *far* prefer princes to smelly old cavemen. Are you *sure* you aren't married to me in that strange world from which you come?"

"If only that inestimable honor and pleasure could have been ours! But we fear that the union of our two . . . houses was merely a pretext invented by a certain unscrupulous impostor to further his infamous goals."

"What! You would call a union of our . . . houses . . . an infamous goal? For shame, sir!"

"An infamous goal for a peasant rogue, to be sure! For a prince of the House of Henley—*that* is an entirely different matter!"

"I am pleased to hear it," replied the Archduchess coolly, stepping back a pace and snatching a glass of wine from a hovering footman. "But here in *this* world, if the truth were known, you are only a prince of the House of Henley by courtesy, are you not? And even that, it seems, is not supposed to be generally known, as Uncle has so tiresomely told me over and over."

"Unfortunately true," sighed the MacNair, "at least for the present time. Eventually the matter will be set aright."

"And in the meantime we all have to pretend that you are some minor visiting royalty traveling incognito? How very tiresome. I *do* love a king!"

"Or even a prince, we believe we recall you saying."

"Or . . . even a prince." Her cornflower-blue eyes glittered. "At least . . . from time to time."

The MacNair stroked the glossy tip of his exquisitely trimmed brown beard and extended his arm gallantly. "In that case—shall we dance?"

"Dance?" She laughed with a loud burst of disconcerting gaiety. "I don't see why not! And perhaps afterwards you can tell me a little more about your world of Champagne. And, perhaps—even about your 'softer' sciences."

CHAPTER
= 26 =

IN A RAGE Kevin Frost crumpled the glossy pages of the *Illustrated London News* and threw it violently across the room. Still not satisfied, he stomped across the periodical room to retrieve the magazine, then slowly tore it into small pieces, which he scattered into the flames in the fireplace.

The Earl of Kensington had observed his temper tantrum with raised eyebrows. "The events of the day distress you to such a point?" he asked sympathetically, lowering his own copy of the *Spectator* to his ample lap.

Kevin Frost turned away from the fireplace to stand glowering before the French windows of Garnaway Castle. Outside was a bleak autumn day of drifting mists and scudding grey clouds enlivened only by occasional sharp bursts of driving rain. The tips of his magnificent mustachios trembled under the impetus of his emotion.

"The cheek of this fellow!" he cried. "Did you see the picture of him in that magazine? Dancing with my . . . dancing with the Archduchess Mireille! Every time I pick up a newspaper or magazine there he is with her! As if . . . as if they were *married* or something!"

The Earl of Kensington sighed in exasperation. "But, my dear fellow, they *are* in France, after all! Even in Franklin it must be generally recognized that the Gauls pay no heed at all to the norms of civilized behavior, and that the nobility are the most shameless of them all—it's a wonder they don't do it openly in the streets! This woman, of course, is

158

an archduchess of notorious repute, while *he* now styles himself Lord Kevin of Deane." The Earl of Kensington snorted vigorously. "A pretty pair of degenerates they make!"

It was not a response calculated to set Kevin Frost's mind at ease. He subsided heavily into a chair on the far side of the room, his chest rising and falling rapidly under the impetus of powerful emotion. If only he had never met the MacNair! If only he had never been lured against his will to France, there to be tortured and tantalized for an entire giddy month by the prospect of attaining the unattainable —only to have it snatched away at the very last instant. Yes, the MacNair had much to answer for!

As his fury slowly subsided he asked himself once again if he had made the wise decision in seeking out the Earl of Kensington at his London town house after his precipitous escape from France. But once again he was obliged to answer himself in the same fashion: What were his alternatives?

In France, or any part of the European continent where the French Empire held full sway, he was in mortal peril. The same was true of his native land. The treacherous escape of the MacNair of MacNair from the peaceful seclusion of his cell in Portland, that fatal blow to the prospects of Kevin Frost, had captured the imagination of the American press. His picture had circulated widely throughout the country and now all forty-six states and territories must be considered inaccessible to him. The only feasible alternative was England, which at least nurtured an organization dedicated to the overthrow of the hateful Napoleon. As the Yeoman Sons of Essex protected themselves, they would also be protecting Kevin Frost. There was obvious danger, of course, in too closely linking his own destiny to theirs, but up till now the Sons of Essex had apparently proven adept in deflecting the wrath of the Bonapartes and their evil secret police.

And finally, of course, mused Kevin Frost, it was here in Scotland that the MacNair had supposedly hidden his priceless crown. If only he could get to it before these half-crazed revolutionaries! With 30,000 diamonds in his pocket he could surely find a refuge somewhere on earth far from Napoleon V or the state's attorney of Franklin. . . .

Reflections of a strikingly similar nature were being entertained by the Earl of Kensington as he dourly considered this pint-sized doppelgänger of the so-called Prince William of England, this one differing only by the preposterous curly mustache that rose up like exclamation points on either side of his nose. Up till now he had proven far less useful than Dennett had initially hoped. "You are *certain,*" insisted Kensington in what had now become a standard litany, "that the MacNair told you *nothing* more about the location of the crown other than that he had concealed it in Scotland?"

"I *told* you: We spent only a few hours together. It was not until the very end of our conversation that he even mentioned the crown at all."

"He gave no hints, no indications, no unconscious—"

"Nothing at all," said Kevin Frost crossly. "Do you imagine that I don't want to find it as badly as you do?"

"That is true, of course," admitted the Earl, who had long since realized that this identical twin of the MacNair of MacNair was certain to be as baldly treacherous and underhanded as his alter ego. If the crown were ever found, never, never, *never* would this obviously criminal deviate be permitted within a hundred miles of it! The Earl of Kensington tugged pensively at the end of his nose. It might, in fact, even be possible to somehow arrange for this Kevin Frost to be surreptitiously returned to France and the tender mercies of the Marquis of Vézelay. Perhaps after he had been suitably stuffed with subtle disinformation. It would be a fitting end to a disreputable career. . . .

But only after they had found the crown, of course!

"Very well," murmured Kensington with a smile of stunning insincerity, "we are, of course, all in this together. Now, then: Back to the task at hand! We have nearly finished our search of the basements. By next week we hope to begin on the ground floor."

With a sigh Kevin Frost rose to his feet. "You still consider it likely that I might be able to . . . teleport this crown to my own head?"

"It is *Dennett* who considers it possible, not I. Possibly if you are ever close enough to it, he avers. You *are,* after all, exactly the same man, right down to the atomic level, as the one who has already been teleporting it all over Europe. In theory there is no reason at all why you yourself should not be able to do the same. That is why Dennett insists on your presence during our search."

"Oh, very well," said Kevin Frost, trying to stifle a profound yawn. "Anything to be helpful." He yawned again. Little sense in telling Kensington that the major portions of his nights ever since arriving in this startlingly opulent castle in northern Scotland had been spent fruitlessly awake as he tried desperately to teleport the magical crown out of its hiding place and onto his own deserving head. . . .

"Perhaps you'll be amused by this," said the Marquis of Vézelay with an exaggerated air of indifference that instantly put the MacNair on his guard. He had accosted the MacNair in the ornate splendor of a private upstairs lounge of the Opera House, Vézelay holding a glass of that tepid sparkling wine which was the closest this world could approximate to champagne, while the MacNair himself sipped from a large snifter of cognac. Across the room the Archduchess Mireille giggled noisily in the company of a large group of equally overdressed ladies of noble birth who had come to refresh themselves during the first intermission of Verdi's monumental *Death of Cleopatra*.

"What is it?" asked the MacNair cautiously, exceedingly vexed to have been sought out by this egregious secret-police man after three blissful though admittedly strenuous weeks in the Elysée Palace in the company of the Archduchess Mireille, twenty-one days during which the Marquis of Vézelay had been held resolutely at bay.

"It's really most amusing," said Vézelay, extending a piece of paper. "It's a warrant for your arrest and extradition."

"What!" The MacNair's heart lurched.

"Ah! But only from a court in the State of Franklin. And for that person known as Kevin Frost."

The MacNair let out an anguished sigh of relief. "*Most* amusing," he said icily. "You will recall, of course, that for the purposes of our present residence in France we are, by order of the Emperor himself, Lord Kevin of Deane, or, if you prefer our French title, le Comte de Domrémy-la-Pucelle. And as we all know, or *should* know, Kevin Frost is a common criminal whose whereabouts are unknown."

"Not so," countered the Marquis of Vézelay. "I know very well where he is. He is, at this very instant, in—"

"Kévin! Kévin, come here at once!" The far-from-sonorous voice of the Archduchess Mireille cut incisively across the loud buzz of the crowded lounge.

"In a moment, my dear. You were saying?"

"I was saying that Kevin Frost can be found at Garnaway Castle in Morayshire in Scotland."

The MacNair was taken aback. "What on earth can he be doing there?" he muttered uneasily, the image of the perilously concealed GODHEAD sharp in his mind.

"Plotting, so I would imagine," replied the Marquis dryly.

"Can't you do anything to stop them?"

"Kévin! Didn't you *hear* me?"

"Kensington and his political party are, I fear, far too powerful to interfere with. But Kevin Frost himself is another matter. The competent authorities in Franklin will be informed at once of his exact location. With any luck at all they will be able to put him out of mischief for the next ten years or so."

"Poor fellow," murmured the MacNair without conviction. "Thirteen years in prison for loving not wisely but too well."

"Your Highness is most poetic." The Marquis of Vézelay leaned closer, his face suddenly animated by a grim smile. "But you haven't heard the best of it. My agents in California recently discovered that—"

"Kévin! What are you *doing?*" The voice of the Archduchess Mireille was disconcertingly close and the Mac-Nair jumped nervously. With a quick smile over his shoulder for the Archduchess the Marquis of Vézelay whispered rapidly into the MacNair's ear. The MacNair's eyes widened and he fell back a pace.

"You astonish me! What terrible irony! Do you suppose that if he had known he would ever have put that Mickey Finn in our drink?" The MacNair looked up to smile placatingly at the Archduchess Mireille, who was scowling ferociously at the two men. "Ah, *there* you are, my dear. I've been looking *everywhere* for you."

"Hrmph! I've *told* you not to drink so much cognac. Now put down that glass at once and come with me. The Countess of Seville wants to hear your story of—"

As he let himself be borne away, the MacNair was wondering if common decency dictated that he should pass along the Marquis of Vézelay's startling piece of information to the really rather unlikable Kevin Frost. Certainly the latter had never done anything to assist *him.* In fact—quite the contrary!

The MacNair shrugged. But why not? *He* was never one to hold a grudge. But on reflection, Kevin Frost could only be in Scotland in the company of the Earl of Kensington for a single nefarious reason: to seize the GODHEAD for himself! Yes, one thing was now certain: He must be removed from any proximity to the crown at once! Yes, he would inform Kevin Frost—but only after he had been securely confirmed in a Portland jail, there to suffer some of the same terrible anguish that he had so willfully inflicted upon a man whose sole desire had been to act as his benefactor. . . .

CHAPTER
= 27 =

"To think that I once hoped you'd be a caveman," giggled the Archduchess Mireille. "My goodness, if you were any *more* of a caveman I'd have to ask my girlfriends in to help out."

"Totally out of the question," muttered the MacNair, who lay spent and inert, his head sunk in the depths of an enormous pink pillow with only the tip of his beard protruding. "It is, in fact, only your own exceptional beauty and charm which incite me to such delightful excess. No one else, not even your—"

The Archduchess snuggled closer, her firm rosy breasts warm against his bare chest, and kissed him moistly on the cheek. "Oh, Bunny, you say the *nicest* things! I don't *really* want to share you with my nasty friends, I was just teasing. I'm just so *happy* that you're a king—well, a prince at any rate—and here with me. I just don't want you to *ever* go away!"

"Never, my dearest!" cried the MacNair gallantly, pulling her tightly against him. "Where, after all, would I be without you—I, a stranger and afraid, in a world I never made?"

"Is that poetry?" asked the Archduchess wonderingly.

"Of a sort. But in a sense it also expresses some of the difficulties I am having in adjusting myself to this world. In my own universe, of course, I have my own high position, with all its concomitant responsibilities. *There* my entire

164

existence has but a single goal: to serve the peoples of my empire. But here—what do I have *here?*"

The Archduchess's cornflower-blue eyes widened in astonished hurt. "But, Bunny, you have *me!*"

"Of course," replied the MacNair hastily, "and you're far more than I deserve! But what I mean is this: Even a prince needs some activity, a higher calling, if you will, something to *do* beyond merely answering silly questions for dim scientists all day long, something which will permit me to fulfill my obligations to society, something which I will be able to call my *own."*

The Archduchess Mireille drew back noticeably in his arms and frowned delicately. "Oh, Bunny, you're not going to start *that* again, are you? I've told you and *told* you that I hardly have *any* money of my own. Everything I have is tied up some way or other that I don't really understand." She let her head fall back to his shoulder and her lips began to gently nuzzle the side of his neck. "Everything you need is right here beside you," she whispered enticingly.

"But that racing stable that the Duke of Finistère has offered me—it would be a *perfect* investment," persisted the MacNair. "Racehorses, after all, pay for themselves with their winnings. They are absolutely self-perpetuating, their upkeep is minimal, a few wisps of straw and suchlike, and the price is so *reasonable*—a mere half million now and the rest in—"

The Archduchess Mireille sat up sharply, the rosy tips of her perfectly conical breasts quivering with emotion. "Kévin, not another word! I *detest* arguing about money—it's so vulgar! How can you—a king—be so . . . so *common?*" Her mouth tightened into a thin line, and with an effort the MacNair hurriedly raised himself from the soft depths of the plump mattress and pulled her warm smooth body back against his.

"Not another word, I promise you," he whispered huskily. "With you I want only to speak of *uncommon* things. Your beauty, your eyes, your—"

"Oh, Bunny, I *do* love you! Hold me, Bunny, hold me *tight!*"

"And later I'll tell you all about champagne," he murmured into her ear, "for that's *another* uncommon thing."

"And the crown," she whispered softly, "tell me about the crown. Tell me how it will look on me on coronation day when we stand in Westminster Abbey and the Archbishop of Canterbury takes it from your hands, its lights all glowing and its diamonds sparkling, and he . . ."

The MacNair rolled his eyes in mute supplication.

The ancient cathedral town of Reims stands on the great plain of Champagne a leisurely two hours' drive northeast of Paris. In his own universe the MacNair had paid a number of visits to this charming old city, for it was here that the world's trade in champagne was centered. Though inferior sparkling wines of a similar nature abounded from Yugoslavia to California, only those wines produced by the authentic *méthode champenoise* in the small triangle of limestone hills to the south of Reims between Epernay and Châlons-sur-Marne could legally be accorded that exalted name.

"I don't see what you find so interesting about this city of Reims," said the Archduchess Mireille rather sulkily as their long black Huit Chevaux drove slowly over the sluggishly flowing Marne in the small town of Château-Thierry thirty miles to the south of Reims. "I think you should stay in Paris at the institute until you find some way of bringing our crown back."

"Today is Sunday, my dearest," replied the MacNair mildly, inwardly wincing at her cavalier use of the word *our*. "There are those, even at the Curie Institute, whose peculiarity is that they insist upon one day of repose per week."

"Well, I think it's *extremely* selfish of them—they *know* how much I want that crown back."

The MacNair sighed plaintively but refrained from speech.

"And another thing," continued the Archduchess as she glowered at a passing herd of brown and white cows, "I simply don't understand why you want to go to Reims just to try their wines. Didn't Uncle's maître d'hôtel and his sommelier *both* tell you that nobody drinks their wine except the Rémois themselves? And even the Rémois do it only because they can't afford anything better."

"Not in *my* world," said the MacNair cheerfully, refusing to let his spirits be dampened by the Archduchess's lack of ardor for their little excursion or the fact that the Marquis of Vézelay and three of his toughs trailed behind them in their own black limousine. Though Paris had been cold and overcast, here it was a perfect morning of early autumn, the sky a faultless deep blue with a few fluffy white clouds slowly drifting over the rich green countryside. A uniformed chauffeur sat rigidly at attention in his glassed-in compartment behind the long low hood of the Huit Chevaux, and a picnic basket from the imperial kitchens awaited them in the trunk.

Beside him on the deep leather seat, a long black cheroot in her gloved hand, the Archduchess Mireille was a vision of expensively clad simplicity. A plain white frock revealed an enticing length of long smooth leg while a small blue bonnet with a wisp of a veil sat jauntily on her curly blond hair. Only the most exacting of aesthetes could have discerned in her profile a slight protrusion of her otherwise admirable cornflower-blue eyes, a mouth that unmistakably had indulged in more than its allotted share of pouting, and a chin that in all honesty barely escaped meriting the harsh word *receding*.

But the MacNair was a man ensnared in the coils of love and to his eyes even these slight defects were nothing more than nature's beauty spots, purposely given his beloved to further enhance—though perhaps only in the eye of the sophisticated beholder, he was compelled to admit—her overall beauty. The fact that the Archduchess Mireille of Luxembourg was the third wealthiest woman in Europe was totally irrelevant, he told himself firmly.

But what was *not* irrelevant was the disconcerting discovery that his angelic-faced lover was also the most notoriously tight-fisted woman in Europe. . . .

Not for the MacNair the unstinting largesse such as he himself would have joyously showered upon his beloved had their positions been reversed, racing Bugattis and blue-water yachts, buckets of caviar and wardrobes of hand-tailored suits. No, the most it appeared he could hope for from the Archduchess Mireille would be a few grudging sous from time to time, disbursed with a sharp homily on the dangers of wasteful extravagance!

It was enough to make a man wonder about the course of true love. . . .

CHAPTER
= 28 =

THE LONG BLACK limousine swept into the city of Reims, closely trailed by that of the Marquis of Vézelay, and slowly made its way through the tangle of narrow streets surrounding the great Gothic cathedral in which for centuries the kings of France had been crowned. The MacNair drank in the passing scene with keen interest, for here was the ancient city of Reims such as it must have been in the Middle Ages when Joan of Arc recaptured it from the English invaders. In his own world most of its medieval buildings had been destroyed by the merciless bombardment of the Germans during the First World War while the hapless inhabitants fled for safety into the enormous underground quarries which over the centuries had been hacked out of the limestone for the extraction of chalk. There in the cool dry caverns the refugees had passed first weeks and then months, side by side with millions of bottles of slowly fermenting champagne.

The Huit Chevaux halted outside the dusty offices of Baudchon et Fils, Négociants en Vins, and accompanied by the debonair Marquis of Vézelay and the skeptical Archduchess, the MacNair was led down into the cellars where two dozen bottles of locally produced white wines awaited his pleasure.

"Ha!" cried the Marquis, stroking his own rather straggly beard. "This is the sort of bodyguarding job I should be given more often."

"In that case," replied the MacNair coolly, "we suggest that you first of all taste each of these wines for possible subtle poisons."

"Your Lordship!" cried Baudchon Père in horror.

"Small matter if he succumbs," explained the MacNair carelessly to the wine merchant. "There is ample room for the body in the trunk of his car."

"Would Your *Highness* prefer me elsewhere?" muttered Vézelay venomously.

"Frankly, yes," said the Archduchess Mireille coldly. "This was supposed to be a pleasure trip. The sight of your—"

"We suppose the poor chap's only doing his job, my dearest," said the MacNair loftily as he bent to raise her gloved hand to his lips, "and your security is, of course, the most precious thing in the world."

"Oh, Bunny!"

The bottles were opened, the wines poured. Their contents were swirled about in large tulip-shaped glasses, held up to the light, rolled about the mouth, and spat discreetly into a small brass bucket. Before his ill-fated venture into the restaurant business in Tokyo the MacNair had once spent seventeen months as the part owner of a modest establishment on the banks of the Garonne in the southwestern city of Toulouse. There he had acquired the charming accent which had so captivated the Marquis of Vézelay as well as an eclectic though well-informed knowledge of wines and champagnes. For by his own choice much of his participation in the duties of proprietorship consisted of sampling the restaurant's well-stocked cellar and subsequently visiting the great vineyards of France for the purpose of restocking its thousands of bottles.

Now he was aghast at the quality of the thin, acid wines which were all the limestone hills of the glorious champagne country could offer. Who would have thought that the judicious addition of a few bubbles could have made such a difference?

Later they picnicked in the cool dark shade of a weeping

willow by a rushing stream in the hills south of Reims. "I don't see why we have to sit out here serving ourselves cold food and having ants crawl up our legs," complained the Archduchess Mireille, "especially when Les Sept Barbus in Reims has just been awarded its fifth star."

"Just think how much more you'll appreciate Les Sept Barbus this evening, then," murmured the MacNair, stifling a soft sigh.

"Oh, very well. What do Englishmen, even princes, know about food?"

"What *is* this celebrated *méthode champenoise* you keep referring to which renders these unspeakable local wines the delight of your apparently civilized world?" interjected the Marquis of Vézelay suavely. "It can't be just the addition of bubbles by simple aeration—"

"Ha!" said the MacNair, fastidiously spooning the last of his chocolate mousse from its crystal glass. "That, we fear, must remain our little secret for the moment. For if any lout could freeze the neck of a bottle, where, then, would that leave even the greatest of kings?"

The Marquis of Vézelay arched his eyebrows. "I had no idea Your Highness was a Napoleonic scholar."

"Napoleonic scholar?" The MacNair squinted dubiously at the secret-police man, wary of some cunning trap. But the Frenchman had turned away to light the cheroot of the Archduchess Mireille and with a baffled shrug the MacNair returned to his own steaming cup of coffee.

Throughout the afternoon the two limousines slowly quartered the narrow roads in the hilly triangle which in the MacNair's world produced champagne and which here supported an occasional vineyard but more often only a living for large herds of woolly merino sheep. Twice they stopped at small vineyards to sample the wares; finally they came to a small seventeenth-century château of plain but classical lines which in the MacNair's world had been a Mecca for oenophilists of six continents.

"This," said the MacNair sadly, "is the Château Beldame." They got out to peer through iron gates at a weed-choked gravel driveway flanked by dark green yews that led to a dry fountain with a broken nymph in front of the château's columned portico. The granite building itself was three stories high with a crumbling mansard roof. Broken shutters revealed shattered panes in the grimy windows. The grounds were barely tended and a distinct air of melancholy hung over the once beautiful estate. "Here is produced the finest champagne in the world."

"Indeed?" said the Marquis of Vézelay with a tolerant smile. "Then here is your great opportunity: don't you see the sign? The property is for sale."

The MacNair scowled darkly. Was this intolerable secret-police man openly mocking his lack of funds, his total dependence upon the largesse of the Emperor and of his miserly niece the Archduchess? He stabbed angrily at the rusty call button set into the concrete gatepost.

The château was locked, but an aged gardener in a ragged blue smock was prevailed upon to show them around the deserted grounds. "Here are the sheds for the fermentation and bottling," said the MacNair, gesturing at a neglected pasture of thorny bushes while the gardener gaped in bewilderment. "Where that small outbuilding stands against the hillside is the entrance to the cellars. An endless limestone cave, you would say, quarried in the sixteenth century, barely lighted and running deep into the hillside. But in the cave, what a noble spectacle: a million bottles of Château Beldame Fin d'Epoque!" His eyes blurred with fond memories. "Never will I forget a bottle of the vintage of '72. It was—"

"Kévin," interrupted the Archduchess plaintively. "I'm tired and cold and not at all interested in this decrepit old ruin or stories about imaginary wines. I want to go *at once.*" She stamped her foot impatiently.

"Couldn't we take just a tiny look at the cave?"

"For goodness' sake, what is there to see in an empty cave that you have already seen a thousand times in the past?"

"The million faded bubbles of a million empty dreams, perhaps?" The MacNair ran his fingers sadly through his beard. "When you fear the consequences of the ungoverned past, why else should you look to see what empty caves might hold?"

The Archduchess Mireille snorted inelegantly and turned

angrily away, but the Marquis of Vézelay looked at him oddly. "Another Napoleonic riddle? Your Royal Highness is a man of constant surprises."

"This isn't the cave where Marshal Baudouin is buried, by any chance?" asked the Archduchess suddenly, a delicate frown wrinkling her smooth forehead beneath the wisp of white lace that fell from her bonnet. *"That* might be worth visiting—if only for a moment."

The Marquis smiled indulgently. "No, Your Highness. Le Cave du Maréchal is some kilometers back along the road we have just come. Perhaps you noticed all the automobiles parked—"

"What is the Marshal's Cave?" interrupted the MacNair.

The eyebrows of the Marquis of Vézelay shot up. "I should have imagined that a Napoleonic scholar of Your Highness's attainments would—" He interrupted himself and tapped a finger against his gaunt cheeks. "But I am forgetting. In *your* world perhaps there *was* no Marshal Baudouin."

"Perhaps not. In what way was he noteworthy, and why should anyone visit his cave? Surely not for the variety of fine Rémois wines which he kept therein?"

The head of the secret police smiled appreciatively. "No, Baudouin was the greatest of Bonaparte's generals after the Emperor himself. It was Baudouin who is generally credited with the decisive victory at the Cotswolds. He was subsequently created Marshal of France and—"

"—and was lost in a cave-in in some silly old cave," completed the Archduchess Mireille impatiently. "They say his bones are still there."

"The Emperor himself decreed that they should be left in peace," explained the Marquis.

"How peculiar," mused the MacNair. "I never before heard of a cave in Champagne collapsing. What was he doing in the cave in the first place?"

"Another mystery," replied the Marquis. "No one knows. Nor why all of his family was with him at the time and perished beside him."

"What a macabre story." The MacNair shook his head.

"Well, then," said the Archduchess, her lips tight, "now

that you're satisfied that it's just another empty cave, could we kindly go—and *at once?"*

"Oh, very well," muttered the MacNair, his thoughts far away on his priceless crown in Scotland. If only he had his blasted crown . . .

CHAPTER
= 29 =

THE FOLLOWING DAY the MacNair formally requested the pleasure of an audience with His Imperial Majesty l'Empéreur de Tous les Français et du Grand Empire des Etats-Unis de l'Europe Napoleon V. For it was evident now to the MacNair that his dreams of the Archduchess Mireille ever financing even a modest winery were totally illusory. As he lay waiting in his great marble bathtub for the barber to appear for his morning shave, the MacNair scowled angrily. For a song he could buy up the entire champagne country between Reims and Epernay and within a few years be the master of an incalculable fortune!

If only he had a song!

Or better yet: if only he had his crown!

But then if he had his crown he wouldn't need to *make* an incalculable fortune—he would already *own* an incalculable fortune. . . .

How unjust life could be!

A single possible solution appeared to present itself. If Mireille, a mere archduchess, was the third wealthiest woman in Europe, wouldn't it be reasonable to suppose that her uncle, the *Emperor* of all of Europe, was even wealthier? What could a few trifling millions mean to him one way or another?

Later that afternoon a page delivered a brief, but hand-written, note from the Emperor himself. If the Count of Domrémy-la-Pucelle would find it convenient to come to his private apartments in the hour following dinner, they might share a cigar and a *pousse-café*.

The Emperor received him cordially in a small gilded salon in which a dozen silver candelabra the height of a man glowed with the light of a hundred long blue candles. Cigars were ceremonially lighted and hundred-year-old cognac poured. With contented sighs the Houses of Bonaparte and Henley sank into deep leather easy chairs. The MacNair blew a perfect smoke ring toward the rococo angels and cherubs who crowded each other upon the ceiling. "As I lay in my bath," he murmured with his head cocked to one side and a finger pensively tapping the end of his Vandyke beard, "I was suddenly struck by how little one actually knows about the *diet* of the brontosaurus. Was this noble beast actually a mere marsh-dweller as is commonly supposed in my own world, subsisting upon reeds and suchlike, or has other evidence been adduced by the scholars of this world concerning this rather vexatious question?"

The Emperor's eyes glittered and his broad chest swelled as he drew a deep breath. . . .

But an hour later when the conversation had been deftly turned to that modest stipend which might be counted upon to maintain the dignity of the Prince's position in France as the Count of Domrémy-la-Pucelle the keen blue eyes of Napoleon V instantly grew opaque.

"At the moment the annual budget is quite out of control, my dear fellow, these senators and deputies across the river are slashing my most vital funds left and right. It is not to be borne!" He slapped the palm of his hand angrily against his deep blue easy chair and rose to stalk over to the mahogany sideboard. "But I fear that it must." He turned with a crystal decanter of cognac in his hand, multicolored glints of light sparkling from its hundreds of facets. "For he who controls the purse controls the nation. Or so my great-to-the-third-grandfather Napoleon is reputed to have said."

"And very truly said," agreed the MacNair gloomily, accepting a large refill of richly aromatic cognac. At the mention of the original Napoleon's name he was struck once again by how little the present Emperor, the sixth in the line, resembled his celebrated ancestor. Even in his middle seventies he was still large and rawboned, with more of the air of a craggy Gascon peasant than what one might expect to find in the person of the titular leader of that civilization which incessantly proclaimed itself the world's arbiter of elegance and breeding.

Very peculiar. Or was it? As the MacNair swirled the cognac around his glass and savored its almost overpowering fullness of aroma, he cast his mind back to the original Napoleon, that almost caricature of a person, small and plump beneath his tricornered hat, his hand forever thrust inside his vest, as if to assuage an unruly ulcer. His son Napoleon II would have possessed one-half his genetic material. His grandson Napoleon III merely one-quarter. His great-granddaughter Alexine I, whose assassination in 1910 had concluded the Great War, only one-eighth. Alexine's son Napoleon IV would have had but one-sixteenth of old Boney's genes in his veins, while the present Emperor Charles-Pierre, Napoleon V, would be reduced to a negligible one thirty-second of the genes of the fabled Bonaparte. Surely that was very little reason to set this amiable brontosaurophile down upon the throne of the most powerful nation on earth?

But undoubtedly this was not the sort of idle reflection which the Emperor relished being brought to his attention. The MacNair swallowed a small sip of cognac and decided to reapproach his subject from another tack. "What I have in mind, of course, is not mere endless charity. Think of it, if you will, as an investment fund for the propagation of those ideas from my own world which—" He expiated for some time on the unimaginable benefits which would accrue first to the French Empire, then to the Emperor's illustrious line, and finally in no small measure to the Emperor himself.

"Extremely interesting," murmured Napoleon V, "even fascinating is not too strong a word. Some of your ideas are absolutely captivating! This . . . what did you call it? video tape recorder—what a marvel! I will give instructions at once for the Curie Institute and the National Telegraphic Center to put all of their resources at your personal disposal. As soon as you having a working model"—his eyes twinkled in anticipation—"we shall discuss means of financing."

The MacNair dug his nails into the palms of his hands. Had this old idiot no conception at all of the technology necessary to elaborate even the simplest VCR, a film to play upon it, and finally a television screen to display it upon? All of this in a world mired at the level of 1920 technology? It was difficult to keep from screaming.

"Your Imperial Majesty is extremely gracious," he said with a dutiful smile. "I shall start upon it at once."

"Yes, please do so. I trust that it shall not take more than a few months at the most." He finished the last of his cognac and wrinkled his forehead in what appeared to be some embarrassment. "I fear that I myself have been coming under no little pressure from my Conseil des Ministres—worthless lot of fellows, wish I could take 'em all out and shoot 'em, just as that idiot . . . hem, as my niece Mireille keeps after me to. . . . They're nothing but politicians and accountants, the whole lot of 'em." He paused as if reluctant to continue.

"You say you are under pressure, Your Imperial Majesty?"

"About your . . . hem! presence here in the palace. All very well, they say, if he really *is* a prince of the blood, but even then only one thing counts with that crowd: results." His fluffy white mustache quivered indignantly. "Results, my dear fellow, results!" He raised the decanter to pour the MacNair another dollop of brandy. "The only result they're interested in, I'm afraid, is this so-called magical crown of yours."

"But I thought—"

"That was supposed to be a secret? How can one possibly keep a secret in a country that has 364 kinds of cheese?" he demanded with some exasperation. "Anyway, they know about it, and now they want it. Not next month, not next week, but *now!* Or if not—out you go!"

"But—"

"Exactly! Just what I told them, my dear fellow! But you know these politicians, I'm sure they're all exactly the same in your own world, hardly gentlemen at all."

"What exactly do they want?" asked the MacNair warily.

The Emperor waved his hand vaguely. "Oh, nothing more than the crown—at least to begin with. That would establish your *bona fides* so to speak, and then we could speak of this whole plan of investment again."

"But if I had my crown"—the MacNair contorted his face into a painful smile—"and I really fear I must emphasize the *my,* then I would, of course, have no need to be standing hat in hand asking for alms like a beggar in Bombay."

"My dear fellow!" cried the Emperor, aghast.

"For I imagine that even here 35,000 gems of the first water would surely enable me to live without causing undue strain to the budget of the French Empire."

The Emperor grimaced and hastily poured himself a rather larger cognac than he had previously taken. "Even there, I fear . . ."

A cold clammy hand gripped the small of the MacNair's back. "You mean—"

"Precisely, my poor fellow. We're all the prisoners of these blasted politicians, aren't we? They mean to declare the crown vital to the security of the Empire and turn it over to the Curie Institute and the Ministry of War. And that, I imagine, will be the last we shall ever see of the crown." He frowned uneasily. "I fear that Mireille will be beside herself."

"I see," said the MacNair bitterly, totally indifferent to the Archduchess's sensibilities regarding *his* GODHEAD. "The glorious French Empire stea— . . . *sequesters* my personal private property, all that remains to me from my native land from which I have been so unjustly kidnaped, and in return I am offered . . . what?"

The Emperor of All the French blinked rapidly as a startling notion suddenly came to him. "What will you be offered?" A faint smile tugged at his lips then slowly broadened as the delightful ramifications became clearer. "I rather imagine that the hand of the Archduchess Mireille of Luxembourg could be arranged for, along with all the capital—in your own name, of course—needed to produce whatever quantities of bubbling wine you might fancy." His bright blue eyes glittered. "And, of course, I see now that you would clearly need a suitable château at some remove from Paris to oversee your vineyards and raise your family. Where, in fact, I am certain that you and the lovely Mireille will live happily ever after. . . ."

CHAPTER
══ 30 ══

"I can't believe it!" exclaimed the Earl of Kensington.

"It's the crown," murmured Sir Norvil Dennett reverently.

"How the devil did it get under my bathtub? The cheek of the fellow! The—"

"Hush," cautioned Dennett. "Put it back—quickly! That way—"

"—that scoundrel Frost will know nothing about it." The Earl of Kensington let his eyes linger for another second on the glittering beauty of the thousands of diamonds, then carefully set the crown back in its dusty hiding place and quietly shut the access panel. "Quick thinking, my dear Dennett."

"Shhh, here he comes now."

When Kevin Frost stepped into the dressing room of the Earl of Kensington's apartment high in the Black Tower of Garnaway Castle, he found the two Englishmen standing in the doorway of the large marble-lined bathroom with impatient scowls on their faces.

"Sorry I'm late, I—"

"No matter, no matter," muttered Kensington irritably. "We've just checked the bathroom—absolutely nothing there. Why don't you start taking some of those clothes out of the closets? With all that wooden paneling there's no telling what kind of hiding places might be concealed there."

"My God," whispered Dennett later that evening as he turned the GODHEAD over and over in his hands, his bushy grey beard bristling with excitement, "there's an entire new technology here. It may be *centuries* in advance of ours!"

The Earl of Kensington hovered anxiously beside the workbench, his eyes glittering in the intense overhead lights of the subterranean laboratory. "Look at those diamonds," he marveled. "How do you suppose that a creature like the MacNair ever came to get his hands on such a thing? And what can the *purpose* of such a crown have been?"

"I don't suppose we'll ever know," said the Master of Garnaway, setting the GODHEAD down on the bench. "A pathological liar is totally incapable of ever telling the truth."

"But . . . do you suppose it's *safe* leaving it here? What is there to prevent him from . . . from doing whatever he does to it and teleporting it to wherever he is this very moment?"

"Nothing at all, I fear," replied Dennett, then added thoughtfully, "but perhaps as soon as the time machine is finished we can move it backwards in time a few minutes or even put it into a bubble outside of time itself—'disentiming' it, as it were. I don't see how teleportation could work over time as well as space."

"But how *long* before the confounded machine is finished?" demanded Kensington testily. "It seems like you and the late Herr Doctor Professor Hubmaier have been working on it for years now!"

"We have been working on it in our *minds* for years now," replied Dennett with one of his superior little smiles which so annoyed the Earl of Kensington. "That of course has been the hard part. But now it's just a matter of machining some of the necessary parts and then putting them together."

"What! As close as that? But you never said—"

"I fear that was going to be my little surprise. Until this evening I thought it might take another month or two. Now that we have the crown, however, and the urgency to safeguard it is . . ." His voice trailed off as he bent over to scrutinize the crown for a long moment. "But look! Just here: See those scratches, those damaged . . . whatever they are, the seven or eight missing stones, that hole in the crown itself. What does all that suggest to you?"

The Earl of Kensington leaned closer, his forehead wrinkled in thought. Suddenly he gasped quietly. "A bullet hole! Look at how the—"

"Exactly," said Dennett with satisfaction. "The crown has obviously been damaged to some unknown extent, possibly in the course of the MacNair's coming into possession of it."

"Ha! Armed robbery, I should imagine!"

"Entirely likely, judging from his character. But you realize, of course, the crucial importance of this damage. It means that almost certainly the crown is not performing whatever function it was designed to perform."

"You mean—"

"That it is, at best, performing in an erratic, haphazard fashion. The MacNair has not teleported it because he is now *unable* to teleport it. For if he could, surely it would not have been left to sit beneath your bathtub all this time."

"You reassure me," said Kensington with a soft sigh. "Then what shall we do with the egregious Frost now that we've found the crown?"

"Turf him out immediately," said the Master of Garnaway absently as he bent over the crown. "Hand him over to the American authorities and let them return him to his well-merited jail. Send him back to Vézelay. Toss him into an oubliette—whatever you like. He's of absolutely no further use to us."

The Earl of Kensington smiled grimly. "It will be a pleasure. I think that on the whole Vézelay—what!"

"My God!" Sir Norvil Dennett jumped back in astonishment from the brilliant lights of the crown which he had just switched on. "The lights, look at the *lights!*"

"My God," echoed the Earl of Kensington in awe, "the lights . . ."

"It was this little switch here," said Dennett wonderingly, using it to turn off the lights, then immediately switching them on again. "Incredible! It must have its own self-contained power source." He turned to Kensington, his eyes flashing. "Do you fully understand the importance of this crown? With it we can—"

He directed an excited gesture at the GODHEAD just as it vanished.

Kevin Frost was in the act of stepping from his bathtub on the third floor of Garnaway Castle when the cold gloomy bathroom was suddenly lit by an impossible brilliance and he simultaneously felt a strange weight upon his head. As if in a dream he raised his hands and slowly, solemnly, hardly daring to breathe, took the crown and set it carefully on the top of the wicker linen hamper at the end of the tub.

For a timeless moment he gaped at its awesome beauty in a state approaching religious wonder, but as he gradually became aware of the heavy pounding of his heart, coherent thought began to return. He had the crown! *He had the crown!*

How had he done it? he asked himself wildly. Yes, he had been standing in the tub, still trying to focus his mind as he had for the last three weeks on a dimly visualized, imperfectly realized crown, and then, and then—there it was!

He was rich beyond imagination!

Kevin Frost clamped his hand over his mouth to smother a cry of triumphant jubilation—just as the door to the bathroom rattled violently and a loud pounding began on the other side.

"Open this door at once!" bellowed the Earl of Kensington. "We know you've got it in there, we can see the light under the door! Open at once, I tell you!"

"Whatever are you talking about?" asked Kevin Frost mildly while his thoughts and eyes rolled desperately about his head as he sought a hiding place for the crown. He splashed water noisily with his foot. "I lie here in my bathtub contemp—"

"Lie? Indeed you lie!" screamed the Earl of Kensington. "We *know* you have the crown!"

"The crown? What—"

Scuffling sounds broke out in the corridor beyond the door and Kensington's rumbling bellow was replaced by Dennett's hardly less impassioned tones. "Frost," he cried, "listen to me! *Turn off the crown!* Turn it off at once, I beg of you! If you don't—*none* of us will have it!"

"Turn it off?" repeated Kevin Frost ingenuously even as he dashed naked from one end of the bathroom to the other, opening cupboards, lifting bath mats, peering under the claw-footed iron tub, and finally draping a large blue towel over the flashing crown and effectively smothering its lights while he tried to gather his wits. "Why would I want to turn off the lights—here in the bathroom? I'd be in total darkness."

He heard a muffled sound that was nearly a sob. *"Please,"* implored Sir Norvil Dennett, "don't you understand? The crown can only be teleported when it's switched on! That *must* be the case! That's why the MacNair hasn't teleported it away already—he must have left it here switched off!"

"Ha!" cried Kevin Frost from the far side of the room, where he had thrown open the small window and was blinking into the cold black night of northern Scotland. A blast of icy air blew against his bare wet chest. Fifty feet below he saw the uninviting prospect of a brightly lighted marble terrace. So much for the window. . . . "So you found it without telling me!" he screamed. "You were trying to keep it from me! And now that it's mine you want me to return it to you! Never, do you hear me, never!"

"Frost, my dear chap," came Kensington's voice, strangely muted as if he were having difficulty speaking, which was indeed the case, for in a rage Sir Norvil Dennett had fixed his long powerful fingers deep in the fatty folds of the apoplectic Earl's bulging neck. "You totally misunderstand us. We located it only a few minutes ago. Naturally one didn't wish to disturb you in your bath. But as soon as you had come out, it was our intention to—"

"But it vanished before we could tell you," interrupted Dennett, releasing his grip on Kensington's throat now that the imbecile nobleman had been sufficiently reasoned with to realize that his mindless bellowing at the fool in the bathroom could only aggravate the situation. "And now we must make certain that—"

"—it doesn't vanish *again!*" concluded the Earl of Kensington in a hoarse whisper.

"You mean the . . . the MacNair could . . . could . . . ?" muttered Kevin Frost in horror-stricken tones. He grabbed the crown, wrapped in the thick folds of the towel, and clutched it as tightly to his bare breast as any mother with a beloved child.

"Of *course* he could," murmured Dennett softly, reasonably. "He's *you,* remember?"

"But . . . but in that case how did *I* . . . ?"

"Because *you* must have been thinking about it—and he *wasn't.* But now that it's switched on, just as soon as—"

"He'll take it *away* from me?" howled Kevin Frost despairingly.

"Exactly!" shouted Dennett. "So, quickly—turn it off!"

"Yes, yes, my dear fellow," wheedled the Earl of Kensington, "do turn it off like a sensible chap."

"My God," muttered Kevin Frost to himself as he desperately tried to unwrap the crown from the tangles of the now seemingly animate towel which resisted his every movement. "I've got to turn it off, I've got to turn it—"

The towel fell suddenly to the floor and he nearly dropped the crown, so brilliant was the startling glory of its iridescent lights. Oblivious to the advice and warnings shouted from the other side of the door, he desperately turned the crown over and over in his hands searching for some means of turning it off. At last his fingers seemed to find a likely switch. He hesitated for a final second, then placed the tip of his index finger against it and had just begun to apply the necessary pressure when—

CHAPTER
$= 31 =$

THE MACNAIR'S THOUGHTS for the past month had come to be increasingly dominated by an almost unbearable craving for his glorious but unobtainable GODHEAD. Without any reasonable prospect of ever seeing it again short of returning to Scotland and somehow switching it on, how quickly life could become tedious in even the most luxurious of palaces! Even, he muttered to himself wearily as he leaned forward to examine his face closely in his bathroom mirror, when an appreciable part of that life is spent in the arms of an apparently insatiable archduchess. Were those actually *wrinkles* that were forming around his eyes, the beginnings of dark bags *under* them?

The MacNair shuffled away from the mirror with leaden feet. Impossible! he told himself resolutely. A good night's sleep and he would be as fit as a fiddle! The perils of middle age simply didn't exist for a man like himself! Unless, of course, middle age was a disease which could be brought on by a life of total indolence in a gilded palace, a life which was nothing less than the triumphant realization of everything he had ever yearned for in his dreary prison cells in years past.

And more! he added hastily. For had he not found Love?

Who else in the entire world was lucky enough to be enamored of the beautiful Archduchess Mireille of Luxembourg, favorite niece of the Emperor Napoleon V? Who else was loved passionately in return by that incomparable

184

beauty? Who else had been promised the hand of the third richest woman in Europe? Who else—

The MacNair sighed loudly from the very bottom of his heart, then stepped into his dressing room to make a meticulous choice from the clothes that hung in neat array. *That* was the snag! Who else had been promised the hand of the third richest woman in Europe—but only on the condition that he forthwith produce his magical, priceless crown? And then turn it over to the French Army!

The MacNair slammed a fist into an open palm. The crown—whatever the future held for him, he had to have the crown!

But, a tiny, barely discernible voice seemed to whisper in a distant corner of his brain, *but if you had the crown, then you really wouldn't need to marry the third richest woman in Europe after all, would you?*

But I *love* her, the MacNair protested.

Do you? If that's the case, then why are you sneaking out on her like this?

I am *not* sneaking out on her! I am merely accepting a dinner invitation on an evening in which she plans to be closeted with a number of her idiotic girlfriends.

And is that why you haven't informed Vézelay either?

The MacNair drew himself up with dignity and made a final jaunty adjustment to his silver and black cravat. The movements of the Count of Domrémy-la-Pucelle are absolutely independent of the approbation of the Marquis of Vézelay: I have no need whatsoever for a nursemaid. Let Vézelay and his merry men spend a quiet evening in their torture chambers. *I* am merely stepping out to dinner.

With an emissary from the Ottoman Empire! How do you think the Emperor—and Vézelay—would react if they knew that?

The MacNair considered the merits of a smart grey homburg with a tiny red feather in its band, then drew it low on his forehead to mask his debonair features. Only *if* they knew, he murmured to himself with an urbane smile, only *if* they knew. . . .

Ziya Gök Hikmet had been encountered a few weeks earlier at Chez Doudoune, one of the innumerable after-dinner cabarets on the Left Bank to which an increasingly weary Count of Domrémy-la-Pucelle had been led in the early hours of the morning by the indefatigable Archduchess Mireille. Its lights were dim, the cacophony relentless. The Archduchess was immediately greeted by loud hoots of pleasure from the fashionable members of *le tout Paris* who jammed Chez Doudoune's converted wine cellar. Algerian absinthe and a Martiniquais cigar were instantly pressed upon her and the Archduchess vanished into their midst. The MacNair uttered a pent-up sigh of relief and presently found himself in a remote corner trading affable shouts with a curly-haired young man from the Ottoman Mission.

"I'm merely the third assistant commercial attaché," cried Ziya Gök Hikmet as he downed his third cup of thick Turkish coffee, "but I'd be interested in hearing more about your idea for sparkling wines. We Turks don't drink—or at least we're not supposed to—but most of the member states of our empire do. In fact we do our best to keep 'em thoroughly sozzled at all times. A new commercial process is always of interest."

"Sound thinking!" exclaimed the MacNair above the uproar. If the blasted French couldn't be persuaded to take a decent interest in their own natural heritage, then why shouldn't he try to strike a deal with the godless heathen? It wasn't as if the French were at *war* with them. . . . "Suppose we fix a meeting in somewhat quieter surroundings."

Ziya Gök Hikmet nodded. "And possibly somewhat more *discreet* surroundings." He glanced meaningfully around the cabaret. "I wouldn't want to insult our delightful hosts by suggesting that the members of the Ottoman Mission come under police surveillance, but . . ." He spread his hands in whimsical surmise.

"A wink is as good as a nod," murmured the MacNair. "Let discretion be our watchword."

Now he and the cheerful young man from the Ottoman Empire sat in a private dining room above a noisy Greek restaurant in the 6th Arrondissement. Heavy plush curtains fell to the richly carpeted floor, muffling the sounds of revel from below. The MacNair was comfortably settled on a plush red settee with his back to the wall so that he faced his host and a cheerful fire in the tiled fireplace. He nodded in qualified approval.

"No one would ever dream of looking for us *here*," laughed Ziya Gök Hikmet. "The hatred of Greeks for Turks is a byword."

"You sound remarkably cheerful about it."

The Turkish diplomat shrugged. "The Greeks hate us—just like all the rest of our empire, the Poles, the Ukrainians, the Hungarians, the Austrians, all those tiresome Balkans. But what precisely can they do about it? Nothing at all! The Greeks have been part of our empire for a thousand years now; they will remain a part for another thousand—whether they hate us or not. In the meantime let us enjoy their great gift to civilization: Greek cooking. Have you ever had their breaded deep-fried cheese as an hors d'oeuvre? Let me recommend it. As well as this bottle of white retsina."

"I thought Turks didn't drink," said the MacNair as he allowed his wineglass to be filled.

"Ha! Only when we're in public—or in Turkey. When we're in Greece—that's another matter! And speaking of wine—I have discussed the matter of your ... champlain—"

"Champagne."

"—champagne with the commercial attaché himself." Ziya Gök Hikmet leaned across the table and lowered his voice. "He was *most* intrigued. He has been in touch with Constantinople. They are *extremely* interested."

"Indeed?" The MacNair drank some of the icy retsina. It tasted exactly as it always had in his own world—like an alcoholic turpentine. He shuddered. "I should not have thought of Constantinople as being a hotbed of wine connoisseurship."

Ziya Gök Hikmet smiled tolerantly. "Ah, how little you know! So much so, my dear Count of Domrémy-la-Pucelle, that the Sultan himself has authorized me, in the strictest confidence, needless to say, to offer you the sum of one million louis d'or for the secret of your process for making champagne."

The MacNair's fingers tightened convulsively around the stem of his wineglass. "One million louis d'or! But that's twenty million francs!"

The emissary from the Ottoman Empire allowed himself a sigh of reluctant admiration. "Monsieur le Comte de Domrémy-la-Pucelle is a determined bargainer. Very well. I am authorized to go as high as *two* million louis d'or. But absolutely no higher, I fear. That is, after all—"

"Forty million francs," breathed the MacNair softly. "Forty million francs!" He gulped the rest of his dreadful retsina and hastily poured another glass. For forty million francs he could buy up everything between Reims and Epernay and have something left over for Burgundy! For forty million francs he could—

Ziya Gök Hikmet sipped delicately from his own glass. "There are, of course, a few minor protocols to be agreed upon."

"Protocols?"

"You would be expected to sojourn for at least a time within our empire."

"Hardly an insurmountable obstacle."

Ziya Gök Hikmet raised his eyes thoughtfully toward the ceiling. "And, of course," he murmured, "merely as an exercise in intellectual curiosity, the Sultan himself would like to have the honor of someday casting an eye upon your extraordinary crown, which—"

"My *crown!*" exclaimed the MacNair in horror. "What do you know about my—"

But the dining room was already filled with the dazzling brilliance of the GODHEAD as it materialized upon the MacNair's head.

Ziya Gök Hikmet gaped in astonishment for no more than a second. Then even as he murmured a soft apology he rose like a tiger and the edge of his stiffened hand slammed into the side of the MacNair's neck. Another five seconds and the still shining GODHEAD had been wrapped in a small blue and red Turkish carpet and the man from the Ottoman Mission had disappeared through the door, his evening an incomparably greater success than ever he had dreamed possible.

CHAPTER
= 32 =

THE MACNAIR FELT himself being vigorously shaken but before he could formulate an angry protest he was suddenly awakened by something cold and wet splashing against his face. Spluttering groggily and shaking all over like a golden retriever, he slowly opened his eyes. Two of Vézelay's plainclothes policemen hovered over him anxiously, one of them holding a glass of potent Greek brandy under his nostrils. The MacNair inhaled the powerful fumes and with the help of the secret-service men painfully pulled himself erect on the settee. His head throbbed and the side of his neck ached abominably. "What happened?" he murmured as he swallowed a cautious mouthful of the fiery brandy.

"We don't know, Monsieur le Comte," replied the policeman who still held the carafe of ice water with which he had been doused. "We had been outside for about twenty minutes when we saw your companion suddenly come shooting out the rear of the building as if the devil himself were nipping at his buttocks. He had something wrapped in his arms and we caught a glimpse of lights flashing, but before we could stop him he jumped into a car and disappeared. Naturally we came to investigate, but all these Turks—"

"Greeks, it's a Greek restaurant."

"Greeks, Turks, whatever they are, they were far from helpful. It took us another ten minutes to find you lying here."

189

"I see," said the MacNair with mounting dismay. So he had been followed after all! He who had taken every conceivable precaution! How was it *possible?* What a nuisance this Vézelay was becoming! What had he ever done to merit such mistrust?

But as the events of his last few moments of consciousness suddenly returned in their ghastly entirety, he fell back against the settee with a sharp gasp. The crown! His GODHEAD! It had actually been in his possession—only to be stolen moments later! And by a Turk! By an emissary of the hated Ottoman Empire! By a secret agent of the Sultan!

Oh, God, what a disaster!

But wait! Could the crown possibly still be switched on? Only minutes had passed since the dastardly attack by Ziya Gök Hikmet. Perhaps disaster could quickly be turned to triumph!

Shutting his eyes, the MacNair leaned his head back against the top of the settee and concentrated his entire being on conjuring up in his mind's eye a vivid image of the blazing GODHEAD pulsing and throbbing with brilliant color. His hands tightened into fists and his face contorted into a grimace as he strained. He could *see* the crown floating before him, so real that he felt he could reach out and pull it to him, and slowly, carefully, gradually increasing the intensity of his command, he *willed* the GODHEAD to him. Beads of sweat popped out on his forehead and he felt his body begin to tremble from the effort. But still the GODHEAD defiantly refused to materialize.

The MacNair slumped back on the settee and groaned feebly as his previous dismay gelled into outright fear. What would his future in France be when the Emperor came to learn of this absurd debacle? Not to speak of the infernal Vézelay! What poison would *he* whisper into the ear of Napoleon V? For it must be reluctantly admitted that to an already biased partisan some of the circumstances of the MacNair's bachelor night out were far from being entirely irreproachable. . . .

Could even the Archduchess Mireille shelter him from their wrath? he wondered desperately.

But once *she* learned that the GODHEAD she herself so

avidly coveted was now in the hands of the Turks—*would* she?

The MacNair let his head fall between his hands, and uttered a despairing groan. He had but a single miserable card to play: He must quickly find a means of bribing these wretched spies before they could report the events of the evening to—

"The Marquis of Vézelay will be here shortly," murmured one of the policemen solicitously. "We telephoned immediately. In the meanwhile is there anything we can do to make you more comfortable? A pillow? A doctor? Another brandy? A blanket? Some hot soup?"

"You are extraordinarily considerate," muttered the MacNair with a ghastly smile. He levered himself up from behind the table and took two halting steps toward the door, his face contorted in pain. "If you would perhaps be so kind as to assist me to the gentlemen's cloakroom . . ."

"At once, Monsieur le Comte!"

No sooner had the door of the second-floor toilet been locked behind him than the MacNair's agonized shuffle and awkward crouch fell away like a cloak as he leapt across the narrow room and carefully slid open the tiny opaque window. He stuck his head into the cold night air to find that he was perched above a darkened alleyway. Peering down into the gloom, he saw that much of it was filled with trash cans but that the area directly below the window was apparently unencumbered.

A moment later he had clambered up onto the metal washbasin and had gingerly maneuvered his legs through the window. His head and torso followed so that he perched precariously on its narrow sill. Twisting about until his entire weight was supported upon his hands, he carefully lowered himself until he dangled at arm's length against the side of the building. Awkwardly he looked down into the alley. At least another seven or eight feet to fall! He moaned softly, but a sudden sharp image of the Marquis of Vézelay spurred him to immediate action. His fingers relaxed their grip and he dropped heavily to the ground. Ignoring the shock that jolted through his feet and knees, he straightened himself up and hobbled quickly to the mouth of the alleyway.

There he peered cautiously around the corner of the building, just in time to see a long black limousine pull up by the sidewalk in front of the restaurant. Hastily he ducked back into the shadows. A moment later he heard the metallic slam of a door, followed by the unmistakable tones of the Marquis of Vézelay. "Wait here, Garigou. I shall probably be returning with our friend the Count of Domrémy-la-Pucelle."

"Very good, Monsieur le Directeur."

His heart thumping loudly in his chest, the MacNair looked back desperately at the far end of the alley. Was there any greater hope in going off in that direction? None that he could see. No more than there was anywhere else in France. . . .

He drew a deep draft of cold damp air into his lungs as he despairingly considered his position. One fact stood out above all the others: *He had to get the crown!*

But already it was probably at the Ottoman Embassy being prepared for shipment to Constantinople in the diplomatic pouch. How long could he tarry here in France while waiting for some accursed Turk to switch it on? And *where* would he tarry? Almost certainly it would no longer be in the arms of the Archduchess Mireille; far more likely in the dungeons of the Marquis of Vézelay on a charge of high treason! The MacNair shuddered. No, that was a fate richly deserved by the Kevin Frosts of the world, but for himself? It was to laugh!

It all came down to the fact that he needed the crown. So much was certain.

And now there seemed but a single way to obtain it. . . .

He let the pent-up air escape from his lungs with a soft hiss as he came to a fateful decision. So be it! he muttered grimly. There was plainly no alternative. . . .

A quick adjustment to his cravat and the MacNair stepped out onto the sidewalk and turned unhesitatingly toward the restaurant in which the Marquis of Vézelay had just disappeared. A few meters ahead of him the secret-police man's Huit Chevaux was parked by the curb, its engine humming quietly. Through its smoked-glass windows he could dimly see the back of the head of the chauffeur sitting stiffly behind the wheel.

The MacNair marched as close to the entrance of the restaurant as he dared, then wheeled sharply and crossed the sidewalk toward the car. By the time the chauffeur turned his head it was to see the MacNair climbing into the rear of his limousine.

"Ah, it's Garigou!" exclaimed the MacNair, pulling the door shut behind him. "How pleasant to see you again. Monsieur le Marquis has been delayed for a spell and has asked you to return me to my residence." The MacNair snuggled deeper into the soft cushions as the car pulled out into traffic. "What a remarkably fine evening, is it not?"

CHAPTER
= 33 =

"You!" cried the Earl of Kensington.

"You?" marveled Sir Norvil Dennett.

"You," muttered Kevin Frost.

"It is I," confirmed Sir Kevin Deane de Courtney Mac-Nair of MacNair. He stood with regal aplomb in the gloom of the great Gothic entrance hall of Garnaway Castle while rainwater dripped from the point of his sleek beard and Benson the butler deftly removed his green plaid inverness coat. A sudden shriek of the bitter November gale pierced the massive stone walls of the castle and the MacNair shivered dramatically. "Surely it must be teatime?" he suggested brightly as he handed his drenched deerstalker to the butler. "Although in my own particular case I believe a large glass of your delectable estate-brewed whiskey will more than suffice. Along, perhaps, with a buttered scone or two." He cast a disarming smile upon the three glowering inhabitants of the castle and let his eye move admiringly about the dark and drafty vastness of the hallway. "How good it is to be back! How I have missed the—"

"This is intolerable!" bellowed Alfred St. John Wester, 7th Earl of Kensington. "You betray us to the French and then you dare—"

"There *is* the matter of a stolen motorcar," pointed out the Master of Garnaway almost apologetically.

"You stole my crown!" hissed Kevin Frost between his teeth.

"Gentlemen, gentlemen!" The MacNair stepped back a pace to regard them with the tolerant good humor of a superior nanny importuned by small but unruly children. "Surely this is not the celebrated Scottish hospitality whose fond memory has sustained me during my many long months of absence! Surely there are more compelling matters of discussion than trivial incidents of the distant past."

"Indeed there are," conceded Dennett as he tugged at the end of his fluffy grey beard. "Where, for instance—"

"—is the—" interrupted Kensington.

"—crown?" concluded Kevin Frost.

"The crown?" The MacNair shook the last remaining drops of water from his beard. "Ah, yes, that tiresome crown! I had imagined that such trifling preoccupations had long since ceased to be of any interest to you. Well, well!" He rubbed his hands briskly. "How good it is to be home again. Now, where *is* that whiskey and scones I distinctly heard you mention? Perhaps when we have warmed the inner man we can turn our thoughts to these other negligible matters."

"Where the devil have you been?" demanded Kensington in a voice devoid of graciousness as they warmed themselves before an enormous fire in the paneled billiards room and devoured the lavishly buttered scones which Benson deftly toasted for them over the flames. "You—or should ▌

say the Count of Domrémy-la-Pucelle?—disappeared from that ruddy palace a month ago, and all of Europe's been like a stirred-up anthill ever since. I am reliably informed that Vézelay is dancing with rage."

The MacNair took a long swallow from his tumbler of pale straw-colored whiskey. "Is he, now? How very gratifying!" He frowned as his mind ran over all that had transpired during the ceaselessly nerve-racking month since he had stepped into the Marquis of Vézelay's chauffeured limousine in the 6th Arrondissement: the desperate encounter with the policeman in Aix-en-Provence; the nightmarish struggle with the perfume smuggler on the stormy seas of the Mediterranean; the devastating betrayal by the preternaturally lovely redhead in Tunisia; the precipitous flight back to Switzerland; the outlandish imposture of the Norwegian burgomaster; the hair's breadth escape from the coastal patrol in Denmark before at last finding blessed sanctuary in England. A month to be excised from the memory!

"Where the devil have I been?" repeated the MacNair. He smiled mysteriously. "You know my methods, Watson," he murmured, and sank his teeth with gusto into a golden scone that overflowed with butter.

"What, what?" The Earl of Kensington turned in bafflement to Sir Norvil Dennett. "What *can* the fellow mean?"

"He means," translated the scientist with complete accuracy, "that he isn't going to tell us. But small matter. Unless he has spent the time in some continental spy school learning new methods of betraying us, it is all really quite immaterial."

"Exactly!" cried the Earl of Kensington. "How do we know that he *hasn't* been sent here by Vézelay to—"

"Your paranoia does you credit," interrupted the MacNair coldly, "but if it is betrayal you seek, I suggest you turn your attention to the gentleman beside you with the peculiarly curled mustachios."

"How dare you!" exclaimed Kevin Frost indignantly, jumping to his feet and gesturing angrily with his scone.

"I should be particularly wary whenever he hands you a drink of his own preparation," confided the MacNair in an aside to the Earl of Kensington. "Like his personality, it tends to be amazingly soporific."

Kevin Frost's eyes bulged with rage but no suitably devastating reply sprang immediately to mind and he sank glowering into his chair, fiercely tugging at his elaborate mustache.

Sir Norvil Dennett sighed plaintively and set down his empty glass. "We shall make no progress with this unseemly bickering." He turned to the MacNair and scrutinized him keenly through his glittering half-moon spectacles. "Let us hold in abeyance for the moment all consideration of your actual status, whether it be Frost, MacNair, Henley, or even Domrémy-la-Pucelle, and come directly to the pith of things: Why, my good man, have you returned to Garnaway Castle?"

The MacNair crossed his legs and leisurely licked the last of the butter from his fingers. "First a question of my own: Why is *that* creature still among you?" He pointed a finger at Kevin Frost. "Surely there is three-star accommodation awaiting his pleasure somewhere in Franklin for the next decade or so?"

"So *you're* the one who betrayed me!" cried Kevin Frost, bouncing once again to his feet. "That's why those confounded policemen have been—"

"Be quiet!" roared the Earl of Kensington. "The question is actually an extremely pertinent one." He turned to the Master of Garnaway. "Why *is* he still here? Kindly refresh my memory, if you will. Before I left for London last month I thought we had agreed—"

"—that he was of no further use to us." Dennett nodded. "But that was *before* he so willfully let the crown out of his possession and before our French friend the Count of Domrémy-la-Pucelle here vanished from Paris with half the French Empire at his heels. It struck me as conceivable that the status of the teleportable crown was still possibly unresolved and that by keeping Frost on hand we might—"

"But that's nonsense!" cried Kensington. "Now that the time machine's finished we no longer care. . . ." His voice slowly tailed off and he blinked uneasily at Dennett.

"And you upbraid *me* for lack of discretion," muttered

the angry scientist, who had a long memory for unflattering gibes. "The fact is—"

"You never told *me*," complained Kevin Frost. "I—"

"The time machine's finished!" shouted the MacNair jubilantly, "the time machine's finished!" He, too, leapt to his feet, but to dance a little jig of delight. The two Englishmen and Kevin Frost regarded him with dour amazement.

"Not entirely," qualified Sir Norvil Dennett cautiously. "There are still—"

"No matter, no matter! I'm sure you'll soon have it in working—"

"If, by any chance, you are thinking that it will be able to restore you to your original universe, I fear that—"

The MacNair waved a dismissive hand. "Of minor importance. Don't you see that the time machine is why I've come back to give you the benefit of my help?"

"Your *help?*" exclaimed the Earl of Kensington, frankly goggling.

"My help," repeated the MacNair with austere dignity. "As you may or may not be aware, thanks to your ignorant meddling with my personal possessions—totally without my authorization, I must point out—the crown by which you set so much store, and for which you were at one point even about to subject me to the basest tortures—"

"A lie!" gasped Kensington.

"Never!" denied Dennett.

"Entirely suitable!" exclaimed Kevin Frost, his eyes gleaming with delight.

"Thanks to your unwarranted interference, I say, the ruddy crown is now in the possession of the—*Turks!*"

Kensington moaned despairingly. "The Turks! How did—"

"No matter," said the MacNair firmly. "The point is, they have it. And I want it back! Since it is clearly the fault of the inhabitants of this castle, I have returned to Garnaway so that they may restore it to me." His flashing brown eyes moved from Dennett to Kensington and back again. "Is that quite, *quite* clear?"

"Entirely, Your High—" began Dennett, who caught

himself, flushed slightly, and finished weakly, "entirely clear."

The fleshy jowls of the Earl of Kensington quivered angrily. "But even if we *wanted* to restore your confounded crown—even granted that it *is* yours to restore, which I do not at all concede—what makes you think that we *could* restore it?"

"Succinctly and accurately put," seconded the Master of Garnaway.

The MacNair cocked his head to study the two men as if they had taken complete leave of their senses. "The fact that you have a functioning time machine, or will have one in the near future, suggests nothing at all to you?"

The Earl of Kensington turned to exchange a glance with Sir Norvil. "What does the time machine have to do with the crown? It's to get rid of Napoleon Bonaparte, not—"

"—to look for missing crowns," finished the scientist, but his brows were wrinkled in thought.

"What he means, you titled nitwits," interjected Kevin Frost rudely, "is why don't you use the machine to go back in time and collect the crown *before* it gets stolen by the Turks?"

CHAPTER
= 34 =

FORTY-TWO MEN had gathered in the high-ceilinged council room just off the vast armory which composed the south wing of Garnaway Castle. Heavily mullioned windows looked out on a bleak winter landscape, and blazing fires leapt high in the great fireplaces at either end of the room. Six enormous brass chandeliers hung from the smoke-darkened ceiling, their thick yellow candles laboriously lighted earlier in the day by a team of footmen. Twelve suits of polished armor stood guard along the wall, and a ceremonial mace lay at the head of the table before the Master of Garnaway, Sir Norvil Dennett.

To the right of Dennett sat the tweed-clad figure of Kensington, to his left Lord Avery of Eventon. Beyond Eventon was Sir Charles Ritcher, the parliamentary leader of the Yeoman Sons of Essex, who had arrived in Cawdor by private train the night before, along with the Marquess of Landsbury and five other Members of Parliament, as well as seven of the party's County Leaders.

The fourteen theoreticians and technicians who had labored with Dennett in the castle's laboratories for the past two years were present, flanking the single German scientist fortunate enough to have been away from Düsseldorf the day Herr Hubmaier had triumphantly blown himself and the rest of the members of the Friends of Goethe Society into total oblivion.

A delegation from the twenty-nine states and principalities which made up the loose confederation known as Germany was led by Prince Konrad of Schleswig-Holstein and the Grand Dukes of Thuringia and Württemberg. The others were Herr Doctor Professor Heinrich Anzengruber, the seminal philosopher of the University of Heidelberg, and four stout industrialists, all of whom had managed to evade the net which the Marquis of Vézelay had spread for dangerous Teutonic subversives and nationalists following the explosion in Düsseldorf.

The MacNair of MacNair, wrapped in an almost perceptible aura of royalty, and Kevin Frost glared at each other from the far ends of the table.

"We have recently had occasion to reconsider the possible dangers of temporal paradoxes," began Sir Norvil Dennett, directing a stony glare at the MacNair. The MacNair raised a supercilious eyebrow in return. How galling had been his fruitless argument for the past three weeks that a letter should be sent back in time to warn him not to dine with that accursed Turk at that unspeakable Greek restaurant!

What a simple, *sensible* course of action!

The MacNair gritted his teeth.

Had not Kevin Frost then immediately spoiled it by proposing that he, Frost, be returned to the Earl of Kensington's bedroom in the Black Tower in order to retrieve the GODHEAD from its hiding place beneath the bathtub?

An angry stalemate had finally ensued when Sir Norvil Dennett stubbornly held out for a simple warning to himself and Kensington—not to turn on the crown in their basement laboratory!

The MacNair cracked his knuckles with a loud, derisive pop. How frustrating it was to find one's very destiny in the hands of lackwits like Dennett and Frost!

The Master of Garnaway turned his eyes away from the infuriating impostor from another universe and continued his remarks. "Even so simple a matter as trying to retrieve a certain object from a period of two months ago has provoked the most intense scrutiny and shown itself to be fraught with peril. If, for instance, that object of which I speak *had* been retrieved, then this very conclave might never have been convoked, and who can imagine how all our personal lives might have been changed thereby? You, Landsbury, instead of sitting here placidly before the fire, *you* might even now be lying dead on a mortuary slab in London, the sad victim of a motor accident in the fog. . . ."

"What!" cried the Marquess, his ruddy cheeks paling.

Sir Norvil Dennett nodded ponderously. "And who knows what other ghastly changes to the time stream we may set loose by carelessly trying to undo the course of history, especially so drastic a course as the murder of Napoleon Bonaparte!"

"But if we can't kill old Boney," muttered a grizzled Scots technician who had labored two years in the underground laboratories of Garnaway Castle, "then what's the use of our bonny machine? What's the point of gathering us here to discuss what we're *not* going to do with it?"

"But we *are* going to do something with it," cried the MacNair, unable to contain his wrath. "We are going to use it to send a message to ourselves in Paris so that—"

"Never!" interrupted Sir Norvil Dennett fervently. "I'll *destroy* the machine before I allow it to be perverted for shoddy personal gain for such as yourself!"

"But—"

The Master of Garnaway sat back in his great chair with absolute finality. "The matter is hereby closed. Now, then, returning once again to the question of Napoleon, it is my considered opinion that ever since the inauguration of our project, we have perhaps been overly concerned with changing the entire course of European history since the fatal Battle of the Cotswold Encirclement. But is it not true that our *real* concern is actually the state of the present world *today?* It is *today* that we suffer under the heel of the tyrant in Paris. And it is this *today*—as it affects us personally— that it is essential to change." Sir Norvil Dennett looked slowly around the hushed room. "Let us suppose, then, if only for the sake of discussion, that instead of killing Napoleon we *kidnap* him!"

"Kidnap him?" exclaimed Sir Charles Ritcher incredulously. "What on earth do you mean?"

"I mean that we remove him from some point in time in which his absence is unlikely to be noticed. We then hold him disentimed in a time bubble outside of time itself, present a set of demands to the present-day French in Paris, and wait for their response. If they are foolish enough not to meet them—well, we still have Napoleon sitting in his bubble. . . ."

Why, the Earl of Kensington had demanded above the ensuing hubbub, was it necessary to find some particular time in which the tyrant could be abstracted from the time stream without his absence being noticed? Why couldn't the time machine simply pick him up during his sleep at 10:30 in the evening of July 1, 1800, for instance, sequester him in his time bubble for however many weeks it took the Yeoman Sons of Essex to negotiate a ransom with Paris, and then return him peacefully to his bed at 10:31 in the same evening of July 1, 1800? "For if you can't do *that,*" declared Kensington dogmatically, "then I don't see what good this so-called time machine really is."

The Master of Garnaway exchanged pained looks with his fellow scientists. "A fair enough question," he sighed, "but our initial tests—*extremely* cautious tests, I might add—definitely indicate that there exists what I might call a Conservation of Time. Once the time machine is used to initially disrupt already past time, all future operations of the machine are limited strictly by the linearity of time that passes *here in our own laboratories.* If, for example, we were to descend to the laboratories this very moment and use the machine to return in time half an hour ago to gather up that decanter of sherry which lies on the sideboard to my left and to bring it forward to our own present time for seven minutes, let us say, we would subsequently be obliged to return it to its previous location precisely seven minutes later than we had taken it."

"You are saying," asked Sir Miles Butterworth, County Leader for Huntingdonshire, "that if we were to snatch up Napoleon at 10:30 P.M., July 1, 1800, and keep him here in the twentieth century for nine days *our time,* we would then be obliged to return him at precisely 10:30 P.M. on July *10?*"

"Such, I fear, is the case," conceded Dennett with a sigh. "The weight of the Conservation of Time would appear to demand it."

"But what happens if you simply *don't?*" demanded Kensington irascibly. "Suppose you say, 'I'm bloody well *going* to put him back on July *3* and that's the way it's going to be!'"

Sir Norvil Dennett had to smile in spite of himself. "That might be what you'd *say,* my dear fellow, but that wouldn't be what you'd *get.* Once you turned on the machine and sent him on his way you'd discover that, like it or not, he would end up reappearing in his own era precisely that amount of time later which he had spent in ours."

"You mean you could *try* to send him back to July 3 but that he'd *still* be returned to July 10?"

"In all our experiments such has been the case."

The Earl of Kensington ran his hands across his shiny scalp in baffled frustration. "Then what *can* we do?"

The scientist tapped his finger upon the table. "The only possible solution is to find a period in which we *can* take Napoleon from the time stream without upsetting all of subsequent history."

Old Lord Evergreen, celebrated as an amateur authority on the life of the first Napoleon, now gathered his forces sufficiently to inflict upon the group an exquisitely detailed disquisition as to why July of 1806 would be the single most propitious moment for the Corsican adventurer to be discreetly removed from his own era.

For it was in that particular month, said Lord Evergreen, that the tyrant had returned from a triumphant tour of a conquered England, suddenly and shockingly divorced his wife the Empress Joséphine, and then completely disappeared from the public eye for the next twenty-three months. At the time, it had created no great stir, but subsequently no completely satisfactory explanation had ever been advanced for the so-called Missing Years, though dozens of historians had devoted their lives to it. Had the all-powerful Emperor suffered a nervous breakdown? A near-fatal illness? A lapse into melancholy or mysticism? Nothing in the voluminous records of imperial Versailles and Paris seemed to hold the answer.

Whatever the reason, at the end of two years Napoleon had reappeared in public with dramatic suddenness, now accompanied by a beautiful woman of mysterious origin, the future Empress Alexine. After their spectacularly lavish wedding in Paris the Emperor resisted any further temptation to lead his hitherto invincible army to a final confrontation with the Ottoman Empire for the total mastery of Europe and Asia. To the dismay of his military commanders, he forsook the arts of war and settled down instead with the Empress Alexine to engender the eleven healthy children who would marry into the royal lines of every state of western Europe. The Emperor was now little seen in public, but for the four decades he reigned before abdicating on his eightieth birthday in favor of his eldest son, Valérie, Napoleon II, he quietly and efficiently worked to impose the reins of French tyranny over a superficially peaceful and prosperous United States of Europe.

"So if ever you want to seize the Emperor," summed up Lord Evergreen, his eyes glinting with excitement, "the Missing Years is the time to do it. But I say," he added wistfully, "if you *should* happen to bag old Boney and pop him into this time bubble of yours, do you suppose you might arrange for me to have a chat or two with the fellow? There are so *many* things I'd like to ask. . . ."

As the MacNair and Kevin Frost continued to glare at each other, uniformed footmen now served coffee and liqueurs while the butler Benson circled the table with a silver tray on which he offered an assortment of cigars and snuff. Fresh logs were thrown on the already blazing fires in the massive fireplaces at either end of the room and for several minutes no one spoke while they swirled their cognac or thirty-year-old Scotch liqueur in gleaming snifters and somnolently watched the blue curls of their cigar smoke drift upward to the heavily beamed ceiling.

At last Reginald St. George Dieudonné, who in spite of his name was a longtime Yeoman Son of Essex and the County Leader for Westmoreland, raised the point that had been troubling him. "But, damn it all, Dennett," he protested, "when one comes right *down* to it, why is it any less dangerous removing old Boney from this time stream than it is simply bumping the blister off? Just because a bunch of confounded historians like Evergreen here spout nonsense about the blighter's Missing Years doesn't mean the bloke was actually *missing* all that time, does it? We all of us know very well he was sitting right there in his ruddy palace, playing whist perhaps, or twiddling his thumbs, but nevertheless *there!* It's just that he didn't care to show his face in public. Are you seriously suggesting that if we take him out of his palace for two entire years no one is going to *notice?*"

"Hmmm," mused the Master of Garnaway, stroking his thick grey beard, "I feel you exaggerate with your emphasis upon 'two entire years,' for almost certainly any plan such as I have proposed could be carried out in a matter of a few weeks at the longest, but I must admit that the point is well taken. Such a gap of even a few weeks would undoubtedly—"

"Ha!" cried Angus McFergus, the tall angular theoretician who had been the first to be recruited by Dennett for his research team. "If that's the only problem, why don't we just *replace* old Boney while we've got him sitting in his time bubble." He raised a knobby finger and pointed it straight at a drowsy Kevin Frost. "Wouldn't you say that if only he hadn't these unco mustachios, this wee laddie from across the sea would be the dead spit of Napoleon Bonaparte himself?"

CHAPTER
= 35 =

"PREPOSTEROUS!" CRIED Kevin Frost, aghast, his hands instinctively leaping up to shield his precious mustachios from the predatory scissors and razors of Garnaway Castle. Instantly he rallied to point out the obvious: If *he* resembled Napoleon, then so did the uncouth creature who called himself Prince William Ernest Augustus. "Shave off that moth-eaten beard of his and see for yourselves!" he commanded with a tremolo in his voice.

But the MacNair's own defenses were superbly organized. If *he* were in the nineteenth century masquerading as Napoleon Bonaparte, he countered, who then would be here in the twentieth, instantly alert to return to Garnaway Castle his teleportable crown the moment some unwary Turkish busybody chanced to switch it on two thousand miles away? For it was obvious that the security of the British Isles demanded that the crown be retrieved before the Ottoman Empire could wrest from it the secrets which might catapult them to domination of the entire world. . . .

"Absolutely," agreed Prince Konrad of Schleswig-Holstein. "In all this discussion of Napoleon Bonaparte we must never lose sight of His Highness's crown." The eyes around the table returned to Kevin Frost.

"Well, I won't do it," he declared defiantly, sitting back in his chair with folded arms, "and that's that!"

"You won't, eh?" muttered the Earl of Kensington. He

turned to Sir Norvil Dennett. "Why don't you have the sergeant at arms step in? He can keep him in one of the dungeons until the constabulary arrive from Forres to serve that warrant that arrived from Franklin last week. As a justice of the peace you are quite empowered to do so." He cocked his head quizzically. "That *was* thirteen years in jail, wasn't it?" he asked Kevin Frost mildly. "Or was it seventeen? Do you know, I've quite forgotten."

Just as Adolf Hitler, the holy embodiment of all that was Germanic, was in actuality an Austrian of humble birth, so was Napoleon Bonaparte as much Italian as French. For the future Emperor of France had been born Napoleone Buonaparte on the Mediterranean island of Corsica in the year 1769, the same year in which that island of perpetual troublemakers had been ceded to France by their longtime Genoese masters with a collective sigh of relief. It was not until the diminutive Corsican was a twenty-seven-year-old general in the army of the Revolution that the spelling of his name had changed to Bonaparte. *What, then, was Napoleon's French accent?* Such was the vital question posed to the Napoleonic scholar Lord Evergreen.

No clear-cut answer was forthcoming, and it was the MacNair who rolled his eyes in exasperation and suggested that a recording device be returned to the palace of Fontainebleau in the early days of the nineteenth century to find out at first hand. Three weeks later four masters of phonetics and linguistics took up residence at Garnaway and began their efforts to replace Kevin Frost's atrocious French-Canadian accent with that of Corsica and the eighteenth-century Paris where the young Buonaparte had begun his schooling.

"Say *oui.*"

"*Ouais.*"

"*Oui!*"

"*Ouais!*"

The eminent phoneticians threw up their hands in dismay while the MacNair looked on derisively from an armchair in a darkened corner of the study. How grotesque were Kevin Frost's ludicrous attempts to shuck off the barbaric accents of his youth! How unlike his own mellifluous tones of southern France!

"Out!" cried Kevin Frost, suddenly spotting the MacNair in the shadows. "Out at once!"

"Oui, monsieur," replied the MacNair in the authentic voice of an eighteenth-century Corsican of lofty birth, *"oui, oui, oui. A votre service, mon cher damoiseau."* And he left the study with a sardonic chuckle.

How curious it was, reflected the MacNair as he strolled pensively through the cold drafty passages of Garnaway Castle while outside its mullioned windows a light snow fell from a leaden January sky, that three dozen supposedly rational men could lend their support to such a ludicrous scheme! Could anything be more grotesque than the notion of a clean-shaven Kevin Frost, small-time bigamist and maladroit con man, being sent back in time to impersonate the greatest historical figure of the ages?

But it was more than merely grotesque—it was actively dangerous! Not only dangerous for his slapstick doppelgänger Kevin Frost should he be unmasked by the intimates and immediate family of the man he was proposing to replace, *but no less for the very people responsible for sending him back in time!*

For an unsettling thought had occurred to the MacNair as he encountered the Earl of Kensington and Sir Norvil Dennett earnestly discussing shotguns in the gun room a few days after the gathering in the council room. "How do you intend to prove to the French that you actually *have* Napoleon?"

The Earl of Kensington smiled over the engraved barrel of a gleaming shotgun in a manner that left the MacNair distinctly uneasy. "I have no doubt that Dennett here will be taking photographs and so forth." His smile broadened. "But beyond that, you yourself will bear witness to the actual process, then *you* will be our emissary to the French with our list of demands. For whom could the French possibly find more trustworthy than His Royal Highness Prince William Ernest Augustus?"

"Absurd!" cried the MacNair, blanching at the thought of the Marquis of Vézelay and the Archduchess Mireille.

"Surely you grow eager to return to the arms of your beloved Mireille? If not, I feel sure that your comrade Kevin Frost could be encouraged to do so with only a modicum of effort, while you yourself were returned to the Fontainebleau of 1806."

"You forget: My place is here at Garnaway Castle, in order to secure the return of my crown from Constantinople," was the MacNair's cold reply. "Such was the decision of the entire assembly of the Friends of Bordeaux Wine. So let us have no more idle talk of my going to Paris to act as your go-between in a sordid kidnaping. Nothing could be more repugnant." The MacNair stalked indignantly as far as the door, then halted and turned with a frown wrinkling his lofty forehead. "But in connection with your fanciful scheme, another objection suggests itself: Suppose the French concede that you do indeed have their beloved Napoleon—and *still* refuse to accede to your demands?"

"Preposterous!"

"Unthinkable!"

The MacNair sniffed skeptically. "I fear you greatly underestimate the natural perversity of the French. I urge you to at least consider my question as a possible hypothesis. I repeat: What, then?"

"What, then?" The Earl of Kensington frowned and turned to Dennett for guidance. But the scientist shrugged in bewilderment. "What, then? Then I suppose that we—reluctantly—dispose of the hostage."

"And in so doing, two centuries of European history undo themselves?"

"Possibly, possibly."

"But suppose that in doing so, it flicks all of you—and, of far greater consequence, even *me*—completely out of existence?"

The ruddy complexion of the Earl of Kensington grew a trifle paler. *"That,"* he said firmly, "is a risk we shall all have to live with."

Not so, mused the MacNair with smug satisfaction as he came to the upstairs library and helped himself to a preluncheon glass of golden sherry from the decanter that sat beneath the Gainsborough portrait of a distant forebear of Sir Norvil Dennett. For his stroll through the castle's corridors had suddenly been crowned by inspiration. The answer to his vexatious question was both simple and irrefutably logical: The dire possibility of being suddenly flicked out of existence was a risk with which everyone in this particular world would have to live—*except for himself.*

For hadn't *he*—and he alone—been demonstrably and inalterably born *in another universe?* How, then, could even the most drastic of changes in the fabric of this present world conspire to undo the fact of his own birth in another? No, no, it was clearly impossible!

His mind at rest, the MacNair cheerfully poured himself another tot of sherry. Clearly he had nothing to worry about!

CHAPTER
$=36=$

As THE ICY month of January, and then of February, passed drearily, Kevin Frost grew increasingly morose and fitful in the profound and ever more detailed study of the Emperor's accent and habits, his exasperatingly numerous brothers and sisters, his scores of advisers and intimates from the army and the government, his decrees and *pensées,* his military campaigns and mistresses.

Did any of these titled English nits actually believe that he—a civilized gentleperson of the late twentieth century—would manage to survive their wild scheme to cast him back into the savagery of early nineteenth-century France? Little matter that he would live in a palace of a luxuriousness beyond present-day conception!

For even if this mad impersonation were to deceive those hundreds of people who enjoyed daily contact with the authentic Emperor of France, how was he, Kevin Frost, to deal with the total absence of hygiene and antibiotics in those far-off days of unplumbed palaces and unpasteurized milk?

Dressed and undressed by a regiment of valets and chamberlains, how would he be able to brush and floss both morning and evening?

Or swallow his five capsules of vitamins and minerals at breakfast time?

Did the Emperor Napoleon jog religiously five kilometers every morning through the royal park of Fontainebleau? According to the eminent Lord Evergreen, definitely *not*.

But what, then, of Kevin Frost's vital cholesterol count?

And had the concept of the bathtub even been *conceived*?

Didn't the nobility of this era merely splash themselves with a beaker of perfume every other week or so when their ripeness became too unbearable for even their own desensitized noses?

Such were the questions that filled Kevin Frost with the profoundest misgivings.

He gritted his teeth in anger. Coerced by the foulest sort of blackmail, he would be exposed to the most intolerable perils while the mortal enemy who was personally responsible for his predicament would be laughing at his misery from the safety of modern-day Paris, where he dallied in the arms of that ethereal love-goddess, the Archduchess Mireille of Luxembourg.

It was not to be borne!

Kevin Frost paced the floor of the enormous bedroom of gilt and crystal and dark red velour which had been reproduced at appalling cost in exact imitation of the splendor of the Emperor's marble sleeping quarters in the palace of Fontainebleau. Already his superb mustachios had been wantonly destroyed and a small but discernible paunch had been acquired through a grossly unhealthy regime of unrestrained gluttony. His hair had been allowed to grow so that now it swept across the top of his broad forehead in a long flowing lock. He wore a fanciful costume of tight white breeches which accentuated the plumpness of his belly, a grey jacket which was purposely cut away to accentuate the chemise of soft green velour with its front of ruffled white lace, and glossy black boots against which the tails of his coat constantly brushed.

Kevin Frost stared gloomily out the window at the dismal February afternoon. From the moment he awoke on his lumpy mattress to the moment his weary head fell against his pillow his entire life was now circumscribed by the constraints of Napoleonic lore. In just a few minutes he could look forward to a tedious examination by old Lord Evergreen about the details of his supposed relationship, both personal and political, with his youngest sister, Maria Annunciata Caroline, 1782–1843, born in—

Kevin Frost groaned. How could he ever have allowed himself to be reduced to such a piteous state? And—what could he do to extricate himself from these perilous straits?

Even as he idly watched the swirling gusts of snowflakes, the startlingly simple solution to his loathsome predicament suddenly presented itself. Automatically his fingers came up to twirl the magnificent mustache that no longer existed. The corners of his lips twitched, then broadened into a toothy smile as he considered the rich ironic justice of the scheme. A soft chuckle became a full-throated laugh and Kevin Frost slapped his thigh in delight.

Hadn't he once before been able to turn his knowledge of certain recondite branches of the pharmacopoeia to his own benefit and the confusion of his enemies?

With a final chuckle he threw himself upon the deplorable imperial bed. Let old Lord Evergreen wait with his confounded school lessons. There was still much to be considered!

Sir Kevin Deane de Courtney MacNair of MacNair ran his fingers through his sleek brown beard and yawned lengthily. How strange it was to see his almost identical self sitting at the dinner table of Garnaway Castle dressed in the nineteenth-century togs of the mighty Emperor! And how disconcertingly cheerful Kevin Frost had been on this, the very eve of his momentous departure into the mysteries of Time!

The MacNair shook his head wonderingly and crossed his icy bedroom to the dark mahogany sideboard beneath a spurious Vandyke which had long ago become invisible beneath its successive coats of darkened varnish. Loosening his cravat, he tossed it onto the four-poster bed piled high with blankets and comforters, devoutly hoping that the maid had remembered to place the hot-water bottle in the foot of the bed. He shivered and lifted the gleaming crystal stopper from the cut-glass decanter of whiskey on the sideboard, then poured out a modest two fingers of the pale liquid for his usual evening nightcap. A splash of peat-colored water from its companion decanter and the Mac-Nair stretched out on his bed to reconsider the events of the day.

A few minutes after dinner he had followed the Earl of Kensington and the Master of Garnaway down the steps to the basement laboratory where the full complement of the castle's technicians prepared to disentime the Emperor of France and encapsulate him in a time bubble. "Aren't you coming?" asked Sir Norvil Dennett of the startling Napoleonic look-alike who lingered at the table.

"Not I," said Kevin Frost, glancing up at the grandfather clock that stood in a distant corner. "If this mad scheme of yours to disentime the Emperor actually succeeds, which I frankly doubt, I see no reason at all to wait about in your cellars until three in the morning to be loaded into your confounded machine." He reached for the decanter of fifty-year-old port. "Another glass of port, then it's off to bed for a few hours' sleep." He fixed the Earl of Kensington with an imperious eye. "You may awaken me at 2:45, no sooner."

Somewhat to the MacNair's surprise the disengagement of Napoleon Bonaparte from his imperial bed in the palace of Fontainebleau proceeded exactly as Dennett had planned. It was now 11:30 on the Continent, and the Emperor, who was a notoriously early riser, had, on the fateful evening of July 27, 1806, retired to his private quarters some hours before.

Now a small mattress was carefully aligned on the floor of the gleaming chrome apparatus which stood in the middle of the laboratory, bristling with cables and instrumentation. The lights were dimmed and the power which had been built up throughout the evening in special accumulators carefully monitored. At last Dennett signaled that all was in readiness. A switch was thrown and with a flicker of lights the time machine began to glow with a soft blue luminosity. Hardly perceptible at first, a keening whine grew louder and louder until the MacNair feared the machinery was about to explode.

"Now!" cried Dennett suddenly, stabbing a red button on the bench before him. Even as the echoes of his cry still rang in his ears, the MacNair was startled by the instantaneous appearance in the middle of the time machine of a naked form huddled on the waiting mattress in the attitude of peaceful sleep. His chest rose and fell in regular rhythm and a faint snore escaped his partially open lips. Long lank hair concealed much of his face, but not for a second did the MacNair doubt that this diminutive figure was the Goliath of the ages, Napoleon Bonaparte himself.

The MacNair shook his head groggily against the mass of pillows behind him, then raised the half-forgotten glass from where it sat on his soft woolen weskit and took another long swallow of his nightcap. How tired he had suddenly become! His eyelids seemed to have taken on the weight of bags of concrete. Could he have had a glass of wine too many at dinner? Or have somehow been affected by the mysterious forces at Sir Norvil Dennett's command which had suddenly encased a still sleeping Napoleon in a perfectly spherical silver bubble? Seconds later, even as the MacNair still gaped in astonishment, the glittering, semi-opaque bubble had momentarily flickered within the structure of the time machine, then vanished with its precious cargo in a wink, leaving only a glowing apparatus now devoid of even its mattress. *Could* it have had some residual side effects? Nonsen—

He found himself yawning loudly and realized that once again he had nearly fallen asleep. With a mighty effort he lifted the glass and let the rest of the incomparably smooth Scotch slide down his throat. His eyes closed for only a moment. How tiresome it was to rise and brush his teeth! In just a moment he would . . .

"Look at him!" cried the Earl of Kensington indignantly. "Dead to the world!"

"As drunk as a lord, you might say," sardonically observed Angus McFergus, who secretly harbored dangerous notions of a severely egalitarian nature.

"But the man's completely incapable!" shouted the Earl in a rage, furiously shaking Kevin Frost's shoulder so that his head snapped back and forth like a puppet's. "Pour some water on him! Slap his face! Twist his toes! Don't just stand there, McFergus, *do* something!"

But there was nothing to be done except call Dennett up from his post in the laboratory where he had been recharging the time machine for its task of sending Kevin Frost back to the now-empty bed of Napoleon Bonaparte in the early morning hours of July 28, 1806.

Sir Norvil Dennett stood by the side of the ornate canopied bed on which the form of Kevin Frost lolled unconscious, still fully clad in the Napoleonic costume which he had worn to dinner. A half-empty decanter of port sat in a pool of sticky red wine on the white marble floor next to the bed, along with an overturned glass. "Drunk himself into a stupor," murmured Dennett, running his hand through his fluffy grey beard. "We should have kept a closer eye on him after all. But he seemed to be doing so well."

The Earl of Kensington snorted incredulously. "Well! Ha! The question is: What do we do *now?*"

The Master of Garnaway turned to him with mild surprise. "Do? We lug his guts down to the laboratory, place him on the mattress, and at precisely 3:04 P.M. we send him back to Fontainebleau, where, entirely naked, he will materialize in the bed of the Emperor of All the French and All the Rest of It."

Kensington blinked in surprise. "We do? In that condition? Is that possible? I should have thought—"

But Dennett had already reached down and with a startling display of strength easily slung the diminutive form over his shoulder. "Really, Kensington," he muttered irritably, "I'm surprised at you. You *know* we have to send him back at 3:04! I've explained it over and over! What difference does it make if he's conscious or unconscious when we load him into the machine? Do you really think I'd let a miserable toad like this thwart our plans as easily as that? For if we *don't* adhere to our precise schedule, we risk—"

"Oh, very well," conceded the Earl sullenly. "I suppose you know what you're doing."

Sir Norvil Dennett stopped at the door to stare at Kensington coldly. "Let us hope that *you* know equally well what *you* are doing when you begin your negotiations with the tyrants in Paris for the return of this miserable creature!" His half-moon spectacles glittered brightly. "For if you don't, I imagine that our French friends will find a way to make all of us devoutly regret that we ourselves did not return to the peaceful days of 1806!"

CHAPTER
= 37 =

A TERRIBLE THROBBING battered the MacNair's temples.
Slowly, groggily, he felt himself swimming up from the
stifling embrace of a tormented sleep and into a dazed
semiconsciousness. His tongue was thick and furry and his
eyelids seemed glued together. He knew without opening
them that the darkness about him would be absolute. A
harsh thirst parched his throat and mouth, while warm
sticky sweat trickled along his naked body. He groaned
weakly and buried his pounding head deeper into the
pillow. What could he possibly have drunk to—

He bolted upright in the blackness with a sudden terrified
start that set his head spinning and his heart pounding
violently against his chest. That whiskey! This awesome,
almost godlike hangover—surely he had experienced its
equal only once before in his life: that ghastly morning he
had awakened with a shaven head in the back seat of a
police car of the State of Franklin!

His puffy eyes still glued together, the MacNair slowly,
fearfully, raised a trembling hand to his chin. . . .

His heart lurched a second time and with a soft cry he fell
back into the soft embrace of fluffy pillows. Once again his
chin was clean-shaven, once again he must have been duped
by that apparently cretinous doppelgänger, the odious
Kevin Frost! Yet *another* Mickey Finn must have somehow
been introduced into his whiskey. . . . In spite of the physi-

cal torments that assailed him, the MacNair could feel his cheeks burning. The humiliation of it, that *he,* the MacNair of MacNair, could be so disdainfully manipulated!

Only now, instead of awaking in 1991 Franklin, he knew with dreadful certainty that if he dared to open his eyes he would find himself in the Napoleonic France of 1806—in the persona of the almighty Emperor himself!

The MacNair pulled a pillow over his head and dug himself deeper into the lumpy mattress. Sleep! he commanded himself despairingly, sleep! When eventually you awake to your icy bedroom in Garnaway Castle, you will find that all of this has been nothing more than a terrible dream. . . .

When the MacNair awoke for the second time, the throbbing in his head had subsided and his eyelids had become unglued. Warily he opened them and saw that he was in a dim underground chamber of some sort, its outlines only dimly discernible in the suffused crimson light that bathed it. An underground chamber? Suddenly his eyes refocused and he saw clearly that he was in the canopied bed of Napoleon's great marble bedchamber in the palace of Fontainebleau. Late morning light barely penetrated thick crimson curtains that stood four meters high. The walls were the same polished marble inlaid with damask panels of yellow and blue silk that the manic Earl of Kensington had re-created for Kevin Frost in Dennett's bleak Scottish castle on the Firth of Moray.

The MacNair fell back with a despairing sigh. So his worst fears were true: he *had* been outwitted by his imbecilic-seeming doppelgänger! Would he *never* learn? He sighed again, from the very depths of his soul, and his face contorted with frustrated rage. The chances of ever again encountering Kevin Frost in order to exact a gruesome revenge were more than merely remote, they were infinitesimal! Abandoned here in 1806, he would simply have to swallow his wounded pride.

Not to mention, of course, having to cope with this tedious and almost incalculably dangerous business of suddenly being thrust into the clothes of the Emperor Bonaparte himself. . . .

But not quite literally, the MacNair corrected himself: He was at the moment actually quite naked. He turned back the pale lilac sheets of glossy satin and discovered in the depths of the bed a wrinkled white flannel nightgown which must have been left behind by the original Emperor upon his being disentimed earlier in the evening. The MacNair pulled it over his head and came to a decision. Sooner or later he would have to expose himself to the world of 1806; there was nothing to be gained by putting it off any further. With a final sigh he reached across the pillows to reluctantly pull the tasseled cord that hung beside his bed.

A liveried footman in a powdered wig glided silently through the deep shadows of the darkened bedchamber and bowed solemnly in the direction of the imperial couch. Then wraithlike, he turned toward the curtains.

"No," grunted the MacNair from the depths of his bed, where he lay hidden with the covers pulled over his chin and a forearm across his lofty forehead, "leave them as they are. Just bring my breakfast—and a large carafe of water. Here, in bed."

"At once, Your Imperial Majesty."

A few minutes later he watched through slitted eyelids as three more footmen in identical black and green livery marched with stiff dignity into the murky light of the bedchamber. The first carried an elaborate gilded tray with a number of covered dishes, the second a silver platter upon which reposed a steaming silver teapot, the third a silver platter with a crystal carafe and a tulip-shaped glass.

They were supervised by a tall grave servant of decidedly superior mien who wore a tight-fitting blue suit with a front of ruffled lace and bright red leggings. His craggy chin had been dusted with talc to ineffectually conceal the stubble of a heavy beard, and wiry black hair poked around the edges of his elaborate powdered peruke. With curt gestures and incisive snaps of his fingers the majordomo silently directed the placing of the tray over the imperial lap and the pouring of hot chocolate and clear water.

The MacNair took a deep swallow of the cool water and then another. Nothing in his entire life had ever tasted so good. He waited until the three underservants had departed, drank again, then finally spoke warily to the impassive maître d'hôtel who stood respectfully in the dark gloom behind the head of the canopied bed. "I shall be spending the day in bed," he said in a harsh whisper.

The majordomo's lugubrious face contorted in sudden worry. "Does Your Imperial Majesty wish to be waited upon by the Count of Lyon?" he asked with the thick accents of Napoleon's native Corsica.

"The leech?" The MacNair shuddered at the thought of being treated by an eighteenth-century doctor and his notions of medical practice. Not for nothing were they called leeches! "Absolutely not." He looked down at his tray and his stomach roiled at the sight of the fluffy croissants on their silver plate. A thin bile rose to his mouth, but he lifted a small steaming cup of overly sweet chocolate and cautiously sipped at it until his stomach settled and his head began to clear.

As he spread fresh sweet butter from a deep silver dish onto the first of the croissants, the MacNair's naturally ebullient spirits began to revive even in the cool reddish gloom of this outrageously opulent bedchamber. So he was to be Napoleon, was he? Then Napoleon he would be!

He chewed with increasing gusto. The first step was obvious. Undoubtedly it would be totally unjust to that inoffensive Empress, Napoleon's wife Joséphine, but which came first: the safety of the MacNair, or the feelings of a woman who had already been dead some 150 years? The answer was plain.

He took another sip of hot chocolate. What of the Emperor's enormous family? Therein surely lay his greatest danger. "The Empress Joséphine," he murmured around a mouthful of soft buttery croissant. "She is still in residence at Malmaison? Hmmm. And Madame Mère—there is no word of her return from Rome? A pity. My four beloved brothers—none of them are near at hand? Alas! And my three excellent sisters—refresh my memory as to their whereabouts. Ha! Madrid, Warsaw, and Oslo, how far away they all seem to be!" He paused in thought for a long moment. So all was as he vaguely remembered old Lord Evergreen instructing Kevin Frost: The Emperor's wife was in her own lavish palace on the other side of Paris, his tiny

Corsican mother was in Rome hobnobbing with the Pope and an adoring retinue of Cardinals, while all his numerous siblings were scattered about Europe.

Excellent!

The only immediate problem was Joséphine, his loving Austrian wife, a scant fifty miles away in her palace of Malmaison. At any moment she might take a notion to journey to Fontainebleau and with connubial devotion join her Emperor upon that imperial couch which up to now had produced no heir to the mightiest throne in the world in spite of all their most frantic endeavors. The MacNair grimaced. Delightful as the encounter might be with the fetching Empress, it was plainly far too dangerous to even consider. Perhaps here in a darkened room he might be able to carry out this mad imposture for the benefit of a handful of servants. But to gull the Emperor's own wife in the most intimate of moments? Inconceivable!

But how could he give the momentous order to divorce the first lady of the Empire? Through the offices of this gloomy butler? So startling and weighty a decision would fall like a thunderclap upon the Empire; it would be totally inacceptable coming from the mouth of a mere servant. So unless he wanted to call in members of his family or high officials of his government he would have to put the order in writing. But he had no notion at all of the Emperor's handwriting!

The MacNair sighed plaintively. Already, merely while lying here inoffensively in bed, he was inexorably confronted by the essential absurdity of this ridiculous imposture. A sudden sweat broke out on his forehead. Never in all his life had he felt himself so trapped by circumstances, so little in control of his own destiny!

Morosely he finished a second croissant and at last broke the lengthy silence. A single possible solution had suggested itself. "Summon a scribe," he ordered, and even in the deep submarine gloom of the chamber the MacNair's eyes seemed to flash. "And then—post a permanent detachment of guards outside the door. Armed and resolute and answering to no one's orders but your own. Henceforth *no one*, with the exception of yourself and whoever you designate for matters of a housekeeping nature, is to be admitted to this apartment under any pretext whatsoever, be he or she the Empress of France, Marshal of the Empire, or Madame Mère herself! Not a single person! Is that entirely clear? Your own head will depend upon it!"

"It is entirely clear, Your Imperial Majesty. It shall be as you desire."

"For your own sake, I most earnestly hope so." The MacNair rubbed his hand ruefully along the itchy stubble of beard that now disfigured his chin. Did he dare to challenge fate by letting his once-luxuriant beard grow out again? He sighed as common sense reluctantly asserted itself. Who could tell what dire consequences a bearded Bonaparte might have for the subsequent history of the world?

"When the scribe has left, you may then return with the barber, one who is entirely mute, I hasten to add. Be certain that he fully seizes the fact that at the merest syllable of tonsorial conversation the razor will be transferred from my throat to his, and for a radically different purpose!"

"All shall be as you wish, Your Imperial Majesty." The maître d'hôtel bowed himself obsequiously from the darkened chamber.

At last, thought the MacNair pensively, a silent barber! Could there be aspects of playing emperor that he might enjoy after all?

CHAPTER
=== 38 ===

THE NORMALLY GRAVE face of Salvetti the maître d'hôtel was even more lugubrious than usual as he bowed low before his imperial master. The MacNair looked up from the small rosewood table in a corner of his vast bedchamber where he sat impatiently skimming through the thick stack of documents which were brought in with his breakfast every morning.

The Emperor of All the French was dressed this afternoon in a loose white blouse of soft cotton; his pants were a faded green velour and his shoes a comfortable pair of fluffy red slippers. A matching set of crystal decanters just behind the red porphyry inkstand on the table contained cognac, Scotch whiskey, and distilled water. The great crimson curtains of heavy velvet that concealed the tall narrow window embrasures that looked out on the royal park of Fontainebleau had been drawn and a bright September sun streamed in through the lacy white gauze curtains that protected the Emperor from the view of those members of the imperial court who occasionally wandered across the manicured green lawn.

In the ceiling far above the table a fan of four handcrafted wooden blades turned slowly but regularly, slightly displacing the damp autumn heat. The design of the blades had been the first of the MacNair's attempts to ameliorate the rather primitive comforts of this extravagant apartment from which he had solemnly vowed not to set foot until the same machine that had deposited him here had restored him to his rightful century. The sketches and an oral description of the fan had been given to his impassive Corsican maître d'hôtel. Four days later a team of artisans had installed the white and gilt device to the distant ceiling. A revolving metal rod disappeared across the ceiling and out into the Palace. Just what kept it spinning outside his purvey was mystery. A squirrel cage? the MacNair asked himself occasionally. Condemned prisoners lashed to a treadmill? One of the newfangled steam engines that were gradually coming into use? The MacNair preferred not to pursue his inquiries. . . .

The majordomo cleared his throat discreetly.

"Yes?" inquired the MacNair of the mournful servant who had suddenly become the second most powerful man in an empire that stretched across all of western Europe.

Salvetti bowed even lower than before. "If Your Imperial Majesty pleases," he said softly in the accents of his native Mediterranean island, "there is, I fear, a certain . . . unrest among the intimates of the Palace."

"Surely not because of the divorce from Joséphine?" replied the MacNair absently, his thoughts preoccupied by the surprisingly difficult task of trying to re-create in the mind's eye the precise design and operation of the twentieth-century porcelain flush toilet. . . . He had forgotten what date the Encyclopaedia Britannica had ascribed to its invention by the universal Bonaparte; but one thing he knew with empiric certainty—it had *not* been invented before July 27, 1806!

"No, Your Imperial Majesty. The necessity of an Empress who can assure the birth of an heir is clearly appreciated. The speculation is far wilder than that: Stories are rife that Your Imperial Majesty is sick and dying; that you are being held a prisoner against your will; even that you are already dead!"

The MacNair rubbed his fingers against the smooth skin of his scrupulously clean-shaven chin as he considered this displeasing bit of news. "I imagine that some of the more courageous—or foolhardy, as the case will prove—are demanding to see for themselves whether their Emperor is alive and functioning and not actually a prisoner of his wily Corsican majordomo?"

The maître d'hôtel's swarthy face flushed with confusion and he bowed until the front curls of his powdered wig nearly touched the creamy marble floor. "I fear that such is the case, Your Imperial Majesty. Naturally I—"

"An instant halt must be put to this noisome speculation," declared the MacNair imperiously. "Which among these intrusive rascals of whom you speak is present at the very moment?"

"At this very moment, Your Imperial Majesty? I believe that the Duke of Marseille, Prefect of Paris, has just left. He has been among the most insistent. But Marshal Baudouin has also been in residence in the Palace for six days now and is becoming increasingly—"

"Baudouin!" The MacNair bit his lip in dismay. Could this be the same heroic Baudouin who was known in France as the Lion of the Cotswolds, the military genius who had turned a possible disaster at the hands of the British into the decisive triumph that had ensured the downfall of Bonaparte's final and greatest enemy?

It seemed only too probable.

And until the moment the Emperor had mysteriously taken to his bedchamber in July of 1806 this lusty soldier had clearly been the second man in France. There was even evidence, Lord Evergreen had said, that before his sudden death he had harbored dark notions about possibly raising himself to the position of *first* man of the Empire.

The MacNair scowled darkly. Wasn't the *real* Napoleon renowned for the incisiveness of his decisions? Best to settle this matter at once, hopefully while this wretched soldier might still be caught off guard. "Very well," he muttered in a soft voice of infinite menace, returning his attention to the papers spread out across the table. "Send him in immediately—along with any others who dare face the wrath of their Emperor!"

As the MacNair nervously awaited the entrance of his celebrated companion in arms, he asked himself despairingly what could possibly be happening two centuries in the future. Six full weeks had now passed since he had awakened in the bed of the emperor! Surely the list of demands which the Yeoman Sons of Essex were to present to Paris as ransom for the safe and unnoticed return of the authentic Napoleon to his imperial throne in 1806 must have been presented by now. And surely the treacherous substitution worked by the detestable Kevin Frost must have been uncovered as well. Once the present-day Emperor Napoleon V and the Marquis of Vézelay knew the actual identity of the man impersonating the Founding Father of the House of Bonaparte, how long could they dare defy the wishes of the Earl of Kensington and his fellow extortionists?

Six long weeks. . . . *Surely* that was enough time!

But why, then, was he, Sir Kevin Deane de Courtney MacNair of MacNair, still trapped here in the confines of the Emperor's bedchamber in the Palace of Fontainebleau? Didn't those idiots in the future realize that every additional hour that passed was sixty minutes in which his brazen imposture might suddenly be unmasked—with the most catastrophic consequences for the next two centuries of the world's history, including their own personal existence?

So why was he still sitting here, quill pen in hand, laboriously counterfeiting the Emperor's signature to documents he barely understood and preparing to meet the challenges of those such as—

"His Excellency the Marshal of France, Baudouin, Baron Cotswold!" trumpeted the majordomo suddenly from the far side of the apartment.

The sharp sounds of heavy boots striding confidently across the marble floor came to the MacNair's ears as he kept his head bent over the pile of papers before him. The sound of the footsteps came to a halt. "Your Imperial Majesty!" cried a loud voice.

The MacNair carefully drew the last two squiggles to the fanciful series of whirls and curlicues that was the official signature of the Emperor Napoleon. At last he looked up with mild puzzlement on his face, the quill pen still in hand. "Baudouin? Ah, Baudouin!" His lips tightened with displeasure and his dark brown eyes glinted in the midafternoon sunlight. "What kindness of an old comrade to come to see if his Emperor is still alive and not the slave of his maître d'hôtel!" The MacNair glared angrily.

If the tall thickset soldier in a bright red jacket with three loops of silver braid across its front and heavy golden epaulettes on each shoulder was chastened by the imperious manner, he concealed it artfully. He scowled down at the diminutive figure sitting before him and reached up to tug at one end of his ragged black mustache. "It was the least I could do," he muttered in the harsh accent of the Jura. He gestured at the quill pen which the MacNair still clutched. "You've hurt your hand?"

The MacNair looked down at his hand in puzzlement. His scowl deepened. "A peculiar question to put to your Emperor!"

"Ha!" The Marshal's shaggy black eyebrows rose and he fell back a step in manifest surprise. "They told me old Buono had suddenly changed but who'd have thought to the point of changing the way you hold your pen? Or the way you greet your old comrades? Or the way you leave them cooling their heels in the corridors for six days while your lickspittle chambermaid runs the Empire in your place!"

The MacNair felt his heart lurch in near panic. Was this the moment he had dreaded for six precarious weeks, the terrible moment some intimate of the Emperor would raise a trembling finger and cry out, "But this isn't Napoleon!" While a million fanciful thoughts whirled through his head he watched the Marshal of France brusquely pull a small chair forward and seat himself upon it without being asked. A light sweat broke out on the MacNair's forehead. Obviously this Baudouin, unless he was a simple madman, was on far more intimate terms with the almighty Emperor than he had realized! Could they once have been childhood friends or youthful schoolmates? The MacNair at once came to a decision.

"My dear friend," he cried, bouncing lightly to his feet and stepping forward to clasp the Marshal's shoulders, "how peculiar you must think me!" With a profound sigh he covered his face with one hand and turned away to pace fretfully to the window and back. "You have no idea how much this business with Joséphine has troubled me. The responsibilities of the Empire, the responsibility of ensuring the succession to the Empire, all of this—"

The craggy soldier snorted sardonically. "Problems arise only if they are permitted to. An obvious solution exists to the problem of responsibility. How many times have I told you, Buono, that if you would only delegate as much of your political authority as you did of your military, you would—"

The MacNair subsided slowly into a blue plush chair on the far side of the room. "I know, my friend," he murmured, "I know. Where would I be—where indeed would the *Empire* be—without your—"

"Exactly!" trumpeted Marshal Baudouin with no attempt at false humility. "Where *would* you be?"

"An interesting topic for philosophic speculation one day when neither of us has such demands upon his time," replied the MacNair evasively, bounding to his feet and crossing the small foyer of his apartment to suddenly pull open the ornate gilt and damask door which led to the rest of the Palace.

Four heavily armed soldiers in pale blue uniforms swung around, their long gleaming sabers rattling softly. Beyond them in the corridor the MacNair spied the majordomo Salvetti standing impassively in the midst of several dozen noisy gentlemen clothed in expensive dress and the distinct air of authority.

"So kind of you to take the time from your own arduous duties to pay me this visit, my dear friend," said the MacNair in ringing tones that carried up and down the corridor as he stood purposefully holding the door open with an outstretched arm.

Marshal Baudouin climbed reluctantly to his feet. "But there is still much to—"

"—discuss about your duties as the new Ambassador to the Court of Helsinki?" the Emperor of All the French and of the United States of Europe cried loudly as those outside the door strained to hear. He sighed plaintively. "How far they will take you from your old comrade," he continued, ignoring the thunderstruck astonishment on the face of the battle-hardened soldier, "but how charming you will find Helsinki itself, a delightful city from all I have been told of it!" He turned to the corridorful of eagerly watching spectators. "Salvetti! Kindly escort the new Ambassador personally to his coach and arrange with the Quai d'Orsay so that he may take up his duties in the nearest possible future!"

With a deft motion the MacNair sidestepped the lumbering Marshal Baudouin and softly fastened the door behind him. He fell back against the pale rose damask, the sweat glistening on the lofty brow over which his Napoleonic bangs now fell nearly to his eyes, and uttered a heartfelt sigh of relief.

What were those muttonheads *doing* in the twentieth century? he asked himself despairingly. What were they doing while Napoleon fiddled and Paris burned?

CHAPTER
= 39 =

"MY LOVE," MURMURED Kevin Frost passionately, "my darling, darling love!"

"Oh, Bunny," whispered the Archduchess Mireille as she wriggled deeper under the tangled blankets and pulled him even tighter into her arms, "how I've missed you!"

"And I you!"

"But why did you suddenly *leave* me like that? You can't *believe* the wicked things the Marquis of Vézelay said about you!"

"I told you, my dearest, solely in order to recover the crown. Our crown," he amended hastily as he recalled those scornfully disparaging words concerning the loveliest, most wonderful woman in the entire world which to his stupefaction he had overheard his detestable doppelgänger addressing one evening to a drowsy Earl of Kensington over large snifters of Scotch liqueur in the downstairs smoking room of Garnaway Castle. *"Your* crown!" he murmured into her delicate pink ear.

The Archduchess of Luxembourg cooed with wordless delight and her superb breasts rose and fell with quickened emotion. Kevin Frost lay back in half-numbed ecstasy as he felt the warm hands of his ethereal Archduchess move lingeringly across his smooth bare chest. He supposed that even the most wonderful woman in the world could be allowed a single small foible or two, and Mireille's single-minded passion for the crown from another universe surely qualified as that. . . .

But what did a crown, even the most valuable crown in a *billion* universes, compare to the love of the goddess Mireille? He lay back in the overheated luxury of the small seventeenth-century hotel room to which he had brought this remarkable woman the evening before after finally tracking her down in the noisy squalor of a Left Bank cabaret, Le Grimace du Singe. A few ecstatic days in the arms of the woman he loved, far from the chill of the icy rains of a dismal grey Parisian March, and then he might be ready to carry out the remainder of the mission that with such apparent reluctance he had let the madmen of Garnaway Castle browbeat him into accepting. . . .

"But I was so *lonely* after you left me," pouted the glorious reason for which he would shortly be subjecting himself to the almost inconceivably precarious hazards of confronting an infuriated Emperor and his hangman the Marquis of Vézelay.

He let his hand run lovingly through her beautiful soft curls. "But don't you remember that I'd been telling you for months how erratically the crown was functioning? As soon as it reappeared only to be stolen by those beastly Turks, I saw instantly that if I were ever to recover it for you I would have to do so from outside Paris."

"But *why,* Bunny?"

"Because the hostile emanations of the Marquis of Vézelay clearly made it impossible for the subtle psionic linkages to be established between myself and the crown."

"I *knew* there was an explanation," breathed Mireille joyously. "So now you *do* have it! And you did it all for me!

And that's why now you've returned to Paris!"

"Essentially that is the case," murmured Kevin Frost warily. "That is to say, I'm *almost* ready to retrieve the crown, but in the meantime I fear there's a spot of rather tedious business to transact with your uncle. . . ." He rolled over and grasped her with a sudden urgency. "Which reminds me: Even though your beloved uncle is, of course, a gentleman of the most scrupulous honor, I think that just to be on the safe side you should . . .

The reception accorded to the personage who styled himself Prince William Ernest Augustus by the Emperor Napoleon V was glacial in the extreme. "You have abused our confidence most shamelessly, sir," he declared in his most imperial manner from where he stood ramrod straight behind his enormous desk in the cold solemnity of his vast office in the east wing of the Elysée Palace. "Your further effrontery in demanding this audience is of even more breathtaking insolence." His icy blue eyes glittered with wrath and his craggy features were taut with barely suppressed fury. A respectful half pace behind the broad-shouldered figure of the Emperor the diminutive Marquis of Vézelay exuded a baleful menace.

Kevin Frost ran his fingers unhurriedly along the sleek lines of the glossy Vandyke beard that was securely attached to his chin. "If such is Your Imperial Majesty's impression, then we must of course apologize most contritely," he replied in an urbane voice totally devoid of contrition. He saw the hateful Marquis of Vézelay cock his head thoughtfully and a puzzled frown wrinkle his forehead. Inwardly he cursed the wretched profusion of French accents with which he had to cope. Parisian, Corsican, Toulousian, French Canadian, why couldn't these ghastly Frenchmen agree upon a single beautiful accent such as the one he had learned in his youth in the forests of northern Franklin? He compressed his lips and drew himself up to his full height. But now, of course, here he was in the lion's den itself, far too late to back out because of a few errant vowels and consonants! *L'audace!* he counseled himself, *toujours l'audace!*

"We conjecture that it must have been the cumulative

effect of the series of terrible physical attacks to which we have been subjected ever since being dragooned into this brutal world of yours," he continued smoothly. "In the half-dazed state in which we found ourselves following that last merciless beating of which even now the circumstances are but hazy suppositions, the single thought which came to us was the recovery of the crown. We must, we suppose, have decided in our half-conscious, half-delirious state that only in England could this English crown be retrieved." Kevin Frost passed a hand wearily across his forehead and shook his head in melancholy recollection. "Dimly we recall stepping into the limousine of our dear friend the Marquis of Vézelay and after that—nothing!"

"Nothing?" exclaimed the director of the Empire's secret police as he wondered why this confrontation evoked such an eerie sense of *déjà vu*. . . .

"Nothing," replied Kevin Frost firmly. "Nothing, that is, until we came to ourselves several weeks later lying in a bed in Garnaway Castle in Morayshire, Scotland, with Sir Norvil Dennett and the Earl of Kensington in attendance. How we came to be there we fear we shall never know." He failed to stifle a small sigh. "Our own supposition is that we were kidnaped by Scottish agents and then held under the influence of drugs while these totally unscrupulous maniacs attempted to draw out our innermost secrets."

"Unscrupulous maniacs?" repeated Napoleon V, for the first time letting his normally expressive face show some animation. "But you refer to your own countrymen, do you not?"

The sigh which Prince William Ernest Augustus, Duke of York, now uttered was prolonged and heartfelt. "If only it were not so," he murmured passionately. "Such men as these . . ." He shook his head in dismay at his inability to find words capable of expressing the enormity of his emotions. Finally, reluctantly, he reached into an inner pocket of his hairy brown tweed suit and pulled forth a sealed envelope which he handed across the desk to the Emperor of France. "This missive from the Earl of Kensington will, we fear, contain a number of disagreeable surprises."

"Indeed?"

Kevin Frost inclined his head in a measured bow and

stepped back a pace. "We beg Your Imperial Majesty to bear in mind at all times that we ourselves are nothing more than a messenger asked to transmit these odious tidings, and that we firmly and irrevocably disassociate ourselves in every way from both the spirit and the letter of the communication. Indeed, it is uniquely in the hope that our own royal presence may signify the extraordinary gravity of the situation, that we have allowed ourselves to become involved even so peripherally with so distasteful an affair."

"Yes, yes, yes," snapped Napoleon V impatiently, "just let me read it, man! Whatever this nonsense is that you're babbling about, it has been several centuries now since we hanged the bearers of ill tidings!"

Ten minutes later the Emperor of All the French and of the United States of Europe looked up from the desk at which he sat in near shock and muttered to the director of his secret police, "Take this man out and have him shot at once!"

CHAPTER
= 40 =

PAPERWORK, PAPERWORK, paperwork! screamed the MacNair silently to himself as he contemplated yet another stack of documents awaiting his attention. Was it for *this* that the megalomaniacal Alexanders and Napoleons and Hitlers had set out to conquer the entire world: that they might then spend the rest of their days drowning in the bureaucratic rigmarole of administering it?

The MacNair grabbed a handful of papers haphazardly.

What an officious busybody this original Bonaparte—a self-styled universal man in the noble tradition of the Enlightenment—had been! Not content with merely bringing first France and then the rest of western Europe under his heel, he had then decided upon the necessity of redefining all their civil and criminal codes.

For Napoleon devoutly believed, as did so many of the lesser dictators who would follow in his tracks, that the state was the absolute arbiter of every conceivable matter within its purvey. Hence this encyclopedic Napoleonic Code, an elaborate and far-reaching revision of everything that touched French life, all rigorously laid down following the strictest precepts of Cartesian logic.

The MacNair scowled disdainfully at the papers in his hand. Look at this nonsense! So many persons per *département*. So many notaries per person. So many clerks per notary. The schedule of fees or the percentage of assets the notary could take when drawing up a marriage contract, a divorce, a testament, a mortgage, a sale of three geese, a rental of two acres of wheat. How many years in prison the notary received for any one of seventy-eight offenses against either the civil or the criminal code. . . .

The MacNair refrained with difficulty from wadding up the entire mass and depositing it in the dark green wastebasket with its silver crest of the imperial eagle. How had he ever come to find himself the prey to such utter boredom? He sighed and impatiently pushed the papers to one side.

While waiting for those imbeciles in the future to untangle his destiny it was high time to leave the paperwork to others and devote himself to the most urgent of tasks: the safety of his own precious hide!

The MacNair pulled at his chin. The most obvious step was to remove the sacred person of the Emperor from this enormous Palace of Fontainebleau with the utmost dispatch. For here Napoleon's own mother, Madame Mère, had her own vast apartment, as did his innumerable brothers and sisters when they were not physically occupying the various European thrones upon which their imperial brother had set them. Here were a thousand idle courtiers and courtesans adept in the arts of palace intrigue. Here was where a disgruntled Marshal Baudouin would certainly strike if he spurned the opportunity of bringing the glories of French civilization to the Lapps and the reindeer. *Here* was simply too dangerous.

For Bonaparte, of course, to decide was to act. Just before midnight two days later a small figure clad in a wide-brimmed black hat and floppy dark brown trousers, a long-sleeved maroon shirt and plain leather jerkin, was led by the lugubrious Salvetti out a tall narrow window of the Emperor's apartment and into the moonless night. Silently the two figures crept along an endless marble terrace until they came to a small coach which was nearly invisible against the looming mass of the Palace. A moment later, with Salvetti beside him in the cramped interior, the Emperor of France was being drawn by four swift horses through the royal forest of Fontainebleau.

Long before dawn the coach had clattered across the cobblestone streets of a sleeping Paris and up to a small side entrance of the darkened Elysée Palace a few short steps from the Place de la Concorde. Two armed soldiers stepped sleepily aside and a drowsy footman appeared with a lighted candelabra held high. Five minutes of walking down dark passages and up even darker staircases brought the trio to the Emperor's new quarters, a third-story apartment at the top of the Palace whose narrow windows overlooked the dark gardens which the MacNair had first glimpsed two centuries in the future from the office of the Marquis of Vézelay.

"Is that the bed?" asked the MacNair, taking the candelabra from the footman and dismissing him with a nod. He turned to his maître d'hôtel. "Post a guard at the door for the remainder of the night. In the morning you will arrange for the transfer of the 4th Corsican Horse from Versailles to take up guard duties for the Palace." He yawned wearily. "For breakfast tomorrow, or rather today: buttermilk pancakes, a selection of finely ground pork sausages, honey which has been warmed until it flows nicely, *salted* butter, a carafe of chilled but previously distilled water, and a pot of coffee. I imagine you will have to threaten the chef with a posting to Manchester before he will allow you to explain how to prepare the pancakes correctly. This you may do."

The MacNair stretched and began to undo the laces of his leather jerkin. "After breakfast we will begin the restructuring of this apartment to more suitable specifications."

Now, ten months later, not long before the first anniversary of his arrival in this, the early nineteenth century, the Emperor of France wearily pushed away the latest drafts of the civil code sent to him by a commission of scholars in the Ministry of the Interior and turned his attention to the project which was nearest his heart: the satisfactory implementation of a modern flush toilet.

The MacNair rose to his feet, stretched, and began pacing the large, low-ceilinged room which served as his working office. Bright red Oriental carpets covered its polished hardwood floor and cheerful June sunlight flooded through the gaily colored panes of the overhead skylights which the MacNair had ordered installed. Its bookshelves were filled with leather-bound books, and large comfortable leather chairs and footstools of the Emperor's own design had replaced the spindly gilt and satin chairs which had been the apartment's original furniture. Three small windows in the side of the steeply sloping mansard roof looked out over the formal gardens of the Palace, and by craning his neck the MacNair could make out through the leaves of the beech trees that lined the Avenue de Marigny the distant window through which one day a mettlesome Kevin Frost would take sudden leave from his audience with the Marquis of Vézelay.

The MacNair shook his head in reluctant admiration at his recollection of that startling moment and uttered a sharp snort. What a wily and resolute rascal was Kevin Frost! What dash, what character!

How he would howl for mercy when the MacNair's fingers someday tightened about his throat!

With a wistful sigh the MacNair resumed his pacing. How curiously difficult it was to design an adequate toilet! Already, to the unspoken wonder of the Elysée's inmates, the Emperor had installed in the large room next to his bedchamber a noble tub carved from a single flawless block of gleaming red Campan Griotte marble. A 5,000-liter copper reservoir had been erected on the roof of the Palace and from there water flowed down to an elaborate boiler in the mysterious regions of the Palace's basements before returning to the Emperor's apartment as scalding hot water upon the turning of a solid gold spigot.

In a small, brightly wallpapered room apart from the actual bathroom, the Napoleonic toilet Mark III had recently been installed, but already the MacNair was filled with schemes for the new and improved Mark IV. Certainly the present one worked, he allowed, with a mighty roar of surging waters that rushed down from the chain-operated tank fixed to the top of the wall, but the toilet itself was still primitive in the extreme, a mere porcelain basin with a metal trap that opened and closed in its bottom, much like those in the trains which had borne the MacNair from New York to Bangor.

The pragmatist in the MacNair was amply satisfied by the fruits of his ingenuity; the aesthete and perfectionist not at all. Only when his labors had finally produced a single self-contained unit in which waters flowed gracefully and silently through a complex series of syphons and concealed outlets would he be truly contented. Humming softly, the Emperor of All the French and of the United States of Europe seated himself at the long table of brilliantly polished wooden inlays and reached for pen and paper. Perhaps if the main inlet were *here* and the secondary flow *there* . . .

CHAPTER
= 41 =

"YOU DON'T *really* believe that Uncle would have had you shot?" gasped the Archduchess Mireille of Luxembourg as she summoned the sommelier to pour another glass of wine for the still quivering Kevin Frost. "*You?* A prince of the blood?"

"Perhaps not," muttered the man who called himself Prince William Ernest Augustus. His eyes moved uneasily around the red plush elegance of Le Vieux Lapin with its breathtaking view of a floodlit Notre-Dame just across the river. "I rather fear that upon mature reflection he would have had me first slowly boiled in rancid olive oil and then nibbled to death by a horde of specially trained rabbits." He passed a hand across his pale brow and tried to dispel the terrible memory of the Emperor's angry command and of that unspeakable list of so-called nonnegotiable demands which the odious Earl of Kensington had so diabolically entrusted him to deliver in all innocence to the Emperor Napoleon. But even now, four hours later, it was as if they had been engraved on the stone tablet of his mind. He shuddered as once again he saw himself—he, inoffensive Kevin Frost!—actually handing to the most powerful despot in the world a list of intransigent orders which commanded that:

The House of Bonaparte-Hanover immediately abdicate from the throne of England and depart, with all its members, for France.

The various Houses of Bonaparte which sat on every European throne likewise abdicate and return to France.

All French military units and missions return to France from wherever they were stationed in Europe.

The twenty-seven German states be allowed to take whatever steps were necessary for immediate unification into a single state.

The so-called European Parliament in Paris be immediately dissolved and all its powers declared null and void.

The divestiture of French capital from all enterprises and companies outside of France be carried out in a period of time not to exceed five years.

An indemnity of five milliards of louis d'or be paid by France to a commission composed of Europeans from every state, who would determine its equitable distribution.

The tyrant Napoleon V and his hangman the Marquis of Vézelay give themselves up to a tribunal of impartial European jurists to be judged for the following crimes against humanity. . . .

Kevin Frost groaned and gulped the contents of his glass in a single swallow. It was a wonder that the towering Emperor hadn't personally strangled him on the spot with his enormous peasant hands! Thank God for the providential foresight which had led him to wheedle the Archduchess Mireille into forcing her way into her uncle's office fifteen minutes after the start of their meeting. He wiped away the sweat that beaded his forehead. Without his beloved Mireille's imperious intervention . . .

Impulsively Kevin Frost pulled the long pale hands of the startled Archduchess across the linen tablecloth and, oblivious of the amused looks of the five-star restaurant's other diners, buried his face against them, covering them avidly with fervent kisses. He felt sharp prickles of moisture well up in his eyes. How much he loved this marvelous woman! How complete his happiness would be if he could only make her his forever!

Later that evening the Prince William Ernest Augustus slept restlessly in his suite at the Hôtel de l'Angleterre on the Rue de Rivoli overlooking the Louvre to which discretion had dictated he return alone after their dinner at Le

Vieux Lapin. As ancient church bells tolled three o'clock all across a sleeping Paris, four burly figures in faded blue coveralls slunk silently into his room. A short time later they emerged with a surprisingly bulky roll of red and blue Persian carpet which they carried down in the service elevator of the hotel and laid carefully in the back of a dark brown Réchard van. . . .

When Kevin Frost suddenly awoke, it was with a burning pain on the inside of his right elbow and a head that swirled and throbbed. He was in absolute blackness. Groggily he attempted to open his eyes but to his dismay discovered that they seemed to be tightly sealed. Just as a sudden awful panic gripped him, a tender hand laid itself reassuringly on his arm and a woman's soft voice whispered soothingly into his ear. "Kevin. Are you awake, Kevin?"

"Yes. What's—"

"Oh, Kevin, we were so worried! What's *happened* to you, Kevin?"

"I don't *know,*" he shouted wildly, "where am I? Who are you? Why can't I *see?* What's the matter with my *eyes?*" He reached up to feel his face, and his fingers encountered a soft material that seemed to be wound tightly around his head. As his fingers began to grope desperately, the hand was withdrawn from his arm and he heard the sound of steps moving away on a hard bare surface.

"That's enough," said a man's voice which was disturbingly familiar. "It's quite conclusive. Take off the mask."

Kevin Frost's head was jerked sharply forward and a moment later he was blinking painfully in the glare of blinding white light. As his vision gradually returned, he saw the outlines of three dark figures standing to one side and realized to his sudden horror that the small man in the middle was the Marquis of Vézelay.

He jerked in shock, but his feet inexplicably refused to move. He sat up on the peculiarly hard bed and saw to his additional dismay that his bare feet still protruded from the maroon silk pajamas which he had worn to bed but that now heavy steel manacles were clamped around his ankles, anchoring him immovably to a bare wooden table. Wildly he turned his head in all directions. He was in a totally featureless white room with a white concrete floor and a high white ceiling from which a number of dazzling lights were suspended. He gasped sharply.

The Marquis of Vézelay stepped forward, urbanely stroking his straggly brown beard, his gaunt cheeks twisted into a ghastly smile. "My dear Kevin Frost," he murmured while his eyes gleamed with pleasure, "how good it is to see you again!"

Kevin Frost threw back his shoulders and straightened his pajamaed torso as much as circumstances would allow. "We fear," he said loftily, "that once again you have fallen prey to the same pernicious—"

"—error which I made once before?" The director of Napoleon's secret police shook his head ruefully. "I think not. Aside from the fact that this particularly well sound-proofed chamber is some dozen meters underground, you will also note that your feet are securely attached. *Here* we shall see no further displays of your acrobatic skills!" He tugged at the end of his beard with sardonic amusement. "Ah! But perhaps you refer to the error of your identity?" He shook his head again. "The fact that we discovered upon a cursory examination you are wearing a cunningly contrived false beard was, of course, suggestive but not entirely conclusive."

Eyes wide, Kevin Frost's hands flew to his beard. It was still securely in place. "But—"

"But it *did* bring to mind what was troubling me during your recent audience with the Emperor—your accent. Was there not still a trace of what was clearly a French-Canadian accent?" The Marquis of Vézelay's smile broadened. "If you will cast your mind back a few moments, my dear fellow, to that soothing, even maternal, voice which greeted you as soon as we injected you to return you to consciousness, you may recall that she was clearly speaking—"

French Canadian! The language of his youth in Franklin! And he had unwittingly replied in like fashion! Kevin Frost groaned in horror and fell back listlessly against the hard wooden slab. How easily he had betrayed himself to this ghastly torturer! Sweat broke out on his forehead and he felt his stomach roiling as the full extent of his predicament became clear. He was manacled in the underground torture chamber of Napoleon's most gruesome hangman! What would happen next?

The Marquis of Vézelay stepped closer and Kevin Frost felt an uncontrollable shudder run the length of his body. "You are, I should imagine, even now comforting yourself with the notion that you are under the protection of the delightful Archduchess Mireille." The secret-police man smiled bleakly and Kevin Frost gasped softly.

Mireille! He had forgotten his beloved Mireille! If only he could—

"Exactly," agreed the Marquis of Vézelay with a profound sigh as his smile instantly vanished. "You *are* under the protection of that nitwitted nymphomaniac. *But,"* he spat sharply, leaning forward so that his glittering eyes were only inches from those of Kevin Frost, "how long, my fine Yankee bigamist, do you think you would remain under her protection if she were to know that instead of being the man who can bring her a priceless crown you are only a wretched—"

"But I *can* bring her the crown," blurted Kevin Frost desperately. "I can even bring it to *you! I've* already done so! I've had it on my head, I've—"

"You see," said the Marquis of Vézelay with a satisfied nod as he stepped back from the table, "you *do* want to cooperate with us, after all, don't you? And if you're a *particularly* candid fellow, perhaps we can all of us keep on pretending that you're actually visiting English royalty." He motioned to one of the two hulking figures in dark blue uniforms, and a small wooden chair was produced. The director of the Empire's Special Directorate drew it close to the bare table on which Kevin Frost was shackled. "Now, then, my dear fellow," he suggested cheerfully, "why don't we start at the beginning?" He cocked his head in anticipation. "What, exactly, were the circumstances in which you first came into contact with this peculiar person who insists that he is from another universe and yet who is so obviously your identical twin?"

CHAPTER
= 42 =

"LET ME BE certain that I have this quite clear," growled the Emperor Napoleon V as he drummed his gnarled brown fingers on the top of his desk. "You are saying that right now, this very moment, in fact, somewhere in the time stream which leads to where the three of us are sitting in this room, my great-great-grandfather Napoleon I is in actuality *Prince William of England?*"

The Marquis of Vézelay nodded reluctantly. "Such would appear to be the case, at least for that period of time beginning July 27, 1806. You may recall that this is the approximate date from which the historians date the so-called Missing—"

"And this *other* Prince William, the one that my idiot niece . . ." continued the Emperor heedless of Vézelay before at last spluttering to a halt before the sheer enormity of the absurd situation.

The director of the secret police gestured at the third man in the Emperor's writing room, the swarthy curly-haired director of the Curie Institute, now fidgeting impatiently in a fragile green and gilt chair. "If Your Imperial Majesty pleases, Dr. Campinotti will attempt to clarify the position regarding doppelgängers. And . . ." He paused before adding delicately, "other matters."

Twenty minutes later the head of the House of Bonaparte sat back in his own outsize chair while he tugged furiously at his fluffy white mustache. His normally ruddy face was pale and his eyes were glazed. "You're saying that we could just *leave* this bloody Englishman or American or whatever he is in the place of Great-great-grandfather and that *he*—this confounded impostor—would go on to become *my* ancestor?" The Emperor shook himself groggily, as if he had been pummeled by a succession of hard blows to the head.

"I believe that it is theoretically *possible,*" replied the director of the Curie Institute cautiously. "For from what we have now learned from this second Prince William, or Kevin Frost if you prefer, based on the several months he spent in Scotland with the actual inventors of this time machine, a Conservation of Time apparently exists. If Napoleon I is brought from 1806 to 1992 for three weeks, let us say, then he irrevocably and inalterably vanishes for three weeks during 1806." He flashed his gleaming teeth. "Which, when you consider it, is only logical: How could the same person possibly exist in two separate times at once?"

"The devil take your logic-chopping!" cried Napoleon V passionately. "What I want to know is this: What am I to *do?* Has Vézelay shown you that list of demands from that madman Kensington? He has?" He leaned across his gleaming desk and pierced the director of the Curie Institute with his icy blue eyes. "If even one *word* of this extortion plot should leak out, the person responsible will vanish instantly and permanently from the face of the earth! Is that *quite* clear, Dr. Campinotti?"

"It is, Your Imperial Majesty," gulped the scientist.

"Hrmph!" The Emperor sat back with his lips drawn tight. "Now that I have threatened *you,* let me assure you that if Your Imperial Majesty gave even the merest *appearance* of asking the Senate to accede to such insane demands, he would find himself thrown into the streets upon the instant! Or worse! He, too, would most probably vanish from the face of the earth—along with the rest of the House of Bonaparte!" He licked his lips nervously. "The merest *hint* of this would be enough to panic the entire world. Which is why we three in this room are the sole people in all of France aware of this disaster; and it is the three of us who must resolve it."

"A question, Your Imperial Majesty," murmured Dr. Campinotti, who was now quite pale. "Have you considered a . . . a straightforward commando raid or something of the nature against these—"

The Emperor waved his hand irritably. "We have photographs of the procedure they have used to booby-trap the time machine and the entire castle. At the slightest threat it would be destroyed, and along with it any chance of retrieving my forebear." He ran his hands through his thick mop of disheveled straw-colored hair. "As I see it, only two choices are possible: Either we accede to their demands and dismantle the French Empire, the greatest force for peace and civilization that the world has ever known. Or we call their bluff and risk plunging the entire world into a chaos beyond imagination." His eyes fell to a somber study of the backs of his enormous hands. "Surely this is the most fearful choice any three human beings have ever been forced to resolve!"

Dr. Campinotti passed a finger through a ring of his curly black hair. "It is, of course, up to Your Imperial Majesty to decide, but it would appear evident to me that for at least the thirty-two days since Napoleon I was disentimed by these Englishmen on July 27, 1806, their substitute Prince William has been taking his place with something more than just a bare adequacy." He leaned forward and tapped an emphatic finger upon the Emperor's desk. "Consider! Napoleon I has been disentimed! His place has been taken by a low Yankee adventurer! Events of unimaginable import whose momentous consequences might be expected to change the entire course of world history!

"And yet what do we find instead?" He shrugged expressively and sat back with a faint smile. "We find that nothing at all has altered! This room, the Senate, the bridges on the Seine, Your Imperial Majesty's silver inkwell on the desk before you, even my own modest salary at the institute—all are as they were before! In other words, this substitute Emperor has so far proved to be a completely adequate substitute for the real one. This would appear to bode well for the future. Who is to say that of the two evils—giving in to the demands of these mad extortionists or taking a chance that Prince William Ernest Augustus actually *does* prove to be Your Imperial Majesty's revered ancestor—that the latter course may not prove to be the wiser?"

A late spring had finally come to northern Scotland. A watery sun peeked wanly through low grey clouds that swept in from the Firth of Moray, and the nine gardeners who tended to the grounds of Garnaway Castle were busy planting bulbs and sharpening their mowers for the first tentative blades of new grass that were beginning to push through the soggy turf. Behind the imposing walls of the castle, however, the prevailing atmosphere was one of baffled fury.

"It can't be possible!" cried Sir Norvil Dennett, the Master of Garnaway. "It's just as that scoundrel Prince William predicted: They're refusing to ransom their Emperor!" He fell back into the deep chintz-covered armchair in a corner of the periodical room with his long face dulled by stunned bewilderment.

Even the Earl of Kensington, who prided himself upon his mastery of the harsh doctrines of realpolitik, was shaken by the monstrous cold-bloodedness with which their hateful adversaries in Paris had applied the tenets of Cartesian logic. He ran his fingers through his bushy side-whiskers. "It may be that they do not clearly understand the position in which—"

"What could be clearer?" asked Dennett sharply. "We have presented them with a choice: Yield to our demands, or we shall dispose of your holy icon, Napoleon Bonaparte. They have replied: Dispose of him in any way you choose. And then use your time machine while you can to flee to the dawn of prehistory to escape our terrible vengeance!"

"Possibly, possibly," allowed the Earl of Kensington dubiously. "It may well be that they are only playing for time, hoping to—"

"Playing for time by telling us to slit the throat of the founder of their empire?"

Kensington winced at the crass brutality of the words. "I feel *certain* that something has been garbled somewhere in the translation," he muttered desperately. "Let me send another message to Henley to transmit to the tyrant, one which more fully explicates the consequences of their peevish refusal to accede to our *extremely* reasonable requests. . . ."

The Master of Garnaway shook his head despairingly. "But suppose they don't? Suppose they absolutely refuse to negotiate with us any further and decide to send a commando to seize the castle and us? Suppose they merely send some of their new Victoire bombers to pulverize us from the air. . . ."

The Earl of Kensington puffed out his cheeks uneasily. "Nonsense, my dear fellow! They know as well as we do that by doing so they would only set off the explosives with which we would . . . oh . . ." His voice trailed off slowly.

"Blow up the time machine, and by so doing, maroon Napoleon I for the rest of eternity in his time bubble. Which is exactly what they're *telling* us to do! Where, then, is our threat?"

"Then *blow* him up, for heaven's sake!" blustered Kensington furiously. "*Then* let's see what the Froggies have to say!"

Sir Norvil Dennett's long thin frame seemed to sink even more profoundly into the depths of the overstuffed armchair. His cheeks were gaunt and above his half-moon spectacles his eyes were haunted. "And possibly throw the entire world into chaos?" he whispered in a voice that was barely audible. "Perhaps snuff ourselves out of existence in the very instant we push the button?" He raised his eyes to meet the Earl's. "Is that what you want, Kensington," he supplicated, "is that what you *really* want?"

CHAPTER
= 43 =

The Clay Bedroom
TALL TREES
Liberty, D.C.

May 7, 1992

My Detestable Uncle,

You are probably wondering [wrote the Archduchess Mireille of Luxembourg] why this letter is being sent to you by air mail from the United States of America instead of from Cannes, and why it is being written on the President's stationery instead of the Hotel Majestic's. Let me tell you.

It is because you have played a filthy vicious trick on me!

You and your abominable butcher the hangman of Paris!

As well as that toad in human form who dares to call himself Prince William Ernest Augustus!

How I hate you all!

But let me start at the beginning.

Now that you are in your dotage, and senility has plainly taken control of your mind, I imagine that you and your other unspeakably odious conspirators supposed that your "dim-witted niece" (oh, yes, I know that's what you really think of me, don't deny it, I *heard* you saying it!), that your dim-witted niece wouldn't be smart enough to notice that ever since the

man who dares to call himself Prince William returned
from wherever he was, he was acting in the most
peculiar manner. ~~All he ever wanted to do was~~ He was
not at all the man of sensibility and utmost refinement
that I had previously known. Nor would he even
produce the crown for me, even though he now swore
that he was able to do so. And every time he went off to
see you or that wretched dwarf Vézelay, he came back
all white and shaky and would just sit by himself
staring out the window ~~not even wanting to~~.

Well, even though of course I'm probably even
stupider than you *think* I am, I knew that *something*
strange was going on, especially when he wouldn't even
tell me what the three of you spent all your time talking
about. So the last time he went to see you, last
Thursday that was, just after he'd got through talking
on the overseas telephone, I decided that I'd find out
just why ~~my Bunny~~ all three of you were acting so
peculiarly.

And it was so easy to do!

Even though this is supposed to be the biggest secret
of all time, isn't it?

(If this is an example of how that low-life Vézelay
runs the Empire's security, I suggest, my dearest
[though mentally incapacitated] uncle, that you have
that miserable dwarf taken to the Zoological Gardens
and thrown into the cage of the stupidest, ugliest
monkey you can find. Then take that monkey and put
him in a neat little grey suit with a lot of shiny silver
buttons on the front and put him behind a desk on the
Avenue de Marigny with a handful of peanuts to play
with and he will certainly do as good a job as your
cretinous toady Vézelay. . . .)

But I digress, do I not?

I imagine that as the dimness of your twilight years
sadly darkens your mind, you long ago forgot the
existence of that discreet egress (or secret passageway,
if you will) which Great-great-great-auntie Alexine had
built into the south wall of the upstairs map room
during the Great War when she feared that Paris might
be invested by the Ottomans. You go up to the third

floor of the south wing and then into the back of the cedar closet next to the laundry room. You press the wall in a certain way and then the passage takes you along to the map room. It's a tight fit for anyone as big as *you,* but when you first showed it to me when I was a little girl of six (a *dim-witted* little girl, I imagine) visiting the Palace during Christmas vacation, you used to squeeze through it with me without any great difficulty.

Last Thursday, when I used it to reach the map room (you should really send someone to clean out the cobwebs from that passage—it looks as if no one has been through it in years), it was just in time to find you and Vézelay and that creature who vaguely resembles Prince William talking about his latest communication from the Earl of Kensington.

I won't bother to repeat the entire conversation, since I know you'd simply forget it as quickly as you've already forgotten the original one, so I'll just tell you that I now know all about the abominable masquerade that this foul creature has been allowed to play on me with the connivance of you and Vézelay.

And I also know that ~~my loving Bunny~~ the *true* Prince William has been kidnaped and sent back to impersonate that hateful Corsican whose damaged genetic material ultimately and so sadly produced *you,* my poor pathetic uncle.

I won't trouble you with all the terrible emotions I felt upon learning about your ghastly plot, since such sadistic beasts as yourselves would only laugh yourselves silly at my tears and distress. So all I *will* tell you is that instead of going to Cannes with the Countess of Mauléon as you thought, I took the night train to Madrid and from there the aeroplane to Charleston in the State of South Carolina. There I hired a limousine to drive me north to Liberty, and, after telephoning, the President and Mrs. Kennedy very kindly asked me to spend a few days with them at Tall Trees.

So here I am in the Clay Bedroom itself, where only the most *special* guests are allowed to stay, writing this letter to you for mailing later this evening.

I never knew how easy it was to write until this morning. That was when I sat down after breakfast with the Kennedys (they're *so* honest and open, unlike *some* so-called leaders we all know) and wrote down an account of every single word that you and Vézelay and that other despicable toad uttered.

In my little account I put down everything I learned about how Napoleon I is being held in a time bubble and how the three of you are now callously playing with the lives and destinies of the entire human race by actually *encouraging* those monsters in Scotland to kill the Emperor or leave him forever in his time bubble.

What do you think (excuse me, I was forgetting of course that *you* can no longer think—do ask your acolyte Vézelay what *he* thinks) will be the reaction of President Kennedy, and the Sultan of the Ottoman Empire, and even of the 300 million people of your own little Empire when they are told about the almost certain extinction which faces them as soon as your co-conspirators in Scotland decide to dispose of our common ancestor?

I think you will be *astonished* by their reaction.

In any case, you will shortly be learning about it at first hand, for it is my intention to arrange for what the Americans term a "press conference" and to reveal the entire sordid story.

Unless, my dear uncle, *unless* you take whatever steps are necessary to *immediately* return ~~my precious Bunny and the crown~~ the *real* Prince William Ernest Augustus to me, here in America where we will be safe from your evil schemes and plots.

Pay heed, dear Uncle! I mean every word I say!

> Your niece,
> Mireille, Archduchess of Luxembourg

P.S. You may send Prince William ~~and the crown~~ directly to Tall Trees, where President and Mrs. Kennedy look forward to meeting him.

P.P.S. "Immediately" means within one week of the receipt of this letter.

P.P.P.S. I forgot to tell you (dim-wittedness obviously runs in the family) what I did with the account I wrote this morning of your conversation in the map room. I put it in an envelope and gave it to the President of the United States and asked him to personally open it upon my disappearance, death, incapacity, or incarceration in a hospital or mental home. So you must hope, my dear uncle, that my health, both bodily and mental, remains sound for the indefinite future.

P.P.P.P.S. I'm having dinner tonight with that *adorable* Senator Huebner from Texas, the Senate majority leader who's always trying to get the United States to break off diplomatic relations with the Empire. I think I'll give *him* a copy of my account also. . . .

"Well?" demanded the Emperor Napoleon V in a terrible voice, his eyes glittering like sapphires in a face that seemed carved from stone. "I thought you said that your service was keeping a discreet eye on the Archduchess Mireille."

The Marquis of Vézelay's slight figure was drawn up ramrod straight in front of the Emperor's desk. His gaunt cheeks were pale and a sheen of sweat covered his forehead. "Yes, Your Imperial Majesty."

"But it didn't stop her from suddenly disappearing from view and ending up at Tall Trees?"

"If Your Imperial Majesty pleases, we thought that with Prince William safely under guard here in Paris—"

"You thought," repeated the Emperor ominously, "you *thought!* As a thinker of the first water, my dear Vézelay, what do you think of the Archduchess's suggestion that you be exchanged for a monkey from the zoo?"

"Your Imperial Majesty, I—"

His Imperial Majesty slammed his enormous palm across the top of the desk with a report loud enough to bring two guards with fluffy white plumes in their gleaming brass helmets rushing into the room, curved sabers at the ready.

"I'll tell you what *I* think," roared the Emperor of All the French and of the United States of Europe in the voice with which he had once drilled troops on the parade grounds of St. Cyr. "*I* think that the Archduchess's suggestion is an *excellent* one!" His cheeks were a bright red and his broad chest rose and fell rapidly. "Take this creature away immediately," he ordered the two guards, "and hold him absolutely incommunicado in a secure place until suitable quarters at the Zoological Gardens can be arranged. And have Colonel Etournaud, the new director of the Special Directorate, report to me at once."

And after *that,* he muttered despairingly to himself when he was alone again in his office, we can try to figure out what to do next to save the Empire from the shambles caused by this pea-brained Archduchess. . . .

CHAPTER
= 44 =

ALMOST TWO CENTURIES earlier, Napoleon I gazed with rapt satisfaction at the final flowering of that humble device which even had he never been Emperor of All the French and of the United States of Europe would have sufficed to make his name forever memorable—as the inventor of the single-piece, silent, indoor flush toilet. Once again he pressed the handcrafted silver handle and watched the mighty vortex of waters swirl with controlled fury around the subtly proportioned curves of the dark blue porcelain basin, then rapidly disappear with only the faintest of gurgles even as the basin was being replenished by a nearly imperceptible flow of water from cunningly concealed apertures beneath the rim. After seventeen months and eleven models, this, the Mark XII, was everything he had dreamed it might be. Now, he told himself, his labors at an end, he could go home. . . .

His spirits suddenly intolerably burdened by the thought of home, the MacNair shuffled gloomily out of his water closet, across the shiny black marble floor of his bathroom, through the dressing room with its meager wardrobe of three or four dozen miscellaneous costumes, and into his large bedroom where already forty-eight pale blue candles burned in gold candelabras. He threw himself fretfully on the canopied bed with its box springs and specially stuffed mattress which he had long ago commanded from the imperial artisans and asked himself despairingly if ever again he would experience the ineffable joy of eating a rubbery hot dog in a gummy roll on a hot summer's evening in Yankee Stadium, a crawfish pie in the Louisiana bayous, sourdough bread and freshly boiled crab in San Francisco, dim sum in Hong Kong, icy champagne, frothing and bubbling in chilled crystal glasses, in—

But wait! The MacNair's eyes suddenly widened. How could he have been so blind for so long? There *was* a way in which to grasp the reins of his own destiny! Its very simplicity must have served to conceal it from him until now. . . .

For the first time in months the MacNair felt his mouth broadening into a smile. A wolfish, predatory smile such as had animated his features at all the climactic moments of his adult life. . . .

En garde, Sir Norvil Dennett and the Earl of Kensington! he cried silently. Beware, Kevin Frost and the Marquis of Vézelay! *Achtung,* the Emperor of France and the Sultan of Turkey, and all the others who had so basely brought the MacNair of MacNair to this pretty pass!

Attention, vous autres! I am about to thwart your most cherished plans!

CHAPTER
= 45 =

"WHAT ON EARTH can be going on in Paris?" wondered the
Earl of Kensington in a troubled voice as he paced nervously back and forth in the afternoon music room of Garnaway
Castle. "The Archduchess Mireille has spent the last five
months in New York on the forty-first floor of the Hotel
Regency surrounded by policemen and bodyguards while
her beloved Prince William has apparently been sent to a
penal colony on Sardinia. The Marquis of Vézelay has
disappeared and—"

Sir Norvil Dennett puffed out his cheeks in exasperation.
"Are you forgetting that the Archduchess's beloved Prince
William also happens to be *our* Prince William, the conduit
by which we are supposedly imposing our will on—"

The Earl of Kensington threw up his hands in despair.
"The negotiations are at an end. What is there to negotiate,
now that the French have dared us to do our worst? What
can we threaten worse than liquidating their original emperor? How many years can we huddle here in Garnaway,
our hands on the switch that will blow up the time machine,
unable to venture forth for fear of being kidnaped or
murdered by French agents?"

"Then what do you suggest?" asked the Master of Garnaway.

But to his distress he watched the dynamic and decisive
Kensington sink limply into a deep yellow armchair, his
normally ruddy face wan and drawn. "Our plans are in

ruins," he whispered bleakly. "Tell me, Dennett, what are we to *do?*"

"*Do?*" repeated the Emperor Napoleon V. "What *can* we do? Up till now we have just barely been able to stave off the demand of the Archduchess that her one true love, the *authentic* Prince William, be returned to her instantly by return mail, along, of course, with his billion-franc crown, by appealing to her reason."

"By appealing to her *reason,* Your Imperial Majesty?" murmured General Etournaud, the new director of the Empire's secret police, with a perfectly straight face.

"Her reason," said the Emperor firmly. "And her keen natural sense of self-preservation. Even *she* appears to grasp the central fact that the only time machine by which we can restore her Prince Charming is in the hands of our implacable enemies. And that by attempting to seize the machine by force we are quite likely to literally blow all of us out of existence."

"I see. So at least we can count on her continued discretion in this matter of—"

"Not at all!" shouted the Emperor, his face red with frustrated wrath. "We can't count on her for *anything!* She may decide to reveal the entire story to the President tomorrow!"

General Etournaud's mouth fell open. "But why would—"

"Because she's the idiot Archduchess Mireille, *that's* why!"

"Do you really think we can trust him?" whispered Prince Konrad of Schleswig-Holstein to the Earl of Kensington as they followed the tall narrow figure of Sir Norvil Dennett and the equally tall but considerably broader figure of General Etournaud down the stone steps that led to the undercellars of Garnaway Castle.

"Not all," replied the Earl, "but what could he possibly do to harm us? He has twice been searched from head to foot, and X-rayed from top to bottom. If he now conceals a powerful bomb inside his stomach, it is cunningly disguised in the form of this morning's breakfast. There will be nine of us and one of him in the laboratory—redoubtable odds for even the most resolute of unarmed combat experts."

"Perhaps, perhaps, but is this really *wise?*" persisted the German prince. "This man is the very symbol of everything we are committed to destroy—"

"What else do you suggest?" shrugged Kensington. "Now that this bird-brained Archduchess is threatening to reveal the entire story, the French are in as great a dilemma as we are. At the moment we and the French are in stalemate—until this nitwitted woman calls her press conference and blows all of us impartially out of the water."

"But—with herself included!"

"It does no good, my dear Konrad, to speak of reason—we are dealing with a hysterical woman!"

Prince Konrad sighed profoundly and stepped into the brightly lit laboratory which housed the time machine. Seven burly Yeoman Sons of Essex stood guard around the time machine itself. General Etournaud blinked in the sudden glare, then turned to examine the room and its equipment until Dennett indicated a straight-backed wooden chair. "*Mon général?*" The Frenchman seated himself with a curt nod and only glared angrily when two Yeoman Sons of Essex stepped forward to deftly shackle his arms behind the chair.

"My excuses, *mon général,*" said the Master of Garnaway, "but you will appreciate the delicacy of our position. . . ."

"Just get on with it," muttered General Etournaud.

"Very well. Everything has been arranged. I need only push this button and—"

The shimmering silver-blue sphere of the time bubble materialized in the center of the laboratory, a glittering jewel which seemed to hover between immateriality and substantiality. Three meters in diameter, it remained motionless in the air, as if resting upon a single infinitesimal millimeter of the bare concrete floor. Dennett manipulated a small lever on the panel before him and it began to sink slowly through the concrete and into the very foundations of the castle. General Etournaud gasped once, then watched in silent awe until the bottom half of the glittering sphere had sunk out of sight.

"Llewellyn," snapped Sir Norvil Dennett, "the chair, the cloak, the hot chocolate—they are ready?"

"Ready."

"Very well, then." The scientist cast a long troubled look at the Earl of Kensington. "You feel *certain* that this is the wisest step to take? Even now it is not too late to—"

The stout Englishman made an impatient gesture. "You understand the quandary in which we all find ourselves. How can we possibly make matters worse by seeing if it cannot somehow be resolved by the most incisive mind of the ages?"

"As you say." With a soft sigh, Sir Norvil Dennett pushed a second button and the glittering silver sphere slowly began to fade from view. "Still, it does seem deuced peculiar to be reduced to seeking the counsel of the very person one has kidnaped and held for ransom!"

How difficult it was, the Master of Garnaway reflected as he half listened to the labored explanations that Kensington and Etournaud were making in French to the diminutive figure seated before them in a blue dressing gown and furry slippers while he sipped a mug of hot chocolate, to convince oneself that here in plain view, only a few feet away from one's very person, was that titan of the ages, the incredible Napoleon Bonaparte himself!

For in spite of the flashing brown eyes and the almost tangible sense of power and assurance that radiated from him, there was no denying the fact that he differed not at all from that bumptious Yankee swindler to whom Dennett had grown so accustomed, that vainglorious peacock who had taken the Emperor's place on the imperial throne, Mr. Kevin Bloody Frost. . . .

Or was it MacNair? Or Prince William of—

Dennett groaned in exasperation. What absolute chaos and confusion! What a miracle it would be if even this genuine Napoleon could find some means of making sense of it all! He cocked his head attentively and fruitlessly tried to follow the rapid string of French that General Etournaud was directing at the glowering Emperor.

"*Assez!*" cried Napoleon suddenly and imperiously, his face flushed a fiery red, his eyes glittering with manic fury.

"Enough!" That was the sole word of the awesome tirade which followed that Dennett was able to understand. The infuriated Emperor's voice grew louder and shriller until to the Scottish scientist the words were a single breathless scream. Rooted to the spot, he flinched nervously as the enraged Corsican suddenly bounded to his feet and hurled the half-filled mug of chocolate wildly over Kensington's shoulder to smash against the wall.

"Your Imperial Majesty," murmured the aghast Earl placatingly, uneasily retreating before the apoplectic Emperor, who now seemed intent on stalking him across the room with a view to sinking his clenched fingers into Kensington's fleshy neck. "If only you'd let us finish explaining. . . ."

"*Gourgandin! Drôle! Lâdre! Coquin! Vilain! Barrique! Pisse-froid! Scélérat! Faux-moine! Putois! Faux-cul! Drôlesse! Ribaud! Tire-chaussette! Canaille! Rosbif! Gratte-genou! Fripouille!*" cried the wrathful Emperor as he marched stiff-legged in pursuit of the trembling Kensington, his eyes bulging and his cheeks a deep crimson. "You *dared* molest my sacred person, you . . . you *faquin! Double-dos! Maraud! Mal-mouché! Butor! Pied-plat! Goddamn! Blanc-bec! Vieille baderne! Paltoquet! Chien! Renifle-orteil! Baudruche!*"

"—all will be settled to Your Imperial Majesty's entire satisfaction!" gasped the Earl of Kensington, who had been backed up against the white concrete wall. His eyes darted desperately to the right and the left as he sought escape from this bantam-cock figure with the maddened glittering eyes who so implacably stalked him. "Dennett! Llewellyn! Holstein! Davison!"

"Ha, *poltron!*" cried the Emperor of France as he neared his helpless quarry while everyone else stood mesmerized by the intensity of the fury that radiated from the diminutive Corsican. With a sudden swift bound the Emperor leapt forward, his lips twisted into a snarl, his fingers clenched like claws. . . .

And as the Earl of Kensington stood transfixed, Napoleon suddenly clutched his chest and with a faint cry of surprise tumbled in a shapeless heap to the concrete floor.

For an eternity only the sound of Kensington's raucous

breathing could be heard. Then an angry, inarticulate shout
came from General Etournaud, who, lashed to the chair as
he was, was trying valiantly to hobble across the laboratory.

His heart pounding with dread, Dennett willed himself to
cross the laboratory and kneel by the huddled figure.
Hardly daring to breathe, he placed one hand on the
burning skin of the lofty forehead and slipped the other
beneath the blue satin nightgown against the cold, clammy
flesh of the Emperor's chest. His own eyes wide, the Master
of Garnaway stared down incomprehendingly at the bulging brown eyes of the most incisive mind of the ages, brown
eyes that were now glazed and unmoving, fixed in an
expression of the most dreadful astonishment.

CHAPTER
= 46 =

AN ARMY travels on its stomach.

*Every French soldier carries a marshal's baton in his
knapsack.*

You can't make an omelet without breaking eggs.

From the sublime to the ridiculous is but a step.

*Go, sir, gallop, and don't forget that the world was made in
six days. You can ask me for anything you like, except time.*

The MacNair scowled at the slim leather-bound volume
in his hand: *Table-Talk—Conversations with His Imperial
Majesty Napoleon As Collated, Recounted, and Annotated
by the Duke of Ogreval.* What a phrasemaker was this windy
Corsican! When he wasn't declaiming to the people of

France and the notables in the Senate, or meddling about with the unending stream of words that composed the Napoleonic Code, he was tirelessly polishing his *bons mots* and *mots justes* for the edification of the rest of an impatiently waiting world.

L'amour: une sottise faite à deux. Ha!

The MacNair drummed his fingers upon the glossy surface of his breakfast table at which he was halfheartedly nibbling at a warm brioche and fresh raspberry preserves while leafing through this fatuous book which his maître d'hôtel Salvetti had brought him the week before. What did all of these phrases remind him of? There was something dimly remembered which nagged at his mind, something which—

Memories suddenly flooded him. Of lunching beneath a shady willow tree in the hills south of Reims with the Archduchess Mireille and the Marquis of Vézelay on a warm autumn's day. Of the secret-police man commenting with sardonic surprise upon the MacNair's unexpected grasp of Napoleonic scholarship. And later that same day, another remark by the Marquis to the same effect.

The MacNair's fingers drummed faster. Why did this suddenly seem so important? What was it he had said to elicit such peculiar comments? He leaned back in his chair, his eyes closed, as he tried to conjure up an exact picture of the moment, the smells of the countryside, the texture of the shiny blue homburg he was wearing, the feel of—

Ha! It was something about champagne! It was . . . it was . . . *If any lout could freeze the neck of a bottle, where, then, would that leave even the greatest of kings?*

And then later on in the day, at the cold and windy end of a wasted afternoon, as they toured the Château Beldam and the MacNair had appealed for the Archduchess Mireille's indulgence to visit its deserted cave, *The million faded bubbles of a million empty dreams—when you fear the consequences of the ungoverned past, why else should you look to see what empty caves might hold?*

Why had the Marquis of Vézelay apparently associated these essentially meaningless epigrams with *Napoleon?* Were they possibly long-forgotten phrases of the Emperor which the MacNair had unconsciously stored away and then brought forth as if they were his own? Possibly, possibly . . .

But in that case what on earth had the Corsican tyrant meant by them? What did *he* know about making champagne?

The MacNair picked up the remains of his brioche, then let it fall to his plate again. Thoughtfully he leafed a second time through the collection of the Emperor's pithy epigrams and witticisms. No, there was nothing here about the necks of bottles or empty caves. . . .

Hmmm. Today, here in 1808, was the 13th of May. That was just shy of twenty-two months that he had been abandoned here. If he correctly understood the gibberish that Sir Norvil Dennett had been wont to sprout about his time machine, that meant that twenty-two months had also passed in the twentieth century since the moment the MacNair had been shanghaied like a drunken soldier and sent back in time. Right now, today, for Dennett and Kensington and the rest of that abominable gang, as well as for Napoleon V and the Marquis of Vézelay, the date must be something on the order of early February of 1994. . . .

And assuming that all of them still existed, the Friends of Bordeaux Wine and the Imperial House of Bonaparte must be anxiously girding themselves for the moment two centuries earlier when the Emperor Napoleon would emerge from the seclusion of his Missing Years and once again stride forth to take the center stage of western Europe.

Would it be too much to hope that they would be paying particularly close attention to whatever actions the secluded Emperor might be taking during these last precarious weeks of the Missing Years, *actions which they now knew to be those of an impostor from the twentieth century?*

With growing excitement the MacNair jumped to his feet and began to pace the sunny dining room. *Suppose, just suppose . . .*

"You say the first Napoleon is *dead?*" cried the Marquis of Vézelay, aghast. "Dead here in the twentieth century?"

"Of an apoplectic fit," amplified his great-great-grandson Napoleon V, "brought on by a surfeit of rage." He stood in the broad window embrasure of his writing room and tersely narrated the startling events, his great hands clasped behind his back while he stared pensively out into the cold drizzle of a grey February morning. "That was nearly a year ago. Since then—"

"A year ago! And yet we're all still here as if nothing at all had happened?" The Marquis of Vézelay sank unbidden into a small gilt chair. Thirteen months of solitary confinement in a military prison in the Vosges Mountains had not added any flesh to his already slight frame or gaunt face. His eyes were now even more prominent than before and his sparse hair and straggly beard were completely grey. He passed a shaky hand across his eyes. "Why . . . why has Your Imperial Majesty summoned me?"

The Emperor of All the French and of the United States of Europe swung around from the window. "Frankly, I'm not exactly certain. Perhaps for your devious mind. Perhaps simply for your company. You are obviously unfit to be allowed to run the Special Directorate but—"

"Ah!" exclaimed Vézelay bitterly. "So that rascal Etour-naud is *still*—"

"Etournaud has defected to the camp of the Earl of Kensington," said the Emperor angrily. "He was present at the time of the first Emperor's death and did nothing to prevent it."

For the first time a faint smile animated the face of the gaunt Marquis. "Yes, I can imagine his subsequent emotions. And my longtime friend, the ardent swain of your delightful niece the Archduchess Mireille, what has become of *him?*"

"Frost? Prince William? That American?" The Emperor snorted. "What do you imagine? He is in a work camp on Sardinia, earnestly weaving baskets and hoeing cabbages."

"Better and better," chortled the Marquis of Vézelay, rubbing his pale hands in glee. "But I can also imagine the unease that Your Imperial Majesty must now be feeling as the time approaches for the first Emperor to emerge from his years of seclusion. Will it *really* be this so-called English prince and almost certain confidence man who will rule all of Europe for the next fifty years? you are wondering. Or, now that the *real* Emperor is dead, may there not be a juncture at which point he was *supposed* to have been returned but now that he no longer exists—"

"All of us will be whisked out of existence any moment," completed the Emperor. "You read my thoughts very well. Which is why I have called you back from your extended leave of absence, my dear cousin." He eyed the Marquis of Vézelay pensively. "Perhaps a hearty meal and a new suit—the one you wear is sitting a trifle loosely upon you—and then you can begin to turn your thoughts to this rather grim situation."

"Tell me, Salvetti," said the MacNair, addressing his saturnine Corsican majordomo, "what do you know about Reims and Epernay?"

"Reims, Your Imperial Majesty? Isn't there a cathedral there?"

"Yes, and a number of caves, both in the city and in the surrounding countryside of Champagne."

"I know nothing of that, Your Imperial Majesty. I am, as you know, from—"

"From my own beloved island of Corsica. Very well, then, bring me as many books and maps of the region as you can."

"At once, Your Imperial Majesty." He bowed low and turned away. Almost at once he stopped. "I nearly forgot. I saw Feroc earlier this morning. He is writing a report which will be ready within a few hours—"

"Feroc—isn't that one of Fouché's confounded spies?"

"Yes, Your Imperial Majesty. I personally charged him some time ago with keeping an eye on Ambassador Baudouin."

"Baudouin!" exclaimed the MacNair, only vaguely remembering the onetime Marshal of France whom he had peremptorily exiled to the northern wastes of Finland. "Isn't he in Helsinki?"

"As far as we know, Your Imperial Majesty. But communications with Finland are, of course, exceedingly slow. What excited the interest of Feroc, however, was the fact that all of the Ambassador's family has recently vanished from sight here in France: his four sons, his two brothers, all of his cousins and relatives."

"Ah," murmured the MacNair, who had picked up some of the Corsican majordomo's conspiratorial view of the world. "The entire clan, eh? Most suggestive, most suggestive."

Salvetti bowed low. "I am pleased to be of service, Your Imperial Majesty. Feroc's full report will be here shortly."

"Excellent, excellent," muttered the MacNair, stalking into his library and throwing himself into a leather armchair. "All I need now is a vengeful hero of France determined to become Emperor in my place. Why can't I simply have a small house on the beach in Hawaii with palm trees and smiling natives all around? And of course, my wretched crown. . . ." He gritted his teeth in vexation. "The one that's caused me all this trouble!"

"If Your Imperial Majesty pleases," said the Marquis of Vézelay with something of his former assurance in his manner, "I have been carefully studying the records of your revered ancestor's Missing Years and have come across an oddity which is *extremely* suggestive."

"Yes?" encouraged the Emperor from his seat before the smoking room fireplace where he sat listlessly cracking walnuts and tossing the shells into the flames.

"Yes. You may recall that during his Missing Years—which are of course the years of the imposture—a number of cryptic utterances and phrases were attributed to him. They have been attributed to a strange mysticism which, depending on your viewpoint, is either a symptom of or the cause of his retreat into seclusion. Many of them remain unexplained by scholars even now."

"Of course they're unexplained," agreed the Emperor. "You and I now know them to be simply the ravings of this Yankee or English madman, whoever he is."

"Exactly!" cried the Marquis triumphantly. "But suppose we were to reexamine them *knowing* them to issue from the mouth of a man from our own time sent back to the eighteen-hundreds against his will. What then?"

"Well, what?"

The Marquis of Vézelay removed a paper from the inside pocket of his grey coat and carefully placed a pair of gold-rimmed pince-nez on his aristocratic nose. "Six weeks before your ancestor's two years of seclusion come to an end we suddenly find *this* in a letter which he dispatched to members of his family, the Pope in Rome, the president of the Senate, and the prefect of every *département* in France: 'Last night I dreamt I soared on the back of a mighty eagle out of Paris and across the countryside as far north as Luxembourg and then south to Reims and then east to the great cathedral of Vézelay where the eagle set me down and I wandered lonely through its catacombs until a voice came to me in the stillness, saying, *The million faded bubbles of a million empty dreams—when you fear the consequences of the ungoverned past, why else should you look to see what empty caves might hold?* And in my dream I was now no longer beneath the ancient church, but deep in a gloomy cavern surrounded by innumerable bottles that stretched off into the darkness and that same eagle which had carried me on his back now appeared before me once again and transformed itself into a lovely young woman all clad in white with golden blond hair and a glittering crown upon her head which dazzled and gleamed as if with a million brilliant fires. And the woman put one hand upon her pale white neck and held forth her other hand to me and spoke, saying, *If any lout could freeze the neck of a bottle, where, then, would that leave even the greatest of kings?'*"

The Marquis of Vézelay looked up from his notes, his eyes glittering with excitement. "Let me relate to Your Imperial Majesty what I recall of a day spent in the company of your niece the Archduchess Mireille of Luxembourg and her erstwhile swain, Prince William Ernest Augustus, known at the time as the Count of Domrémy-la-Pucelle. . . ."

CHAPTER
$= 47 =$

NO WONDER LIFE SPANS were lower in the bad old days, thought the MacNair miserably as he was bounced and flung about the inside of the small plain carriage that raced along the roads of northern France in the silver light of a full moon. All this pounding on the kidneys and other vital organs must surely be a factor in their early demise. . . .

The thick velvet side curtains of the carriage were partially drawn and it was far too dark in its interior to read the map that was folded beside him, but the MacNair was certain from the harsh sound of the horses' hooves and of the metal rims of the wheels that they were now clattering through the cobblestoned streets of the sleeping town of La Ferté-sur-Jouarre on the banks of the Marne. Even now, twelve years later, he recalled with a nostalgic twinge that town's gastronomic temple of *ancienne cuisine* the Auberge de Condé and the superb meal of *foie gras en gelée* followed by sweetbreads in a sauce of pink champagne he had once devoured in the company of a pert brunette from Venice. He peered fruitlessly at the shadowy forms of the passing buildings and wondered if the restaurant would ever exist in this perverse universe to which the unspeakable Herr Doctor and Professor Hubmaier had so maliciously brought him.

Wedging himself immovably into a corner of the jolting carriage, he reflected that if all now went according to the plans which the most scrupulous logic had devised, then shortly he would once again be in a position to find out.

Soon, so very soon. . . .

The jolting of the carriage took on another rhythm and the clatter of hooves and wheels was suddenly muted. He looked out into the night and saw that they were once again in the sleeping countryside, racing along one of the long straight roads which the Emperor had decreed for the easy movement of his armies. If that had really been La Ferté-sur-Jouarre, then they were already nearly halfway to Reims—another eighty-two kilometers, the MacNair remembered from his perusal of the map before he and Salvetti had sneaked out earlier that evening from a side entrance of the Elysée Palace. He tugged nervously at the soft brown leather cap which concealed much of his face and felt along the seat beside him to reassure himself that the two dozen sealed bronze caskets were still there. He felt himself in the grip of an exhilarated anticipation. What, he asked himself anxiously, awaited him in Reims?

By the time the MacNair's carriage reached the city the streets of early morning Reims were already crowded with farmers and peasants on their way to market. For several miles the towering spire of the great cathedral had been visible across the slowly lightening countryside, but here in the early nineteenth century no unsightly sprawl of suburbs had grown up around the city proper: One moment the carriage was on a broad dirt road passing between farms and pastures, the next on cobblestones passing between stone and mortar buildings that were already centuries old.

The MacNair knocked vigorously on the front panel and the carriage came to a halt. Red-faced peasants in heavy blue clothing with baskets of vegetables and squawking poultry under their arms eyed him curiously as he climbed down from the coach, but none of them seemed to recognize their almost mythic Imperial Majesty in this small agile figure in dark maroon corduroy and light brown jerkin who was wedging himself into place on the driver's bench between Salvetti and the hulking driver.

"Straight ahead," said the MacNair to the driver. "And then I think it's off to the right."

But after forty minutes of fruitlessly driving back and

forth along the twisting streets of Reims the MacNair gave up as hopeless the task of trying to find the ancient building which in 1991 had housed the wine shippers of Baudchon et Fils. Very well, he sighed to himself, he would just have to start searching for the caverns on his list.

His ultimate goal was the great cave of the Château Beldame, before whose entrance he had once stood bickering with the Archduchess Mireille and the Marquis of Vézelay. But *that* was miles to the southeast of Reims and dozens of others could be visited on the way. A like number existed within the city itself, but even in disguise it seemed best to avoid onlookers as far as possible. With a sigh he turned to the driver. "South," he ordered, "to Epernay."

A mile to the south of Reims a recent map had indicated that just to the west side of the main road could be found the former quarry still known as Les Frères Blaireaux. A tangled mass of shrubs and hedges now covered the rocky hillside indicated by the map and no quarry or cave was in evidence. The MacNair ordered the coach to a halt. He and Salvetti swung down from the driver's bench and pushed their way through a break in the bushes along the road. Disheveled and cursing, they came out in an overgrown pasture in which a large flock of merino sheep were grazing placidly some distance away. A few hundred yards to their left they spied a sheepherder standing motionlessly beneath a broad elm and the MacNair dispatched his Corsican majordomo to question him about the supposed cave.

"Blast it," muttered the MacNair when Salvetti had returned, "now that *he* knows we're here we'll have to go through all that rigmarole with the surveyor's equipment." They returned to the carriage, then once again marched into the pasture, this time with the driver and Salvetti carrying leather satchels and ungainly instruments. The MacNair ordered them about officiously while they made their way to the half-concealed opening of the cavern which they now found without difficulty behind an outcropping in the hillside. "You wait here and keep everyone away," he told the driver. "If anyone should be impertinent enough to ask our business, we are the 4th Brigade of Engineers of the Imperial Army, attending to the confidential business of Marshal Duchêne. Dangerous explosives are being stored. Traps are being set. Guards, vicious dogs, and spies have been posted. You may take whatever other measures are necessary to discourage them. Is that clear, Sergeant?"

"Yes, my colonel," snapped the grizzled sergeant with a ragged salute.

Four lanterns were lit and Salvetti and the MacNair carried them awkwardly through the broad mouth of the cavern along with the satchels and surveying equipment. The ceiling here was twenty feet overhead and they were a hundred yards into the hillside before the light from outside began to fade. They passed a turning in the passageway and were suddenly in almost total darkness. The MacNair retrieved a small bronze casket from one of the satchels, and, abandoning their surveying equipment, the two men made their way ever deeper into the blackness of the abandoned limestone diggings, their smoking lanterns casting small circles of flickering orange light.

At last the MacNair came to a halt and peered around the blackness in growing dismay. Here he was in a cavern, one that in his own world was almost certainly used to store champagne. But now that he was here, what *exactly* was he to do? His sudden brainstorm of stashing away a number of boxes in abandoned caves in the hope that someone in the future might think to look for them had seemed brilliant at the time. But now . . . ? Somehow he hadn't expected an abandoned quarry to be quite so . . . so *abandoned!* Where was he to *hide* the wretched casket?

But now that he was here, he had to do *something!* With a sigh, he sent Salvetti to retrieve a small geologist's hammer from the satchels. When he returned, the MacNair indicated a spot in the soft limestone wall about head-high and gave instructions for him to pound out a niche big enough to receive the bronze casket which he juggled impatiently in his hands.

Twenty minutes later the MacNair jammed the small metal box tightly into an aperture barely large enough to hold it and crammed as much as he could of the bits of limestone that Salvetti had displaced in the space around the gleaming casket. He rubbed two handfuls of gritty powder over the exposed surface in the hopes of masking its gleam from a casual glance. But hopefully it could still be spotted by someone with a powerful light and a powerful enough motive for searching.

He chuckled maliciously to himself in the eerie orange light cast by the smoking lanterns as he and Salvetti made their way back toward the entrance and the bright morning sunlight of Champagne. Would preventing the end of the world be considered a powerful enough motive? he wondered.

Or at least the end of the world such as those who were clearly responsible for his present contretemps would understand it. For in the small bronze casket now hopefully hidden away for retrieval two centuries in the future the MacNair had enclosed a pithy message that would, he hoped, make instant sense to the right eyes:

To my dear friends the M. of G., the E. of K., the P. of S.-H., the M. of V., the A. of L., and N. the Five, Greetings from the past:
Your friend P.W.E.A.H., D. of Y., thinks of you often, and begs to remind you that in less than two weeks the Sleeping Beauty is due to awaken from his two-year slumber. But he can state with certitude that the Sleeping Beauty is no longer interested in acquiring the hand of the lovely A. He now has in mind one of the innumerable daughters of the S. of the O.E., thereby cementing an alliance with that cheerful paterfamilias. With what joy he looks forward to the offspring of that momentous union! How they will spread across Europe!

You may recall the birthplace of N. as already being outside France: now married to a luminary of the East, P.W. will of course move the center of his own activities eastward to Italy, or possibly even as far east as Greece. France, never fear, will always remain dear to him as a model dairy farm and producer of firewood, and he will do his utmost to encourage these wholesome activities to the total exclusion of any other. . . .

Once his family is well established (a very *large* -

family, he is certain) P.W. will then have sufficient leisure to devote the rest of his days to seeking out the direct forebears in Germany and England of his good friends the M. of G., the E. of K., the P. of S.-H., and all the others in Morayshire of whom he retains the most piquant memories. You may be sure that he will do whatever lies within his power to encourage them to maintain an absolute and lifelong celibacy. . . .

In fact, he can absolutely *guarantee* all of the above consequences unless the t.m. in G.C. is *instantly* put into operation and used to return the writer of these tidings to the same ambience enjoyed by all of his above-enumerated friends.

>Sincerely, oh, *most* sincerely,
>(H.R.H.) P.W.E.A.H., D. of Y.

"There!" muttered the MacNair half aloud. "If *that* doesn't get them moving . . ." I suppose I'd better be prepared to spend the next fifty years as Napoleon Bonaparte, he concluded to himself gloomily.

CHAPTER
= 48 =

THE MACNAIR HAD somewhat grandiosely ordered the construction of an even two dozen bronze caskets; still accustomed to thinking in terms of automobile travel along paved roads, he had vaguely planned to conceal each of them in a different cave within two or, at the most, three days. Now the sun had long since disappeared behind the hills to the west and in the soft summer twilight the MacNair and Salvetti were scrambling through the thorny bushes that concealed the partially blocked entrance of only the third cavern they had been able to locate. The road from Reims to Epernay lay only a hundred yards west of this rocky crag that suddenly sprang from the gently rolling hills of the surrounding countryside, but was completely hidden from view by a nearly impenetrable thicket of blackberry bushes that grew along its shoulders. The carriage itself had been pulled into a pasture and the driver sat dozing on his bench.

"The last one today," cried the MacNair to his saturnine majordomo with rather more zestful enthusiasm than he actually felt, and picked up a lantern in either hand to lead the way through the crumbling stone archway into the still dry blackness.

The floor of the cavern quickly dipped and turned to the right. Within a dozen yards they were out of sight of the small circle of pale sky, and the darkness became absolute.

The MacNair pressed ahead, the lanterns held high, one elbow brushing the limestone wall to his right. His shadow jerked and blurred to all sides of him, while just behind him he could hear the footsteps of his faithful Corsican as he advanced with his own lanterns, a bronze casket, and a number of small implements for digging.

"This will do," said the MacNair, halting at a stretch of wall which was indistinguishable from the rest. "You might as well dig here."

"Yes, Your Imperial Majesty."

The MacNair took a lantern for himself and sat down in the gloom some distance away with his back against the rough underground surface. For a seemingly interminable time he watched his majordomo laboriously chipping away at the wall in the orange light of the other three lamps. The pounding of the hammer and pick echoed loudly through the unseen tunnels and caverns that surrounded him, and the MacNair gritted his teeth in vexation. Very soon now he would have to reconsider his plans. If it took all day to deposit a mere three messages, how long would it—

He was startled by a sudden silence and what appeared to be a faint light approaching from the darkness to his right. His heart lurched in his chest and he jumped hastily to his feet. He glanced at Salvetti, who was standing motionless, hammer in hand, then back at the flicker of bobbing orange light. The vague outline of legs in motion could be seen in the cone of light cast by the lantern. The MacNair gulped convulsively. "Is that you, Sergeant?" he called hesitantly.

"Oui, mon colonel," came the hoarse reply, and with a loud exhalation of pent-up breath the MacNair slouched back against the limestone wall in heartfelt relief. It was only as the clatter of footsteps grew louder and the glowing lantern neared that he thought to ask himself just why his driver should be—

But by then it was far too late, for to his horrified shock he found himself looking down in the circle of light at the glossy leather boots of at least eight or ten men. Before he could do more than open his mouth they formed a tight ring about him, hemming him in implacably against the cavern wall. The lantern dipped and as if in a bad dream he saw

that half a dozen enormous flintlock pistols were now
aimed directly at his stomach.

The MacNair drew himself up and expanded his chest
like a pouter pigeon. He ripped the floppy leather cap from
his head and flashed a look of imperial fury at the half-
visible men around him. "What the devil do you rascals
think you're up to?" he cried wrathfully. "Do you have the
slightest idea of who—"

"—you are?" said the same hoarse voice that had answered him a moment earlier. "Of course we do—Your
Imperial Majesty!"

"Ah! That's better, then," sighed the MacNair. "Now
then, put away those ridiculous weapons before you do
yourselves a mischief and—"

"—then explain ourselves? Gladly, Your Imperial Majesty." The pistols trained on the MacNair were unwavering
but the lantern was slowly raised until it illuminated the
man who held it. He was tall and broad, with a wide-
brimmed hat that swooped at a rakish angle across his
forehead. A thick pirate's mustache drooped beneath his
fleshy nose. The MacNair stared at him in baffled dismay.
Was this someone he was supposed to know? One of his
brothers or—

"You don't recognize me?" The man grunted with sour
amusement and swept the hat from his head. "Look well,
young Buono—on your old mate from our beloved cadet
school at Brienne, Yves-Louis Baudouin, Imperial Ambassador to the Court of Helsinki!"

"Baudouin!" gasped the MacNair. "But . . . but what are
you doing *here?*" He cast a quick glance to where his
majordomo, Salvetti, stood silently against the far wall.
"And how did you *know* I was here? *No one*—"

"—except yourself and Salvetti knew, eh?" The marshal's laughter boomed through the cavern. "That was quite
enough, I fear."

"You mean—Salvetti?"

"Salvetti. Once he came to understand the full extent of
your madness it was easy enough to realize that another
emperor would soon be stepping in to protect France from
your pitiful follies and delusions. And as the second man in

France, the right-hand man to a madman, where would that leave *him* unless—"

"—he betrayed me to you himself," concluded the Mac-Nair bitterly. "Sound strategy, of course, very sound, very Corsican."

The Lion of the Cotswolds chuckled complacently. "Exactly. This strange expedition of yours to the caves of Champagne coincided perfectly with my own, shall we say, discreet arrival from Finland, and after gathering up my family, of whom you see the male members around you, we—"

"—followed me here. I see. And just what are your intentions in regard to your Emperor—and to Salvetti, of course? You will demote him to being but the third man of France, perhaps?"

"Salvetti? The chambermaid?" Baudouin's eyes turned to the lugubrious majordomo. "Step forward, my good Salvetti, that you might claim your just reward!"

The Corsican nodded gravely and set down the tools he was still holding. Scrupulously avoiding the eyes of the MacNair, he stepped away from the limestone wall—to be flung back an instant later by a ragged volley of gunfire. Eyes wide with surprise and horror, he slumped slowly to the ground, where he twitched once, then lay motionless.

As the echoes of the shots slowly died away in the distant depths of the cavern, the MacNair fixed Marshal Baudouin with a cold eye. "As you say, his just reward."

The Marshal nodded. "Who could ever trust a Corsican —particularly one who had already betrayed his master once?" He sighed heavily. "A pity that it should have to come to this between old schoolmates, but there it is! Really, Buono, I'm astonished at you! Coming alone to a cave in the middle of nowhere, with no one at all aware of your whereabouts—what kind of a grasp of tactics is *that?* It's simply *asking* for trouble! Too bad, too bad. You really should have listened to me when I wanted to discuss the delegation of authority. And now . . . Well, now, I fear, this gloomy cavern will prove an excellent spot for his mysterious excellency the Imperial Bonaparte to vanish forever from human ken." Baudouin's heavy hand fixed itself around the MacNair's biceps. "Right this way, Your Imperial Majesty. We'll just stroll down to the end of this cave, and when I return I'll take a look in that box to see what your final folly was all about."

CHAPTER
= 49 =

"YOU'VE BEEN DOING *what?*" demanded Napoleon V.

"I've been searching every cave and quarry within a hundred kilometers of Reims," replied the Marquis of Vézelay, with a barely concealed air of triumph.

"And . . ."

"And in the twenty-seventh cavern I came to—I found this!" He brought forth a small bronze casket, dull and blotched with age.

"What is it?" asked the Emperor curiously, leaning across his desk.

The Marquis's face grew instantly grave. "If I read it aright, a message to us across the centuries from our old friend Prince William, the erstwhile Duke of York."

"My God!" cried the Emperor, his craggy face aghast after he had twice read the message on the piece of heavy white paper which the Marquis of Vézelay took forth from the casket. "My God, my God, my *God!* He's about to flick the United States of Europe out of existence with a snap of his fingers!"

"Not to mention the House of Bonaparte," noted the Marquis with a certain ambivalent relish to his voice. "We could both of us be sitting here talking, just like *this,* and hey-presto! we're gone, just like *that!"* He snapped his fingers loudly.

"But what am I supposed to *do?"* moaned the Emperor of All the French and of the United States of Europe.

"That, Your Imperial Majesty, is why *you* are Emperor, and I am not. I know only that you will do what you *have* to do!"

The Emperor's icy blue eyes skewered the sardonic Marquis as he stared at the former secret-police man with ill-concealed loathing. "I should have left you in your retirement home in the Vosges," he muttered furiously. "Very well. There is clearly but one thing to be done. Arrange a meeting with these damned madmen Kensington and Dennett. Just the four of us. Give them any safeguards they want in order to get them there."

"Any?"

"Any, damn you! Up to and including a total amnesty. But hurry!" His eyes turned to the grey winter sky that showed through the bare branches of the leafless shade trees in the Elysée park. "How many more days remain in the Missing Years? I don't think we have much time at all. . . ."

While Sir Norvil Dennett and Alfred St. John Wester, 7th Earl of Kensington, bounced slowly north in a chartered trimotor airplane to their rendezvous in Iceland with the Marquis of Vézelay and a personage to be known only as Mr. Brown, several thousand miles to the west Mary Louise Babcock, widow of the late lieutenant governor of the State of Franklin, had taken $9.45 of the income generated by the $2,341,849.12 held in trust by the Fiduciary Bank of Salem, Massachusetts, to purchase a railway ticket from Portland to New York. At the same time that the two anxious Englishmen were being ushered into a small waiting room at the American embassy in Reykjavík, the lithe auburn-haired beauty was being shown into the morning room of the triplex apartment in which the Archduchess Mireille had taken refuge at the Hotel Regency on 61st Street.

The equally slim Archduchess stood rigidly at the side of a glistening grand piano appraising the other woman with a distinct reserve. Only her voice betrayed her emotions. "You said you had something to communicate concerning . . . concerning a certain Kevin Frost?"

Mary Louise Babcock had not been invited to remove the heavy fur coat she wore as protection against the wintry gales that battered New England in this February of 1994. Her lovely lips twitched in a faint smile of tolerant derision. People of *real* importance, governors and senators, she had known all her life; she had lunched with two vice-presidents of the United States, played golf with a secretary of state, and dined with a president; she was far from being over-whelmed by a pop-eyed archduchess with a receding chin from some measly place called Luxembourg. "Yes," she said coolly as she draped her coat carelessly over the nearest chair, "I have distinct reason to believe that he is, in fact, that same person known to you, and to the sensational tabloids, as the Count of Domrémy-la-Pucelle. Or is it the Duke of Deane?" She sank gracefully onto the arm of a divan and crossed her long elegant legs. "You Frenchmen seem to have so *many* names!"

"Kevin . . ." murmured the Archduchess Mireille as she fell back onto the padded piano bench beside her. "What do you know about him?" she whispered huskily.

Mary Louise Babcock's brilliant green eyes glittered fiercely. "I know only that he is my husband, and that I want him back!"

"Let me see," said Sir Norvil Dennett, carefully marking figures on a piece of paper. "You say that Napoleon's Missing Years are considered to run from July 27, 1806—that's the day we exchanged him with Prince William—to July 4, 1808, the day he suddenly reappeared at the American embassy celebrations with the woman who was to become the Empress Alexine?"

"That is correct," murmured the Marquis of Vézelay with a quick glance at the glowering personage known as Mr. Brown.

"One year, eleven months, and seven days," said Dennett thoughtfully, adding a second row of figures to the page. "Prince William was returned to 1806 nearly two years ago, on March 21st, 1992. And today is the 23rd of February. He tapped the pencil thoughtfully against his bushy grey whiskers. "We would appear to have at the most five days to accede to Prince William's demands. At the end of that time . . ." He shrugged his shoulders meaningfully.

The craggy face of Mr. Brown was grim. "Your time machine is in working order?" he snapped in French.

"Oh, yes, entirely so."

"Well, then—use it to return this . . . this Prince William at once!"

"You are forgetting, Mr. Brown: If we return Prince William, then who—"

"—will appear at the Fourth of July party at the American embassy?" concluded the Marquis of Vézelay. "And then go on to reign as Napoleon I for the next forty years?"

A long sullen silence ensued as looks of mutual hatred were exchanged across the shabby wooden table in the conference room of the American embassy.

"There's only one thing to do!" cried the Earl of Kensington at last, his normally ruddy face nearly purple with emotion as he slammed his fist onto the table before the startled Mr. Brown. "And if your bloody hangman here has had him killed, then it's just too bad for the lot of us." He glared venomously at the totally unabashed Marquis of Vézelay. "Just what have you done with this idiot Kevin Frost?"

The two women had collapsed into each other's arms and were sobbing together in companionable misery when the telephone began to ring insistently. Dabbing at her eyes with a white cambric hankie, the Archduchess Mireille lurched unsteadily across the room. *"Oui, c'est elle-même. Oui."* She put her hand over the receiver, her eyes wide. "It's Uncle Bonbon," she whispered in bleary surprise. "I wonder what—" She returned the receiver to her ear and her voice hardened instantly. "Yes, Uncle, I hear you! How odd that you should call at this moment: You must have heard that I have just scheduled that press confer— What? What? *What?"* She let the telephone drop to her lap while a faint tinny voice continued speaking unheeded. Her cornflower-blue eyes had grown round with wonder. "He wants me to become an empress," she whispered to an uncomprehending Mary Louise Babcock, "he wants me to become a real empress!"

Fourteen months had passed since the flight of the Archduchess Mireille to New York and the subsequent death of the Emperor Napoleon Bonaparte of an apoplectic fit. Though not entirely a stranger to a life of enforced reclusion in the United States, Kevin Frost had nevertheless not relished the fourteen months he had spend tending vegetables on the hot and arid island of Sardinia in the Mediterranean between France and Italy. Even the allotment of a half liter of harsh red wine with his evening meal did little to kindle his enthusiasm for the Emperor's hospitality. Nonetheless he glowed with health: His incipient paunch had disappeared, his arms and chest bulged with muscle, his eyes were clear, his face was tanned.

Now he was asking himself despairingly why he had suddenly been summarily marched from the fields by six taciturn soldiers in full battle gear and taken by them still in his khaki work clothes to a military airfield an hour's drive away. Could the same beloved Mireille who had once so cruelly abandoned him without a word have at last relented and importuned her imperial uncle into releasing him from this bitter imprisonment?

Or—his heart leaped up and began to pound violently in his chest as he was roughly trundled aboard a twin-engined army plane whose propellers had already been turning over as their car swung onto the airfield—or had his longtime nemesis, the rancorous Marquis of Vézelay, at last convinced his patron that the time had come to dispose of lovable Kevin Frost—permanently?

The hatch slammed behind him, he was strapped into a plain metal seat, and the craft lurched forward. A moment later it was airborne and swinging out across the gleaming blue sea. Kevin Frost clenched his fists tightly and tried to control his mounting panic.

The Archduchess Mireille—or a forgotten grave?

What was his destiny to be?

* * *

The American embassy in Reykjavík was a modest two-story dwelling of faded brick not far from the building that housed the Althing, the world's oldest parliament. At the request of the French and British ambassadors a small room had been set aside and a formal guarantee of safe conduct offered to the participants by both the Icelandic and American governments. Now that small upstairs conference room, previously the site of three meetings between the two Englishmen and the two Frenchmen, became even more crowded as a door opened simultaneously on each end of the room.

"You!" cried the Archduchess Mireille indignantly.

"My love!" exclaimed Kevin Frost, his eyes agleam with incredulous delight as he stepped across the room and attempted to enfold his beloved in his sinewy arms.

"Kevin!" gasped Mary Louise Babcock, now stepping into view from behind the burly figure of the straw-haired Mr. Brown. "What's happened to your mustache?"

"Mary Louise! I mean . . . who *is* this woman?" blurted the appalled Kevin Frost, turning just in time to receive a stinging backhand across his right cheek from an enraged Archduchess. He lurched and stumbled, the better to receive an even more vehement forehand across his other cheek from the infuriated beauty he had so basely scorned in the State of Franklin.

For the first time in many months the once normally cheerful Mr. Brown felt a faint smile struggling to animate his face.

"Bravo!" cried the Marquis of Vézelay gleefully as the man who had so poignantly contributed to his own downfall staggered about the room in shock and bewilderment. "Again! And again!"

"Enough!" shouted Mr. Brown, his icy blue eyes gleaming. "We have serious—"

"Uncle!" gasped the Archduchess Mireille, for the first time becoming fully aware of Mr. Brown's presence. She raised her hand and stepped forward purposefully. "You said you were going to make me Empress! You said nothing about harboring this slimy toad of a—"

"Please, my dear, please!" begged Mr. Brown, retreating

warily to the other side of the table, "everything will be explained. But first—just who is this . . . charming lady and why—"

"I'm Mary Louise Babcock," stated that charming lady between clenched teeth, "and I have come to see if that toad on the other side of the room is actually the man I married and the man I love!"

"What!" cried the Emperor of 300 million souls, his mustache quivering with emotion, "so ravishing a creature as *you*—married to a . . . to a . . . such as *this?*" A scornful flick of his hand dismissed the miserable Kevin Frost.

"Ha! What a notion! *That's* not the man I married!"

"What?" cried the Marquis of Vézelay, his head spinning in total confusion. Could there now be a *third* Kevin Frost somewhere?

"I don't know *who* he is, and I don't care! But that's not the man I love!" Mary Louise Babcock turned to the stunned Archduchess of Luxembourg and, pulling her tightly against her own superb bosom, kissed her compassionately on her lovely forehead. "Thank you for bringing me with you," she whispered. "He's all yours, and welcome to him!"

CHAPTER
= 50 =

"PICK UP THAT carcass and bring it along," growled the Lion of the Cotswolds to the desperadoes who still encircled the glowering MacNair with their ridiculous-looking but deadly flintlock pistols. "We'll dump it along with the other." His fingers tightened on the upper arm of the MacNair and he jerked him suddenly forward. "This way, Buono, right this way."

The MacNair snorted angrily and jerked his arm free from the Marshal's grip. "The devil you say," he muttered in a black rage, and stepped forward to knee the astonished hero squarely in the lower regions of his dark blue jacket. The Marshal of France staggered back with a sharp gasp, just as a sudden white light of impossible brilliance exploded soundlessly in the darkness of the cavern. Its blinding intensity lingered for what could only have been a few seconds, but it was more than enough to dazzle the MacNair and the men around him.

But the MacNair's reflexes were quicker and infinitely more motivated than those of the hulking Marshal Baudouin *et famille:* even as he tried to blink away the flashing lights and colorful stars that danced before his eyes, he lashed out powerfully with a heavy workman's boot and heard a satisfying scream. An instant later he was clambering across a sprawled body and running blindly into the darkness. . . .

Shouts and curses echoed behind him, and above his

labored breathing he heard the sound of racing footsteps. The same dazzling light flashed again, somewhere behind him this time, and kept him from running at full tilt into the pitted limestone wall. He skidded on the powdery floor as he tried to change direction, just as a pistol shot exploded deafeningly and the wall beside him cratered and spat rock at his face.

The MacNair gasped in terror and turned sharply to his left—now at least he had the wall beside him to give direction. His fingers brushing the rough surface, he ran desperately into the darkness. More shots exploded behind him and the whine of passing bullets lent speed to his already flying feet. The blackness embraced him.

Suddenly the passageway around him lit up again with the harsh white glare of a third explosion, but one which now was far behind him and cast his long black shadow some twenty yards before him. The cries and curses of the family Baudouin were distinctly weaker, and definitely receding into the distance. His chest pounding violently, the MacNair found a last reserve of strength and rounded a corner in the passageway to find himself once again thankfully engulfed by a total darkness.

His fingernails still rasped along the wall beside him as he stumbled haltingly along the uneven floor. A chilling thought suddenly struck him—*was he even going in the right direction?* Suppose he was even now plunging ever deeper into the cavern, about to totter at any moment into a bottomless abyss . . . ?

His tortured breath was loud in his ears. Too late to stop now, he muttered wildly. Whatever those soundless explosions were that had so providentially diverted the murderous Lion of the Cotswolds, they had given him a last desperate chance to save himself. Best to take full advantage of it without idiotic thoughts of suddenly tumbling helplessly through the darkness, falling, falling. . . .

The MacNair pressed on into the blackness.

An infinite time later, just as he thought that his laboring lungs could gasp no more, he became aware that the inky blackness that enfolded him was quickly receding. He plunged on with renewed strength, even as his chest heaved and his legs nearly buckled, and in a moment of the greatest exhilaration he had ever known he saw the twinkling stars of the bright night sky in an oval just before him. With a strangled sob of exhaustion and relief the MacNair lurched out of the hillside and into the cool fresh breeze of southern Champagne.

For a single delicious moment he paused to gulp cool air deep into his lungs, and then with his wildly pounding chest still burning agonizingly, he staggered twenty yards across the pasture to the dark mass of a thick bush and oblivious to all its thorns collapsed into its inky center.

As he lay crouched in its concealment, his pulse racing and the blood pounding in his ears, to his shock and horror he became aware of a darker silhouette slowly detaching itself from the hillside near the mouth of the tunnel and moving against the clear evening sky. His eyes widened. It was obviously a man, and moving inexorably toward his hiding place. The MacNair clutched his legs against his chest and desperately pushed himself even deeper into what was supposed to be his sanctuary.

But it was all quite useless. The darkened figure moved unerringly to the bush, then stopped and appeared to be staring directly down at the MacNair. The MacNair gulped silently and tried to tell himself that in an instant he would burst forth from his refuge and strangle this terrifying menace with his bare hands. . . .

Adrenaline pumped through his body, leaving him trembling and light-headed. He tensed his legs in readiness and prepared to—

"So *there* you are," sighed the unmistakable voice of the Marquis of Vézelay. "Do come out of there, Your Royal Highness, and let's be on our way. I imagine that the Emperor's soldiers have rounded up those desperadoes by now and we can return to the business of concealing your little casket with its poignant message. There's been entirely enough nonsense already this evening, don't you think? If that casket isn't in place two centuries from now for me to find, then I don't know *where* we'd all be!"

CHAPTER
== 51 ==

"BUT THIS IS monstrous!" cried the Earl of Kensington indignantly from where he stood in a large cluster of men in the brightly lighted laboratory of Garnaway Castle. "You clearly promised us a general amnesty!" He rattled the shackles which bound his wrists.

"So I did," admitted the Emperor Napoleon V coldly. *"I* promised you amnesty, and *I* have kept to my word." He stepped forward and let his arctic-blue eyes run across the motley group of sixty-three Englishmen and Germans who were crowded together under the watchful guard of twenty-eight heavily armed soldiers. Beside the Emperor stood a dozen more grave men in formal morning wear. "I, however, am not responsible for actions of the heads of other states. One of your ransom demands, you may recall, was the call for total independence of all the European states. Very well, here is formal proof of their independence: The heads of all the European states have unanimously decreed you and your colleagues to be far too dangerous to be permitted to continue playing with your time machine. Even your own British Parliament concurred in this decision."

"An infamy, a mockery!" declared Prince Konrad of Schleswig-Holstein passionately from the midst of the dispirited crowd of prisoners. "You have no concept of honor!"

"You would prefer the guillotine, as was the consensus

decided upon by my confreres?" asked Napoleon dryly. "I should have thought that my own plea that all of you be exiled instead would have—"

"Exiled to first-century Easter Island," cried Sir Norvil Dennett hotly. "You call that preferable to your—"

The Emperor shrugged. "*Somebody* has to be responsible for the mysterious civilization that grew up there two millennia ago. Dr. Campinotti informs me that it might as well be Les Amis des Grands Vins de Bordeaux and the Friends of Goethe Society as anyone else." A wintry smile crossed his craggy features. "Just think, man, you may well turn out to be the forebears of those Polynesian vikings who—"

"Bah!" snorted the former Master of Garnaway, turning his back to the Emperor of All the French and the United States of Europe.

Napoleon V shook his head sadly and turned his gaze across the laboratory to Dr. Campinotti and his team of assistants from the Curie Institute. "Are you ready, Doctor?"

"All is in readiness, Your Imperial Majesty."

"Then dispatch the first group."

Ten bitterly protesting Yeoman Sons of Essex were herded forward at bayonet point by soldiers representing the fourteen states that along with France composed the United States of Europe. The tight confines of Sir Norvil Dennett's time machine closed about them. "What about these handcuffs?" shouted Sir James Stuart vehemently, rattling his shackles in the face of an impassive Norwegian soldier. "We'll starve to death if—"

"The keys will accompany the last ones through," replied Dr. Campinotti placidly. "Tools, foodstuffs, and various supplies have already been sent ahead. Even the splendid contents of this castle's remarkable wine cellar." He flashed his magnificent teeth in a dazzling smile. "Or should I say, sent behind. Ah, well, little difference." The hum of the accumulators had been building up for the past ten minutes and now it suddenly reached an almost intolerable pitch. The Emperor grimaced in discomfort and raised his hands to his ears. With a glance at the instruments before him the director of the Curie Institute moved his finger to a button on the panel. A moment later the ten Yeoman Sons of Essex had vanished into the distant past.

"Remarkable," muttered the Prime Minister of Portugal to the Emperor, "and now they're already on Easter Island in the year 1 A.D.?"

"So I assume," shrugged Napoleon V. "Once they've all been sent back we'll use the machine to check up on their presence on the island, and then I fear we'll all of us have to bear witness to the tedious business of making certain that everything concerned with this infernal machine is destroyed forever."

"Only too willingly," agreed the Grand Duke Ingvar of Sweden. He leaned closer to the Emperor and lowered his voice. "You will excuse the possible impertinence, I am sure, my dear Charles-Pierre, but once the machine and all the papers relating to its construction have been destroyed in front of us, what, then, is to assure the rest of us"—he indicated the thirteen other heads of state—"that Dr. Campinotti and his colleagues would not be able to—"

"—reproduce the machine for themselves for their own purposes? Or for the exclusive service of France? An excellent question, my dear Ingvar." The Emperor nodded grimly. "And one to which I have devoted considerable worry." His cold blue eyes grew even frostier and he moved his lips closer to the younger man's ear. "I fear that it is a monstrous injustice to the good Dr. Campinotti and his colleagues, but as soon as they have finished dispatching the rest of this group of madmen, they, too, will be . . ." He gestured meaningfully.

The eyes of the Grand Duke widened. "They, *too,* will be sent to Easter Island?"

"What else would you have me do?" The Emperor sighed plaintively. "Poor loyal Campinotti, a hard end for such a distinguished scientist."

"There *will* be the wine cellar," pointed out the Grand Duke thoughtfully. *"That* will surely be a comfort to—"

"You'll all regret this bitterly!" shouted the unrepentant Earl of Kensington furiously as he was herded forward into the time machine. "I'll see that all of you scoundrels pay!

You'll bitterly rue the day! I'll—"

Dr. Campinotti's finger came down and then there was only silence.

CHAPTER
= 52 =

ON THE SAME fine spring day, April 11, 1994, that the Emperor Napoleon V was in Scotland grimly presiding over the destruction of the infernal machine that had so nearly brought about his downfall, a number of infinitely more tender affairs of the heart were transpiring in various parts of Europe.

In the towering mountains of the Jura in the eastern part of France a hermetically sealed military reservation was nearing completion. Within its tightly guarded borders the Duke of Vézelay, recently reinstated by a grateful Emperor as the head of the Special Directorate, was strolling slowly through a rolling meadow toward a picturesque stone village on the banks of a tumbling stream. Four heavily armed soldiers dressed in the baggy blue uniforms of the Grande Armée of Napoleon Bonaparte trailed three paces behind. Great banks of black storm clouds were massed around the peaks of the surrounding mountains, but here on the lush green meadow a bright sun warmed the frail Duke and the hulking figure who slouched beside him in the nineteenth-century costume of a Marshal of France.

"I'm sure that you and your family will be quite content here," murmured the newly elevated Duke to the Lion of the Cotswolds. "Surely you recognize the familiar sight of your own little natal village? Thanks in part to an extremely generous grant from the University of Texas, it has been re-created exactly as it was in the year 1808. How stimulating you will find the other inhabitants of the village, historians, ethnologists, and sociologists from the Sorbonne and Texas for the most part, all of them dressed in the costumes of your era and living exactly as you yourselves do! How fascinating it will be to participate with them in the rich work of the mind!"

"Women," growled the old soldier irritably. "You've interfered in our affairs for no reason at all, kidnaped us and locked us up like monkeys in a zoo for the rest of our lives, and now you natter on about the rich work of the mind! What *I* want to know is this: What about our wives and—"

"Dear, dear," admitted the Duke of Vézelay, coming to an abrupt halt, his lips pursed. "Well, well, do you know, that never occurred to us when we blew up that cave behind you. You really should have brought them along with you to that cave of yours." But his gaunt face quickly brightened. "I imagine that the scholarly contingent from the University of Texas will certainly include any number of earnest lady Ph.D. candidates—what a scholastic coup it will be for them to participate at first hand in the lusty courtship rites of the gallant flower of Napoleonic France!"

"I don't care if it has a flush toilet *and* a marble bathtub with hot water," declared the Archduchess Mireille with sharp disdain eight days after making her first public appearance at the American embassy's celebration marking the Fourth of July 1808. "I am *not* going to live at the Elysée—it has far too many unpleasant memories of Uncle Bonbon. Besides, it is *far* too small for an empress."

"Very well, my dear," replied Kevin Frost absently as he disdainfully fingered one colorful costume after another in the Emperor's dressing room on the third floor of the Elysée Palace. What a garish taste his doppelgänger the MacNair of MacNair had displayed in the matter of his wardrobe! "What, after all, are mere toilets and bathtubs? Others can always be installed elsewhere."

"*Exactly!* Spoken like a *true* Emperor!" The blond Archduchess was unable to restrain from hugging herself and quivering with glee. "Oh, Kevin, it's going to be so *wonderful* being an empress! First we'll move into the Malmaison, and then after that's been fixed up, out to Fontainebleau. And, of course, for really *large* parties there's always Versailles. . . ."

"Very well, my dear," repeated the Emperor of All the French. "But don't you think that first we should—"

"Oh, Bunny, I was forgetting the coronation! And the wedding! Can we have the Pope? Can we have it in Westminster Abbey? What about the crown? Even if it doesn't light up, I could have one made with thirty or forty thousand diamonds, couldn't I?"

"For the Empress Alexine?" smiled Kevin Frost indulgently. "The most beautiful woman in *any* universe in *any* century? I don't see why not."

"And afterward . . ." The future Empress nibbled her lower lip delicately. "Perhaps we can have that awful Marquis of Vézelay *finally* taken out and shot, just as I was *always* telling Uncle to do."

"Nothing would give me greater pleasure," agreed the Emperor fervently, "but I fear that the blackguard has contrived to remain in cowardly safety in the twentieth cent—"

"*Mince alors!* I was forgetting that. . . ." The lovely cornflower-blue eyes of the Empress were troubled for a moment, then sparkled radiantly. "But wasn't he the sixth or seventh Marquis? Doesn't that mean that somewhere right here in 1808 there's a first or second Marquis of Vézelay? We can take *him* out and have him shot!" The Empress Alexine impulsively pulled Kevin Frost to her superb bosom and hugged him tightly. "Or guillotined! What a surprise *that* will be to that nasty old Vézelay!" Her luscious red mouth found Kevin Frost's eagerly. "Oh, Bunny, what *fun* we're going to have!"

"Yes, my dear," fervently agreed Napoleon I, Emperor of All the French, as he pulled the former Archduchess firmly toward the great canopied bed that awaited them in the next room, his mind already jumping ahead to the eleven splendid children he was destined to propagate in the course of the next momentous decade. . . .

"Are you *really* the . . . the Kevin Frost who was in jail in Portland?" asked Mary Louise Babcock, her magnificent green eyes turned downward to the sparkling silverware and crisp white tablecloth of the Cochon Truffé. Her long slim fingers nervously twisted the stem of a crystal wineglass. "I feel so odd being asked out to dinner by someone whose identity I'm not even sure of."

Sir Kevin Deane de Courtney MacNair of MacNair stroked the glossy fullness of his magnificent Vandyke beard as his eyes feasted hungrily on the beauty of the ravishing creature across the table. Even the five-star restaurant's famed specialty, the lobster soufflé with Nantua sauce, lay ignored on the plate before him. "I am that person," he admitted, drawing himself up to his full height while his flashing brown eyes glinted in the light of the great crystal chandelier above their table. "*But,*" he added after a significant pause, "I am in *no way* that uncouth Kevin Frost who has treated you so abominably. I am," he declared magnificently, "the MacNair of MacNair!"

"What a peculiar name!" Mary Louise Babcock's glorious eyes looked up to hesitantly meet his, while the corners of her lovely mouth twitched in a tentative smile.

"No more so than the effect which you have upon me."

"I have a peculiar effect upon you?"

The MacNair reached across the table and fervently squeezed her unresisting hands. "Ever since I glimpsed you first, for the barest instant touched your fingers, in that loathsome cell in Portland, I have been nothing more than your abject slave," he whispered ardently. "*I,* the MacNair of MacNair, a slave! A slave forever to your beauty, to your—"

"Oh, Kevin," sighed Mary Louise Babcock, her eyes suddenly glittering with tears. "You *know* I loved you, but . . . but all these *complications!* How do I *know* what to do?" The tears began to roll unheeded down her peach-blossom cheeks. "Sometimes you're Kevin, sometimes you're MacNair, sometimes you have a mustache, sometimes you have a beard, sometimes you're in jail, sometimes you're a friend of the Emperor of France, sometimes you're pretending to be married to me, sometimes you're making love to that scrawny blonde with the overbite, sometimes you—"

"Hush," soothed the MacNair tenderly, reaching across the table to dab gently at the tears that stained her cheeks, "hush, my dearest, and I'll tell you a little secret. One that the Marquis of Vézelay told me one night at the opera and that I unfortunately never got around to passing on to Kevin Frost."

"A secret?"

"A secret. You recall that the reason you found me languishing so cruelly in prison was the marriage which the scoundrel Frost had contracted years before with some woman from Martinique named Jacqueline Groussolles?"

Mary Louise Babcock's face grew taut. "I most certainly *do* recall! It is a dark cloud which will hang over me for the rest of my life."

"No more." The MacNair gestured for a hovering waiter to replenish his glass with the Graves '89 which sat in a heavy silver bucket on an adjoining serving table. His eyes darted about the restaurant as if wary of eavesdroppers. He lowered his voice and bent forward. "The Marquis of Vézelay, for reasons of wounded pride, was eager to discover whatever he could about Kevin Frost. His agents in California eventually discovered—and interviewed!—the woman known as Jacqueline Groussolles."

"*Known as . . . ?*"

"Known as. Her real name is Mildred Hennigan and she has a police record in seven states and a federal territory. She was interviewed in Eureka State Prison for Women, where she is even now serving a four-year sentence for fraudulent conversion. Vézelay learned that she actually was from Martinique, but had moved to the States at an early age. She started out in the old badger game, but then became more ambitious and took to marrying elderly or feebleminded men of means. After milking them of their resources she would move on to the next marriage. In the case of Kevin Frost her preliminary intelligence work was obviously at—"

Mary Louise Babcock's astonishing green eyes had grown

round. "But then that means that . . . that she was never legally married to Kevin at all!"

The MacNair squeezed her hand tightly. "And that in turn means that Kevin Frost *was* your legal husband!"

"Was? *Is!*"

"You forget, my dearest: Kevin Frost is in nineteenth-century France with his hand stuffed into the front of his vest, busy with the Empress Alexine glumly siring the House of Bonaparte. He will not be returning."

"Yes. I *was* forgetting." Her eyes met his. "But that means that . . ."

". . . that if you will have me, *I* will take the place of the most fortunate man on earth, the Kevin Frost of Portland, Franklin!"

CHAPTER
= 53 =

As THEY HONEYMOONED on the Riviera, only one thing was needed to make the MacNair's happiness complete: the restoration to its rightful owner of his priceless GOD-HEAD. For three weeks, whenever he had an unencumbered moment, he concentrated his keenest mental resources upon the bejeweled crown, willing it with all his being to materialize upon his head.

Obstinately it refused to heed his commands.

But even this galling circumstance was in some small measure mitigated by the knowledge that even now the canny Yankee trust officers of the Fiduciary Bank of Salem were lovingly tending to the orderly fructification of the beautiful Madame Frost's moderate fortune, here pruning a stock, there judiciously reinvesting in a municipal bond, now clipping a gilt-edge coupon, now foreclosing on some widow's mortgage, but always and eternally, for the rest of her days, distributing to Mary Louise Frost that welcome quarterly payment of her income.

Never again, the MacNair told himself cheerfully, would he be reduced to the horrid straits of having to study English genealogy in the hopes of mulcting some half-crazed insurance broker. He smiled tenderly at the radiant source of all his newfound happiness and raised a glass of an unpretentious local rosé from Provence to her in fond salute. A moment later he was lost in rapturous contemplation of the ineffable depths of his beloved's glittering green eyes. . . .

On the twenty-second day of their honeymoon he opened the door of their corner suite on the top floor of the Hotel Negresco to find two of the Duke of Vézelay's plainclothesmen standing respectfully at attention. Six minutes later, in spite of his most emphatic protests, he was in a long black limousine speeding toward the small airport on the shores of the Mediterranean that served Nice.

Three hours after that he was ushered into the director's quarters on the fourth floor of the Curie Institute in Paris, where to his dismay he found the director of the secret police impatiently pacing the floor.

"What!" exclaimed the MacNair with carefully mimed astonishment. "You're still in existence, then?"

"Whatever do you mean?" glowered Vézelay.

"I felt *sure* that Kevin Frost would have looked up some of your more remote ancestors with a pair of pruning shears by now and . . ." He shrugged as if it were a matter of little importance. "Ah, well, perhaps someday when he has the leisure. . . ."

"Most amusing," murmured Vézelay uneasily, his face becoming a deathly white as the MacNair's meaning sunk home.

"Isn't it, though? I wonder when you suddenly vanish if we who remain shall still remember you, or if all of our very memories will also change in consequence? An interesting point of speculation, don't you think? Now that I'm here at the institute," suggested the MacNair cheerfully, "why don't we ask the director?"

"Later perhaps," muttered the Duke between clenched teeth. "In the meantime the Emperor has asked me to place a proposition before you."

"A proposition?"

"Yes. I take it that all of your most frenzied efforts to retrieve your crown by telepathic means have proved unfruitful?"

"Have they?" asked the MacNair jauntily, his eyebrows raised. "Perhaps even now it reposes in my bank vault in Liechtenstein."

The Duke of Vézelay had regained a little of his color. He snorted derisively. "Not likely! For the Special Directorate happens to know, in fact, just exactly where it is at this very moment!"

"Indeed!" The MacNair's eyes flashed. "And just where is that, pray tell?"

Vézelay waggled a finger. "Ah! For that we must first come to the proposition which I mentioned earlier."

"Very well, then: Make it."

The secret-police man leaned forward. "It is speculated by the scientists here in the institute that the crown has gradually been losing its inner power, its *élan vital,* whatever it is that enables it to be teleported around Europe by you and your egregious twin, now the revered founder of our noble House of Bonaparte."

"And if this is so?"

"It means that you will never again set eyes upon it. Unless—"

"Unless what?"

"Unless you agree to utilize what the institute believes to be a telepathic amplifier at a certain specified time when we *know* that the crown has been switched on."

The MacNair felt his pulse beating faster. "And if I were to do so?"

"First we must have a formal agreement. The crown itself will become the property of the French government—"

"*What?* Never!"

"—while the individual diamonds remain your property."

"You mean—"

"What are thirty or forty thousand paltry diamonds to the wealth of the French Empire?" asked the Duke of Vézelay magnificently. "We will gradually replace those on the crown and turn the originals over to you to do with as you please."

"This agreement will, of course, be drawn up by a notary of my choice, be registered with the clerk of court, and furthermore be witnessed by the Emperor Napoleon V himself?" asked the MacNair suspiciously, hardly able to credit his remarkable fortune. What on earth did *he* care about the crown as long as he had the diamonds?

"It shall be as you say," said the Duke of Vézelay grandly. "Shall we step along to the Palace to draw up the document? His Imperial Majesty is anxious to learn at first hand your impressions of the far past."

"I fear that he will find little enough to interest him," replied the MacNair, shaking his head dolefully. "In all my time there I saw nary a brontosaurus."

The ambassadors from over a hundred nations sat rigidly in their gilded seats of honor only a dozen yards from the spot where Abdul-Medjid II was to be invested as Sultan of the Ottoman Empire under the great dome of Hagia Sofia in Constantinople. The old Sultan Suleiman VII had been dead now for well over a month but it had taken that long for the thousand members of the ruling family to decide upon his successor from within their ranks. Now they were solemnly gathered, along with ten thousand lesser dignitaries from the far corners of the Ottoman Empire, to witness the majestic ceremonies of his investiture.

All morning long the stately pageantry had proceeded, broken only by calls to prayer, and well into the afternoon. Now, as evening neared and thousands of heads sagged wearily upon slumping shoulders, the culmination of the ceremonies approached. The French Ambassador, the Duke of Brittany, leaned forward in his seat with apparent keen interest, his long fingers templed in front of his mouth.

"The Caliph al-Mustarshid-billah of Baghdad has appeared from behind the throne to the left of the Sultan," he murmured in a voice so low as to be inaudible to his neighbors, the ambassadors of Brazil and of the United States of America. "He is carrying before him a red velvet cushion. On it is what appears to be a rather ostentatious crown. It is obviously quite heavy. It must be inset with many thousands of diamonds—I can see them glittering from here. . . ."

Two hundred yards away, in a small blue panel truck parked in a crooked lane just off the great plaza of Hagia Sofia, three technicians specially sent from France hovered over the equipment concealed in the rear of the truck. While two of them made delicate adjustments to the apparatus, the man who wore the earphones was repeating into a small microphone the words which the Duke of Brittany was murmuring into his own tiny transmitter.

On the far side of the city the words from the panel truck were received in a bare room on the top floor of an ancient four-story tenement. Three husky Frenchmen stood uneasy guard while the fourth, who also wore a headset, spoke rapidly into a telephone.

"He's speaking Basque," explained the Duke of Vézelay to the keyed-up MacNair of MacNair in the underground laboratory of the Curie Institute. "The most difficult language in the world. Even if the line is tapped—and *all* lines out of Constantinople are tapped—no one will be able to understand a word."

The MacNair ignored the secret-police man, for his eyes were fixed on the man sitting on the stool before him, a telephone receiver held to his head. The MacNair's own lofty brow was bare, unencumbered by any of the elaborate devices he had expected to have attached to him upon his descent into the vault. For not long before his unexpected sabbatical to Easter Island the institute's late director Dr. Campinotti had reluctantly concluded that all of his unremitting efforts to construct a shelter to harbor the GODHEAD from telepathic phenomena had perversely succeeded only in unwittingly developing a psionic amplifier.

Now the MacNair sat in that superbly shielded vault deep in the bowels of the Curie Institute where more than two years before the appalled Archduchess Mireille of Luxembourg had suddenly felt the weight of the Tirthankara

Mardumjar's glittering crown vanish from her head.

"The Caliph is raising the crown," murmured the French Ambassador from the hushed stillness of Hagia Sofia.

"He is holding it in his hands above the Sultan's head," repeated the French agent in the blue panel truck.

"Now an acolyte has stepped forward and touched the crown," translated the Basque into the overseas telephone.

"The crown has suddenly burst into an explosion of lights," cried the Basque in the vault of the Curie Institute. "Its radiance fills the great cathedral. A murmur has gone up from the thousands of spectators. Now it is being lowered onto the Sultan's head—"

And then the GODHEAD was sitting firmly on the MacNair's own head, its glorious fairyland of glittering colors as magical and exhilarating as the moment he had first glimpsed it so many horrible tribulations earlier.

The MacNair raised a clenched fist in sudden exultant joy.

The GODHEAD was back!

At long, long last the crown was his!

EPILOGUE

WEARING NOTHING but a pair of knee-length bathing tights, Sir Kevin Deane de Courtney MacNair of MacNair plodded morosely through the golden sands of the beach at Cannes, his arm around the slim waist of his lovely auburn-haired companion. Palm trees waved against a pellucid blue sky and the docile Mediterranean lapped softly at their feet but the MacNair's jaw was slack and his normally flashing brown eyes were dull and unfocused, as if turned inward upon some terrible inner vision.

At last he broke the silence. "Can you imagine it?" he whispered wistfully. "Once again I held in my very hands a crown whose value once approached 100 million dollars."

Mary Louise turned adoring green eyes to the dynamic bantam cock of a man beside her. "How lovely the crown must be," she breathed softly. "As soon as we return to Paris you *must* take me to see it."

"If you really want to, my dear," replied the MacNair with a sigh that seemed to issue from the very bottom of his soul.

"You don't sound very enthusiastic. Is there something wrong?"

The MacNair shrugged briefly and pulled himself closer to her warm glowing skin. "A minor contretemps, perhaps. You will recall that I incautiously signed a solemn agreement with the Emperor himself and the French government to give me all the original diamonds on the crown?"

"Of course." Her eyes widened in dismay. "Don't tell me that now they've reneged on—"

"No, no. They are scrupulously carrying out the letter of the agreement." The MacNair pursed his lips and sighed a second time. He shuffled his bare toes in the sand. "I can still hear the words of the first scientist at the institute to look at the crown once we'd switched the lights off. 'How peculiar,' he said. 'Are these supposed to be *real* diamonds? Possibly it's all this teleporting back and forth, but now they seem nothing more than rather tarnished lumps of carbon.'"

Mary Louise stared at him with rounded eyes. "You . . . you mean we're *penniless?*"

The MacNair raised his melancholy brown eyes to meet hers with an expression of weary resignation on his face. "Not *entirely* penniless," he muttered. "The Emperor *has* seen his way clear for a modest pension for services rendered. I daresay that along with your own revenues it will see us through, though not in any great style, of course. Ah, well, that château on the Loire I had my eye on would clearly have been too big for just the two of us. When we return to Paris we shall look for an apartment on the Ile

St.-Louis. Only for the spring and fall, of course. In the winters we shall—"

"Kevin," said Mary Louise in a subdued voice, digging her own toes into the sand and looking over her shoulder at something invisible far out to sea. "I . . . I'm afraid I have to tell you something."

"Tell me something? Well, of course. Tell me what a fool I am." The MacNair looked up at the light of his life with concern and curiosity. Why did her voice have such a peculiar tremolo to it?

Her delicate Adam's apple bobbed twice. "I . . . I suppose I should have told you sooner, but . . . but in all the excitement of meeting you and . . . and everything, it just didn't seem important."

"Important?"

"You . . . you recall that everything I inherited from my first husband—"

"—the $2,341,849.12?" The MacNair made a slight gesture of airy indifference. "I vaguely recall the mention of some such figure or other."

Mary Louise took a deep breath, lifting the rosy tips of her perfect bare breasts nearly to the MacNair's chin. "Well," she said with brittle defiance as tears suddenly began to run down the sides of her face, "I *had* 2 million, all right. Or at least the Fiduciary Bank of Salem had it in trust for me. But now . . ." The tears flowed faster. "Now my lawyer Mr. Fraser tells me that the bank is closed and that they've . . . they've defalcated with it and—"

"Defalcated," repeated the MacNair, while his heart and breathing seemed to come to a sudden abrupt halt. "You mean they've *embezzled*—"

Mary Louise threw herself into his arms and buried her face against his neck. "Embezzled, stolen, defalcated, I don't *know!* All I know is that it's gone!" Her warm tears fell against his bare shoulder. "Oh, Kevin, it's all my fault, now neither of us has any money! Whatever are we going to do?"

The MacNair wrapped his arms around her warm back and pulled her tightly to him. Even as his hands patted her gently he drew himself up to his full height as if he were on a military parade ground instead of the sands of Cannes.

"*Do?*" he repeated with a rather sickly smile as he hugged his beautiful, ardent, devoted wife, now as poor as the proverbial church mouse. "Do? What else *can* we do except to go to Reims?"

"But what would we do in Reims?" she sobbed.

He kissed her tenderly on the tip of her delightful nose. "Surely you haven't forgotten that pithy saying of the Emperor Napoleon I? *If any lout could freeze the neck of a bottle, where, then, would that leave even the greatest of kings?** Why, it would leave him in Reims, along with the woman he loved, reinventing champagne and restoring for good the fortunes of the noble House of MacNair!"

APPENDIX I

THE MACNAIR REPRESENTS himself to the Friends of Goethe and Les Amis des Grands Vins de Bordeaux as being from a world in which William IV, who reigned as King from 1830 to 1837, did *not* marry Adelaide, Princess of Saxe-Meiningen, but rather Mary Louisa Victoria, Princess of Saxe-Coburg-Saalfeld, who in the real world of the Mac-Nair married the *brother* of William IV and eventually became the mother of Queen Victoria.

In the MacNair's imaginary genealogy three children were born of this fictive union of William IV and Mary Louisa Victoria: Frederick, George, and Edward. Upon the death of his father in 1837 the eldest son, Frederick, ascended to the throne. It is through the line of Frederick I, therefore, that the MacNair of MacNair, in his guise of

---

*For a possible explanation of this still baffling tag line, and additional lore concerning the noble art of making champagne, see Appendix III.

William Ernest Augustus, Duke of York, is descended. The present King in the MacNair's fictitious world is Frederick IV and he, the Duke of York, is his third son.

APPENDIX II

IN THE UNIVERSE of the Earl of Kensington Napoleon I was born Napoleone Buonaparte on the island of Corsica in 1769. He reigned as Emperor from 1805 through 1849, abdicating on his eightieth birthday in favor of his eldest son. He died peacefully in his sleep in the year 1860 in his ninety-first year.

His eldest son, Valérie (1809–52), reigned for only three years as Napoleon II, from 1849 through 1852. He was thrown from his horse at the age of forty-three and killed instantly.

He was succeeded by his own eldest son, Georges-René (1831–67), although he was but twenty-one years old. Misfortune continued to stalk the House of Bonaparte, for Napoleon III died of pneumonia at the age of thirty-six.

At the time of his death his sole issue was his thirteen-year-old daughter, Alexine (1854–1910). Her uncle the Duke of Burgundy served as regent for five years until she acceded to the imperial throne in 1873 upon her eighteenth birthday. She was assassinated in 1910 at the age of fifty-six.

Her eldest son, Michel-Yvon (1873–1956), reigned as Napoleon IV for the next forty-three years. Following the example of his great-grandfather, he abdicated upon his eightieth birthday in favor of his eldest son in 1953. He died three years later, in 1956.

Charles-Pierre, the present Emperor, was born in 1917 and acceded to the throne at the age of thirty-six. He had enjoyed a reign of thirty-eight years at the time of the Earl of Kensington's comments.

APPENDIX III

IN THE MACNAIR'S original world, true champagne—which takes its name from the former French province of Champagne—can only be produced in a strictly defined area between Reims and Epernay, although innumerable other sparkling wines of varying qualities are bottled all over the world. Some of these wines owe their delightful effervescence to the introduction of bubbles by aeration, others to a natural fermentation of the wine itself.

But the only method permitted by a zealous French government for producing true champagne is *la méthode champenoise,* supposedly discovered by the fabled Dom Pérignon, a monk at the abbey in the vineyard town of Hautvilliers in the early eighteenth century.

Champagne can be made of either red or white grapes. What is essential to the process, and what distinguishes *la méthode champenoise* from all others, is its strictly controlled fermentation. An initial fermentation takes place while the freshly pressed juice of the grapes is stored in bulk, either in barrels or in vats. When this newly alcoholic wine is subsequently bottled a few months later, additional sugar and yeast are inserted into each bottle. These induce a second fermentation, and the bottles are set aside to age for a number of years.

As the wine continues to ferment, an important residue

of dead yeast accumulates in the bottle. All of this must be scrupulously removed before the champagne can be sold, a delicate business when dealing with a highly pressurized bottle. Herein lies the trick which may explain the Mac-Nair's cryptic remark to the Marquis of Vézelay.

Over a period of several months, each of the millions of bottles stored in the great caverns between Reims and Epernay is gradually tilted and rotated by expert workmen called *remueurs* until it is eventually standing on its head in a special rack, with all of its accumulated sediment now collected in the neck of the bottle.

The neck of the upside-down bottle is then passed through an icy brine so that the entire contents of the neck are quickly frozen. Once again upright, the cork is then removed and the glorious pressure of the champagne itself propels the frozen lump from the bottle, purging itself of the dead yeasts which were responsible for its remarkable transformation from inadequate and unpalatable wine to the "king of wines and the wine of kings."